PRAISE FOR *CONSORT OF FIRE*

"The fiery breath of a dragon pales in comparison to the incendiary heat of this epic erotic fantasy."

—Kirkus Reviews

"By combining life-or-death stakes with off-the-charts eroticism, Rocha keeps the pages flying. The scalding sex scenes drive both plot and character development and incorporate the fantastical world-building in fascinating ways. This is an exciting start to what promises to be a thrilling new series."

—Publishers Weekly (starred review)

"The story layers are peeled back slowly enough to immerse readers . . . Rocha's new offering is set in a rich, erotic fantasy world, filled with lush characters and a magical landscape of secrets, power, and betrayal."

—Library Journal

"Interwoven with the history, the curse, and the intended murder is an overarching plot that will leave readers eagerly anticipating the next book in the Bound to Fire and Steel series."

—Booklist

"A glorious, epic, and erotic firestorm of a book! I could not put it down!"

—Nalini Singh, New York Times bestselling author

QUEEN
OF
DREAMS

Mercenary Librarians

Deal with the Devil
The Devil You Know
Dance with the Devil

Bound to Fire and Steel

Consort of Fire

QUEEN
OF
DREAMS

KIT ROCHA

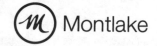 Montlake

Published by Montlake, Seattle

www.apub.com

Amazon, the Amazon logo, and Montlake are trademarks of Amazon.com, Inc., or its affiliates.

ISBN-13: 9781662513206 (paperback)
ISBN-13: 9781662513213 (digital)

Cover design by Hang Le
Cover image: © Maksim Shmeljov, © BaYaoPix, © Weerachai Khamfu, © Wirestock Creators, © Nuwat Phansuwan, © Aaditya Puranik / Shutterstock; © serikbaib / Getty

Printed in the United States of America

To the Broken Circle.
You know what you did.

A REMINDER OF HOW WE HAVE COME

TO THIS PLACE

In the days before we marked time, the world was simple. We hunted in the forests and fished the lakes and streams. We cultivated crops and rejoiced when they thrived. There was poetry and art and gaiety, for the world was bountiful and we thrived off its generosity.

But there were those who did more than thrive. Those who heard the whispers of the world itself. They were the Dreamers, those whose will could shape the world, because they could touch the Everlasting Dream and make the wishes of their hearts become true. As word of their power spread, people came to follow them—first as leaders, and then as living gods.

But the gods didn't always agree.

Three thousand years ago, the Dreamers fought a terrible war that nearly shattered the world. The one who had started it—the Betrayer—escaped with his followers to the unexplored lands to the west.

The seven remaining Dreamers recognized that their power had become too great, and withdrew to their castles and their keeps, content to let mortal rulers rise in their place. They agreed to guard the borders and protect the land in exchange for three promises: that the Mortal Lords pledge not to take more from the land than it could give, that we protect the people as the land's heart, and that every one hundred years we send an heir to serve as the Dragon's consort, tying our bloodline to the High Court for another generation.

And so we made the pact with the High Court on the first day. For two thousand and nine hundred years, we sent our heirs to the keep, even as dark rumors built that they suffered under the growing tyranny of the Dragon's wrath.

Thus came the rule of King Dalvish II. Raised under the tutelage of an unaging priest from far beyond the Western Wall, Dalvish was eager to break the oaths that prevented his court from exploiting the rich trade offered by the Empire. When his priest discovered two orphaned children with unusually dangerous magic, Dalvish made the decision to adopt one as his own, passing her off as his heir—the princess he would sacrifice to the Dragon's wrath on the first day of the three thousandth year of our pact.

The girls were trained as their natures bade—sweet Princess Sachielle was ruthlessly tutored in seduction and deception. Her handmaid, Zanya, was given brutal lessons in violence and death. One would lure the Dragon to her bed, and the other would slay him there. To ensure their obedience, the priest wove a curse around Sachielle's very life—if they failed to kill the Dragon in fifty days, her soul would be ripped from the Everlasting Dream, her life ended.

A simple enough plan. But even simple plans go awry when hearts are involved.

King Dalvish II could not have anticipated how the love between Zanya and Sachielle made them stronger. Nor could he have imagined that the Dragon would see in the pair the answer to his own unending solitude. If he had simply broken the curse and taken them to his bed, it would have been bad enough.

But it was the truth of the orphans' identities that changed everything.

For three thousand years, the High Court has walked the world as gods. But now something new takes its first steps—something magnificent and terrifying. A power that transcends the petty idea of gods.

Zanya, driven to claim her full power by her need to save Sachielle, has been revealed to be the pure essence of the Endless Void itself, born into human flesh. In her triumphant awakening, she slew the High Priest and King Dalvish II, plunging the Mortal Court into chaos.

And our own Princess Sachielle? Though she has evidenced no similar magic, the rumors whisper that she is the spirit of the Everlasting Dream. The power of creation itself.

And that the Betrayer intends to claim her as his Empress.

Chapter One
WITCHING MOON

Their mistake had been taking the time necessary to burn the witch.

The smell of charred wood and fabric still blanketed the chill morning air in Emmonsdale. Zanya stood on the platform where the execution had been intended, ignoring the villagers' occasional nervous whispers and sidelong gazes. Under any other circumstances, she would have been the sole focus of their agitation and unease. But not today.

Today, the man in front of her drew their enraptured attention. As reluctant as she was to admit it, he certainly deserved it.

The Dragon was spectacular when he was in his element.

Ash wore his usual armor, a style ancient before they'd started counting time. Leather and brass had been polished to a shine that couldn't hide the hard usage over thousands of years and countless battles. The cuirass protected his massive chest but left his shoulders and upper arms bare, where light-brown skin stretched over dangerous muscle.

The greaves covered his strong legs from ankles to knees, but the leather strips hanging from his thick belt did little to hide his massive thighs.

Facing down three dozen of the Mortal Queen's heavy cavalry in their shiniest steel, he looked barely dressed. He hadn't even bothered to unsheathe the sword that rode across his back.

Not one soldier seemed willing to charge him.

A weak cough rose behind Zanya. She stole a glance over her shoulder to where the Huntress was cutting the bonds of the accused witch. Elevia's jaw was tight as she sliced at the rough rope, but she gave no other evidence of what must be considerable rage. The old woman's smoke-induced cough was the only injury she'd suffered from the attempted execution, but if Zanya and the rest of the High Court had come even a few moments later . . .

But they hadn't. They'd arrived at the village just as the flames surged toward the old woman's legs. The fire licking at her heavy woolen skirts died with Ash's first step into the square. The torches held by her would-be executioners had snuffed out next, the flames sucked away as if the world had inhaled.

By the time they reached the crowded square, the only fire left in Emmonsdale danced in the Dragon's eyes. The Lord of Fire had not been amused. The weak cough—a reminder of the old woman's suffering—was unlikely to improve his mood.

As Zanya expected, the noise shattered the silent standoff. Ash stepped forward, the entire weight of his formidable attention on the leader of the queen's soldiers.

The man's ornate gilded pauldrons marked him to the world as a guard commander. The stiff set of his shoulders, cruel ice-blue eyes, and familiar condescending sneer identified him to Zanya as Velez, the youngest son of House Sandrake. His noble blood combined with some natural ability had secured him a swift rise through the ranks of the royal guard to a trusted position near the former king's right hand.

His gleeful sadism had made him one of Zanya's most dedicated tormentors.

He had courage, Zanya would give him that much. The rest of the soldiers fought to control horses who had picked up on their riders' fear and wanted to flee. Only Velez sat rock-steady in the saddle and drew his sword, leveling it at Ash.

"You were warned twice already," he announced, arrogance dripping from every word. "When you murdered our king, you severed any duty we owe to your wicked and corrupt court. These lands are under our protection now. Leave this place, or die."

Ash didn't ask him how a handful of mortals expected to expel a dragon god who had roamed this world for over three thousand years. He didn't point out that it had, in fact, been Zanya who thrust a dragon-hilted blade deep into the king's chest, ending his life. He didn't even raise his voice.

The low rumble of his words still made the earth shiver. "When you are burning healers at the stake, your protection leaves much to be desired."

"We're not burning healers," Velez spat. "We're cleansing this village of heretics."

Zanya could not see the Dragon's face, but from the way the soldiers inched back, she imagined flames had appeared in his eyes. His voice was gentle malevolence. "And who do you name heretic?"

"Anyone who speaks out against our gentle queen and calls for treason."

This produced an uneasy murmur through the crowd. A handful of villagers already sported bruises and shackles—those who had tried to interrupt the burning, Zanya guessed. They knelt by the soldiers, hands bound at their backs. Those who still stood free gripped makeshift weapons—staves and scythes, one or two sizable kitchen knives. The blacksmith held a hammer loosely at her side. Several burly young foresters hoisted the axes they must have been using to chop wood.

The soldiers might have cowed this village before, but the arrival of the Dragon had strengthened their resolve. If his men came for the healer again, the people would fight back.

Velez ignored this obvious fact with true aristocratic hauteur. "Every villager must turn over false idols and any token of the traitorous High Court. The queen commands it."

Zanya highly doubted the queen had done any such thing. Princess—now Queen—Anikke had celebrated her fifteenth birthday only a few moons prior. Zanya had been there, purportedly nothing more than the handmaid hired to accompany Anikke's eldest sister when Princess Sachielle was sent to do the family's duty by becoming the Dragon's consort.

Anikke had been utterly ignorant of the undercurrents at that awkward family celebration. She hadn't known that Sachielle was no more related to her by blood than the palace cook was. Or that King Dalvish II had found Sachi as an orphaned toddler and concocted a plan to spare his own blood from the magic that bound the royal family to the High Court when they sent their centennial sacrifice. Anikke had had no idea that the doting father who watched benevolently as his two daughters shared a slice of cake had been torturing Sachi from the moment he'd brought her into his household, doing everything in his power to hone her into a weapon of seduction and deceit.

Into an assassin.

Anikke had been oblivious to all of it, shyly excited from the kind attention of the older sister she looked up to but rarely got to see, and heartbroken when she realized this was the final birthday they would spend together. Sachielle was bound to the High Court, the latest in a string of sacrificial consorts. It should have been the end.

Only Sachi had lived, and King Dalvish II had died. And now Anikke was a child queen, sheltered and ignorant of the true conspiracies entangling her court and her family. It mattered little if her uncles Doven or Bodin, or her aunt Tislaina, were the ones issuing orders on behalf of the grieving queen. Whoever was in charge wanted vengeance for the life Zanya had claimed.

And they'd take it out on their own citizens if the High Court didn't stop them.

Fortunately for this village, the Dragon alone was more than capable of stopping them. The backing of his fellow gods—the Huntress, the Wolf, and the Lover—was practically overkill. None of them needed Zanya at all. But Ash had asked her to come, as part of her training.

Zanya was a god now, too. Of a sort.

The restless murmuring of the villagers died as Ash took another step forward. He stood with his feet parted, like a wall with the strength of the earth that answered the call of his magic. "There will be no burnings. No confiscations. You will leave this village."

Velez slashed his sword through the air—a flashy move that was more bluster than skill. "The heretic and the prisoners come with me. Unless you'd like to see how much of sweet little Emmonsdale we can bleed out before you can stop us."

Was he a fool, or did he truly believe he could stand against a god? Of course, it had been centuries since the Dragon had walked casually among the people. Stories had twisted him into a vicious and rageful monster, a beast with no self-control who devoured the weak and defenseless. Zanya had learned the lie beneath those words over the past weeks—but only the cruelty had been a falsehood. Not his power.

The Dragon could erase Velez with a flick of his fingers.

The disdain in Ash's tone said as much as he stared at the lord over his flashing sword. He hadn't even deigned to draw his own yet. "This is your last warning. Turn around and go."

Velez responded with a sneer. He thrust his sword into the air, and the men behind him drew their weapons in a clatter of steel. Over the sound, Zanya heard the softest sigh drift back . . . Ash, frustrated that he would be forced to violence.

Then one of the soldiers screamed. His horse reared, revealing the knife buried in the soldier's throat. The soldier next to him whirled his horse and cut down the villager who'd launched the attack.

And chaos exploded as the good folk of Emmonsdale went mad.

If it had been Ash against the soldiers, it would have been no contest. He would have cut through them as if they had no more substance than air. Zanya had seen him do it before—deftly disarming and unseating cavalry soldiers with lazy ease, so precisely in control of the battle that he didn't even need to kill them. Just a handful of painful bruises, a few broken bones, and the gut-deep reminder that they had no hope when they faced the Dragon.

The civilians complicated everything.

They were angry and desperate, and they had no intention of leaving the soldiers who had threatened their healer with mere bruises. They came at the mounted soldiers with murder in their eyes, and any whisper of remaining discipline collapsed as the knights scattered, each one fighting his own private battle for his life.

A child's scream of fear rose over the clash of steel. Zanya pivoted, but Aleksi was already there, plucking the child out of danger as Elevia guarded his back. Magic exploded behind Zanya in a prickling wave, and a giant wolf leapt past her, its eyes glowing molten gold.

Ulric, she thought, but had time for no more as his growl rumbled across the square. The Wolf was the god of the forest and all wild things, and the horses of the queen's soldiers answered his call with terrified obedience. One after another began to rear and buck, doing everything in their power to dislodge their riders. The deft ones managed to fling themselves clear of their saddles. The less fortunate . . .

Zanya turned from the sight of the two foresters descending on a soldier, axes flashing in the warm morning light.

The violence called to her, sweet and chaotic. The clash of steel, the harsh cries. The sound a sword made when it sliced through air. Through armor.

Through flesh.

People fought and died all around her, and a dark part of her reveled in it. No, not a dark part of her—the *true* part of her. The inner self with which she still grappled, even as the power of it pulsed in her veins.

For centuries, the High Court of Dreamers had been the most powerful entities who walked their lands. Gods in human form, each with power over their own domain. Earth and fire answered to the Dragon.

The air and water obeyed the Siren. The Wolf called to the wild places, while the Witch walked those that bordered life and death. Anything the Lover touched grew, fertile and bountiful. And the Huntress never missed a mark, whether she hunted game or knowledge.

Their powers flowed from the Everlasting Dream, a place of pure hope. The heart of creation.

But destruction had a home, too. The Endless Void.

And Zanya was that elemental chaos, born into human flesh.

A handful of weeks wasn't enough time to come to grips with the truth of something so unfathomable. Guilt still flooded her as she caressed the hilt of her sword, her blood singing with how good it would feel to draw it and strike down her enemies. Not the usual kind of guilt, either—not sickness at the weight of death. At the reality of causing it.

Zanya's only guilt came from how little guilt she felt when her sword struck true and blood flowed. For her entire life, the world had been brutally, painfully simple: there were enemies, and there was Sachi. To protect Sachi, she would bathe in the blood of those who came against her.

But the world was no longer simple. She had power now, too much to use recklessly, and that was all that stayed her hand now as the violence sang to her. That had been the Dragon's command to her: to watch. To learn. To not engage, unless she was called upon.

All of those noble intentions crumbled when she saw Velez melting through the shadows.

He'd abandoned his horse and skirted the main battle, leaving his men to their fates. His target was clear—the old woman and the cluster of apprentices still tending to her.

Thought ceased. Instinct took over. Zanya reached for the shadows that had always obeyed her, wrapping herself in their caressing darkness. The power to summon them when she stood in broad daylight was new. So was what she did next, an internal *twist* that carried her into the Void for a heartbeat. There was no time in the Endless Void. No distance. Every place touched it, and it touched every place.

She didn't even have to take a step. But she did, bursting from the Void and her protective wreath of shadows directly into Velez's path.

He recoiled, fear flashing through his eyes before rage replaced it. "Abomination!"

Zanya drew the sword the Huntress had gifted her, and it felt like a feather in her hand as she smiled. "Will you name me heretic, too? Try to burn me?"

"You should be burned," he spat back. "Purged from this world. You were always unnatural, but now evil surrounds you like a dark halo."

Yes, that had been the price of claiming the power she'd needed to save Sachi's life. For twenty-five years, Zanya had known she was *other*, but for the most part she'd been able to hide it. Now anyone who looked at her could see the truth. Her mind and heart might feel fragile and human, but her body and spirit were anything but.

And her power came from the Void.

"I am what I am." Zanya advanced. "What I have always been."

"Foul and corrupt," Velez snarled. "Just like your traitorous mistress."

Ice crept through her, far more dangerous than the heat of battle hunger. He could insult her all day if he wished, but if he turned that poisoned tongue toward Sachi . . . "You will not speak of her."

"Will I not?" he taunted, raising his sword. "The queen is still mourning the betrayal of her beloved sister, you know. But soon enough she will dry her tears and listen to the counsel of her elders. And on that day . . ." Joy lit his face. "Oh, the price on dear Princess Sachielle's head will be legendary."

It was all bluster and lies. Sachi was safe at Dragon's Keep. The castle sat at the top of a mountain, in the middle of a caldera lake. It was so well fortified as to be impenetrable, and entirely self-sufficient besides. As long as Sachi stayed safely within its walls, nothing and no one could hurt her.

But Velez wanted to. The hunger for Sachi's pain lit those blue eyes, just as it had when he'd done his best to beat Zanya into submission during her endless training sessions. Once, when she'd been just fifteen, her trainers had tossed her into the sparring ring with seven men armed with swords. She'd had only a simple wooden practice knife for defense. The soldiers had been promised one gold piece for every time they drew her blood.

The wealthy heir of House Sandrake hadn't needed the fifteen gilded coins that had glistened in his palm at the end of the night. Oh no. He'd made her bleed for the pleasure of it.

The same memory shone in his eyes. "I still have my gold coins," he murmured, swinging his sword in a lazy arc. Testing her. She swatted it away with a clash of steel that only widened his grin. "When I strike Sachielle's golden head from her pretty little neck, I'll put the reward next to them."

He couldn't. He *wouldn't*. But the ringing of steel and the low, tormenting sound of his voice twisted through her, dragging her back to that claustrophobic time during her training. Her heart beat faster. Fear tasted like ash on her tongue. When he lunged at her, her body brought her sword up out of pure muscle memory, her block jerky and uneven.

"She always was your weakness, wasn't she?" Velez taunted, his eyes glinting as he circled, the tip of his blade flicking out in another testing advance she barely managed to block.

Where was the heat of battle she'd just savored? Where was that terrifying darkness that reveled in the kill? Her breath came too fast, and her limbs moved too slowly, as if the chains she'd slept in most nights in the capital still weighed her down. She could feel the cold iron around her wrists.

She's little more than a feral wolf.

She could hear their laughter. The guards. The cocky young lords. Velez, smug and safe on the other side of the bars that caged her, his handsome face curved in a cruel grin.

The king would do better to put her down.

9

Zanya bit her lip and tasted blood, bright and metallic. The king couldn't put her down. She'd driven a blade deep into his heart. She'd knelt in a puddle of his blood and watched the life go out of him. He could never hurt Sachi again.

He could never hurt *Zanya* again.

She knew that. Somewhere in her mind, she knew the truth. But her body wouldn't obey, wouldn't calm. Fear raged through her as Velez swung at her in earnest, his sword coming so close she barely managed to block the blow. His body pressed in, his face staring at hers across their crossed blades, the deadlock as intimate as a kiss.

"I always knew I'd be the one to end you." In his voice, she heard the echo of every man who had promised her misery and pain from the first time they'd put a weapon into her hand at less than ten years old.

Rotten to the core, every last one of them. Twisted and wrong, willing to hurt Zanya and Sachi if it gained them lands and riches. Willing to hurt them just for the joy of having power over someone helpless and afraid.

Shadows curled up her body. Zanya tasted her own blood on her lips. Remembered Sachi's blood on her hands, spilled in an attempt to escape the curse these mortal bastards had placed upon her.

They'd come so close to losing everything. So close Zanya still woke every night, sobs of terror trapped in her throat.

"No." It hurt, like she was speaking through broken glass. Her entire body pounded with the frantic beat of her heart. She remembered being small and wounded and helpless—

But even when she'd been all of those things, she'd always fought back.

"No?" Velez mocked. He broke their stalemate with a surge of muscle, and suddenly a dagger glinted in his hand. A flick of his wrist scored a line of bright pain across her cheek, and his dark laughter curled around her. "How about I send you back to Princess Sachielle in pieces? A fitting gift for a traitor."

Rage roared up from within, shattering her fear. Shadows enveloped her, and Velez hissed and stumbled back, all playful cruelty swallowed by superstitious hatred. "Witch!"

"Worse," Zanya whispered.

Then she struck.

Her sword shimmered in the sunlight like black diamonds as she swung it with all her strength. Velez flung his own up to block it, but Zanya's blade slid through it as sweetly as it would have cut through flesh.

"What—"

The choked word was all she let him have. He was still gaping at his cleaved weapon when she reversed her swing and sliced through his neck. But it wasn't enough. She could still hear the pounding of that fearful heart—her heart, her childhood heart—and a snarl erupted from her lips as shadows caressed her fingers. She punched into his chest and tore his heart free, crushing it in her fingers as if she could silence the frantic beating inside of her for good.

Time wobbled. The top half of his sword bounced in the dirt with an odd clang. A moment later his head joined it, his face still twisted into an expression of horrified realization.

It took another moment for his body to topple over. In that quiet, stately heartbeat, she realized the rest of the village had gone deathly silent.

Zanya heard the creak of her leather armor as she stepped back. She heard her own harsh exhalation, as well as the sound of Velez's blood as it dripped off her sword and splattered on the dirt. She forced her fingers open and released the mangled heart, letting it fall next to its heartless former owner.

She couldn't hear her own pulse anymore. She couldn't hear anything but the wind and the drip of blood and the unnatural stillness of so many people too aghast to even whisper.

Then gentle, insistent hands closed around her upper arms, digging into her armor and pulling her back. Elevia.

"Come away now, Zanya," she murmured.

Velez's empty eyes stared at the sky, his mouth twisted in shock. There was no thrill in seeing him vanquished, just the sick feeling that somehow, even in death, he would still manage to claim this day as his victory. Whenever she played the vile games devised by those at the capital, she always lost. One way or another.

"Come," Elevia repeated softly. "He belongs to the vultures now."

Zanya shuddered and turned her back on the nightmare from her past. "He always did."

Chapter Two
WITCHING MOON

Week One, Day Nine
Year 3000

Usually, Sachi didn't mind the waiting.

Or, more accurately, she understood it. Ash would never sit idly by as the people of the Sheltered Lands were threatened—even if that threat came from within, at the hands of their own rulers. Neither would Zanya. She'd experienced firsthand the sort of cruelty that House Roquebarre would gladly visit on its own subjects, and she would stop it wherever and however she could. In their hearts, they were soldiers.

So Sachi understood. Fire burned. Water was wet. Soldiers went to war.

And when they did, they left people like her behind.

The night breeze picked at Sachi's hair, blowing the loose locks around her face. The days weren't so bad. Dragon's Keep was large, with enough of a permanent population of crafters and acolytes to qualify as a settlement. There were always plenty of tasks to occupy the lady of the keep.

But the nights, when the keep's tavern awoke but everything else fell asleep? The nights were lonely, quiet and interminable. She spent most of them sitting in the consort's garden, looking out over the courtyards and the caldera, waiting for her lovers to return.

"My lady?"

Startled, Sachi turned to the petite, battle-hardened blonde who served as her personal guard. "Ambrial. I am so, so sorry—"

"But you weren't listening." Ambrial favored her with a small, forgiving smile more suited to a holy woman than a near-mythic warrior. "Understandably, your thoughts are elsewhere."

"To put it mildly."

"We don't have to speak," Ambrial offered. "Silence has its worth."

"No. I asked you to distract me, then promptly refused to let you. I'm beastly."

Ambrial hid another, more amused smile behind her hand. "As you say, my lady. Shall I begin again?"

"Please do."

"Then I'll tell you about the sundering of the continents." Ambrial squared her shoulders. "Back when the gods we know were young, the earth was . . . different. The Dream had shaped it into one land surrounded by one sea. United and harmonious. Then came the War of the Gods."

Ash had spoken of it, though rarely, as if the pain of it all was still too fresh. The Builder, as he was then known to his fellow gods, had sought to exploit the earth's resources in order to further his construction projects and industrial progress. But he'd taken things much too far, stripped and scarred the land beyond its ability to recover naturally. The Builder became the Betrayer, and when the other gods had tried to stop him . . .

War.

"None of the gods wanted to fight their brother, but they'd exhausted every avenue of diplomacy and appeasement. So, in order to spare the others the pain of marching against one of their own, the Dragon claimed the fight as his, and stood against the Betrayer alone."

Oh, Ash. It was so him that an ache rose in Sachi's throat, a noise caught somewhere between a laugh and a sob. There was nothing he wouldn't take on himself, no agony he wouldn't endure to protect his family.

"The earth itself wept as the Dragon and the Betrayer fought. The very ground beneath their feet tore apart in protest and crashed back together in grief, raising the Western Wall, along with a brand-new range of mountains along the border. Fire burned across the plains, blackening the soil, and then over the deserts, so hot the sand turned to glass."

The visual pierced Sachi's mind, bringing with it an image of the twisted vista so clear, she felt as if the very real expanse of it stretched out before her.

Ambrial drew in a shaky breath. "The Dragon and the Betrayer fought bitterly, slamming one another against the torn earth with such force that their infantries were knocked back, unable to intervene. So they continued to fight, just the two of them, shattering rock and hot glass, leaving craters so deep we can still see the scars today."

The evocative words slipped beneath Sachi's skin, thrummed in her veins, lit her senses until she could hear the sky howling and smell the rent earth. She closed her eyes and swore she could feel the hot sand beneath her bare feet. She clenched her fists and tasted the iron tang of blood in her mouth.

The wind whipped Sachi's hair around her face now, driven by hot gusts that stung her cheeks.

When she opened her eyes, the garden had vanished. So had Ambrial, and the consort's tower, and the whole of Dragon's Keep. Sachi stood in a desert, so vast that it seemed to never end. Dark clouds roiled overhead, turning over and over in a dizzying tumble, interrupted only by sharp, jagged flashes of lightning.

Sachi squinted. In the distance, so far away she could barely make out the shapes as human, two figures clashed. Watching them *hurt*, and Sachi's pulse sped. Out of instinct, she started to move toward them, but her feet were so heavy she could barely lift them.

Suddenly, the figures shot high up into the air, arcing through the sky as if propelled by some unseen force. When they slammed back to the ground, raising a plume of sand as they slid across the desert floor, they were much closer. Sachi almost lost her balance and fell as the earth rumbled and shook.

Sachi managed to stay on her feet, but then she rubbed the grit from her eyes, and she nearly sank to the sand anyway. One of the people fighting was Ash, and the other was a red-haired man with a short beard. Both were bruised and bloodied.

Realization overwhelmed Sachi, and she swayed on her feet. She was watching the distant past unfold. The War of the Gods, when the earth—along with Ash's heart—had been sundered by greed and treachery. Was it merely her imagination, fleshing out Ambrial's story in vivid detail? Or was she literally seeing a vision of the events of long ago?

It *felt* real, so Sachi surrendered herself to the vision. Every bit of her, body and soul, right down to the marrow, *longed* for Ash—to call out, to go to him. To rescue him from this dreadful fight that no one could ever win.

She knew she couldn't intervene, but still she stepped forward just as the red-haired man—*the Betrayer*—drew back his arm for a brutal punch. To her shock, he stopped, as if his attention had been drawn by something.

And then he looked up at her.

His brow furrowed as his gaze fixed unmistakably on her, roving over her face. Sachi froze, afraid to move. Afraid to break the spell, but also of what might happen if she inserted herself any more fully into this ancient, long-past moment.

Then the man exhaled, the sound full of shock but also a strange sort of yearning. "Are you real or a dream?"

The moment shattered as Ash roared and pushed him back far enough to plant both feet on the man's chest for a solid kick. The Betrayer went flying through the air, screaming.

Sachi reached for Ash. Her fingers barely grazed his bare shoulder before she, too, was flying, only *away*, back through time, through space.

Back to herself.

She gasped in a breath. Ambrial half stood over her, having started to rise from her seat, concern etched on her pale, delicate features.

"Are you well?" her guard asked anxiously.

Sachi laughed, but it came out sounding too high and a little breathless. "Fine. I'm fine. I just drifted off into my own world again, that's all."

"Yes," Ambrial said slowly. "Yes, my lady. I believe that you did."

She sounded too serious, as if, on some level, she understood. As if she'd somehow *seen* the truth, and Sachi didn't know what to say.

In the end, she didn't have to say anything, because the blaring of horns brought her to her feet. They weren't the sharp, discordant blasts she'd heard in drills, meant to signal an attack. These horns were deep, mellifluous, heralding the arrival of the Lord of the Keep.

"Ash," she breathed into the night breeze. "Zanya."

She hit the curved exterior stairs, the endless stone steps that led down from the consort's garden to the castle's battlements. She ran along them, brushing past the stationed guards in her haste to reach the next set of stairs.

By the time Sachi reached the courtyard and the wide wooden gate that secured it, the returning group had made it to the Godwalk. The small towers that served as the court's base of operations at Dragon's Keep rose on either side, casting the new arrivals in a dizzying mix of shadow and light from the windows.

Panting and breathless, Sachi clenched her hands into fists to keep from clutching her side. But the breath she *did* have deserted her entirely when she caught sight of Zanya's blood-streaked face.

"You're bleeding," she gasped, stumbling forward.

Ash was there immediately, his soothing grip steadying Sachi's steps as his voice washed over her. "It's not hers. She only got a scratch, and it's already healed."

"I'm fine." Zanya caught Sachi's hands before they could make contact. "I promise I'm fine. But I'll ruin your dress."

Sachi yanked her hands free and threw her arms around Zanya's neck. "Damn the dress," she rasped. "And damn you for scaring me like that."

She held on, trembling with relief, as Zanya patted her back, insensate to the gentle murmurs in her ear until she heard one word: *Velez*.

An icy chill slithered up Sachi's spine at the mention of the loathsome man, and she drew back. "Velez was part of this attack?"

Elevia snorted. "He was. And now he's part of your very lovely velvet dressing gown."

"Oh." Sachi's stomach turned—not from the reminder of the blood soaking her gown, but at the implications. Velez was an important person, well-regarded among not only the courtiers but the extended royal family, as well.

Zanya's jaw tightened as she avoided Sachi's seeking gaze. It didn't matter—Sachi knew her well enough to read the tangle of emotions on her face. Defensive guilt, stubborn satisfaction . . . and a whisper of the pain that had chased them both from the capital.

Ash sighed softly. "It was a complicated situation—" he started, only to be cut off by Ulric's rough snort.

"It was a disaster," the Wolf said shortly.

Sadly, Sachi suspected it was an understatement. Ulric had a particular talent for that. But that was a private conversation, one she needed to have with Ash and Zanya alone.

So she took their hands and smiled tightly at the others. "I'm so pleased you all made it back. But I need to see to my lovers just now. You understand?"

Ulric inclined his head respectfully before turning to the massive stone building that served as his home when he was in residence at Dragon's Keep. Elevia followed, staying close behind him instead of breaking away to her tower next door.

Aleksi hesitated, then nodded. "Tomorrow?"

"Tomorrow." Ash put one hand at the small of Zanya's back and pulled Sachi to his chest with the other.

They could have walked back through the castle and up the endless steps, but Zanya was too anxious to be away from watchful eyes. Shadows twirled out from her in a wild, eager storm, abruptly spinning darkness around the three of them. The world vanished, replaced with the momentary sensation of falling, and Sachi's feet hit the plush woven rug at the foot of her bed.

This was *her* chamber, *her* space, and she sprang into action. She pointed at Ash, then at the hearth, where she'd already hung two fresh kettles of water to boil. "You, light that. Then fetch me some bathing cloths, please. And *you* . . ." She turned to Zanya, who stood there with a wary expression. "Let's get you out of that armor."

Zanya took a step back, already fumbling with the blood-encrusted buckles. "I can do it."

Sachi batted her hands away, then tried to brush away a spot of blood beneath Zanya's eye. It only smeared. "I'm going to do it. And you're going to allow me."

"You don't need to get blood on your hands," Zanya whispered, but she wasn't fighting it anymore.

"I know what I need to do," Sachi countered.

Behind Zanya, the fire burst into cheerful flame as Ash knelt beside the hearth. He pressed one large hand to the first kettle, and the water began to steam. In moments, he'd filled a silver basin and brought it to Sachi.

"I know what I need to do," she repeated as she dipped the edge of a cloth into the water, then washed the blood from Zanya's cheek. "It's not much, but I can take care of you."

19

Zanya's eyes drifted shut. She stiffened when Ash stepped up behind her, but when he only reached for the buckles on her armor, she swallowed hard. "At least let me clean the armor."

The guilt in her voice made Sachi's chest ache. "Camlia will pout if we don't let her handle it, and you know it." She paused, dipping the cloth into the water to rinse it. "Tell me what happened out there?"

A shudder. Zanya flexed her fingers wide, then curled them into fists. "I let Velez goad me."

It was no less than Sachi had expected, but hearing her suspicions confirmed made her stomach twist painfully. "Oh, darling. *No.* You can't let them do that to you."

Ash's nimble fingers freed the final buckle, and Sachi leaned back to let him pull away Zanya's breastplate. The black, quilted gambeson vest she wore beneath hid the blood better, but there was still plenty of it. Too much. When Zanya opened her eyes, their dark-brown depths were almost swallowed by shadows—shadows and *rage.*

And so Sachi knew what her lover was going to say before Zanya parted her lips. "He threatened you."

"Of course he did. Velez was many unsavory things, but he wasn't stupid." And he'd dedicated years of his life to tormenting Zanya. Whether he had been drawn by the promise of lavish compensation, or whether he just *liked it,* Sachi didn't know. But a single word would have dragged Zanya back to all those dark places.

Sachi couldn't ask aloud, not with Ash hovering beside them, his own rage so carefully banked. But she *could* ask, after a fashion, so she tilted her head and caught Zanya's gaze, held it questioningly.

Zanya stared back for one heartbeat. Two. On the third she looked away, her voice dropping to a hoarse whisper. "He told me he'd never spent the gold he won that day. That he planned to stack it next to the gold he earned for taking your head."

Bastard.

Ash paused, the unlaced gambeson half off Zanya's shoulders. "What gold?"

"It's all in the past," Sachi deflected, pinning him with a sharp look. "Ancient history."

His jaw clenched, but he acknowledged her unspoken order with a tight nod before starting in on the buckles of Zanya's bracers. "The fight was chaotic," he offered quietly, making quick work of the right arm before switching to the left. "The villagers attacked the soldiers, and I lost control of the situation. Zanya shouldn't have been—"

"Don't," Zanya rasped hoarsely. "Don't make excuses for me. You left me unattended for the time it takes to brew a pot of tea, and I—" She choked, as if she didn't even want to describe what she'd done in front of Sachi. "I need to be *better*."

"Well, you'll both have to forgive me, but I'm laying the blame where it belongs—squarely at Velez's boots. He spent his life putting violence into the world, and it finally came back to him." Sachi grasped Zanya's chin. "He got what he deserved. Say it."

Zanya swallowed hard. Tears glistened in her dark eyes, but the shadows swirled away. They were just brown now, beautiful and sad in the firelight. "He got what he deserved."

"That's right." While Ash knelt to remove Zanya's greaves and boots, Sachi finished cleaning her face. "There. Do you feel better now?"

Zanya exhaled with a shuddering laugh. "No. Maybe?" She swiped a hand over her eyes, dashing away tears. "There is one good thing about this, I suppose."

"What's that, my love?"

"Velez knew how to hurt me." She reached up to stroke Sachi's hair. "Most of the people who could have said that are dead. And now he's joined them."

Sachi quelled a shudder. "We won't be running from that place forever. I promise, Zanya."

She closed the distance between them, sealing the vow with a soft peck before seizing Zanya's mouth. In response, Zanya's possessive fingers plunged into Sachi's hair.

There was an edge of something desperate in her kiss, wild but also vulnerable, as if she were trying to center herself with the familiar comfort of Sachi's lips. Sachi let her take control of the kiss and rubbed her hands soothingly up and down Zanya's arms.

For a moment, it seemed like it was working. Zanya tightened her grip in Sachi's hair with a throaty moan and backed up a step, bringing Sachi with her. But with the next step, Zanya collided with the wall of Ash's chest. His large hands covered Sachi's, steadying them both.

And Zanya vanished in a swirl of shadows, leaving Sachi stumbling into Ash's arms.

Not again.

Ash sighed softly and rested his chin on the top of her head. "I shouldn't have startled her."

"It's not your fault." Zanya had been accidentally taking to the shadows often since her manifestation, and it was always worse when she was upset. "On a night like tonight? I should have expected it."

"Maybe I shouldn't have taken her with us." Ash pulled back and tucked a disheveled strand of Sachi's hair behind her ear. "Too many people from that cursed palace hurt both of you. Neither of you have had time to deal with the pain of it."

"We'll manage," she whispered. "But what about you? You must have been frightened when Zanya—when she—" The words choked off as a sob welled in Sachi's throat.

"Shh. Shh, Sachi. You were threatened, and she acted on instinct. An instinct I understand all too well." He tugged her close again, running a soothing hand over her hair and down her back. His lips were warm against her temple. "I've had over three thousand years to learn patience and control. She's had a bare handful of weeks. She *will* learn."

Ash wouldn't let anything happen to Zanya. Sachi knew that, but it was scant comfort when she was left at home, alone with her ignorance and Ambrial's stories. "It's the not *being* there, Ash. Not knowing what you two have faced or how you are until you return. It's killing me."

"I know." He stroked her hair again. "You've been so understanding, to stay here. I promise it won't be forever. Just until—"

A clatter sounded from the bathing chamber, accompanied by muttered curses. Zanya stalked out, barefoot and flushed with embarrassment. She shoved her windswept hair back from her face and met Sachi's eyes reluctantly. "I'm sorry. I didn't mean—"

Sachi cut off the apology with a shake of her head and a gentle smile. "Where did you go this time?"

"Our cave by the capital." Zanya looked down at her dark pants. The cuffs were damp and smelled of seawater. "The tide was in."

"We'll go back for a proper visit soon, I promise." She held out her hand and waited for Zanya to take it. "Now, I'll run you a bath, and then we'll go to bed. You need the rest—both of you."

Ash brushed a kiss to her cheek, his smile the gentle one that only she got to see. "As my consort commands."

Sachi went about her task, mulling over her vision from the gardens. It had felt real, but how was she to truly know? She supposed she could press Ash for details to confirm, but she hated to do it, even at the best of times. The wounds he had incurred during the War of the Gods were as fresh now as they ever had been. She didn't want to hurt him over what could very well have been a simple flight of fancy.

And tonight, after all that had happened? She could *never* do that to him.

No, she would find out on her own. Perhaps she'd ask Camlia if any portraits of the Betrayer existed within the keep. That way, at least Sachi would know that her vision of the past had been a true one, and not something her mind had conjured.

As for the fact that the suspected Betrayer had seemed to see her, *speak* to her? That, she would take to Ash and the rest of his court . . . but only once she knew for certain.

For now, she had her lovers home and safe, and that was what truly mattered.

Chapter Three
WITCHING MOON

Week One, Day Ten
Year 3000

Spring always came slowly to the mountains. Even with the sun well overhead, its light shining cheerfully in a cloudless blue sky, the breeze that tugged at Ash's hair as he leaned against the parapet held the bite of lingering chill.

Not that anyone crowded around the practice yard below seemed to notice.

The clash of steel rang on that same cool breeze, each impact so fast it formed an eerie sort of music. At the heart of the chaos, Zanya cut a graceful, brutal path through each of the Raven Guard in turn. She wielded newly forged double blades like they were an extension of herself, blocking blows from Remi's axes as easily as she parried Malindra's longsword.

Isolde rushed her from behind, but Zanya spun and raised her crossed swords, catching the downswing of Isolde's mighty war axe. Then she kicked the other woman squarely in the chest with enough force to send her smashing through the wooden fence around the practice ring and hurtling toward the keep walls. Isolde exploded into a mass of ravens in the instant before impact, regrouping in a flutter of wings before reforming as a woman kneeling in the dirt, panting.

"They're using powers now," Ash noted, watching Kardox's doomed attempt to close with Zanya. Moments later, he skidded across the dusty ground to join Isolde, and Zanya spun to catch Ambrial mid-swing, disarming the knight. Another mass of ravens formed, flying in all directions to narrowly escape the swing of Zanya's second blade.

"They have to," Ulric rumbled, watching the mayhem below play out through golden eyes that saw too much. "I haven't tested her fully, but she's stronger than them now. Maybe stronger than me. And her speed . . ." He huffed. "And she hasn't even mastered that shadow trick yet. Once she does, she'll be impossible to hit."

She might also spend a full night in their bed. Ash had tried not to take it personally, the way Zanya tended to startle and vanish beneath his touch, but he felt as if he were back at the beginning with her again. He'd seduced her with violence the last time, playing on the hunger for dominance that lurked beneath her skin. On her eagerness to defeat a fellow predator.

A dangerous spark, and he'd reveled in the deadly attraction between them. But this wasn't a game anymore. This was the rest of their lives . . . and this time Ash had to seduce her with safety. When she trusted him enough to be vulnerable with him, he expected the shadows would stop stealing her away.

Today, in the training yard, there was nothing vulnerable about her. The five members of the Raven Guard were legendary warriors. Ash had seen them devastate battlefields. They dominated any fight they walked into, because they'd been extraordinary even before death had claimed them. With the strength of their rebirth and the power to change forms . . .

And, five against one, Zanya was making them *work* for it.

Ash didn't know if he was terrified or fascinated—a common problem when faced with Zanya at the best of times, and an inconvenient one when every instinct he had screamed at him to descend on that practice yard. He wanted to be the one who tested her. Who pushed her. The one who honed that rough brilliance into the warrior she would become.

Something beyond a legend. The god of destruction itself.

She would be glorious.

Ulric sighed.

"What?"

"That look on your face." The Wolf shot him a disgruntled look. "This is how we ended up with a slaughtered lordling yesterday. She needs a teacher willing to grab her by the scruff of the neck when she gets out of line—"

A growl rose out of Ash's chest, utterly beyond his control. Deep beneath them, the earth responded with a rumble that made the castle walls shiver.

"See?" Ulric said mildly. "You can't play both lover and trainer, Ash. You can't spar with her because it heats your blood and then go easy on her just because you're feeling protective."

"I'm not going easy on her," he muttered.

Ulric just stared at him.

Fine, he knew it for a lie. A newborn god with the power to kill could not be coddled. He should have spent the night walking her through her loss of control, stripping away excuses and defense. He should have made her *see* that someone with their strength had no cause to recklessly slay a mortal. There were a thousand ways she could have ended the confrontation. She should have been forced to list them all, until the responsibility of her power lived in her bones as pure instinct.

Unbidden, the image of Zanya's back rose in his imagination. Light-brown skin marred by delicate, raised scars—a childhood of lashings and abuse that had left their mark. The only reason she didn't have more was because she'd begun healing too fast for the scars to set. Zanya understood brutal training all too well.

It was *all* she understood.

A lifetime of pain, and only a scant few weeks to begin believing that she might have a future beyond it. How could he cage her when she had barely tasted her first gasp of free air? "You're right. I have seen the scars they left on her body and soul. I cannot bring myself to add to them."

"I know," Ulric replied, his voice gentle. "She needs to feel safe. That is a lover's role, and you're very good at it. But she must be taught to control herself, old friend. Yesterday, she struck the head from a noble brat none of us will miss. Next time, it could be the head of a guard who startles her, or a servant who wakes her from a bad dream. Next time, it could be you. Or *Sachielle*."

Ash gripped the stone before him and watched as Zanya twirled and tumbled, steel flashing bright under the blazing sun as she parried and slashed and blocked. Kardox was panting for breath, his weariness showing in his sluggish attacks. The twins, Remi and Isolde, looked exhausted. Ambrial was next to fall victim to one of Zanya's vicious kicks, and unlike Malindra, she didn't transform in time. Her body hit the stone wall hard enough to shake it.

They'd been going since sunup, and Zanya didn't even look winded.

"You're right," Ash admitted, hating the words and knowing them for truth. "I can—"

"No," Ulric cut in. "*Not* you, for all the reasons we just discussed. You will be her lover and her protector. But Elevia and I will be her teachers, the ones who draw the lines she must not be allowed to cross."

Three thousand years of friendship was the only thing that allowed Ash to relax his grip on the parapet. Elevia and Ulric would be unyielding when it came to teaching Zanya the responsibilities and safe usage of her new powers, but they would not be cruel.

And he would be freed from these conflicting instincts.

"Thank you." Ash watched as Zanya disarmed Kardox for the final time. The man held up both hands to yield, and Zanya spun as if anticipating the next blow. None came. She'd exhausted the entire Raven Guard. Disappointment tightened her features for a heartbeat before she masked it, sheathed her swords, and moved to help Kardox back to his feet.

Would restless energy still drive her from their shared bed tonight? His steward had reported that she haunted the halls more often than not, startling servants as she endlessly paced the corridors with shadows curled around her like attentive guardians. It had been too many centuries since he'd first manifested his power to remember if he'd felt that same restlessness. Physically? Perhaps. The increased vitality and stamina could be unsettling.

But Ash suspected Zanya's problems were more deeply rooted. For two decades, she'd spent every moment training for one purpose—to kill the Dragon. She was an assassin trained for a job that no longer existed. Everything she'd been taught to do, to want, to *be* . . .

A whistle sounded from the base of the tower. Ash leaned over far enough to see Elevia standing there, her hands propped on her hips.

"Well, come on, then," she called up to them. "This silly little war isn't going to strategize itself."

Feeling too restless to bother with the stairs, Ash hopped up onto the parapet. Wings might have made the five-story drop more graceful, but it would take a much greater fall to hurt him. Especially when the earth seemed to gentle beneath his landing, shivering to disperse the impact before firming beneath his feet. He smiled and stroked fond fingers over the cobblestones before rising.

He met Elevia's raised eyebrow with a mild smile as a massive wolf landed deftly beside him. Golden eyes glared balefully before the creature shook its fur. A ripple of magic followed, and Ulric resumed his human form. Those gold eyes still looked grumpy, though. "Are we feeling too melodramatic for stairs today?"

"Only a fool keeps the Huntress waiting," Ash replied mildly.

"Flattery will *not* get you out of this," Elevia shot back.

"Don't worry, Huntress." Ulric slapped Ash on the back so hard he almost staggered. "We had the talk. Ash has agreed to step aside."

"Well, that's a relief. I was starting to think I'd have to physically move him out of our way."

Ash sighed but was spared coming up with a witty retort when Zanya approached them. She'd toweled off her face and tied her black hair back into a neat braid, erasing any proof that she'd just spent an entire morning in frantic combat.

She still nearly trembled with barely leashed energy as she fell into step beside them. "Are we going to the meeting now?"

"We are," Ash confirmed. "And after that, Ulric and Elevia have offered to take over as your official trainers."

"Official?" Zanya raised one dark eyebrow and glanced at the Huntress. "What does that mean?"

"It means I won't be nearly as indulgent as Ash," Elevia replied, "but you'll probably learn more. *If* you're willing to put in the work."

The Huntress knew exactly how to bait a trap. Zanya's dark eyes practically gleamed at the challenge—her hunger to pit herself against them and find her own strength was insatiable, and for the first time in her life she was around people eager to encourage her to do just that. "I am."

"Good," Ulric said. "We'll start after the meeting."

The cobblestone path opened into the market square, where plenty of folks were out doing their midday shopping and selling. Some of the transactions that went on between the residents of Dragon's Keep operated on a barter system—those who grew crops or tended animals traded with those who excelled at crafts or provided other services. But many more sold their surplus to Ash's steward, Camlia, who paid premium prices in High Court tokens. Cold cellars deep beneath the castle, blessed by Aleksi's touch and wrapped in Inga's magic, held goods and produce in stasis for long months, ensuring that there would always be fresh food for sale for the residents of Dragon's Keep.

Some of the shops they passed held food from Ash's cellars. Others plied freshly cooked meals, or handmade crafts and goods. A few stalls were always claimed by daring traders who braved the intimidating climb to reach the castle and were rewarded with brisk sales of harder-to-obtain items—books always went swiftly, as did luxuries from the capital.

Only two outside traders were here today, and both watched Ash's party cross the square with wary eyes. Whatever rumors had been seeded by the court of the Mortal Lords in the past weeks had clearly found fertile ground, if even those who had trusted Ash enough to cross into his domain now eyed him with discomfort.

Then again, those wary gazes might be following Zanya. Even mortals seemed to see the darkness around her now, an impossible aura of glittering shadows that whispered of danger. Those accustomed to moving among the High Court had taken it in stride. But outsiders . . .

Outsiders had always spooked more easily.

But there was nothing Ash could do about it right now. They left the market behind and stepped onto the Godwalk, the long row of towering estates that housed the High Court when they were in residence.

It had pleased Ash to build his friends extravagant homes within his domain. Each of the six buildings could have been called a modest castle in its own right, with fortified gates leading to spacious courtyards, and multiple stories of well-appointed rooms leading to towers that climbed toward the sky.

Bright, colorful banners hung down the front of each stone edifice when its owner was in residence—Inga's vivid pink was missing on the right, but the Lover's deep-amethyst standard stirred in the breeze. Surprisingly, so did the Siren's sapphire blue. "Dianthe's here?"

Ulric shrugged. "She didn't come through the front gates."

No, she wouldn't have been able to without fanfare. Then again, the Siren could go anywhere water touched. She'd described it once as passing through the ocean at the heart of the world, which didn't explain why she could dive into the water on the other side of the

Sheltered Lands and surface in the fountain in her courtyard here at Dragon's Keep as easily as stepping from her bathtub. Ash tried not to think about it much—especially after a disastrous attempt to take him with her in their youth had been his closest brush with death outside of the War of the Gods.

Drowning in the heart of the ocean sounded much more poetic than it had felt.

On the left, the Phoenix's orange banner remained painfully absent. The Wolf's dark green was a typical sight, as Ulric spent as much time in residence here as he did in his own modest keep in the Midnight Forest. They passed it and turned toward Elevia's home, her golden banner waving proudly above their heads as the group headed through the open gates into her neatly organized courtyard.

Since her actual home was so near, Elevia treated her section of the Godwalk like a hunting lodge. Hounds bayed and scampered about the courtyard, which was filled with tanning racks, game-processing tables, and heavy cauldrons bubbling on tripod stands over low fires. There was even a small smokehouse, bleeding fragrant woodsmoke into the clear blue sky. Outside, two racks bore rows of fish—one set brined and ready to go into the smokehouse, and another that had just come out and was about to be packed into barrels.

They crossed through a smaller gate and into the cooler darkness of the main building. Elevia led them to the left, to her war room.

Walking into it always felt to Ash like what it must be to walk into Elevia's mind. The vast space was well-lit and ruthlessly organized. The far wall was lined two stories high with bookshelves packed with so many volumes, he'd often imagined she owned a copy of every book ever put to print. A row of knee-high shelves held tightly rolled maps of every village and defensible structure in the Sheltered Lands. More cabinets held neatly organized correspondence from hundreds of sources scattered across their lands. Some she kept in records. Most she stored in her head.

Very little happened that Elevia did not hear about eventually.

But the main feature of the room was a massive wooden table over six paces long on which the Sheltered Lands stretched out before them in breathtaking miniature. The western mountains carved up into the air, knife sharp. Delicately painted waterfalls plunged down their sides into the main river that flowed the length of the table and spilled into Siren's Bay. The Midnight Forest's deep-green pines spilled into the Witchwood's maples, the individual trees stretching out branches as fine as eyelashes from which tiny, brightly colored leaves trembled. The gentle rolling curves of the Burning Hills gave way to lush green around the Lover's Lakes. The sparkle of water seemed so real that sometimes Ash expected to see tiny waves blowing in the breeze.

At the war table's head, Sachi perched on a stool with her hands folded in her lap, waiting patiently.

Ash hurried to her, concern rising. "Sachi, are you well?"

"Quite." She blinked up at him, her momentary bemusement quickly supplanted by an affectionate smile. "And you?"

"I'm fine." He hesitated. "You don't have to be here for this, if you don't wish it. You've suffered enough at the hands of those in the capital."

"Which is precisely why I asked her to join us. The time she spent in the Mortal Lords' court could offer insight beyond any we possess." Elevia propped her hands on her hips and pinned Ash with a flat stare. "If you have a problem with it . . ."

"I can do this, Ash," Sachi told him quietly. "She's right. You don't know them the way I do."

"No one does," Zanya said flatly. She'd circled him to stand behind Sachi, a protective shadow who traced soothing fingers down Sachi's arm. "None of us would last a week trying to navigate court politics. But she found a way to dominate them, even with no real power."

Pride was clear in her voice. Ash acknowledged it with a dip of his head. "I never meant to question if you *could*." He brushed his thumb over Sachi's cheek. "I just hate the idea that you must. I'd rather protect you from it."

Sachi wrapped her fingers around his wrist. "Likewise."

"Glad we're all in agreement, then," Elevia said wryly, just as Aleksi strolled through the door with Dianthe on his arm. "You're late. And *don't* blame it on Dianthe."

"Wouldn't dream of it." Aleksi smiled easily. "It was entirely my fault. A thousand apologies."

"Perfection takes time." The Siren teased her fingers playfully through Aleksi's hair to dishevel it. "I wouldn't want to rush him."

But Elevia didn't laugh, or even smile. She was wholly and completely focused on the task at hand. "Shall we begin?"

Dianthe moved to the foot of the table, hovering over the bay that bore her name. Ash took his place at the head, facing the mountains that cradled his keep. Instinctive positions, reflecting how they had always guarded the continent between them. While fire and earth had always sung in his veins, the Siren controlled the moods of the sea and the temper of the winds. It made them stronger than the others, their gifts being so immediately tied up in the rhythms of their very world.

It also meant responsibility lay heavily across them both whenever that world was threatened.

Ash might be the nominal leader of the High Court, but it was Dianthe who spoke. "Huntress, tell us what you know."

"The answer to that, sadly, is *not much*." Elevia walked around the table to stand next to Dianthe and indicated the capital. "We know that the death of Dalvish II left a power void at court. The king's heir, Princess Anikke, was too young—and perhaps too inexperienced—to effect a smooth ascension to the throne. Which has left us with a handful of power-hungry regents ruling the Sheltered Lands with a malleable child as their figurehead."

Aleksi shook his head. "A regrettable situation."

"Mmm. Especially since their attention seems to be firmly focused in this direction." She nodded toward the red flags that marked the sites of the attacks Ash had been forced to answer. "They're obviously making repeated—and, let us note, successful—attempts to draw Ash out of his highly defensible keep. The question is, to what end? Sadly, I've thought of numerous possibilities myself, and Aleksi keeps adding more to the list."

Ash bit back another sigh. "Dare I ask?"

"The two likeliest options are the simplest." Aleksi ticked them off on his fingers. "Either they're so arrogant they think they can kill you, or they're trying to give the Betrayer a clear chance to do it."

His former brother might well take a chance to kill him, if he thought he could. But the last time the two of them had clashed, they'd called it the War of the Gods—and they'd nearly broken the world in two.

The Betrayer had spent the last three thousand years building his own Empire and consolidating his power. Did he still fear a clash between them? Or was he sure he would win? "So those are the obvious reasons," Ash said. "What are the less obvious ones?"

"Sachi," Zanya growled. "You said the Betrayer wants Sachi."

"Oh, yes. The Betrayer wants Sachi," Elevia agreed. "Just as I'm sure the regents want *you*, Zanya. You murdered their king in his own bed-chamber. My spies tell me there was even a witness—Dalvish's favored mistress, cowering in a false closet, her arrival thwarted by yours. They must be desperate to be rid of you, just in case you decide to perform an encore, this time on one of them."

Zanya's hands curled into fists at her side, but she said nothing. Her expression said enough—anger and guilt did battle across her expressive features, a conflict sparked by the sure knowledge that her actions yes-terday would only make things worse. Ash wanted to reach out to her, but she wouldn't welcome it. Not here, in front of the others.

Sachi spoke. "How do we determine what their reasons are?"

"We don't, my lady." Elevia shrugged. "Their motivations are of no real consequence. Ash is not prepared to stay home while they murder innocents, and neither are any of the rest of us." She glanced around the table. "Any refutations on that point?"

"You know there will be none," Dianthe murmured from the foot of the table. She was dressed in her usual vivid blue—today in a sleeveless tunic that revealed the golden tattoos weaving across warm brown skin the entire length of her arms. Her eyes, normally a deep brown, glowed an electric blue as her tone dropped. "Though no more of the regents' troops will be moved by river or sea. They will have to cross overland."

"And those movements will be observed and reported back to me, so we should be reasonably aware of their comings and goings." Elevia stared down at the table, her gaze practically boring holes in the Western Wall. "No, what we *need* is actionable intelligence about the Betrayer. Let the regents writhe like fish on a hook. *He's* the one who could wreak real destruction."

Ulric's fingers traced over the base of the Burning Hills. "Has there been any word of the Phoenix?"

"Vague rumors," Elevia answered. "Dianthe has already dispatched Einar to investigate the latest one, but as of now, I can offer nothing solid."

"Einar can track a whisper in a whirlwind," Dianthe said. "So far, he's found nothing, either."

Aleksi frowned down at the table. "Then we have to locate the Phoenix. It's our only way forward. We must know what they've discovered about the Betrayer's plans."

"Agreed." Elevia sighed. "But all we can do is keep looking."

"I can try."

It was Sachi's voice, soft but sure. Every gaze swung to her, but she faced down the table of gods with the steely dignity that had entranced Ash from the start.

Her spine and spirit might thrill him, but the thought of her setting foot out of this castle with the Betrayer determined to claim her kindled a dangerous protectiveness in him. And the idea of her lost in the vast expanse of the Empire? "Sachi, we've spoken of the danger—"

"I won't have to leave the keep," she reassured him. "But you said the Phoenix has a particular affinity for the Dream, yes? Perhaps I can use that. Find them in the Dream."

For an endless heartbeat, he simply stared at her. At her big blue eyes, her upturned nose, her lushly curved lips that smiled so readily. She had golden hair that flowed down her back like sunshine, and golden skin that . . .

He'd gotten so used to her over the past weeks that he'd stopped seeing it, the same way he'd stopped seeing the magic that flowed from the other members of the High Court. But even in a room cut off from sunlight, Sachielle glowed, as if an iridescent rainbow of light exploded from her in all directions, a light that screamed of joy and hope. The exact inverse of the moody, deadly midnight glitter that surrounded Zanya.

Zanya's traumatic and dazzling manifestation had left little room to forget exactly what she was now—the power of the Endless Void cloaked in human flesh. The essence of an ancient primordial power, destruction and chaos.

There had been no equally dramatic awakening for Sachi, but her power still hummed beneath her skin as a gentle warning. And Ash *knew* what she was, in the depths of his soul. Zanya's equal. Her mirror.

The Everlasting Dream, given human form.

How reckless he had been, to ignore such a potent weapon in their armory. They had no idea what she could do if she set her mind to it. And he hadn't bothered to ask, because even with Zanya's instability and wariness, the last few weeks with Sachi had been like a fairy tale. After centuries of enduring the fear and horror of consorts trained to loathe him, he'd been gifted with this sweet ray of sunshine.

Sachi had slipped into his life as if she'd always belonged there, taking up the long-neglected tasks of a string of unwilling consorts with earnest joy. His steward adored her. The servants worshipped her. His castle, too long shrouded in tense dread and darkness, had come to life under her hands.

Ash had waited three thousand years for the consort promised to him by whispers in dreams. But that hadn't been the only promise, had it?

The Dragon's consort will break the Builder's chains, and the people will dream again.

It was pure selfishness to hoard her in his castle like a private treasure. Especially when he knew she was meant for so much more.

Exhaling softly, he nodded. "We should have asked if this was something you could do."

"It isn't. I mean, I don't *know* that it is." Sachi took a deep breath. "I should start at the beginning."

She rose and turned away, then faced the others once more. "I've always been able to slip through the Dream in the smallest of ways. I was accidentally stumbling into others' sleeping dreams—and nightmares—when I was still a child. As I grew older, I found I could do it purposefully. Enter their dreams . . . or bring them into mine."

"It isn't the same thing, though," Elevia pointed out. "A dream is just a tiny, superficial sliver of the *Dream*. Like a—a shallow pool in a small corner of a vast hall."

"I know, and I always assumed my abilities were limited to just that. But something happened." Sachi met Ash's gaze. "Last night, right before you returned."

Were her full powers finally manifesting? Sachi still clung to the idea that she was mortal, even when the truth seemed so obvious to everyone around her. "What happened?"

"Ambrial was telling me about the final battle of the War," she whispered. "When you faced the Betrayer alone. I was listening, and I was thinking of you, wishing you were there . . . and then I saw it. A vision of that last battle. I was watching it unfold before my eyes, like I was standing right there."

She held up a hand, cutting off Elevia before she could speak. "I thought the same thing, believe me. I've always had a very active imagination. But I could *feel* this—the burning winds, the shards of molten sand cutting my face." Sachi inhaled raggedly. "And then he spoke to me. The Betrayer. He looked me dead in the eye and he *spoke to me.*"

The edge of the table cracked, cutting a jagged line through the mountains on the western border. Ash stared blankly down at his own hands, unable to comprehend the meaning of his fingers digging splinters into the wood. Unable to handle the irony of this pristine, delicate copy of their world shattering beneath his hands.

The world would not survive another confrontation between him and the Betrayer. And Ash was terrified that was exactly what was coming.

"Do you know if it was true?" Elevia asked, softly this time. "Was it *him*, Sachi?"

"There are no likenesses of the Betrayer to be found in Dragon's Keep," Sachi answered, her voice equally soft. "So you'll have to tell me."

She produced a paper from a hidden pocket, carefully smoothed the creases, and laid it on Elevia's war table.

The Betrayer's mocking visage stared up at Ash, rendered in Sachi's delicate, impeccable hand.

Ash forced his hands open and used over three thousand years' worth of hard-won self-control to keep his voice even. "I've never heard of this. Of reliving the past in the Dream."

"The Everlasting Dream touches all places," Dianthe said, watching him from across the table with wary eyes. She of all people knew how close the world had come to shattering last time. She'd been the one helping him hold it together. "Perhaps it touches all times, too. Haven't we all met seers who can glimpse what is to come?"

"Glimpses," Ulric countered. "Mere wisps of the Dream."

"Well," Aleksi breathed. "I hope you'll pardon me for saying so, love, but it's about bloody time."

"*Aleksi,*" Elevia admonished.

"I am simply saying, we don't bat an eye when Zanya physically whisks one of us across the country in the span of a heartbeat. But now we're going to quibble over the lines between the present and the past?"

He held up both hands and shook his head. "Count me out of that, I just want to hear more."

Sachi smiled at him. "There is no more. The shock of it pulled me out of the vision. But . . . it made me think. Perhaps we've been going about this search for the Phoenix the wrong way."

"We did try searching the Dream in the beginning," Dianthe pointed out.

"Ash tried," Aleksi corrected. "Which is not the same thing at all. No offense, darling."

None taken, because it truly *wasn't* the same. The Everlasting Dream might whisper to Ash, but it did so through the world itself. He'd always felt strongest with the earth beneath his bare feet and the wind in his hair. The ephemeral nature of the Dream slipped too easily through his fingers.

Like Sachi almost had.

He lifted a hand to her cheek and indulged himself by smoothing his thumb over her jaw and focusing on the subtle glow of her, on the radiant diamond rainbow that lived inside her.

Magic in its purest form. Because whether she believed it or not, *he* did. Just as Zanya contained within her the power of the Endless Void, Sachi was the Everlasting Dream manifested in human flesh. They would be fools not to take advantage of her power. And yet . . .

"I worry," he said softly. "Promise me you'll take care."

"I promise, Ash. For you, anything."

On Sachi's other side, Zanya's jaw tightened. But she avoided Ash's gaze, staring stubbornly down at the map.

"Right, then." Elevia picked up a piece of her shattered map and eyed it balefully. "We all have our orders, so let's be about them. Stay ready."

Chapter Four
WITCHING MOON

Week One, Day Ten
Year 3000

When Ash had told her that she would be training with Ulric and Elevia from now on, Zanya had expected grueling swordfights and bouts of hand-to-hand combat fierce enough to exhaust the nervous energy that coursed through her. Truth be told, she'd been eager for the chance to test herself against the dark, dangerous power that curled around the Wolf and the Huntress—power that spoke of over three thousand years of strength and training.

Instead, Ulric took her back to the Huntress's war table. The damage Ash had accidentally inflicted had been seamlessly repaired, as if it had never happened.

Elevia stood at the head of the table dressed in her usual leathers, her blonde hair braided tightly around her head. She propped her hands expectantly on her hips. "Have you come prepared, young one?"

Zanya flexed her fingers. "I don't know. Ash said you'd be training me, but . . ." She gestured at the table. "I thought he meant swords, not tactics."

"Blades are superfluous, and you are *not* ready for tactics. Not yet."

Confusion rose, but Zanya found no relief in Ulric's stormy expression. She wet her lips nervously. "Is it about learning self-control? Because I killed the soldier?"

"Let's start with what you can *do*," Elevia suggested. "You can transport yourself and others across distances. What are the parameters of this ability?"

At least she had an answer to this. "I can only travel to a place I've been before. Or to a person I have a connection to."

"What happens if you try to pinpoint an unknown place or person as your destination?"

She'd tried, once, in the dizzying aftermath of accepting her full powers. She'd stood with Ash and Sachi in her arms and tried to take them back to Dragon's Keep, to Ash's bedroom. "The shadows gather around me, but I can't . . . *step*. Not until I think of a place I know."

Elevia pulled out a chair and gestured for Zanya to sit, remaining silent until she complied. "Does it have to be a place you've been, seen with your own eyes, or will comprehensive study of a location's layout and function suffice?"

"I . . . don't know."

"You can transport people. How many? Are some easier than others?" Elevia barely paused for breath. "What about objects? Other creatures? Does mass factor into this at all?"

"Or distance," Ulric rumbled. "You say you can travel to someone you've met. What about someone *I've* met? Can you travel to a place I've been if I'm with you? What happens if someone's standing right where you mean to come out? Could you travel to a moving boat? *From* a moving boat? Could you carry the boat with you?"

"And these are just the questions we can think of right now, about this particular thing." Elevia tilted her head. "What about the Terrors?

Can you unmake any Terror, or only one you summoned into our realm yourself? Will they obey your commands? Will they defend you, fight for you? For Sachi?"

Zanya's stomach lurched. "No."

For a long moment, Elevia just *looked* at her. "No, they won't do these things," she asked softly. "Or no, you refuse to even think about this?"

"No, I won't use Terrors as a weapon." It was hard to hold Elevia's gaze, but she didn't let her own waver. "It's not an option. I won't try."

"Why?"

The memory fought to rise, and Zanya choked it down. Bits and pieces still trickled through—the helpless screams of villagers. The sound of rending flesh. Blood, the scent strong and metallic and not nearly as upsetting to her as it should have been.

Sachi's horrified sobs.

The Huntress's sharp gaze saw too much. Zanya broke and looked away. "Please."

Silence. Then, "Fair enough. What else can you do?" Elevia leaned over Zanya's chair. "When you know all these answers, *then* you'll be ready for swords and tactics. But not before."

Relief flooded her when she realized Elevia wouldn't push it. Childhood memory faded, taking the screams of agony and her own bitter shame with it. Ulric and Elevia weren't like her trainers in the capital. They weren't here to shape her into a tool fit for their hands and their purposes, and they wouldn't force her to learn against her will. Having the depth of her ignorance of her powers laid out before her like a banquet wasn't *enjoyable* . . .

But they wanted her to learn everything she could be. And they'd help her get there. New anticipation buzzed along her nerves, and she lifted her chin. "I didn't come prepared," she told the Huntress, meeting her eyes squarely. "But I want to be."

"Good," Elevia murmured. "Then let's begin."

◆ ◆ ◆

Sunset found Zanya up to her chin in hot water, soaking muscles that ached for reasons she could not begin to imagine.

But I want to be.

Had she spoken those words only this afternoon? She felt at least a dozen years older. How young and innocent she had been. How foolishly energetic. Groaning, Zanya sank beneath the surface as if the hot water might do its work on her aching skull.

Only if she stayed beneath it long enough to drown.

Zanya had naively thought that controlling her abilities would be the hardest part. Through ruthless, methodical experimentation, Ulric and Elevia had shown her the truth—mastering the magic that seethed inside her was a distant dream if she did not first *understand* it.

So they'd experimented. Over the course of an afternoon, Zanya had visited every corner of the Sheltered Lands. Distance seemed to make no difference in the difficulty, but what she brought with her did.

Objects were the simplest—she transported stacks of pillows as light as feathers and cartons of ingots meant for the blacksmith with equal ease. Physical contact seemed to be the limiting factor—if she could pick it up, she could move it.

Mortals proved equally uncomplicated. Though she'd had to grit her teeth to endure being locked in a circle of a dozen of Elevia's retainers, as long as she had physical contact with all of them, she could move them as far as she wanted with no strain.

The High Court themselves were the first stumbling block. She'd traveled with Ash and Sachi plenty of times and knew the feel of them—a *heft*, as if she had to lift them before she stepped. Nothing that could challenge her, but not so effortless as the mortals, either. But transporting Elevia was harder, as if the world resisted her attempt to carry the other woman into the Void. Ulric was even worse, and the first time she'd tried to carry them together, she'd felt the strain.

Elevia had leapt upon the variation, a huntress fixed on the target of a mystery, and so the experiments had continued. Zanya had carried them across the country to the Witchwood, where Inga had proved an eager passenger. Traveling with the Witch wasn't so bad—the Void seemed as intrigued by her as she was by it. But when the time came to transport the Lover . . .

Forming shadows around Aleksi had felt like strapping a mountain to her back. Carrying him with her the single step it took to travel to his Villa felt so momentous, her arms physically shook when they stepped into the bright sunlight of his courtyard. So had his. She'd offered to leave him at his home to spare him the return trip, but he'd pointed out with a sigh that Elevia would never forgive him and held out his hand.

Carrying him back had been twice as bad somehow. He'd arrived at Dragon's Keep looking as ragged as Zanya felt and immediately begged off further trips.

He'd been granted a reprieve. So had all the animals, after her attempt to travel with a horse had resulted in a beast so panicked it had taken Ulric an age to calm the poor thing. He'd been the one to flatly forbid any more attempts with wild or tame creatures, and by that point Zanya was all too eager to comply.

The animals had been spared. Zanya had not.

She hadn't realized she could still be driven to limp-kneed exhaustion, but by the time Elevia and Ulric were satisfied with their experiments, she'd barely made it back to her quarters and into the tub. Their final words chased her there, cheerful approval that might as well have been a threat: *"A good baseline. Now we can truly begin."*

Staying underwater until she drowned sounded less exhausting than facing the whole thing again tomorrow. But Zanya had never been one to quit.

She surfaced to find a sympathetic Sachi hovering nearby with a towel draped over her arm. "Long day?"

Zanya fought the urge to whimper. Actually *whimper*. "The Huntress and the Wolf decided Ash was going too easy on me, and they intend to rectify the situation."

"Were they right?"

Of course they were. Zanya and Ash still balanced precariously on either side of Sachi, two people bound together by their shared devotion to their princess. Lust had been easy enough to kindle, but trust between predators was much harder. And Ash was so damn *protective*, as if he couldn't tolerate having the tiniest hurt befall anyone under his care.

And apparently, Zanya now fell under his care. The unnaturalness of it made her anxious in an entirely unfamiliar way. "They were too right. He coddles me when he should not."

"Why should he not?" A trace of indignation colored Sachi's voice as she unfurled the towel and held it up. "He loves you."

"No, he loves *you*," Zanya countered, rising. "What he and I have is far more complicated."

She reached for the towel—which had been warmed—but Sachi clung to it stubbornly, wrapping it around Zanya's wet body herself. Then she held out a hand, steadying her as she stepped from the bath.

Finally, she spoke. "Love *can* be complicated, and it can look different for everyone. My feelings for Ash are not the same ones I carry for you, but that's all right. They both sing like love to me."

"Because you have a generous heart." Zanya cupped Sachi's cheek and stroked a thumb over the soft fullness of her lower lip. "You love so openly. It takes me more time. I suspect it usually takes him more time, too, but who could resist you?"

"I would have thought you too tired for flattery tonight." But Sachi blushed as she rubbed the towel over Zanya's skin. Then she retrieved a similarly warmed robe of sumptuous black silk and eased it up Zanya's arms. "Come. I've set a chair in front of the fire. I'll brush your hair."

It was a complete reversal of the roles they'd been locked into by their trainers in the capital. And truth be told, Zanya had never minded this part. Tending to Sachi, pampering her . . . There'd been pleasure in that. She loved taking care of her.

But there was pleasure in being tended to, as well. Especially when that sweet flush stole over Sachi's cheeks and she lowered her lashes. Demure yet eager, the way she looked sometimes when she sank to her knees and offered to please Zanya.

So she followed Sachi to the chair. She dropped into it, the tired ache in her muscles a fading memory as warmed silk slid over her skin and Sachi's gentle fingers stroked through her hair. "Have you decided to be sweet to me tonight?"

"Whenever am I not?"

"When you want to be bad." Zanya closed her eyes, the pleasure of Sachi's touch sinking into her. "I've noticed how eagerly Ash rewards your misbehavior."

A musical laugh floated up as Sachi dragged her fingers slowly through Zanya's wet hair, carefully detangling the strands. "I couldn't deprive him of his fun. Besides, you know how novel it is for him, the fact that I'm not scared or nervous. I would never take that away."

Zanya supposed that made sense. It certainly explained how her sparring matches with Ash tended to spiral out of control, as if the danger she represented were the finest aphrodisiac. The first time she'd felt him hard and aroused beneath her had been with her knife at his throat.

And the last time she'd felt him hard beneath her had been the night she'd almost killed him.

Her heart skipped a beat. Zanya focused on the familiar touch of Sachi's fingers to ground herself. "Have you . . . since we came back to Dragon's Keep? With him?"

It took Sachi a moment to answer. "No. But you'd know that already, if you ever stayed in bed instead of getting up to pace the castle grounds all night."

"Night isn't the only time you can have sex," Zanya countered. "And I wouldn't be angry, if that's what you think."

"I know you better than that, Zan."

"I just don't want . . ." She tilted her head back and stared up into Sachi's beautiful eyes. "I'm the one having problems. I don't want to get in the way."

"You aren't. You *couldn't*." Sachi smiled, then sighed. "What are you really trying to say, love?"

Zanya lifted her head and gazed into the fire. Was it her imagination that the flames seemed to dance, even without the Dragon here? Did they rise and fall to please the woman Ash loved? "You have a place here. Maybe we never expected you to actually fill it, but you *do*. You're the Dragon's consort. This is your tower. You have duties and responsibilities. I don't know how I fit in."

This time, Sachi's laugh was more rueful. "Where do you fit in? You're the Endless Void, Zanya. Part of their court. Demand your own tower on their Godwalk, if you please." Her voice softened. "Or you could simply stay where you have always belonged. With me."

Zanya had spent the entire day in brutal training, trying to learn how to handle the responsibilities of her new powers, but the idea of demanding her own castle among the High Court's estates still felt untethered from reality. Even sitting here, while Sachi tended to *her*, felt wrong.

"A single moon ago, everyone agreed that I belonged in whatever closet was assigned to house your maid." Zanya closed her eyes as she bared the full depth of her insecurity. "At least they trained you to *be someone*. I'm barely literate, Sachi. Ignorant of everything but violence. How am I meant to sit at a table alongside *gods* as if I'm one of them?"

"Because you *are*." Gentle arms slid around her neck, and Sachi's next words stirred her damp hair. "And because you're the bravest, most determined person I've ever met. You're smarter than your trainers ever realized, and *I love you*."

The words worked their usual magic. No matter how desperate their circumstances, no matter how bleak their chances, Sachi's touch had a way of lifting any burden. As if hopelessness simply could not exist in a world where a creature as bright as Sachielle lived and breathed and adored you.

It must be partly her nature. Some innate magic tied to what she was, the literal essence of dreams. Zanya should ask Ash if he felt the same way when Sachi stroked light fingers over his skin and whispered his name in that breathless voice. If it eased one darkness inside him while stoking another—a hunger to wrap that brightness in protective arms and guard her from a world that would dim her light.

That was the darkness that wound through Zanya now, languid and dangerous. "Sachi?"

"Yes, love?"

"Come here."

Sachi laid the hairbrush on the dressing table with a soft click, then slowly walked around Zanya to stand before her. "How may I serve you?"

She looked ethereal, her simple white shift translucent where Zanya's wet body had pressed against hers. The blaze of the fire behind her outlined her curves and gave the wild spill of her golden hair its own molten highlights. The hunger inside Zanya that never truly slept exploded into a craving so deep, it took all her self-control not to lunge for Sachi and drag her to the ground.

Her fingers flexed on the arms of the chair—and the wood cracked beneath her grip. Panic jolted through her, followed by the first kiss of shadows rippling around her legs and up her body. If she hadn't been so *tired*, they probably already would have taken her away, but she caught herself and forced them to dissipate.

Sachi slid to the floor, her hands on Zanya's knees. "Stay with me."

"I'm afraid to touch you," Zanya whispered hoarsely. "I'll hurt you."

Sachi shook her head, her fingers already edging beneath silk. "I'm not afraid."

Of course she wasn't. Zanya loosened her grip on the damaged chair, but she couldn't bring herself to touch Sachi. Not yet. "I threw one of the Raven Guard through the fence surrounding the practice grounds this morning and fractured the keep walls. How can you trust me when I don't even know my own strength?"

"Because you're just like Ash. You don't want to hurt me." She lowered her head and licked the inside of Zanya's knee, sparking a shiver of anticipation. "You'd die first."

"I'd never do it on purpose," she agreed, breathless as the robe gave way under Sachi's clever fingers. Silk slid over her skin, caressing her breasts and her aching nipples. Warm breath feathered higher on her inner thigh as Sachi edged her knees wider. She wanted to sink her fingers deep in that golden hair and twist tight. "But you're so good at making me lose control."

"Don't think of it that way," Sachi urged. "Think of it as letting go."

Zanya dared a single touch—a fingertip she traced over Sachi's flushed cheek and down to the adorable point of her chin. Gently, so gently, she used that fingertip to lift Sachi's gaze to hers. "Is that what you want? Do you want to make me let go?"

"I want you to stop thinking so much," she answered in a yearning whisper. "You don't have to give up your control, just . . . stop clinging to it so damn hard for a little while."

Zanya could deny Sachi nothing when she turned those wistful blue eyes on her. The arms of the chair might be dented and wobbling now, but the back was as plush as the seat. Zanya relaxed into it and scraped her fingernails lightly over Sachi's scalp. "You know what pleases me, love. Be sweet for me."

Her reward was a brilliant smile as Sachi surged up to kiss her. For an endless moment, that was enough—the joy of getting to simply *kiss* Sachi openly and without fear. She could take her time enjoying the taste of her, including the hints of ginger and lemon from her tea, and the soft noises she made when Zanya licked past her lips to tangle their tongues.

Sachi was the one who broke away first, sinking back down to her knees. Her fingertips trailed up Zanya's calf, followed by the soft brush of her hair. Then more kisses—Sachi's open lips pressing to the sensitive spot just inside her knee. A graze of teeth. Her tongue, teasing its way up Zanya's inner thigh as Sachi's fingers stroked her hips, the curve of her waist, her outer thigh, her knee . . .

A slow burn so exquisite, Zanya felt her head tip back. She wished she could thread her fingers back into Sachi's golden hair, but the only things she dared to grip were the much-abused wooden arms of the chair. "Is this what you call sweet? I would call this teasing me."

Sachi only glanced up at her, a wicked gleam in those blue eyes, and licked higher. Familiar fingers danced their way over her hip, moving lower. Zanya's breath sped, her body tense with anticipation as the two meandering paths converged on a single target.

When they reached it, Zanya gasped. Knowing fingertips stroked her. Parted her. Left her exposed for the hot touch of Sachi's tongue. The pleasure of it bloomed bright and so hot her hips jerked up in spite of her attempts to stay still. Sachi only hummed in satisfaction and pressed her against the chair before licking her again and again, each knowing stroke a silent demand that Zanya's body answered eagerly.

Heat flooded her limbs. Tension braided itself tighter within her, until even Sachi's firm touch couldn't still the restless movement of her hips searching for the pressure that would release the gathered need and let her soar.

But Sachi didn't give it to her. Instead, she slowed her caresses. Her mouth drifted lower, licking through her folds, her tongue driving deep, as if to savor the arousal she'd sparked. Zanya groaned her frustration—a groan that twisted into a sharp cry when Sachi stroked her free hand up to pinch one tight nipple.

The nip of almost-pain shot straight to her core, tangling with the languid pleasure there. Her fingers spasmed, and another sharp crack came from the left arm of the chair as it started to list sideways. "Sachi—"

"Let go," came the soft plea, and Zanya squeezed her eyes shut and shoved her fingers into her own hair, gripping it as clever fingers found her other nipple, and the harsh jolt left her squirming helplessly.

It shouldn't have been like this—so intense, so close to madness from just a few touches and the caress of Sachi's tongue. But when Zanya dared open her eyes, the sight was what shattered her.

Sachi, golden and glowing, backlit by the firelight in her barely there gown. Her cheeks were flushed with the pleasure of pleasing Zanya, her blue eyes bright with love. She captured Zanya's gaze and refused to let it go as she fucked two fingers slowly into her, the sound utterly obscene in the quiet, otherwise broken only by the crackle of the fire and Zanya's hoarse breaths. She was so wet the glide of them only taunted her with what she needed—more.

Of course Sachi knew. Her tongue swept out again, rough and swift over Zanya's clit. And then there were three fingers filling her, and it was too late for slow. Sachi fucked her, twisting deep, timing each advance to coincide with a flutter of her tongue that had Zanya's pulse racing out of control.

This time, she didn't slow. That braided tension twined tighter and tighter until Zanya thought she'd die of it. Her right hand clenched tight. Wood cracked in the distance. She didn't know what it was. Only that Sachi's golden hair was finally, *finally* beneath her fingertips. She wrapped her fingers in that silken glory and savored Sachi's moan as pleasure twirled higher and higher, as her fingers curled tighter and tighter—

Sense came to her at the same time as release, her orgasm riding a wave of bright, terrible panic. Shadows exploded with the force of her body's tremors, wrapping her in their embrace, and she had no conscious thought left except one.

Protect Sachi. Protect—

Zanya landed naked on cold stone, the shock of it overwhelming with her body still shuddering through release. Disoriented and reeling, she forced her trembling limbs to obey her, rolling onto her side and then her knees as her gaze swept the unfamiliar surroundings.

A burning hearth. Rough-hewn walls. Vast darkness. A comfortable-looking leather chair large enough to seat two people . . .

. . . or one dragon god.

Ash started to his feet, tossing aside his book as panic filled his eyes. "What is it? Is Sachi—?"

He cut off with a sharp inhalation, and humiliation burned through Zanya when he abruptly turned away. She already knew how sharply he could smell Sachi's arousal. With the last shivers of orgasm still rocking through her, Zanya must have reeked of sex and need. No doubt her full flush and disheveled hair told the entire story.

She'd never been self-conscious about her body before, but *this* sort of nakedness was enough to make her wish for oblivion.

A warm weight fell over her back. A robe, the soft fabric smelling strongly of Ash, and she scrambled to shove her arms into the sleeves and fasten it around her. Only then could she force herself to take slow breaths as she climbed to her feet.

Facing him made her face burn all over again. But there was only gentle concern in his gaze as he perched on the arm of the chair. "Is everything all right?"

She didn't know how to answer. Now, instead of dying of humiliation, she felt as if she'd been caught doing something illicit. They'd never really discussed the boundaries of . . . whatever this thing was. His assurances that he would not be threatened by Zanya's prior claim might hold when he was enjoying the intimacy of his consort's bed . . .

But no one had been getting much intimacy lately, mostly because of Zanya. "I'm sorry," she whispered awkwardly. "I wasn't—I wasn't trying to leave you out."

"I didn't imagine you were." He rose and took a step toward her, but froze when Zanya stumbled back. Retreat was against everything in her nature, but she felt too off-balance, too *raw* to push a challenge like this. His robe might cover her from chin to ankles, but she still felt naked.

Ash sighed softly. "She is your lover, Zanya. You do not need my permission to enjoy each other. My only concern is if . . ."

Zanya wet her lips. "If?"

He shook his head. "You look exhausted. And Sachi must be worried. Go back to her, and we'll discuss it another time."

Pulling the robe more tightly around her body, Zanya shook her head. "Sometimes I don't understand you at all."

A tiny smile quirked his lips. "I find you equally perplexing. That is why we'll talk. Later. I'll sleep in my bed tonight."

"No."

"No?"

Zanya found her pride and stepped forward, staring up into his face. "Sachi sleeps better when you're near. Give me a moment to talk to her, but come to bed with us. Please."

The Dragon watched her with those ancient brown eyes for a long time before lifting one hand. He moved slowly, as if afraid she'd shy away. When she didn't, he used one fingertip to catch a stray lock of hair that had tangled in the collar of the robe and smoothed it back behind her ear. "As you wish, Zanya."

Her body was still too sensitive to tolerate the touch. It prickled over her skin in dangerous temptation. She could have simply turned and left his quarters and endured the walk back across the stone bridge to Sachi's tower, but she wanted to be *gone*. The shadows twirled around her, and she took the step into the Void, pausing there a moment in the peaceful, floating darkness, where no one could see her cheeks flame.

With mortification? With desire? She still wasn't sure. But a few deep breaths in the familiar emptiness restored her equilibrium enough for her to step back into Sachi's quarters with her expression under control.

She found Sachi curled up in her massive bed, a lamp still shining on the bedside table and a large book open in her lap. Just like Ash, another thing the two shared in common. Insecurity tried to rear its head again, but Zanya stamped it down and offered Sachi a nervous smile. "I'm sorry? But I'm back."

Sachi's answering smile was gentle, soothing. "Where did you go this time?"

In response, Zanya gestured to the robe. She was a tall woman, but it had been tailored for Ash and was correspondingly massive. The sleeves covered her fingertips, and the hem almost dragged the floor. "Ash was reading, too. I startled him."

"I imagine so." Sachi tugged the heavy covers back and nodded to the middle of the massive bed. "Do you want to talk about it or get some sleep?" The corner of her mouth kicked up in a sudden, wicked grin. "Or try again?"

"With my luck, if we try again I'll end up in the middle of the market square. Or in Castle Roquebarre's throne room." Her usual nighttime attire was laid out on a padded bench near the bed, no doubt left there by quietly competent maids attending all the tasks Zanya used to do.

She shrugged out of Ash's robe and pulled on the loose pants and sleeveless top. Then she climbed into the bed and knelt facing Sachi. "We do need to talk."

"All right." Sachi closed her book and set it aside.

"I'm learning," Zanya said haltingly. "Ulric and Elevia aren't going to go easy on me, but maybe that's what I need. I used to know my body and my strength. I trusted myself. I need to learn how to trust myself again."

"So you'd like to be celibate for the time being?"

"No, it's not—" She cut off the panicked denial and forced herself to take a breath. There was no judgment in Sachi's loving expression. No disappointment. It made it easier to whisper the vulnerable truth. "I want to try, but I need for it to be okay if it takes time. If I keep messing up."

"Take as long as you need." Sachi grasped her hand, squeezed it. "Ash and I can wait."

Anxiety squeezed her chest tighter. "No, that's what I *don't* want. It's too much pressure, Sachi. If you want to bed him, you should. You don't have to wait for me."

For what seemed an eternity, Sachi just *looked* at her, her searching blue gaze roving over Zanya's face. Then, finally, "All right. I understand."

Relief eased the pressure inside her, and Zanya managed a shaky smile. "I would ask if I should do the same if the situation arose, but I'm not brave enough to face the Dragon on my own."

"He would gladly take you." Sachi's voice was tender and serious, skating right past the half-joke. "And I would be glad to know that you felt cherished and safe, as I do."

The words stirred a different sort of ache, a quiet yearning that had nothing to do with feeling cherished and everything with knowing that the violence inside her could meet its match in the Dragon. With him, she didn't want to feel safe. She didn't *need* to—because the Dragon could handle it if she let go of *everything*.

Of course, she'd have a hard time fucking him if she kept vanishing every time he touched her.

"We'll see." Zanya relaxed back onto the bed and pulled Sachi with her. "I may be worrying for nothing. A solid week of Elevia and Ulric making me transport people and supplies and gods and horses back and forth across the Sheltered Lands, and I'll either have perfect control of my powers or I'll be too tired to vanish and you can have your wicked way with me regardless."

Sachi giggled. *"Scandalous."*

"Not unless I bring you with me the next time I'm coming on your tongue." Zanya buried her laugh in Sachi's golden hair. "Imagine all the places we could have arrived. Though given the unpleasant day Aleksi had while traveling with me, appearing in his courtyard might have given him a treat."

"Or we could have wound up on Camlia's desk, crushing all her very important correspondence."

"While I'm sure she would take it in stride," Ash's voice rumbled from the balcony, "she would certainly find a way to blame me for upsetting the order of her castle."

Sachi sighed. "Entering the room without explicit permission is far less rude than eavesdropping, my lord. Please do *come in*."

Zanya turned to find Ash strolling into the room. He closed the door and pulled the thick curtains that kept out the late-winter chill before crossing to the bed. His gaze caught Zanya's, one brow raised in silent question.

She was in Sachi's normal spot in the middle of the bed. Usually they curled up on either side of her, two protective monsters guarding their love—but if she moved now, it would feel too much like a rejection. So she tugged the blankets back on her side in equally silent response.

The mattress dipped under his weight. Ash propped himself up on one arm and leaned over Zanya to brush a kiss to Sachi's lips before lying down, his body a line of fire not quite touching Zanya.

Sachi lowered the lamp. The fire was still blazing merrily, and she settled down in the sharp shadows cast by its flames, a contented smile curving her lips. "Good night."

"Good night," Ash murmured from her other side, and the solid weight of his arm settled across Zanya's body. In the soft firelight she could see his fingers splayed possessively over Sachi's hip. She heard Sachi's soft sigh of contentment. Their warmth cradled her, contained her . . . *surrounded* her.

But they were still three pieces that didn't quite fit. How could they? Zanya herself was in pieces, and she hadn't quite figured out how to put all her sharp edges back together yet. She could only hope that training with Ulric and Elevia would help.

Zanya might not have much practice in dreaming for the future, but she knew this was where she wanted to belong.

Chapter Five
WITCHING MOON

Week Two, Day One
Year 3000

Sachi didn't know how to fail.

To some, that might have seemed like a good thing, a statement of eternal victory. But it wasn't, because of course it didn't mean she *never failed*. It simply meant she didn't know what to do when she did. How to pick herself up and carry on instead of falling to self-recriminating pieces.

It wasn't a flaw she liked to consider, much less admit, but there it was, all the same. Though it couldn't exactly be called a fault, could it? It wasn't as if she simply *disliked* the idea of being terrible at something, anything. No. She'd spent the last twenty years acutely aware that failure of any sort meant something worse than defeat—the shame of punishment. Unendurable pain.

So was it really any wonder she couldn't abide the thought of it?

She clenched her fists and pressed the naked soles of her feet harder against the bare stone of her chamber floor, anchoring herself in her dream. Her favorite chair by her favorite window was bathed in late-afternoon sunlight. Even with her eyes closed, she felt its warmth on her face, seeping through her velvet dressing gown.

She could do this. She *must*.

But she hadn't counted on Elevia's warning to hold so wretchedly *true*. Sachi's previous forays into the Dream had been tentative explorations of but a small corner of it, like splashing up to your ankles in a tide pool. Now, she was trying to dive right through the heart of it, in search of one tiny beam of light.

How did one begin to search the vastness of all the oceans for a single shell?

Perhaps this was more like Zanya's gift of traveling through the Void than Sachi had previously considered. That seemed to require certain levels of acquaintance—with the destination, with the journey. Even with her companions.

And so it was with Sachi's dreamwalks. The dreams of those she knew were like living tableaux, staged masquerades into which she could slide with no effort, as if her very knowledge of them had laid their souls bare to her. She'd never even attempted it with dreams of an absolute stranger. She saw them sometimes, in that formless space that she knew as the Dream—blurry bubbles of emotion that seethed with nostalgia or desire, fear or confusion. Peering into them was like trying to look through a thickly frosted pane of glass. She'd never dared to try to penetrate those barriers.

Maybe searching for someone was bound by the same limitations. Since she'd never met the Phoenix, it could be sheer folly to even attempt to find them in this boundless—Everlasting—dreamscape. But she had to try.

She *had* to, for Ash's sake. She had to do everything in her power to prevent another showdown between him and the Betrayer. Ash wouldn't survive it. Not because he couldn't stand against his brother, but because seeing the earth torn asunder *again* would kill him.

"They're not *really* brothers, you know."

The cheerful voice materialized behind her. Sachi whirled around, but saw only bright, unending emptiness.

"Sevastyan was an only child. His mother wanted many more, but that was not to be."

The rasp of stone on stone enveloped Sachi, along with the distinctive crackle—and warmth—of a fire. When she turned this time, a woman sat before her, grinding some sort of large grain or kernel on a wide, concave rock.

The woman was *old*, with sun-scorched skin the color of tea-stained paper. It gave her the contradictory appearance of being tough and delicate at the same time, with deep creases in her cheeks and around her eyes, especially when she smiled. But her hands—about those, there could be no doubt. They were still strong, capable. Her hair was long and gray, held back from her face in simple braids secured by leather ties worn soft from age, just like her. She was dressed very much like Elevia or Ulric, in homespun and leather and furs, except that every item she wore was a different shade of purple.

The woman hummed as she finished grinding the dried grain, gathered it in one aged palm, and dropped it into a kettle boiling over the fire. She smiled as she stirred, then finally settled back on her heels with a sound of satisfaction.

Sachi stepped closer, drawn in by the sweet domesticity of the scene, warmed as much by the woman's smile as by the fire. "May I?" she asked, indicating an empty spot on the furs beside her.

The woman looked up at Sachi with a mild confusion that quickly gave way to joy. "Of course! Sit, sit. There is always room for you at my fire, and the night meal is almost ready."

The furs were plush, heated by the flames, and Sachi pulled them around her body as she settled in. "It smells delicious."

"It's venison stew." The old woman leaned forward to stir the kettle again, groaning softly as she shifted her weight. "I had to trade three coils of good, sturdy rope for this haunch."

"That's very expensive." The words left Sachi's tongue without thought, unbidden, but she knew at once that they were true.

"Aye, very." The woman looked up and winked at her. "But wait until you taste it. The first stag of Isere's Moon is good luck, you know."

Sachi *didn't*, but the mention of Isere snagged on a memory—standing under the trees with Ash in the Midnight Forest, watching magic drift down around them as he told her the story of the lovers who became their moons. A story his grandmother had told him as a boy.

"You're her," Sachi whispered. "His grandmother."

"My name is Saga." Her eyes twinkled with mischief—and love. "Tell me, does he still sneak extra puddings?"

"He doesn't have to," Sachi answered honestly. "The Dragon can have anything he wants. Everything."

"Hmph." Saga frowned skeptically as she turned away and prodded the fire beneath the kettle.

Sachi stared at the old woman, bewildered. How could this be? The Dream was a mysterious place of wild wonders where almost anything was possible, but not this.

Never this.

In all her many lessons, Sachi had never once heard of an intact spirit dwelling within the Dream. The priests taught that death was as much of a homecoming as it was another beginning, a return to the Dream so complete that the departed became one with it. Their very soul would melt into the Dream to await what came next.

But here was a woman who had lived long before the time of the gods, stirring a spitting fire back to blaze under a fragrant stew.

"I'm sorry," Sachi whispered. "But . . . are you *real?*"

"The cheek!" Saga gasped in outrage, but it turned to laughter before Sachi could hasten to apologize. "To be honest, it seems more fitting that *I* should ask *you*."

"That's fair." The first step, perhaps, to determining the answer to Sachi's question was to get more details. "Where are we? And when?"

Saga looked out, past the fire. As she did, shadows began to appear in the nothingness, shadows that swirled until they took the shapes of sky and earth, buildings and animals. People.

"This was the best day of my life," she murmured, smiling. "Not the greatest or the most important, but the one filled with the most pure happiness. The most peace."

Perhaps the priests in the capital were wrong, and *this* was the real promise of returning to the Dream. Your own little corner of it, where you could relive your happiest moments. No troubles or strife, just a quiet, gentle rest.

Sachi didn't know.

"Now, then." Saga's gnarled hand settled over Sachi's, warm and seemingly very real, indeed. "Tell me—how is my boy?"

"Worried," she answered immediately. "About so many things. Whether he'll have to fight again. Whether his efforts will be enough this time to secure a victory. Whether the cost will be too high, even if victory comes."

"Those are far from idle concerns, my child. They are worries born of wisdom. Experience."

"I know. But it's hard because I can't help him."

The woman's brows knit in confusion. "Why not? Aren't you his consort? His mate?"

"I'm . . ." But the words died on her lips. Sachi couldn't bring herself to admit the truth, not even here. Not even to a woman who'd been dead for thousands of years.

I'm not enough.

She didn't say it, but Ash's grandmother nodded anyway. "I understand. It's impossible, isn't it?"

Sachi felt helpless, adrift in the face of her own shortcomings. "Then how am I to do it?"

Saga seemed to consider that for a long time. Then she said, "Realize, Sachielle, that this may not be about skill, or preparation, or even luck. That the task you see before you is not your true test."

Sachi's head was beginning to spin, and she shook it to clear it. "Then what is?"

"You must learn to be who you are." Saga's eyes burned, bored into hers. "Are you ready to walk this path?"

"No," she confessed. "I'm *scared*. Terrified."

"No. You doubt, and that's not the same thing at all." The old woman's hand tightened around hers. "I cannot give you the answers you seek, for they lie within you. Only you can decide what they are."

Sachi's mind reeled. It didn't really seem like the sort of thing a person could just *decide*, whether or not to be a primordial force of existence older and more powerful than the entirety of the High Court.

Saga cocked her head to one side. "A shame you can't stay for the meal, child."

Sachi opened her mouth to ask why, but sudden pain jabbed her in the side. The Dream melted, stripped away in an instant, until only the vaguest sense of it remained.

She opened her eyes in her bed, where Zanya had rolled over and shoved an elbow into Sachi's ribs. Gently, Sachi slipped into the space Zanya had vacated and let her have the rest of the bed, giving her room to sprawl.

It left Sachi cuddled close to Ash. As he looped an arm around her waist and murmured sleepily, she studied his face in the soft moonlight, looking for any hint of resemblance to the woman she'd seen in the Dream. They had similar eyes, she supposed, and the same nose. And Sachi could tell that, had he grown old instead of taking his place among a pantheon of immortal gods, Ash would have carried the same laughing lines around his eyes that Saga had worn.

Could Sachi do this? Could she accept that this might be her destiny, as well? She'd barely even begun to entertain the notion of a life beyond Dalvish's court, beyond her suicide mission to destroy the Dragon. Now she had to try to fathom an eternal existence?

It seemed too much to comprehend, but she knew she could do it, because she would have Ash and Zanya. She wouldn't have to watch and mourn as injury or old age stole them away, leaving her behind with an empty bed and even emptier heart. She would spend the ages with them.

She *desperately wanted* to spend the ages with them.

Was that enough to unlock her destiny? It couldn't be, or the unfettered Light of the Dream would be pouring through her at this very moment. And Sachi didn't feel any different.

You must learn to be who you are.

Perhaps that wasn't as metaphorical as it had sounded at first blush. After all, Sachi knew what she'd been trained to be, what she'd been meant to do to complete her assigned tasks. But those were external definitions, forced on her by a king who hadn't cared what lay beneath Sachi's blue eyes and fair skin. To him, she was merely a tool to be sharpened.

So who *was* she, really? She enjoyed music and dancing, the feel of soft fabrics against her skin. Sunrises, though she relished sleep a bit too much to see many of them. She couldn't abide bullies or bear to see injustices go unchecked, and sometimes she worried that the skillful manipulation that had been part of her training had seeped into her very pores, become a part of her that could never be torn away.

She loved Zanya, who had always been so fiercely protective no matter how scared she was. And Ash, who was equally fierce and so *lonely* that it permeated everything about his life, like ice slowly opening cracks in a solid wall.

Silently, Sachi recited everything she knew about herself, repeating the words until she drifted back into a quiet, dreamless sleep.

Chapter Six
WITCHING MOON

Week Two, Day One
Year 3000

Outside of those brief, awkward moments the previous night, Zanya had never been inside the Dragon's Tower.

Sometimes it was easy to forget that he was the Lord and Master here. Ash's steward, Camlia, ran both castle and keep with an iron fist and a proprietary interest passed down through generations. Her son-in-law managed the crafters' quarters. A niece oversaw the gardens. When it came to the castle's security, the Raven Guard arranged the watch and trained new guard recruits.

There were few places in his own castle where Ash claimed ultimate authority. In spite of Sachi's protests, he even remained diffident about the consort's tower. He always came to them and waited for permission to enter. As comfortable as he seemed there, he clearly considered it Sachi's—and Zanya's—territory. He walked there as a welcome guest, never its master.

But the Dragon's Tower was, without question, *his* territory. No one entered without permission. The number who had permission was vanishingly small—a handful of trusted servants, Camlia and her grandson, who served as a page, and . . . Well, that was it, as far as Zanya knew. He did not often invite friends to visit with him there, and he never invited retainers for meetings. Even Zanya and Sachi had not earned an invitation to his bed.

The Dragon's lair was off-limits.

And Zanya was about to invade it. Again.

At least she intended to use the door this time. She crossed the bridge between their towers, pausing only briefly to admire the spectacular sunset beyond the western peaks. The skies lit up in a dozen gradations of pinks, blues, and violets, all of it bleeding into a deep twilight already awash with stars. It was tempting to linger—with the larger Creator's Moon dark and the smaller Destroyer's Moon barely more than a crescent in the sky, the stars shone with unusual ferocity— but pride forced one foot in front of the other until she stood in front of the massive wooden door to the Dragon's Tower.

Pride might have carried her to the threshold, but nerves made her hesitate, getting the feel of her body before she lifted a hand to the door. A scant week ago, agitated and distracted, she'd attempted to pound on the cook's door and had instead put her fist through it, causing a mild domestic crisis until Camlia arrived to smooth things over.

And that was the crux of all this, wasn't it? The reason she was here? Even knocking felt fraught now. The first tap of her knuckles against oak was too soft, too tentative. She gritted her teeth and rapped harder. Three *thuds* echoed on the other side, and she jerked her hand away as the door suddenly disappeared.

Ash stood in its place, tall and disheveled, caught between his daytime attire and the casual way he usually appeared in Sachi's quarters. His feet were bare, and his belt was gone. Dark trousers hung low on his hips, and his chest was completely uncovered. Zanya found herself staring at it, tracing the rare scars that crisscrossed his light-brown skin and the flexing muscles she could almost feel beneath her fingers.

"Zanya?"

She jerked her gaze back to his, hoping the shadows hid the flush that warmed her cheeks. "We need to talk. I thought we could . . ." She gestured behind him.

She hadn't expected his hesitation or the wariness she could almost taste on the air. But before she could snatch the words back, he'd stepped aside, pulling the door wide. "Come in."

She almost missed the days when he'd called her *handmaid*. At least the title had provided some distance compared to the way he wrapped his tongue around her name, the way he managed to sound exasperated and fond and hungry to taste her all at the same time.

Hurrying past him with her gaze averted, she made it all of three paces into his quarters before she lifted her head.

She froze. And stared.

She'd been too flustered before to retain more than the vague impression of stone walls and fire-kissed darkness. But the room in which she stood was massive enough to swallow the great hall at Castle Roquebarre. Unlike Sachi's quarters, there were no elegant walls dividing the tower into a dozen different rooms, nor were there plastered ceilings to give the space some sense of proportion.

This room took up the entire top of the Dragon's Tower. He could have stood in the center in his massive dragon form and spread his wings wide without brushing either wall. And while tapestries softened the area around his desk and near his hearth, where the chair she'd found him in before sat, most of the walls were rough-hewn, as if she'd stepped into a mountain cavern.

The splash of water dragged her attention to the side, where five wide steps led up to the edge of a bathing pool sunk deep into the floor. Sachi had one, too, but where hers had been lovingly carved smooth and edged with tile, this massive pool more closely resembled the hot springs they'd swum in during the royal progress. A crystal-clear waterfall hot enough to steam cascaded improbably from above, forming a natural shower. Massive candles dripped wax into niches carved into the stone, and their light reflected off the spray of water droplets like diamonds.

Darkly stained wooden tubs held flowering vines that crawled the walls, a living tapestry in vibrant reds and golds. The plants only enhanced the feeling that she'd wandered into some magical cave—or a dragon's den. She traced the path of the climbing vines to where more steps led up to an even larger dais.

The bed—

No. She would not think about the bed right now.

Zanya whirled, putting her back to it, only to find that Ash had returned to the chair in which she'd found him last time. A matching chair of worn, padded leather sat nearby, with a simple table between them. Ash poured a goblet of wine that smelled sharply of cinnamon and spiced berries and placed it next to the empty chair. "Sit."

There was an edge of command to the word that made her balk. Darker instincts stirred, demanding that she challenge him, but Zanya bit them back. If she'd learned one thing from watching the High Court interact, it was that constant displays of dominance were the provenance of the insecure.

The time would come soon enough to remind him that he could not command her.

So she sat and picked up the goblet. The mulled wine was warm and sweet on her tongue, with the bite of spice and cinnamon that she loved. "It's good."

"Mmm." Ash sank back into his chair, his goblet held lazily in one hand. "So. Do you wish to dance around it for a while? Inquire about my day? I can make small talk about your training."

Yes. Anything to put off the moment when she'd have to face this awkward truth. Zanya took another deep sip and let the soft warmth of the wine sustain her. "I never was much for dancing."

"Neither was I," he admitted. "Look at me, Zanya."

She did, and she almost immediately regretted it. Those beautiful brown eyes held endless sympathy, and the kindness of his words almost broke her. "I thought you were only vanishing when I touched you. I thought it was just me."

The gentleness scraped at raw nerves unaccustomed to such care from anyone but Sachi. But it was the sadness lurking beneath that truly made her heart ache. All this time, he'd thought she was rejecting him. She almost wished it were so. It would be less humiliating than the truth.

"It's not just you. It's not about you or Sachi at all. It's me." She swallowed hard, and it took effort to hold his gaze. "I've always been a coward. And now I can't hide it anymore."

"A coward?"

His voice held disbelief. Irrationally, that only irritated her more. Bad enough to be forced to reveal her shame, but to be met with incredulity? "Obviously I'm a coward. Why do you think it took so long for me to have sex with you?"

"Because that is who you are." He shifted forward, and the feeling of the room changed. As if a great and terrible rage gathered beneath his carefully neutral expression. Like a storm looming on the horizon. "Some people feel desire in an instant. Some feel it only rarely, or once affection and love have grown. Some never feel it at all." Thunder broke across his face in a stormy frown. "There is no wrong way to feel or not feel desire, and there is certainly no cowardice in it."

He said it with such conviction, but he missed the point entirely because he still didn't understand. "I desired you," she countered in a low voice. "Maybe not as swiftly as Sachi, but far more swiftly than I would have liked. But I was afraid, because desire makes you vulnerable. So does pleasure. And I don't like to be vulnerable."

Ash tilted his head and studied her, and she could tell he was sifting through his memories, imagining every time they'd touched. How carefully she'd arranged every encounter to center Sachi's pleasure, or his.

Even alone with Sachi, those moments of being helpless to the pleasure were a thrill she savored and feared in equal measure. The more she craved that loss of control, the deeper her terror grew. And now her instincts had a very literal response to the panic that seized her when orgasm swept away her control—flight.

"I don't think that's it at all."

His voice was so deep and so close that she started. She'd been so tangled in her thoughts that she hadn't heard him move. But he knelt in front of her now, his hands on either arm of her chair, so tall that even on his knees, they were close to eye level. Heat surrounded her. Though he wasn't touching her, she felt caged.

When caged, Zanya always lashed out. Disdain coated her voice. "You think you know me better than I know myself, Dragon?"

"I think I'm learning you. And perhaps you flee from me because you do not wish for me to see you vulnerable." A slow smile curved those full lips. "But I know there is no discomfort on this earth you would not overcome in order to please Sachi. You have no self-preservation where her safety and joy are concerned. If your instincts are carrying you away from her in moments of release, it is to protect *her*. Not yourself."

Perhaps he knew her a little bit, after all.

Without releasing his gaze, she drained the mulled wine from the beaten copper goblet and held it up between them. Curling her fingers together should have been impossible, but the copper bent like soft taffy with the flex of her hand. The goblet collapsed in on itself, crumpled like a piece of paper in her fist.

"I didn't understand," Zanya rasped, sudden tears stinging her eyes. "I told you not to hold back with her, but I didn't know. I thought I was strong before. Now? I could grab her and crush her bones without even realizing it. I could hurt her *so badly.*"

Strong fingers pried hers open. Ash took the mangled cup from her hand and set it aside. His thumb ghosted over her palm, a soothing touch that raised goose bumps. "You're going to learn. It won't be overnight, but it will happen faster than you think. Your instincts will catch up to what your body can do, and you'll learn to trust them again."

Zanya shuddered and closed her eyes to block out those compelling brown eyes. "You have to protect her until I can."

"I'll protect you both, always."

"No, not like that—" Zanya swallowed. "In bed. Whether I'm there or not. Maybe—maybe she could sleep in your bed until I have more control—"

"No."

It was so unexpected, the tone so sharp, Zanya's eyes flew open. The sympathetic brown eyes—Ash's eyes—were gone. The Dragon stared at her instead, flames filling his gaze. When he spoke, his voice had dropped to a dangerous rumble. "It's not a good idea for either of you to sleep in my bed."

It was such an abrupt reversal that Zanya blinked. "Why?"

Ash lunged to his feet and stalked away, and warning prickled down Zanya's spine. Not of magic, but of the predatory instinct that told her danger lurked. With every step he took, Ash seemed more . . . untamed. There was a feral edge to him that set off alarm bells when he abruptly stopped, his back to her. Firelight caressed strong muscles as he exhaled roughly.

"This is the only place in the castle, the only place in this *world*, that belongs only to the Dragon. When I'm here, I'm closer to my other self. Less human. Less . . ." He trailed off, then glanced back at her, and she recognized that stare. It was the predator who peeked out when they sparred. The one who played with her to see who would come out on top. "Less accommodating."

Something that would no doubt fulfill all of Sachi's fondest wishes. Zanya felt more hesitant. "Are you saying that you'd hurt her?"

"Not physically." His gaze swept toward the bed, and for the first time Zanya realized there were silver rings decorating the stone wall above the vast surface—silver rings strung with delicate chains. "But there are ways to scare a person that hurt just as much."

Zanya might not be experienced in the sexual games people played, but neither was she naive. And she knew Sachi. "I thought you'd been fucking people for thousands of years. If you're worried that Sachi would be upset if you chained her to your bed and played conquering possessive Dragon with her, you aren't very observant."

He huffed, a sound torn between frustration and amusement. "That's the point. It wouldn't be a game." And suddenly he was *moving*, lunging toward her in a blur of movement that would have been too fast for a mortal to see.

But Zanya wasn't mortal anymore.

Her brain told her his outstretched hands were aiming for the back of the chair. He only meant to loom over her, to grind in his point by using his speed and the size of his body. To scare her a little, if he could. There was no threat here, but her body reacted the way training had taught it—on instinct.

And training told her the precise moment to lift her leg and plant a foot in his chest. He stumbled, off-balance, hands flailing for the back of the chair, which was already tilting backward under the force of his advance. She waited until momentum was in her favor and extended her leg, sending him flying over her head.

Of course, the chair was still going down, and it was too late to stop it. She flipped free of the smashed remains and rolled up into a defensive crouch, only to find Ash in a mirror pose a few feet away, his eyes ablaze.

Not just rage in those fiery eyes, but heat, too. It unspooled inside her in reaction, the same damned spark that made her want to fight every last member of the High Court. Was it desire? With the others, not quite. There would always be something arousing in the challenge of a fight, in the flex of muscles and ruthless competence and the hunger to triumph, to *conquer*. She felt that heat with the Raven Guard, with Elevia, with Ulric . . .

But not like this. Not this hot. Not this . . . dark. She wanted to tear this room apart until they were both breathless and bruised, and then . . . And then . . .

And then *what?*

She was breathing unsteadily, even though the exertion couldn't have winded her. "If you want to tie Sachi to your bed and play the conquering Dragon, what do you want to do to me?"

His slow smile tingled like he'd stroked a hand over every inch of her body. "Sweet, deadly Zanya. You're not ready for the things I'd do to you."

Pride made her bare her teeth at him in outright challenge. "Oh? Have you got something more deviant up there than chains attached to your bed?"

"Are you brave enough to find out?"

No, not remotely. But she was in too deep now. Keeping a wary eye on him, she rose and ascended the steps that led to his bed.

Now that she was closer, she could see that the walls on either side had been carved with recesses, like irregular shelves. She approached the ones on the left side and found the items you'd expect when a man had chains on his headboard. Leather wrist cuffs with shiny buckles, lined with the softest fur. Larger ones undoubtedly meant for ankles, perhaps even arms or legs. Silken braids of rope. More lengths of chain.

Another shelf held long, hand-carved boxes that looked as if they should contain daggers. Curious, Zanya traced her fingers over the dark-stained oak and flipped the latch. But it wasn't a dagger she found resting on the velvet. Made from swirling glass and decorated with intricate ridges, the phallic toy rivaled Ash in size. She'd never seen its like before, but had no trouble imagining its uses—or the sounds Sachi would make as Zanya—

Ash's footsteps echoed behind her. Zanya jerked her fingers away and moved on to the next shelf. Jar after jar of potions lined this one, with delicate handwritten labels. They ranged in color from blood-red to the palest gold, and had evocative names like Dragon's Blood and

Night of Fire, Witchwood Euphoria and Empath's Kiss and Lover's Touch.

"Not as wide a selection as Aleksi's, but Inga has never been stingy. And she delights in concoctions that enhance sensation."

If the wine she'd had at the Lover's Villa on union night was anything to go on, Zanya was sure the contents of these bottles could heat the blood in ways that defied imagination. But it wasn't so terribly shocking. "I expected worse. This is all very tame for a fearsome monster."

A final step brought the heat of him against her back. His breath tickled her ear. "What did you expect? Whips? Shackles? I have those, too, though I confess they've never been to my tastes. Pleasure has always been my torment of choice."

She agreed with him, personally, but she still tried to laugh it off. "Is that really a torment?"

"You know it is, Zanya." Fingers touched her shoulder. In this painfully intimate moment, even the lightest brush over her skin felt illicit enough to tighten her nipples into hard points. Shadows started to stir around her fingers, a tentative offer to whisk her away from temptation. She struggled against them, pride stiffening her spine.

She would not flee from him. She would not give him the satisfaction.

His touch traced lower, down her arm, ghosting over one of her scars as his voice wove a spell around her. "Pleasure strips you bare, reveals your soul. It makes you vulnerable, just as you said. And that's what I crave in my bed. Pleasure so deep it strips away all artifice, all masks."

Sachi's dream come true . . . and Zanya's nightmare.

Warm fingers stroked back up over her shoulder. His knuckles grazed the side of her neck, streaking fire straight to her core. When his lips touched the shell of her ear, she sucked in an unsteady breath. "And it goes both ways," he murmured. "The satisfaction I would take in every screaming, sobbing orgasm, the greedy way I would demand more and more . . . That reveals me for what I am. Possessive and ravenous and insatiable."

"The Dragon," Zanya whispered.

"Exactly." His thumb traced along her jaw. "And do you know what I think, Zanya?"

She was breathing too hard. She wanted to lean back against him, rub against his heat. She wanted to tilt her head and bite his fingers in warning. She wanted to whirl and bear him to the floor, pinning all this heat and strength beneath her. Claim it as her own. Answering him was almost impossible. "What do you think?"

"I think you're just like me." He pressed a gentle kiss to the top of her ear. "Possessive." His lips grazed the shell of her ear, and her knees almost buckled. "Greedy." He spoke the last word directly against her ear, setting her aflame. "Insatiable."

She certainly felt all those things. She drew another unsteady breath, but her voice broke on his name. She gave in to the need, pressing back against him, rubbing against his heat even as the shadows threatened again. Her heart was beating too fast. She didn't know if it was fear or need.

Gentle hands gripped her shoulders and turned her, leaving her staring up into Ash's serious brown eyes. His lips were so close to hers that his low words felt like a kiss. "I will take care of Sachi," he promised, even as the shadows climbed Zanya's body. "In bed and out of it. And when it becomes too much, Zanya—when you need to *feel* without worrying about hurting her—you will come and hurt *me*."

Then he was kissing her, hot and demanding, his tongue driving between her parted lips with such domineering challenge that she raked her fingernails over his scalp in an instinctive warning that resulted in a rumble of pleasure. Her entire body pulsed, overwhelmed with the need to meet that challenge, to drive him to the floor, to *conquer* him—

The shadows seized her, jerking her away to the blank safety of the Void, where she hung for an endless moment, gasping for breath that would not come.

Oh, the irony of it all. For years she'd been a helpless human, training to kill a dragon she loathed. Now she was a god, belatedly aflame with the desire that would have made her mission to destroy him so simple . . .

And now she feared hurting him.

Laughter stole the breath she'd barely regained, laughter that echoed through her empty world as she let her body and blood cool.

She *would* learn to control these powers. And then Sachielle *and* the Dragon would be hers.

Chapter Seven
WITCHING MOON

Week Two, Day Two
Year 3000

Perched on a cliff high above his keep, Ash stared toward the west.

The mountain range in which he made his home plunged steeply down toward the crashing ocean. The water that seethed there had no real name, as if its presence were inconsequential. When people spoke of the vast span between their shores and those of the Empire, only one name ever came to their lips.

The Western Wall.

Most commonly, the name referred to the string of rocky, hostile islands that filled the ocean between their respective shores. Some were larger than the Midnight Forest. Some were small enough to fit in one of the Lover's Lakes. They all rose, jagged and angry, from the dangerous waters that crashed against their shores, like the ancient stone teeth of some mythical beast.

The Kraken had told him once that the Western Wall was a range of mountains every bit as formidable as those in which Ash made his home—but only the highest peaks rose above the water. Plenty more lurked beneath the waves, eager to tear open the hulls of unwary sailors and smash their boats into kindling.

Ash could remember when the entire expanse had been a rolling meadow dotted with wildflowers.

No one fully understood the sundering of the continents. Not even him, and he'd been there, on that blasted plain where fire had turned the sand to glass and violence had turned the glass to bloody shards. The world had tried to tear itself apart beneath his feet, ripping what had been one land into two.

The violence of it would have destroyed them all. So Ash had thrust his bloodied hands into the earth and begged the world to heal itself. To thrive. To give him another chance to be the protector it had deserved.

Instead, the world had decided to protect *him*. The crash of continents had altered the faces of both countries, as if parts of what would become the Empire had *disappeared* beneath the Sheltered Lands, shoving up angry mountains that spit lava. Water had flooded in from the North and South Seas alike, burying what had been beneath its inky depths.

In the aftermath, there had been silence. And the Western Wall.

Of course, these days, those who referred to the Western Wall might be speaking of a person instead of these mountains. The stark, difficult-to-navigate chain of islands should have been a welcome home for pirates and raiders from the Empire, bent on causing mischief. But only one ship hoisted its colors proudly in these waters.

The Kraken.

The Dreamer and the boat shared the same name. And truly, they might as well have been inseparable. Only a direct order from Dianthe could pull Einar from his ship, and he never stayed on land for long. Einar was the true Western Wall, a warrior whose fierce and deadly crew patrolled the shores for invaders or mischief with a dedication that no doubt gave a healthy swath of the Empire nightmares.

And he was down there now, prowling the coast, seeking vulnerabilities even as he chased the last known word of the Phoenix.

Ash's instincts demanded he should be doing the same. Flying patrols over the Sheltered Lands, trying to spot the movements of soldiers or what the queen's people intended next—

—*falling directly into their trap,* Elevia's voice reminded him wryly, present even when she was not.

Ash sighed.

Elevia was likely right. She usually was. There was a reason she had served as the general of their armies. The Huntress could look at a situation from multiple sides and glean plans within plans with a patience that eluded Ash.

He preferred confrontation of the more direct sort. Face your enemy. Make them stop.

Reaching down, he ran his fingers over the ice-covered rocks beneath his perch. He let his power push into the earth and felt the immediate push back, like a puppy surging up in anticipation of attention. He smiled and closed his eyes, letting his power twine with that eager presence.

You know the people who belong to us. The people who love you. Warn us if they are in danger.

How much did the earth actually understand? He'd never been sure, but the curious touch twirled around him as pebbles clattered down the cliffside. Then the sensation faded.

Laughing at himself, Ash summoned his wings and leapt. Fire consumed his body as he fell, and the dragon burst out of it, spiraling easily down to Dragon's Keep. After doing an obligatory sweep to check his domain—and a showy backflip to entertain some of the children who played in the market square—he alighted on the top of his tower and shifted back.

A narrow set of stairs led down to his balcony, which opened into his room. He might not feel the chill of the highest mountain peaks the way someone else might, but the blissful heat of his bathing pool still beckoned. He shed his clothing haphazardly as he navigated the steps, then dove beneath the water with a satisfied rumble.

He came up directly beneath the waterfall. Water heated by the energy deep in his volcano sluiced over his head and ran down his body, washing away the stress of the day. He gathered a handful of the cleansing liquid one of the crafters made for him, inhaled the bracing scent of the Midnight Forest, and smiled as he went through his usual evening routine.

Some things always managed to settle his nerves.

Of course, stepping from beneath the waterfall to find Princess Sachielle in the heart of his domain did the exact opposite.

Sachi stood near the leather-covered bench at the foot of his bed, her head tilted back as she studied the tapestries on his walls. Her feet were bare, and she wore layers of red and orange, sheer robes belted with intricate gold braid. The vibrant colors brought out the gold in her skin, but that wasn't what stirred something primal in him.

She looked like she was already wrapped in his flames. An offering to the Lord of Fire.

"Sachielle." His voice came out a low rumble.

"I didn't knock," she said casually, but with a devilish gleam in her eye. "Since you once told me that, as I am your consort, your quarters are open to me at my convenience."

Yes, he undoubtedly had said as much. He'd made the offer to a string of consorts out of duty until the words became rote. It had been a thousand years since one had last taken the words at face value.

Of course, judging by the wickedness in the smile she couldn't quite hide, Sachi knew *exactly* what she was doing. "I take it Zanya spoke with you?"

"Zanya often speaks with me." Sachi licked her lips. "What is it you truly wish to know, my lord?"

Every instinct screamed at him to lunge for her. To capture her before she could escape his domain, even though *escape* seemed to be the very last thing on her mind as her bold gaze drifted over his naked body. Ash tightened the leash on his self-control. "Did she warn you, Princess? Every night, I have come to your bed as a well-behaved guest. But the Dragon rules as master in mine."

"I would expect no less." Sachi smiled. "But if you think Zanya's whispered words to me were of *warning*, my lord, then you are mistaken."

"Is that so?"

She took a single step closer, the sheer fabric of her robes parting to reveal one bare leg as she moved. "What she delivered to me was a promise."

No amount of self-control could choke back the heat of arousal. Of *yearning*. After so many centuries of consorts shrinking away from him in terror, it was intoxicating to be wanted for exactly what he was. For *all* of what he was. "And where is Zanya tonight?"

"With Ulric and Elevia. Training."

Ulric had mentioned the plan to take her on overnight excursions to see if her powers were stronger in darkness. This must be the first of those . . . and Zanya had sent Sachi to him, primed and eager, with a promise to Sachi that amounted to a command to Ash.

Take care of her.

It was an easy enough command to follow, but caution held him rooted in place. "We can return to your rooms, and I will ravish you as relentlessly as you could ever wish. But if we stay here, it will not be a game. Be sure, Sachi."

She didn't answer right away. Instead, she drifted closer, until she was close enough to take his hand. She placed it over her racing heart, held it there, and whispered his name.

"It's never been a game for me," she confessed softly. "Even when it was supposed to be. So *yes*, my lord. Ash. I'm sure."

He spread his fingers wide, the water from his bath turning the light silk translucent. The pad of his thumb skimmed the tightened bud of her nipple, driving a gasp from her parted lips. Her heart thundered beneath his palm. Her eyes begged for this—for the moment they should have had the night of their binding, if the fear of her curse and her mission hadn't twisted her into knots he could feel through their bond.

A bond they no longer shared. It had snapped at the moment of her death, leaving a void inside him that had once been full of the vivid *presence* of Sachi. Her return to life had not brought that magical awareness back . . . but Ash knew exactly what to do.

Ignoring his nudity and the trail of water he left in his wake, Ash swept Sachi up in his arms. She barely had enough time for a startled laugh before he'd ascended the steps to the dais where his bed sat. He set her on her feet and turned to the recessed stone shelves along the wall.

The bottle he wanted was no bigger than a plum, its contents the same dark purple with pink swirls that caught the light. He held it up so Sachi could see the label—Empath's Kiss. "Aleksi and Inga designed it," he told her. "Five drops on your tongue, and you'll be linked to anyone else who takes it. It will be like we're bound again."

"It will reassure you?" she asked, her gaze locked on the small vial.

"Yes. I will feel what you feel, and I will be able to keep you safe."

Sachi reached for the vial. "Am I to assume the converse is also true? That I will feel what you feel?"

"Yes." He took her hand. "It might be overwhelming at first, so be sure you want this connection."

In response, Sachi simply opened her mouth. Waiting. The sight shot fire through his veins, and he quickly tilted his head back and let the sweet elixir fall onto his tongue, which tingled in the wake of that burning heat. The tingling swelled into anticipation as he placed five wine-colored drops of the liquid on Sachielle's tongue.

He'd barely closed the glass bottle when the anticipation sharpened into aching desire and a relief so intense it weakened his knees.

No, those weren't *his* knees in danger of giving out. He let the bottle clatter to the stone shelf and caught Sachi as she swayed. "Princess?"

She gripped his arms, nails digging into skin, and moaned. Ash sank his fingers into her hair and tilted her head back, trying hard to keep his voice even. "Look at me, Princess."

Slowly, her lashes lifted. And her eyes, normally clear and blue, reflected the reds and glowing golds of a raging fire.

His fire, as if he'd already claimed her, inside and out. The wild possessiveness he usually kept so carefully in check snapped free of its chains, and he hauled her up his body until her face was even with his. "Last chance," he growled, letting the hunger rage through him. Letting her *feel* it across their newly forged bond. "Now you know how deeply I crave you. Do you still wish to stay?"

Her chest vibrated against his as she echoed his growl and arched closer. "I will not leave," she rasped, "because you're *mine.*"

The vow utterly shattered him. With a growl, Ash seized her mouth. His tongue swept over her lips, demanding entrance and surging forward the moment she parted them. He savored the taste of her, the feel, her eager, willing submission . . .

And he gave himself over to the Dragon.

Chapter Eight
WITCHING MOON

Week Two, Day Two
Year 3000

Sachi had felt the kiss of fire before. Washing over her skin, *under* it, scorching every part of her. She knew what it was to burn. But this? Was something beyond her experience, even her comprehension. It was different from their previous bond, less emotional and more physical. Less muted and more viscerally immediate.

And so she *felt* the moment Ash loosed his tight grip on control. His kiss didn't change, but *he* did. A tension melted out of him, as if he'd been holding himself very, very still and had simply . . . relaxed.

There was nothing soft or languorous about it. His arms were steel around her, and his fangs grazed her lips and tongue. His kiss was rough, needy. But for the first time . . .

Entirely *him*.

Her breath caught, and her eyes stung. When Ash lifted his mouth from hers, she realized he was sitting on the end of his bed with her on his lap, her legs locked around his hips.

She licked her lips and felt a wave of foreign but familiar lust wash through her. Ash raised a hand to stroke her jaw. Flames danced down his arm, eager and sweet. They encased his fingertips, and when they faded, his broad fingers ended in formidable claws. He drew them up her face, the sharp points kissing her skin with aching tenderness.

Perhaps he still expected her to flinch or jerk away. Instead, she tilted her face to his touch, scraping her cheek against one claw. It stung, but only for a moment, and then heat rose in place of the pain.

"I've told you a thousand times," she whispered. "I am not afraid of you."

His lips curved into a dangerous smile, and something heady and satisfied throbbed deep within her. He traced that single claw down the vulnerable column of her throat and growled a command. "Stand up. Undress for me."

"Heresy." Sachi caught one layer and rubbed the gauzy fabric between her fingers. "These aren't meant to be carefully, systematically removed. And certainly not by me."

His fingers curled around the back of her neck as his thumb stroked over her pulse. "Already you disobey. Do you want so desperately for me to tear them from your body?"

She turned her face to hide a smile. "Very well. You've shredded enough of my clothing."

That throbbing need followed her as she slid from his lap. It pulsed beneath her skin, between her thighs, as she slowly untied the braided belt around her waist.

He held out a hand in silent command.

"So imperious." She gathered the braided silk in one hand and placed it on his outstretched palm. "Dare I ask what you plan to do with it?"

Ash stroked his thumb along the soft cord, but his gaze never left her. "Do you remember the night we were bound together?"

How could she ever forget? She'd been numb with nerves but vibrating with promise, ready to bed him as soon as humanly possible.

Because it was the proper thing to do, both as his newest consort and to satisfy the most immediate goal of her long-term mission.

But mostly because she had *wanted to.*

"I said and did all the right things, but you saw right through me." The memory was enough to elicit a rueful laugh. "I was a terrible seductress."

"You were a maddeningly adept seductress," he countered, his voice low and dark, like distant thunder. "I could feel your fear like a knife through the heart. I should never have even crossed the threshold of your chamber. But the *thoughts* you conjured in me . . ."

Another pulse of hunger made her hands tremble, but she lifted them to the fastening on her outermost robe anyway. "Illicit thoughts, I hope."

"They'd wrapped you in cords like this, as an offering." He stroked the braided rope again as his gaze followed her fingers. "I wanted to know how they'd look against your skin. If you'd like it as much as I would."

"Being tied up, my lord? Or being at your mercy?"

"Both." He rose with predatory grace and circled her slowly. "But I forgot all that the moment you wrapped your lush lips around my thumb and sucked. Wicked, wicked girl. I almost put you on your knees then, in spite of everything."

The heat of his body at her back made her want to sway toward him, but she remained still. "That would have made for a far more enjoyable night."

"If only I hadn't been able to sense your fear," he murmured. His hands touched her shoulders, claw-tips curling into her robe. With one effortless tug, he shredded the fabric and left it hanging around her in ribbons.

A rumbling growl rattled in her own chest even as another reached her ears. Ash closed a hand around her throat and dragged her back against him, his lips brushing her ear. "You aren't scared now."

Her only thoughts were of whether he'd slide that hand down to toy with her breasts, or up and into her mouth in a lewd echo of that thwarted seduction. "I never was, Ash. Not of you."

"So you tell me." He used his free hand to strip away the shredded robe, leaving her completely naked and pressed against his equally bare body. His cock was a line of steel against her lower back, hotter than the rest of him. But every inch of him *burned*, especially his claws as they ghosted back up her body to tease around one tight nipple. "Though I can feel the truth of it, sometimes I still don't believe. Even the consorts who came to my bed willingly came nervously. Especially when they met the Dragon."

"Then they were shortsighted fools," she whispered. They'd deprived themselves of something more than pleasure or companionship or even love.

They'd deprived themselves of *Ash*. Of his warmth, his humor. Of the protectiveness and caring that formed the very heart of him.

Fools, indeed.

His mouth brushed her ear as he turned them toward the wall, where a massive mirror stood next to a wardrobe. Their reflections stared back, her skin gilded by firelight as he loomed behind her in shadow. A trick of the light—or exactly what the Dragon wanted the fire to show. Her, on display, pinned against his body by one gentle hand at her throat.

"You're so beautiful," he whispered against her ear. His other hand traced the swell of her hip. "So soft and sweet."

She'd never thought much about her body. For the longest time, it had merely been a tool, the greatest weapon in her arsenal. Then, with Zanya, she had known for the first time what it was to truly hunger. But she hadn't considered her own dips and curves, the supple lines that made up the shape of her.

Now, through Ash's eyes, she could finally see. Wet heat pooled between her thighs as she drank herself in with *his* gaze, his carnal appreciation both tempered and multiplied by love.

"Is this how you like me?" Hot anticipation slid through her as she raised one hand and drove her fingers into his hair. Then it tightened into a knot of pure satisfaction as she clenched her fist, pulling Ash's hair. "Sweet?"

"I like you every way." His growl vibrated through her body everywhere they touched. Fangs pricked her ear. "Especially bad. Sweetness is so much more rewarding when I've coaxed it from you."

"With your claws around my throat? Or by teasing me until I give in?"

In answer, fire sprang up around the hand on her hip. It was a sharper sort of flame, almost like a caress, one that stung and soothed in equal measure. As she gasped for breath, Ash drew his hand up, along her side, to her bare breast. The magic followed in his wake, lingering on her skin in a literal trail of fire.

Sachi whimpered, and Ash's cock twitched against her back.

Slowly, he circled her nipple with his claw. With the heat of the fire in play, it felt almost like a pinch—or a bite. She fell back against him, leaning on him for support as the flames spread to the other side of her body, and the fire consumed her.

She stared at their reflections. She burned, fingers of flame licking over her skin. But Ash was burning, too, and that made her smile through the hint of pain. "Sometimes I think you try to scare me."

"No, Sachi." The flames traveled down her body like phantom hands, warming her inner thighs. She held her breath as they began a slow journey back up, but they stopped just short of entering her. "I've held back. I've always held back. Until now."

"Don't." She wanted to arch her hips to the fiery caresses, drag Ash's hands and claws and mouth *closer* somehow, but she remained still. "I crave every part of you, Ash. Everything you are."

The hand at her throat vanished, and his gaze caught hers in the mirror. "On your knees, Princess," he ordered gently. "Show me what you can do with those wicked lips while I play with you. If you can break my willpower before I make you come, I'll give you a reward."

Sachi turned. "And if I fail? What is your reward?"

"Then I will feast on you until I'm sated."

"Fascinating." She slid to the floor, careful not to touch him as she knelt before him. His skin *steamed*, the last of the water burning off of him as he stared down at her. Her hands trembled, so she locked her fingers together, then leaned forward and licked the tip of his jutting erection.

The contact *sizzled*, and Sachi swallowed a moan as Ash gathered her unbound hair and wrapped it around his fist. He didn't pull, barely even *breathed* as she slowly closed her lips around him, but the silken promise was there, all the same. For now, he was in control. But eventually—if she teased, coaxed, pushed him high enough—he would give in.

And then he would take.

So she teased, gliding her tongue around the crown of his cock. She moaned when she felt Ash's sensual torment as he slid into the molten depths of her mouth. She coaxed, lightly drawing her fingernails down his thighs. And she *pushed*, taking him deeper and deeper, until Ash sucked in an unsteady gasp.

His fist tightened in her hair. His hips jerked, thrusting deeper still. Then he froze, and here it was—the moment he would usually have pulled back. But that flash of hesitation melted with a groan as she pressed closer, digging her nails into his hips.

Fierce, feral satisfaction washed over her as he hauled her back by the hair until the head of his cock just brushed her parted lips. He loosened his grip so that she could rub her cheek against his rigid length. "You're so eager to please."

She couldn't deny it, so she didn't try. "Does your challenge still stand, my lord?"

"Oh, yes." The gentle tug at her hair made her scalp tingle. "I thought to give you a head start, but I don't think you need it."

Fingers of fire spilled down her spine, a ghostly caress that somehow felt like the softest kiss and the sting of nipping teeth at the same time.

The fire split midway down her back and circled her body, surging up to tease around her breasts in ever-narrowing circles.

Everything was wet heat and a grinding need that settled at the base of her spine and made her entire body ache. There was no way she'd be able to resist her searing pleasure along with his, but it didn't matter. Either way, Sachi would win. So she turned her attention back to Ash's cock, wrapping her fist around the base and squeezing with every pulse of pleasure that rocked her.

A growl escaped him and rumbled through the room. The flames spiraled to tight points, as if a pair of mouths had closed around Sachi's nipples and sucked so hard her vision blurred. Only the heavy, slick glide of Ash's cock on her tongue muffled her scream. He shuddered under the reflected wave of pleasure, his hips jerking again, driving him deeper.

"It's too bad Zanya can't see you now," he rasped, his gaze alight with wild fire as he watched her lips stretch taut around his cock. "Can you feel her fingers sliding down your back and over that sweet, curvy ass?"

Sachi's eyes widened. She *could* feel it, the phantom trace of a touch that moved exactly as he described.

Her knees wobbled as he went on. "Has she ever spanked you, Princess? I've seen you act like such a bad girl, almost begging her for it."

The fiery touch spread out over her ass, stroking teasingly and then sliding lower, between her parted thighs.

"I could teach her how. Hold you down for her and show her how to do it so it hurts just the right way." His voice deepened. "Do you know how hot she'd get, watching you squirm? Listening to your whimpers? Slipping her fingers inside you only to find out how wet you get when someone takes you the way you need to be taken?"

The words washed over Sachi, *through* her. She trembled with the effort, but still she couldn't stop herself from straining toward the fiery touch. It pushed inside her, at first a sensation more of heat than pressure. But as Ash continued to rasp his filthy, delicious words, the heat expanded until it felt like fingers fucking in and out of her body.

"I'd keep spanking you, and Zanya would fuck you with as many fingers as you could take until you fell apart for her. How many would it be, Sachi? Three? Four?"

Sachi moaned around his cock. Her legs were quaking now, just like Ash's hand in her hair. Just like his voice, dark and quavering and *hungry*.

"Would you still want more?"

She came with a sudden pulse of pleasure that startled her with its intensity, and she barely managed to throw her head back before her jaw clenched. The orgasm went on and on, curling her toes and tightening her muscles until they ached. Ash groaned, but his fire stroked her through it, calming and consoling.

Then his strong arms closed around her, lifting and steadying even as his voice soothed her. "Good girl. Good, sweet girl." The words rumbled against her temple, and she found her forehead pressed to his shoulder. "Can you look at me?"

He held her effortlessly, as if she weighed nothing, and yet Sachi could scarcely draw breath. "You won," she gasped.

"I won," he agreed, turning toward the bed. He let her slide down his body until she was kneeling on the soft sheets at the foot of the wide mattress. He cupped her face, his thumbs gliding over her flushed cheeks before tracing her lower lip. "But it was close. Your mouth is so hot, your tongue so sweet."

The room was still tilting wildly, as if she had literally become drunk on pleasure. So Sachi pulled Ash into a kiss, unsure if it would center her or send her spinning even harder, knowing only that she needed it.

He knew, too. Of course he did. He kissed her with indulgent pleasure, as if he had all the time in the world to explore the way her lips moved against his, the way they parted when he teased her with his tongue. He kissed her until the world stopped tilting, until the spinning started inside her again as every slow drag of his tongue promised something beautiful.

Only then did he break away, his lips hovering over hers. "Crawl to the head of the bed. Do you see the chains?"

Sachi swallowed a moan. "I do."

"Hold on to them and offer yourself to me."

No elaboration, no further instructions . . . but Sachi knew what he wanted. Here, in his lair, he could take anything as his due. But what he desired, what he truly *needed*, was her willing surrender.

She crawled up the bed on her hands and knees. She remained in that position as she wrapped the warm chains around her arms and gripped them with her hands, her elbows on the plush mattress and her ass in the air.

A wave of dark craving swept through her, eliciting a sharp gasp, and she looked back at Ash. For a heartbeat, she saw the fiery outline of wings flare out behind him. Then the bed dipped and he was on her, his hands gripping the chains above hers, his chest a wall of heat at her back.

"Do you remember your welcome feast?"

"Before—" Her voice broke as his lips brushed the top of her spine . . . and slid lower. "Before or after you fled, my lord?"

Fire kissed her fingertips before weaving down her arms in the wake of his fingers. "After."

"I enjoyed dessert." She bit her lip as his fingers traced over her waist and the flare of her hips. "And far too much wine."

"All I could think about was tasting you. I wanted to launch myself off that mountaintop and land in the courtyard. I didn't care if the whole court watched me lay you out on the table and spread your legs wide."

Her cheeks flushed, but she couldn't be *too* scandalized. Not after the night they'd spent under the moons and stars at Aleksi's home. "That might have required speaking to me."

He bit the back of her thigh in warning, then pushed her legs apart. "You would have been my feast. I would have savored you for hours." He licked her then, a slow circle around her exposed clit, followed by a quick flick of his tongue. "I *will* savor you for hours."

Her voice sounded high, breathless. "I had no idea you'd given it so much thought."

"Liar," he rumbled. He punished her with another teasing nip, this time on the curve of her ass. Then his tongue returned to her clit, hot and ravenous, teasing a little before thrusting into her, as if he craved nothing more than the taste of her.

Sachi jerked, rattling the chains. She writhed as every wet caress sent a shock of pleasure up her spine, but still she kept her grip on the chains. Her nipples began to ache, and at first she chalked it up to the sheer depth of her arousal, or maybe the friction of her upper body rubbing against the soft furs beneath her. But then the ache *bloomed*, and she understood.

Ash had set her on fire again.

He stroked her, with his tongue and with his magic, until she was teetering on the brink. Then, as Sachi strove for release, he backed away, softening his caresses and quieting his fire. When she could breathe again, at least enough to gasp his name, he started all over again.

He did it again and again, pushing her up and then easing her back down. And every time he did, his fire spread a little more. By the time it had completely engulfed her, Sachi was begging, nearly insensate with desperation.

"Shh," Ash whispered. The sound barely penetrated Sachi's haze of need, but she could feel the emotions behind it—longing and lust, both tinged by something deeper, warmer. "I'm here, my love."

"Don't stop this time, don't—"

And he didn't. He pushed her higher, demanding more than her pleasure or even her release. Demanding her *surrender*. He thrust his tongue inside her, growling when she shuddered, shrieked. When her legs quivered and she almost collapsed to the bed.

He fucked her until he had to grip her hips to keep her from squirming away. And it was his fingers on her flesh that sent her flying, not just the pressure but the absolute satisfaction that flooded Ash as he held her captive to the demands of his ravenous lips and lashing tongue. Unable to escape, to do anything but come in his mouth.

Sachi fell into it, arching toward Ash's tongue with a long, low moan that slowly turned into a scream that she muffled against the inside of her arm. The world blurred, and her entire body shook—from ecstasy, yes, but also from the thrill that snaked through her.

There were no words to describe it, what it was like to *feel* Ash's determination, his shocked pleasure at her responses. His longing to be *loved*.

Ash didn't release her as he feathered tiny kisses over her lower back. Each one made her shiver anew, and she breathed his name again. When Sachi collapsed to the bed on her side, he continued those featherlight kisses across her hip.

He rubbed his thumb over the inside of her thigh. "Are you with me?"

How could she come so hard, with the taste of her own pleasure on her tongue, and still be so hungry? "I'm here." Now her voice sounded low, hoarse. "I'm here, Ash."

"Good girl." His thumb drifted higher, gliding through the slick evidence of her desire, until he reached the deliciously sensitive heart of her and bit off a curse. "You're so wet for me. So ready to be fucked. You'll take anything I give you, won't you?"

Carnal appreciation for her own curves filled Sachi again. She untangled one hand from its golden chain and trailed it up her rib cage, over her collarbone. A light graze across one nipple left her shuddering and cursing. "*Fuck*, yes."

Reaching for the chains once again, she rolled to her back with a hungry moan and draped one leg over Ash's shoulder, opening to him. Two fingers slicked through her folds, spreading wide to part her. At first, she didn't know why . . . until she looked down her body to find him watching her intently.

The moment their eyes met, fire touched her again. Not a single flame, licking lightly across her skin, but a searing heat that felt like the pressure of his tongue, only it moved so *fast*, almost vibrating on her clit. She cried out, her hips bucking, but he held her tight with his other hand.

"That's it," he soothed, his fingers splayed on her stomach. His massive hand held her in place, pinning her to the bed so she couldn't escape the writhing flame. "That's the Dragon's tongue. Can you take it, Sachi?"

"Ash—*fuck*—"

He worked his finger inside her next—just one, but she was already so sensitive that she whimpered.

"By the first flame, you're squeezing me so tight. So close to coming again." He licked the inside of her knee with a groan. "What do you want, Princess? Do you want another finger?"

She gripped the chains so hard they almost cut into her hands. "Yes, please."

He pushed two fingers into her this time, fucking deep. The slick sound of it made Sachi shake, and she bit her lip to hold back a moan as a sharp stab of hunger pierced through her.

Oh, but Ash felt it, echoed it with a rough groan. He leaned over her, his free hand on the bed next to her face, holding his weight as he pressed his lips to her shoulder—and curled his fingers inside her.

He licked her nipple next, and Sachi's tongue tingled. She arched, chasing the sensation, only to shudder through a shocking bolt of pure ecstasy when her thigh slid against the hard, pulsing length of his cock.

Fascinated, Sachi rubbed her leg against him harder, then choked on a cry when Ash accompanied the hot rush of pleasure with a deep, hard thrust of his fingers.

"Are you trying to make me come all over you, Sachi?" He curled his fingers again as he pumped them in and out of her.

"I want—" The words broke on a sound that was half sob, half growl. "You're so hard it hurts. How can you want this much and not be going mad?"

He looked at her, his eyes glowing white-hot. "Because I know it will be worth it."

Sachi splintered. This time, her inner muscles clenching around his fingers doubled the sensation, prolonged it, and she bucked wildly under his touch.

"I'm not going to stop fucking you," he whispered. He withdrew his fingers, but only to add a third, stretching her open with a searing heat that had little to do with his magical flames. The heel of his hand pressed against her swollen clit with every thrust, and Sachi's scream almost drowned out his hoarse words.

"Take it for me, Sachi. Take the pleasure."

She lost count of her orgasms. It seemed like she'd always been coming, arching her back and pleading as her toes curled and her body tensed and released, over and over. Instead, she marked the time by *Ash*.

There was his voice in her ear, urging her on. "Sweet girl, you can take it."

His skin beneath her grasping hands and scraping fingernails. "Go ahead and scratch me. I like feeling your nails in my skin."

His fingers inside her, wide and talented, demanding even as his words teased. "I wish Zanya were here to see you like this. Flushed and shaking, so wet and ready she could fuck you with her whole hand."

And the hungry fire, always the fire, sizzling over her skin, under it. Burning her alive, holding her over the edge of a chasm so deep and fathomless she would never survive the fall.

But Ash kept going. "That's it, Sachi." His low, smooth commands now trembled with a metallic hint of tortured desire. "Just like that. Let it come."

She barely recognized her own voice, either. "I can't, Ash."

He stroked her hair back from her damp cheek. He kissed her, the sweet gentleness a contrast to the possessive thrust of his fingers and the way that fiery tongue flicked her closer and closer to madness. "For me, Sachi. One more."

"I *can't*."

"You can." His teeth closed on her nipple, a sharp bite that broke through the rolling waves of unceasing bliss and made them crash in around her until only darkness remained.

She came back to herself sprawled on her back, with Ash stroking a soothing path up and down her side as he pressed soft kisses to her forehead. "There you are," he murmured.

Panting, Sachi stared up at the ceiling and willed it to stop spinning. "Are we certain?" she laughed, only half joking.

Suddenly he was there, blocking out the world. He braced his weight on either side of her head, caging her in flexing muscle and heat. A tenuously banked fire lurked in his gaze as he stared down at her, and across their bond she felt his ravenous hunger spark her own again, somehow even stronger than before.

"We can stop now." His voice was dark with need. "Or you can take more. For me."

The chains still hung down above her head, abandoned in the throes of pleasure. Sachi reached for them, winding them around her arms and hands once more. "For *us*."

Words couldn't describe the feelings that flooded her—primal satisfaction, accompanied by a jolt of something that Sachi almost wanted to call shock tinged with hope.

It made her heart ache, this tentative yearning. After thousands of years and probably just as many lovers, Ash was still terrified by the possibility that he might incite her fear, just by being himself. No wonder he controlled himself so rigidly and refused to ever let go. All he wanted was to be accepted, and it was the one thing the world had denied him.

Until now.

Sachi gripped the chains, using them for leverage as she pulled her upper body off the bed until her lips hovered just under Ash's. Then she whispered, "Don't make me wait."

He moved so suddenly that Sachi dropped back to the mattress, but he didn't follow her down. He straightened, running his hands over her curves as he sat back on his heels . . . and pushed her thighs wide.

"Watch." He gripped his cock in one hand and guided it into her. "Watch me take you."

As wet as she was from his fingers and the endless, slick pleasure, the gentle but insistent invasion still threatened to overwhelm her. She arched her hips, trying to take him faster, but Ash held her firmly in place as he slowly rocked deeper.

He took his time, merely growling in response to her whimpered pleas, teasing her with his words. "That's it, take all of me. I know you can."

By the time his hips were tight against hers, Sachi was writhing on the bed. He'd warned her that having her here—in his bed, in his *lair*—would unleash something feral in him, and that his desires were darker than she'd imagined.

What he hadn't said, at least not aloud, was the fundamental truth that whispered across their bond: nothing short of her complete and utter surrender would satisfy him.

So Sachi gave in. She melted before him, grinding against him as much as his iron grip would allow.

Yes.

He finally released her, but only to wrap his hands around her spread thighs. "Hold on."

And then he fucked her, fast and deep, harder than she'd anticipated, but so, so good. He used his near-bruising grip on her thighs to drag her into every greedy, unapologetic thrust, and Sachi wanted to scream from sheer relief. It was more than desire. It was more than bliss. It was a kind of madness, coming and feeling the tightness of her own body at the same time. Seeing herself, flushed and screaming, even though she was looking up at Ash. Fucking and being fucked, pleasure and breathless, persistent need weaving together until every sensation threatened to tear her apart.

This moment was *theirs*, shared and amplified because of it. "I love feeling how fucking good this is for you." His hair hung over his forehead as he drove into her again and again, and Sachi longed to smooth it back. "Tell me you want more," he groaned, words that sounded less like a command and more like a plea.

An easy answer, one she felt in her soul. "I always want more, Ash."

Fire flashed, and he lifted a hand to her chest. His claws scraped over her skin, lightly at first, then harder. He circled her nipple, teasing the hardened flesh, then closed tight in a rough pinch.

"*Ash!*"

Both hands traced down her body and across her inner thighs, his claws leaving thin red lines in their wake. "Tell me."

"Always," she panted. "*Always.*"

He cupped his hands under her knees and pushed them up, over his shoulders, as he leaned over her, using his weight—and another deep, angled thrust—to pin her to the bed. Sachi's vision blurred, going red and orange and then white around the edges of her field of vision. Fire, she realized vaguely, and a gorgeous, sparkling array of colors that filled the entire room with light.

The room burned, and so did she. Sachi clutched at Ash's shoulders and back, the chains forgotten, her nails pricking his skin until he threw back his head with a hiss. His claws did the same to her, scratching the delicate skin of her thighs until she could no longer separate the pain from the pleasure of coming.

"Can you still take more, sweet Sachi?" He rode her orgasm, every powerful thrust setting off another shower of sparks, until she couldn't even scream.

She had to whisper her answer. "I'll take anything."

Ash drove a hand into her hair. He slid the other beneath her hips, canting them for his next thrust.

Look at me.

Sachi wasn't sure if he said it, or if his need for it was so strong that their bond whispered the idea into her mind. But she obeyed, opening her eyes to lock onto Ash's beautiful face.

Love me.

I do.

The flame ignited between them once again, the one he'd called the Dragon's tongue. It slipped over her clit, curling around it. Sachi felt Ash's arousal reach a delirious, fevered pitch as he watched her writhe against him, riding his cock and the searing caress of his magic until everything was burning.

And then Ash bit her, his fangs scoring the sensitive skin of her neck.

Sachi's breath caught on a hoarse cry. Then she couldn't breathe at all, so great was the pressure of the orgasm quaking through her, and it didn't matter, because no one could survive this. It was too good, too much pleasure—

And then it *exploded* in a rain of pure fire that swirled around them, blocking out everything but the two of them. And then even that deafening blaze was drowned out by Ash's inhuman roar as he came. Her entire body tightened, sharing his orgasm as he spilled into her with a few final, desperate thrusts.

Sachi wasn't sure how long it took him to move, but when he began to stir, she opened her eyes and caught a glimpse of falling ash . . . and a few glittering hints of pure white light still twinkling above the bed.

Then Ash rolled over and pulled her with him. He was still inside her, his cock pulsing in time with the aftershocks that gripped her. She hissed lightly when he pulled her even closer, and he hummed a soothing noise of apology.

"It's good," she assured him. "Just . . . a lot."

"I know." His eyes shone. "I feel it, too."

Sachi laid her head on his chest and listened to the strong thump of his heart beneath her ear. She'd missed this. They'd both been so busy— and, in a way, stepping lightly around one another. They might be lord and consort, joined and formerly bound, but there was still so much distance between them sometimes. So many things they didn't know.

But they could find out.

Sachi lifted her head, loath to lose this sense of physical closeness but driven by curiosity. "Is your name Sevastyan?"

He blinked at her, brow furrowing. "Wherever did you hear that?"

"In the Dream." It was all she knew for certain, and she rushed ahead to explain. "There was a woman. Your grandmother, I think. We spoke, and she told me things. But she couldn't have been *real*, right?"

Ash stroked his fingers through her hair, his eyes troubled. "No one has called me by that name since my grandmother died. Even my mother called me Vash. And by the time the High Court formed, I'd been Ash for so long . . ." He trailed off, his fingers still moving restlessly. "You spoke with her?"

"Yes, I think I did. Even though I know it's impossible."

"Are you so sure it is? A year ago, I would have deemed much of what Zanya can do to be impossible." His fingers slid down over her shoulder to linger over her heart, where not even the tiniest scar marked her desperate attempt to shatter a curse. "You died, Sachi. But she took that death into herself and delivered it to another. Everything I've ever learned about the world says that cannot be. But she isn't *of* this world. She's made of the darkness and stardust that created it, and so are you."

There had to be a way to know for sure. "She had silver-blonde hair gone gray, wound up in braids, and brown eyes—the same color as yours—that crinkled at the corners when she laughed. Her clothes were all shades of purple, even the furs, and she was cooking a stew over an open fire. The first stag of Isere's Moon."

"It's good luck," he murmured, then laughed softly. "I haven't heard anyone talk about the first stag of Isere's Moon in three thousand years. Not even Elevia keeps to the old ways anymore. Maybe it *was* her. How else could you know?"

Perhaps I pulled it from the Dream itself. The words died on her tongue. As an explanation, it was no less fanciful and impossible than a conversation with Ash's long-dead grandmother. If Sachi could do either of those things, then it had to be true. She had to have, at the very least, an unimaginably strong connection to the Dream.

And that had to be worth *something*. "I will find the Phoenix," she promised Ash quietly. "And I will find out what they know. I won't let you go through another war, I swear."

He upended them in a surge of muscle, laying her back on the bed. With his head propped on one hand, he smoothed the damp strands of her hair back from her face and smiled. "Do you know why I've taken a consort every one hundred years? Why I continued to do it, even when they came to me full of hatred and dread?"

"No." She'd tried and tried, but she hadn't been able to figure out why he would persist in tormenting himself.

"Because three thousand years ago, when we stood on shattered land and begged the Everlasting Dream for a path forward, we heard a whisper from the world. A prophecy, I suppose you'd call it, though none of us have ever spoken of it outside the halls of the High Court."

"What did it say?"

"That the Dragon's consort will break the Builder's chains, and the people will dream again."

Sachi ached for him as the final piece of the puzzle slipped into place. "You kept trying because you were looking for someone special."

"I kept trying because that was what I owed the world. I didn't protect it back then." Regret shadowed his features as he stroked the backs of his fingers over her cheek. "I let harm come to it, so the Dream asked me to wait for the person who could win the fight without destroying us all. And then it sent me you." He stopped with his thumb pressed against her lips. "Every one of us heard the prophecy, but I also heard something else. A promise inside the whispers."

"Tell me," Sachi murmured.

His gaze held hers, searching. "It was a promise that I would never be alone again."

A question lurked beneath the words, one she could clearly sense across their ephemeral bond. One she could answer, gladly and freely.

So she did. She stretched up and whispered the words against his lips. "You won't, Ash. Never. You will always have me."

He slipped his arms around her with a groan, and Sachi poured every bit of her devotion into the kiss, putting her vow into action as well as words.

Chapter Nine
WITCHING MOON

Week Two, Day Two
Year 3000

The bluff beyond the Phoenix's tower had a glorious view. Even with the Creator's Moon still barely a quarter full, the stars shone bright enough to wash the distant landscape in silver. Zanya could trace the long path they'd taken down the northern side of the Burning Hills during the royal progress, to where the rolling valleys flattened into lush farmland. Moonlight reflected off the distant lakes, tiny pinpricks like distant stars that had fallen to rest upon the earth.

Had it only been a few weeks ago that they'd ridden past those lakes? Zanya had scoffed while relating the childhood story they'd all been taught—that the Betrayer and the Dragon had battled one another across those verdant plains. That the force of their bodies slamming into the earth had created the lakes, and that the Witch had filled them with her tears.

Inga might not have filled the lakes with her tears, but the violence of Ash's fight with the Betrayer truly had torn gashes in the world. At the time, it had been difficult for Zanya to fathom violence on a scale that left craters a furlong wide and deep enough to swallow a palace. Even with her own unusual strength and sturdiness, it had seemed impossible. Surely bodies would break before the *earth itself* did.

Then again, Elevia had kicked her *through* a stone wall two hand-spans thick this afternoon, and Zanya didn't have a mark on her to show for it. Her body had met rock with force enough to turn it to dust, and there were no broken bones, no bruises. Not even a twinge.

But Ash had felt pain when they'd made those lakes. She'd stolen the memory of it from him once, using her affinity for nightmares. She'd felt the shattering of his bones, the rending of his flesh. Whatever war those two had waged had been violence beyond even her fertile imagination.

And the Betrayer wanted to steal Sachi away.

That was reason to train until she dropped. To learn everything she could. Ash had barely survived the last battle against his so-called for-mer brother. Zanya knew he dreaded another confrontation. Not what the fight would do to his body, but what it might do to the world itself.

A simple enough problem to fix. After all, Zanya had spent her life training to assassinate a god. Why not kill one who actually deserved it?

Gravel scraped softly behind her. One crunching footstep, heavy and deliberate, which meant it was Ulric, warning her of his approach. Elevia would have circled wide and come at her from the front. The rest of the party was more comfortable leaving her alone. Zanya tossed a few more branches into her little fire, and it flared as Ulric stopped by her side.

He raised one eyebrow in silent question. Zanya huffed and wrapped her arms around her knees. "Go ahead and sit, if you want."

The Wolf sprawled gracefully next to her, one knee cocked with his foot on the ground, the other leg bent over it. He rested his elbow on that knee and stared out over the bluff. "How are you feeling?"

"Not so bad."

"Tired?"

"Not really. But not restless, either." The anxious energy that had driven her from bed most nights since her transformation had vanished, probably spent during long days under Elevia and Ulric's punishing training routine.

"Good." He picked up a twig and tossed it onto the fire. "Tomorrow will be a long day. We intend to anchor you to as many strategic sites across the Sheltered Lands as we can. The next time we need to get somewhere in a hurry, you can take us there."

Zanya felt her lips twitch into a self-deprecating smile. So much for her grand dreams of assassinating the Betrayer. Her tutors had a far more mundane use in mind for her. "So now I'm transportation? A pack mule?"

"Did you honestly expect Elevia to ignore such an advantage, with war both at our backs and on our doorstep?"

Zanya supposed she hadn't really considered it. The gods did miraculous things every day, and Ash could turn into a giant dragon and fly anywhere he wanted to go. "Is it really so unusual? Has no one ever been able to do this before?"

"Not like this." Ulric's serious tone erased her smile. "There are some, like Dianthe, who can travel physically using the Dream, but they're rare. Most of them use water to do it. Dianthe calls it the heart of the ocean, a place they can travel through that touches every other place water dwells."

"Can she take people with her?"

"Not unless they can breathe underwater. She tried it with Ash once, just after I met them . . ." He trailed off, and when Zanya glanced at him, his eyes glowed a soft gold in the firelight. "I've never seen the Siren so scared. She thought she'd killed him."

The Wolf's usually hard face had softened with the memory, a shared moment over three thousand years old. And, for a heartbeat, envy squeezed Zanya's chest tight. How she wished she'd known the High Court when they were young and untried. When they were testing their powers and sometimes failing catastrophically. Maybe then it wouldn't be so hard to imagine herself as one of them. "I'd like to have known Ash before the Betrayer. He must have been different."

Ulric smiled, small and sad. "It's true. The war took something out of him. He feels the world in ways the rest of us don't, and we almost shattered it. He feels responsible for letting the Betrayer go too far."

Everything in Zanya rejected that. "It can't have been his fault."

"No," Ulric agreed. Then, after a pause and a wary look at her, he amended, "Mostly not."

"Mostly?"

She hadn't realized how much protective anger she'd packed into one word until he lifted a placating hand. "It's complicated, Zanya."

"Then explain it."

"He always let the Betrayer disrespect him." Ulric grimaced. "The *Builder* cared about progress above all else. Taming the wild places, advancing our technology. Digging into the earth to find what treasures it could yield and using them, even when what we already had was good enough. He had no respect for those who couldn't embrace his vision. Like me—the wild places have always been mine to protect. But my power didn't threaten him the way Ash's did."

Because Ash had power over the earth itself. There was nothing the Builder could have created that Ash couldn't have torn down. Fire was threat enough, but Ash could part the earth and ask it to swallow anything—building or village or city—whole.

No, Zanya could not imagine he would have cared for such a threat. Which reminded her of something else. "Inga told me that the Betrayer called me an abomination. That he thought you all should kill me."

Even in the firelight, Zanya could see his sudden flush. "Did she tell you that I considered the same?"

"No." Inga had likely been too protective of Ulric to break such confidences. Anyway, she hadn't needed to. The pain of his clear mistrust had cut deep in those first days, but Zanya covered it with a smile. "You weren't subtle about it, though. I don't think you lie any better than I do."

A noise rumbled up out of him, but whether it was a laugh or a growl she couldn't say. "No. I do not."

He turned to face her, and Zanya tensed. The firelight flickering over his tanned skin and golden eyes reminded her of the first time she'd met him, at the feast to celebrate Sachi and Ash's bonding. She remembered the dark temptation of all this dangerous magic, the way her inner predator had risen, hungry to test herself against him. It wasn't the same sexual heat she felt when Ash touched her, but there was a sensuality beneath it that she couldn't deny.

She could remember dancing with him that night. The spark she'd felt, awakening parts of her she'd thought long buried. Sachi had been her only safe outlet for affection of any kind, and she'd come close to hating the Wolf that night for reminding her just how small her world was.

All of it was still there as he reached out to brush a wayward lock of hair back from her eyes. His own glowed that gentle, molten gold—the gold of the Wolf. "My nature, at its heart, is pure survival," he murmured. "And it had been several thousand years since I was last forced to face my own mortality so squarely in the face. I was unfair to you, little sister. I won't make that mistake again."

Zanya's heart pounded. Tears stung her eyes. She watched him raise one arm in silent invitation, and any sexual awareness shattered under the sudden overwhelming *longing* for what he offered her—that tantalizing promise that had almost destroyed her during the consort's progress.

Acceptance. Acceptance of *all* of her, even the deadliest parts. And not just impersonal tolerance, but the friendship that tied these ancient gods together. The camaraderie and belonging she'd craved so deeply that it had become an ache inside her worse than any heartbreak.

He was offering her family.

Zanya edged closer, leaning into him. His arm came down around her shoulders, his big hand resting lightly on her arm, as if he didn't want her to feel trapped. She expected it to be awkward, but it wasn't. They fit together, both creatures born of survival and honed into weapons. Monsters who belonged to the wild places. No wonder she'd loved the Midnight Forest so much. It sheltered the same darkness that thrived at the heart of her, a darkness that held its own impossible beauty.

She didn't know how long they sat there in comfortable silence, gazing out into the star-swept night, but the fire had burned low by the time quiet footsteps approached.

"I hate to interrupt," Elevia murmured, "but it's time to get back to work."

Zanya sighed, but she didn't protest. As soon as Ulric's arm dropped away, she rose and kicked dirt over the embers of the fire. "Are we traveling again?"

"No. We need to talk about your Terrors."

It was a struggle not to flinch back. "I said I'm not doing that. I don't want to summon them."

"I understand that," Elevia replied evenly. "But they're part of you—"

"They are *not*," Zanya interrupted, shoving away the words as if she could also push back the shame that lingered deep inside her. "It's only happened a few times. Complete accidents."

"Which is exactly why you have to develop a measure of control." She took a single step closer. "You need to be the one to decide when or even *if* they appear. *You*, Zanya."

"You don't know what you're asking!" Memories that Zanya had spent a lifetime avoiding crashed over her, fueled by that shame. She buried them in words. "I've seen the scar on Ash's arm. None of you heal from wounds inflicted by Terrors. What if I accidentally summon not one Terror but an *army*, and then I can't control them? You could die. *Everyone* could die." She turned to Ulric, appealing to the survival instincts that she knew ran deep in him. "Do you want to face an army of Terrors?"

"No." It was the Wolf who spoke, those eyes glowing gold in the darkness. "But Elevia is right. You can't run from a part of yourself. And we trust you. You won't let them hurt us."

As if it were that simple in the chaos of a Terror attack. Terrors were nightmares given form, spawned from the very earth. Some were embodied by pure Void magic. Others took on the twisted form of whatever debris and detritus could be cobbled together. She'd seen bones and sticks, rocks and discarded weapons—the materials didn't matter. Only the power holding the nightmare together.

Void magic. *Her* magic. The only thing that could mortally wound a god touched by the Dream.

The only thing inside her terrible enough to horrify Sachi.

"I'm not doing it," she rasped, turning away. "It isn't worth the risk. Maybe I can try sometime when I'm alone, but not here. Not like this."

"Zanya—"

But Elevia got no further. She and Ulric both stiffened and fell silent as they looked at one another. Then Elevia took off at a run.

"What is it?" Zanya asked.

"Horses, coming in fast."

A reprieve. For a moment, Zanya felt the sweet flood of relief. Guilt followed swiftly as Ulric took off, and she realized the implication.

Riders crashing into their camp at night meant trouble.

Zanya ran after Ulric as he loped to where Elevia had intercepted a trio of riders. Even from a dozen paces Zanya could tell that their horses were lathered from an impossibly long run—and that the riders reeked of smoke and blood.

Her stomach churned. At Elevia's side, one of her lieutenants sounded the whistle that meant *form up*. The Huntress whirled as Zanya reached her side. "Can you carry us back to the town where they tried to burn the healer?"

The Huntress's guardsmen formed a loose circle around her. It would take effort, but she could do it. "As many as can touch me. Though I can't bring the horses, obviously."

"That's fine." Elevia numbered off several to remain with the mounts. The rest gathered close, murmuring apologies as they pressed in all around her. Zanya extended her arms to either side, grasping Ulric's shoulder on one side and Elevia's on the other, waiting until everyone had found a way to touch her. "Are we ready?"

"Go," Elevia ordered.

Blessing their rigid training, Zanya closed her eyes and summoned the shadows. They swirled up at her feet, eager and caressing. Taking a deep breath, she called more, letting them swirl wider—down her arms, past her fingertips. They grew to encompass a dozen of Elevia's hardened fighters in swirls of pure midnight. When Zanya could *feel* the weight of every last one of them, she stepped into the Void.

And out into a nightmare.

Chapter Ten
WITCHING MOON

Week Two, Day Three
Year 3000

Somewhat predictably, Sachi was so sated from Ash's attentions that her sleep was dreamless and warm, with all the restful nothingness that came with being truly exhausted. But something tugged at her from within the darkness, kept drawing her back toward consciousness.

I won't let you go through another war, I swear.

There was something she was meant to do, a task she'd taken on with all the fervent sincerity of a vow.

I will find the Phoenix.

Yes, that was her task. Sachi struggled through the darkness until she found the light. She stepped into it, surrounded herself with the unending white expanse of the Dream, and marveled because it was getting easier to find her way. Before long, walking the Dream would be like breathing, so integral to her existence that she wouldn't even have to *think* about it, much less try.

Unfortunately, it wasn't getting any easier to *locate* her quarry. Sachi had never met the Phoenix, had only tasted echoes and hints of their essence and power once, at their tower. It had radiated from the blue flames outside their temple, the ones Ash had called the Phoenix's fire.

Sachi had feared it a little at the time, the notion that simply walking through that inferno could reveal the truth that lived at the very heart of her. But now? She longed for that revelatory flame. Perhaps she'd ask Zanya or Ash to take her there again. She could walk through that gauntlet of blue flames and finally, once and for all, *know.*

The crackle of a fire behind her made Sachi smile, and she turned, fully expecting to once again greet the spirit of Ash's grandmother.

Instead, she faced a wall of fire.

Startled, Sachi stared at it, wondering if she'd somehow conjured the Phoenix's flames from nothing. But this blaze didn't consist of delicate, dancing blue fire. It looked more like the sorts of protective walls that Ash sometimes raised.

Sachi's smile returned, and she stepped forward. Had her heart somehow brought her back through the Dream to him?

And was he dreaming of her?

Stepping through the flames didn't hurt, but it didn't deliver her into Ash's embrace, either. She found herself in a cave, though it looked like nothing she'd ever actually seen before. It wasn't like the dark cavern of salt and stone that she'd shared with Zanya on the edge of Siren's Bay. This was a network of narrow tunnels, seemingly carved from sand.

"Hurry along, now." A soft, low voice echoed through the tunnels like the murmur of a rushing river. "We don't have much time."

It came from Sachi's right, so she turned to follow it, rounding corners mainly by instinct. She had no idea *where* she was, but she knew she was meant to be here.

"Here, sit. Have some water." The voice was closer this time, so close it could have been right next to Sachi's ear. "Brynja, find some blankets. They're freezing, but we can't risk a fire. Not here."

A fire. The words tugged at Sachi, and she found herself approaching the nearest wall. She placed her hand on the surface, and it vibrated beneath her touch like a struck cymbal. Then the wall rippled slightly, as if it wasn't quite solid.

Sachi walked forward again, *through* the sandstone.

She emerged in a small cavern lit only by a tiny blue flame. Sachi watched, fascinated, as it floated through the air and alighted on someone's outstretched palm like a bird. The person, whose head and face were mostly wrapped in light-colored cloth, peered into the darkness with eyes that burned blue.

"Phoenix."

Their eyes narrowed, and they yanked the cloth away from their face with a vicious tug, revealing delicate features and a dark mustache and goatee. "Who's there? Identify yourself."

"I . . ." The Phoenix had been missing for decades; did they even know that Ash had taken another consort, let alone who Sachi was? She didn't know what to say, so she moved closer. Out of the shadows.

Golden light suffused the cavern, illuminating half a dozen huddled figures in the corner, as well as two more hovering just behind the Phoenix. None of them reacted to the sudden wash of light.

None except the Phoenix. They held up a hand and squinted against the sudden brightness, which seemed to alarm their companions.

"What's happening to them?" one demanded anxiously. "Nyx?"

The other just looked on in reverence. "They're having a vision."

For a moment, everything in the cavern seemed to blur. Sachi blinked, but the wavering veil only intensified. It was like looking through a thin fall of water, a transparent but very tangible barrier, and Sachi sucked in a breath as understanding washed over her.

The Phoenix wasn't in the Dream at all. They were wide awake, going about their business in the actual, physical world. *Sachi*, on the other hand, was most definitely in the Dream . . . and merely peering out of it.

The Phoenix ignored their companions, who continued to fuss and fret, and fixed their gaze on Sachi. "It's *you.*"

Relieved, Sachi nodded. "Then you know me?"

"Of course I do. Everyone does." The Phoenix stripped away the rest of their head covering, revealing hair that was dark at the roots but almost white at the ends. They ran a hand roughly through their hair, sending it tumbling across their forehead. "But if you're here, that means we're out of time."

"No," Sachi denied, "but everyone has been looking for you. The rest of the High Court, they need to know—"

"Yes." The Phoenix drew near—close enough to touch, save for the shimmering barrier between them and Sachi. "Tell the others it's to be war. They must prepare. I'm coming for them as soon as I can."

"Sachi!"

It was Zanya's voice, echoing all around them, so distressed that the veil between Sachi and the Phoenix thickened, almost solidified.

The Phoenix reached through it to grip Sachi's hand. "Tell them."

"I will," Sachi promised. "Be careful. Stay safe."

"You, as well."

With a violent jerk, Sachi tumbled from the Dream. For a disorienting moment, her body was in Ash's huge, warm bed, but her mind was still leagues away, across a continent, in a cave beneath the Betrayer's Empire. She fought to pull herself back together, to take just one single breath.

"Sachi!"

Finally, she managed a gasp. Ash stirred beside her, but he didn't wake, so she shook his arm. "Ash. *Ash,* wake up. Hurry."

He blinked up at her, then rose on one elbow, his entire body tense. "What is it?"

"It's Zanya," she choked. "Something's wrong."

Shadows swirled at the foot of the bed, blocking out the dying firelight, then coalesced into a bloody, soot-streaked Zanya.

"You need to come," she rasped. "Both of you."

Chapter Eleven
WITCHING MOON

Week Two, Day Three
Year 3000

Zanya's shadows carried them into chaos.

Ash could sense the flames even before the shadows receded. They raged out of control, feeding on wooden buildings and thatch roofs that had little protection against the fierce burn. His instinctive push to quiet the flames did nothing—something unnatural had kindled this fire, something he had never felt before.

Trusting Zanya to keep Sachi safe, Ash raced toward the inferno. Another thrust of his magic met a resistance he'd never felt before—a sickening twist, as if the flames themselves were . . . *ill*. Poisonous and wrong.

"Ash, wait!" Elevia shouted. "This isn't normal fire!"

It was possible the Mortal Lords had been dabbling in weapons meant to foil the powers of gods. It was equally possible the Empire had provided this as a distraction. Its source didn't matter. Only stopping it did.

Cautiously, Ash approached the leading edge of the fire. The heat of it felt unnatural, but not deadly, so he reached out. Flames leapt to his fingers, crawling up his arm. It stung, like dragging something rough over sensitive skin, but it didn't burn him. Not until he tried to draw the fire into himself.

Scalding agony erupted beneath his skin. He gritted his teeth, weathering the pain, and tried to quench the fire, but it wouldn't dissipate. It raged within him, seeking an outlet. He knelt, holding his fingers spread wide above the dirt—and hesitated.

Sending the fire into the earth might bank it, but every instinct he had screamed against it. This sickness should not—*could not*—go back into the ground.

"Ash?" Sachi's voice sounded behind him, rough with worry—and pain.

Their potion-induced temporary bond lingered, but Ash could do nothing about that now. "I can draw it into me," he growled. "But there's no way to bank it without poisoning the earth."

Suddenly Zanya was there at his side, her shadows swirling. She hissed in pain when the flames reached for her, and Ash struggled to expand the circle of his protection. It saved her from burning, but agony still seethed in her dark eyes as she grabbed his hand.

"Use me," she ordered. "I think I can send it into the Void."

The Void. Vast, endless. It was pure destructive power, grinding everything into the dust that fueled creation. Whatever wrongness might be at the heart of this could not withstand an annihilation so complete.

But Zanya was so new to her powers. If she slipped or lost control, the flames could consume her. "Are you sure?"

She scowled at him. "Now, Dragon. While there may yet be people left to save."

Bracing himself, he released the fire again. It raged down his arm, toward their joined hands. She gasped when it crawled across her wrist, her skin reddening beneath the wild flames. But almost as soon as it touched her, shadows spun down from her shoulder, surging toward the fire. They smashed together, twisting into a column that flared upward.

Then the shadows began to swallow the flames.

They *could* do this. But they must move quickly.

Ash wrapped his free arm around Zanya, dragging her against his chest. "Hold on to me," he shouted over the sudden surge of flames. "Don't let go. Not for anything."

The vicious heat seemed to lift her hair on a hellish breeze. "I won't," she promised, clinging to his neck. "Do it."

Someone behind them screamed a warning, but Ash ignored it. With Zanya held protectively in his grasp, he raced toward the heart of the conflagration. His power swirled the fire around them in massive sparks of color, churning through the sickly greens and blues, replacing it with healthy golds and oranges.

He felt when they reached the source of the blaze. An unnatural liquid coated the earth, burning a bioluminescent green he'd rarely seen outside of Inga's more fantastical creatures. Ash wrapped all the protective power he had around Zanya and roared over the flames, "Now! Open yourself to the Void!"

Shadows stretched out in all directions. Ash pulled the sickly fire toward him, starting with the flames that licked at their feet. It churned around them, battling his own fire and the tendrils of shadow. They were too small, thin ropes of midnight trying to entangle the blazing vastness of the sun. Zanya's breath heaved against his ear, her agony evident. He could protect her from burning, but not from the pain . . .

Fool. She's too new. Too untried—

And in trying to resist his overprotectiveness, he'd put her in jeopardy. Sachi would never forgive him if he lost Zanya. And he'd never forgive himself, either.

Zanya's head fell back. Her eyes flew open, and they were pure black. No iris, no white. The kind of blackness you could only find at the farthest depths of the ocean, or deep within the earth. Places that had never even known the touch of starlight.

Her mouth opened in a silent scream.

And that untouched darkness exploded, swallowing them both.

A wind rose around them, a vortex of fire and darkness. The force of it threatened to buffet them apart, but Ash wrapped both arms around Zanya as that ghostly wind lifted her feet from the ground.

The dark whirlpool expanded. Ash clung to Zanya and *pulled* with everything in him, commanding the flames to converge upon him from all directions. It should have overwhelmed them both, but as fast as he pulled, the wild, dark power swallowed the inferno. He barely had time to feel the agony as it washed through him and vanished.

"Not so fast!" he shouted, but the darkness swallowed the words, too. Zanya's black eyes stared past him, unseeing. She'd thrust both arms out to her sides, her hands balled into fists. Her mouth moved, but whatever sound she made was lost to the roar around them.

The unnatural fire collapsed, spinning away into nothing. The remaining flames stretched out into impossibly thin strands of glittering gold, lost to the Void. Ash couldn't see the rest of the village, couldn't see their people, couldn't see *anything* except Zanya and the shadows.

Shadows that swirled around him now, tasting. Hungry. He felt a tug at some intrinsic part of him deep inside. The fire that lived within, that pumped his very blood.

The power that made him the Lord of Fire.

The strength went out of his legs. He hit his knees, still clinging to Zanya. The toes of her boots barely brushed the dirt, as if only his weight kept her from launching skyward. "It's done, Zanya!" he screamed.

She stared down at him, her eyes still flooded with shadows, her hair floating on a breeze that didn't exist. The tug inside him sharpened into pain—just for a moment—and then she shuddered in his grip. The whirlwind died. Shadows turned to mist, revealing a glimpse at the world outside them for the first time.

Her boots thumped against the blackened dirt, and she swayed, bracing one hand on his shoulder to keep her balance. She closed her eyes. When they opened, she was Zanya again—warm brown eyes and a brow furrowed with concern.

"I'm sorry," she whispered.

"No apologies." He squeezed her hand and rose. "You did what needed to be done. And you did well."

She exhaled, then looked over his shoulder and went stiff.

Ash turned slowly. The moonlight illuminated what had been a thriving village only a few days ago. He recognized the distant tree line, a few outbuildings. He recognized the shocked, ash-streaked faces of the few survivors hovering outside the circle of charred, burned destruction.

Emmonsdale. The village where the Mortal Queen's soldiers had tried to burn a healer as a witch. Where Zanya had killed Lord Velez, and the villagers had fought back.

Apparently, the new queen had decided to make an example of them.

"Sachi!"

Zanya broke away from him, staggering through the blackened ruins all around them. Ash followed in time to see her sink to the ground. Sachi was already there, her pristine white nightgown covered with soot and blood. She cradled a body in her arms, and her fingers trembled as she tried to smooth the corpse's matted hair.

Ash's stomach lurched when he recognized the dead woman's face.

It was the healer that Velez had sought to burn. The woman Ash had saved, only so she could die a different death. An equally pointless one.

"She never hurt anyone." Sachi's voice was hoarse, either from the smoke or from screaming. "But they had to make her pay, didn't they? For our interference."

Confirming it would only break Sachi's heart, but Ash couldn't bring himself to lie to her.

"Come away, Sachi." Zanya gripped Sachi's arms, gently urging her to rise. "You can't fix everything."

"I don't need to fix everything," Sachi snapped, then sobbed as tears streamed down her face. "Just something. *Anything*. One godsdamned thing."

Zanya looked distraught. But Ulric crouched before Sachi and lifted her chin. "Then help us fix this," he rumbled quietly. "The soldiers who burned the village told them that anyone who forsakes their rightful queen will suffer the same. What do you know of the girl?"

It took a moment for Sachi's sobs to subside, but when they did, a fierce light filled her eyes. She went still, so still she barely breathed, and the last flashes of her emotions deserted Ash, as if she had just gone blank. Fear gripped him before he recognized her stillness for what it was—a predator considering an attack.

"No." Sachi's voice had steadied, cooled, and she shook her head as she finally rose. "The *queen* is a child. Barely fifteen. If the order for this destruction came from House Roquebarre, then it likely came from her regents."

Elevia crossed her arms. "Tell us."

"Dalvish's three siblings—Doven, Bodin, and Tislaina. Easily dealt with on an individual basis, whether through diplomacy or bribery." She paused, her eyes still flashing but her expression grave. "But their united front poses a problem. As long as they stand as one, they are formidable. And brutal."

The Huntress hummed. "Then we should find a way to divide them."

"No. We face them with a weapon rarely seen at Dalvish's former court—the truth." Sachi paced the scorched ground. "The arrangement between the mortal rulers of the Sheltered Lands and the Lord of Earth and Fire was codified by treaty. A treaty that Dalvish violated."

"Presumably by trying to murder Ash," Ulric muttered.

"Not exactly. The true breach was when they sent me to serve as his consort." She stopped and faced Ash. "They promised you an heir, my love, but they sent you an orphan. You have recourse."

"Not to put too fine a point on it, but why would they give a *shit* about his recourse?" Elevia asked. "As Ulric just mentioned, they did try to kill him. They must assume they've lost any claim to his protection."

"Oh, they absolutely won't care about that. But they'll care about losing the lands granted to them in trust by the terms of the treaty." Sachi ticked a list off on her fingers. "The entirety of the Blasted Plains plus nearly half of the Burning Hills, including portions of the fishing lands and farmsteads to the east and north."

Ash could barely remember the specifics of the negotiations. He'd been reeling in the aftermath not only of war but of losing the Builder to pride and avarice. But something Sachi said prompted a recollection. "The capital."

"Yes," Sachi confirmed. "Parts of it, anyway. Most interestingly, Castle Roquebarre. You could take their home, Ash."

All he wanted was for the killing to stop. "Will it work?"

"I'll make it work," Sachi murmured fiercely, then glanced at each of them in turn. "I will go to Anikke with proof of her army's brutality. If it turns out that she knew about—or, Dream forbid, *approved*—this order, then we'll know."

"Know what, exactly?"

"That killing a tyrannical king wasn't enough." Sachi stared down at a smoldering tuft of grass, then crushed it beneath her slipper and met Ash's gaze. "And we must also now depose a queen."

Ash stared at Sachi. He'd known she was hungry for knowledge and history, and Zanya had once noted offhand that she would have made a formidable scholar. But he'd never seen that curiosity and focus turned quite this ruthlessly toward political practicalities.

It was almost as frightening as it was dazzling.

"Good. Then that's settled." Sachi's eyes burned, and her chest heaved. "I met your friend tonight. The Phoenix."

His heart leapt. "In the Dream? You found them?"

"I did. They were . . ." Her brow furrowed. "Smuggling refugees out of the Empire, I think. I found them in some sort of cavern or tunnel system."

"Sachi." Elevia stared at her with appraising eyes, as if seeing her for the first time. "Are you saying they were awake? That you spoke to them—"

"In the real world, yes." Sachi caught Ash's gaze. "I never left the Dream, but they could still see me."

"That's—" Ulric bit off the word with a glance at Zanya. *Impossible* still lingered in the air, but no doubt he dared not say it when they'd just witnessed Zanya channel the corrupted power of a fiery maelstrom into the Void.

Impossible was a concept they all might do better to forget when it came to these two.

Ash believed. "What did they say?"

"That they're coming for you as soon as they can, but you must prepare." She swallowed hard. "It's to be war."

Ulric cursed softly. Zanya looked away. Ash met Elevia's gaze and saw resignation but no surprise, as if she'd known all along that this day would come no matter how zealously Ash ran from it.

The days of denial and avoidance were coming to an end. Ash would have to face his ancient enemy again . . . and pray the world survived it.

Chapter Twelve
WITCHING MOON

Week Two, Day Three
Year 3000

Sachi lay between her lovers, wide awake and thinking. Ash's arm was slung across her midsection, and Zanya's leg over both of hers, as if they could protect her even in sleep. Even in dreams.

Her throat ached. So did her eyes, though they were red and sore from the smoke and from crying, not from screaming. Everything still smelled and tasted of charred wood and thatch, and she *hated* it. That destructive fire had made a mockery of the warmth of Ash's nurturing, protective flame, and no amount of wine had been able to wash it all away.

The drink had also done little to calm her racing thoughts. *Why* did she feel responsible for the brutality visited on that village? Everyone knew she wasn't really Princess Sachielle of House Roquebarre; she was an orphan, a nameless nobody. An impostor. This wasn't her family. These weren't *her* atrocities.

But a tiny, persistent voice in the back of her head called her a liar. Dalvish had not been her family, and neither had his wife or siblings. But they couldn't very well maintain that Sachielle was their daughter and heir without having her live with them as a member of their household. So Sachi had spent years playing older sister to tiny little Anikke.

In that way, sometimes lies could become real. Anikke was born after Sachi had already been installed at court, and no one who had known the truth had been foolish enough to share it with the child. So she had believed, with all her young heart, that Sachi was her beloved sister.

Did that not make it so? What *was* a family if you could not build one out of love as surely as you could out of blood? If Anikke was not truly her sister, then she was, at the very least, the closest thing Sachi had ever known.

Which made discovering the depth of her involvement in these military actions more than a matter of practicality. It made it a matter of Sachi's heart. It would shatter into a million pieces if she learned that Anikke had ordered the troops to march on Emmonsdale. To murder its citizens.

But it would also shatter if she were to find out that she'd left a helpless, defenseless, *innocent* girl alone to fend for herself in that pit of vipers.

So Sachi had to try, but how? Should she attempt to reach Anikke through her dreams? On the one hand, it could yield the information she sought. On the other, it could alert Anikke that not everything was as it truly seemed with her wayward supposed older sister.

No, the risk was worth it. It had to be. It was Sachi's best chance not only to assess the situation—and Anikke's role in it—but to gather intelligence beyond what the Phoenix might know. Sachi could materially contribute to the war effort for once.

After all, people said things in dreams that they would never say aloud to another soul.

And if she planned to seek out Anikke in her dreams, now was the time. The queen might not even be suspicious of such a thing if followed closely by Sachi's arrival in the capital. The Mortal Lords *were* said to possess magic. That was the very thing that demonstrated their divine right to rule, wasn't it? Any proper royal might expect to have prophetic dreams.

Her course decided, Sachi closed her eyes and took a deep breath. Ash stirred beside her, and she stroked the back of his arm until he fell still once more. Then she slipped away, into the Dream.

This time, her journey began in darkness instead of the open white expanse she'd come to expect. She took tentative steps forward until plastered walls with gray stone peeking through materialized in front of her.

Castle Roquebarre.

She knew this hallway. It was near the kitchens and the back stairs, the ones where she had often lingered when she hoped to catch a glimpse of Zanya. Sachi dragged her fingers over the stone, skipping over the heavy tapestries that decorated the walls, approximating windows where none existed.

She had to get to Anikke. So she hurried to the stairs, a stone set carved in a spiral, and began to climb.

What would she say? Sachi considered it as she mounted step after step in a dizzying circle. The truth was too harsh for a setting like this, as likely to drive the girl from sleep in startled fear as to convince her.

Sachi passed a landing and nearly stumbled. This floor did not house family or servants, but . . .

Nikkon. She stared at the hall, with its deep-black carpet and golden wallpaper. This entire wing had been his, and he'd relished its privacy and convenience. It placed him close to Sachi's chamber, and he could come and go as he pleased, with only the servants the wiser, and everyone knew *they* didn't matter—

It had served him well, this little pocket of the castle.

She kept climbing, but her traitorous feet refused to carry her away from the black carpet. It began to spread, oozing onto the pale gray of the stone, and Sachi jerked away—

She turned, and found herself in a cavernous hall filled with golden light and glass *everywhere*. There weren't just windows, but entire curving walls comprised of clear and colored glass, floor to ceiling. The effect was as striking as it was disarming, and Sachi spun in a dizzy circle, trying to take it all in.

Then she saw *him*. The Betrayer.

She almost didn't recognize him as the same man from her vision. He was dressed in court clothes, velvet and linen and leather, all in the finest and most vivid shades of green. His head lolled against the wood as he drowsed on his gilded throne, and he looked . . . *young*. Completely different with his skin not slicked with blood and swollen from Ash's fists.

This was the lurking enemy, the monster of all their nightmares? He looked so normal that Sachi had taken several steps toward him before she caught herself and froze.

Everyone at Dalvish's court had looked normal, too. Beautiful, even when their hearts were harder and blacker than coal.

What do I do? Make contact? She'd never seen anyone sleeping within a dream before, and she had no idea what would happen if she tried to shake him awake. Would he become aware but remain within his dream state, or would the interruption thrust him, entirely and unceremoniously, from sleep?

In the end, she crept forward, because she couldn't bear to squander the chance to ask him *why*.

Between one step and the next, his eyes flew open. Even at a distance, their hazel depths sparked with color—golden honey one moment, then the sharpest green.

Sachi stopped again, her chest heaving. Even when she walked in Zanya's dreams, there was a slightly unfocused quality to her lover's gaze that spoke of fleeting images and the blurry, changeable nature of sleep.

The Betrayer, on the other hand, looked directly at her. No, *through* her, as if he could perceive her on a level deeper than sight alone.

Something was not right.

She blinked, and the Betrayer was *there*, standing in front of her, his strong hands closing tight around her arms. His beautiful mouth curled into the smile of a true believer faced with their destiny.

"I knew you'd come to me."

For a moment, everything went white, and all that existed was the punishing hold on her upper arms. Sachi struggled until that, too, disappeared in a whirling rush that stole the scream from her throat.

She dropped through nothingness and emerged in a huge bed, tangled in the covers . . . with the Betrayer, now dressed in his nightclothes, still gripping her arms.

And she was wide, *wide* awake.

"No," she gasped.

The Betrayer rolled from the bed. Sachi was still struggling her way free of the blankets when he returned with a small silver cylinder in one hand. He gripped her chin with the other and stared down at her, determination warring with false regret in his cool gaze.

"I'm sorry we have to start this way," he murmured. She slapped at his hands as he pressed the cylinder against her neck, but he was far too strong to fight. "You'll understand in time."

Sachi felt a sharp sting. Moments later, her vision began to blur, and everything got heavy, so *heavy* . . .

She fell back against the pillows. "Where . . . ?"

"You're in my home, of course."

Panic surged through Sachi, but her body refused to react to it. Her mind screamed to fight, to run, but the darkness was upon her. And Sachi knew there was no fighting it.

A thumb stroked her cheek. "My Empress."

Sachi tried to turn her head, but the darkness won. It always did.

Chapter Thirteen
WITCHING MOON

Week Two, Day Three
Year 3000

Ash knew the moment Sachi vanished.

He was awake before his arm, which had been draped over her, hit the mattress. The depression beside him in the pillow still smelled like Witchwood roses. He could still feel the warmth of her last breath, exhaled against his shoulder. Sleep made him groggy as he groped at the blankets and flung them away, his mind scrambling for meaning in the space between his body and Zanya's.

"Sachi?" Zanya rolled to her knees, sliding one hand through the emptiness, as if she couldn't believe Sachi wasn't in it. "Where—?"

Realization hit her at the same time full wakefulness did.

"Zanya, *wait!*" Ash flung out a hand, but it was too late. Shadows gathered around her in a violent storm, tearing through reality with the force of Zanya's panic. His hand swung through air, but a heartbeat later Zanya exploded from the shadows, swaying on her knees, her eyes nothing but blackness as she curled her hands into fists.

"I can feel her," she snarled, and the shadows contracted again. Pressure built like the warning before a violent storm, and the shadows ejected Zanya with so much force she flew off the bed.

"Zanya, you can't—"

She was already scrambling to her feet. Shadows stabbed through the room like daggers, weaving around her. "She's *right there*. I can feel her, but something is blocking me."

She tried again, and again—like a disoriented bird battering itself against a glass window. Ash kicked free of the blankets and lunged for her, but only succeeded in stumbling through the empty space left behind before the shadows spat her out again. He grabbed at her shoulders. "Zanya, *stop!*"

Tears streaked her cheeks. "She's scared! I can feel it! Wherever she is, she's *terrified!* I just need—"

She collapsed into shadows again. But this time, she exploded back out of them as if thrown by a giant hand. Livid marks crisscrossed her arms and her face, glittering with painful menace.

"You're hurting yourself," he growled.

She shook her head. "I don't care."

He lunged again, but she had already slipped into the writhing shadows. A scream rose from within their depths. Zanya's scream, echoing down an endless tunnel. It raked claws of despair down his spine as it grew louder.

That was a scream of frustration. Of rage and denial. Of *agony*.

The shadows exploded into mist. Zanya hit the floor, her body limp. Ash dove for her and turned her over, feeling frantically for her pulse. Her heart was beating too fast for her rasping breaths, and those glowing lines looked like scars, only they bled freely as he swept her up into his arms and bolted for the door to the bridge.

"*Inga!*"

The stairs would take too long. Wings of fire sprouted before he hit the center of the consort's bridge. Zanya's body melted through his shimmering arms only to be caught with painstaking gentleness in his massive claws. She'd never looked as fragile as she did now, small and bloody and painfully *still*, the only movement her long black hair trailing down as he launched himself into the sky with a commanding roar that rattled the entire castle.

One powerful sweep of his wings brought him to the Godwalk. Inga was already in front of her tower, a robe half-tied around her body and her own dark hair flying wildly in the wind from his wings. There was no room for his dragon form in the space between buildings, so he transformed in another gout of fire, clutching Zanya protectively to his chest as they plummeted to the cobblestone walkway.

Stone shattered under his feet as he landed. He ignored it and spun to Inga. Shock held her immobile for a terrifying moment, then she shook her head and finished tying her robe. "Take her inside, at once. To my workroom."

Ash barely saw the brightly colored garden that formed Inga's courtyard. Ethereal butterflies fluttered out of his way as he raced through it and into the main castle. Where the Huntress had set up her war room in the matching tower, the Witch had built some fantastical combination of a greenhouse, a still room, an experimental laboratory, and a sickroom.

"Here."

Inga unfurled a clean white sheet over a waist-high wooden table. Ash set Zanya down as gently as he could, smoothing her hair back from her bloodied cheeks. Inga's voice was soft behind him as she spoke to the servant who'd trailed them inside.

"Fetch Aleksi. Hurry."

"Elevia and Ulric, too," Ash rasped.

The metallic scent of Zanya's blood made his own boil. He'd been so focused on her panic that there had been no room for his own. But it raged beneath the fragile shell of calm he'd constructed, a maelstrom so vast it could swallow this whole castle and return these mountains to dust.

Somehow, he had to say the words without breaking. "Sachi is gone."

"Gone?"

Ash focused very closely on Zanya's forehead, on coaxing back the lingering, stubborn pieces of hair that stuck to her bloody skin. He must not break. "She vanished from our bed. Zanya tried to follow her, and this was the result. She said that something was blocking her. It looked as if she was slamming into a wall and being thrown back."

Inga set the tip of her fingernail beneath Zanya's breasts and whispered a word. Her gentle magic prickled over Ash's skin as she dragged her nail down, cutting the shirt all the way down to its hem. It fell open, revealing the same pattern of crisscrossing wounds marring Zanya's skin. They still bled sluggishly, the smears of it concealing the actual wounds until an assistant brought a bowl of warm water with a wet cloth. Inga wiped away the blood, leaving oddly raised marks that glittered an iridescent silver.

"Almost like a web." Inga traced one of the scars with her fingertip.

Ash felt his fragile shell cracking. "I don't care what it is," he snarled. Zanya's light-brown skin usually had a healthy, sun-kissed glow, but she was drawn and sallow now. The restless energy that had so plagued her had been replaced by a stillness that stoked panic in his soul. "Just tell me you can fix it."

"I can try," Inga responded, still stroking one of those shimmering scars.

One of Zanya's hands spilled from the table, her fingers clenched as if reaching for Sachi. Ash folded his hand around hers and hissed in shock. "Her skin is cold."

"I know. I think she's fighting the . . . infection."

"The infection?"

Inga held out her hand and twisted her wrist. A familiar knife appeared there, dark and as long as Zanya's forearm, with distinctive shimmering waves of midnight in the steel. A remnant of the way it had been forged—and the dark power that had gone into the forging.

Void-steel.

The last time Ash had seen that knife, Zanya had been trying to kill him with it. How it had come into Inga's possession or why she'd *kept* it was beyond his imagining. But the presence of the only kind of weapon that could easily slay a member of the High Court fractured the brittle shell holding back his panic.

He leapt onto the table, hovering protectively over Zanya and forcing Inga back with a growl. A mistake. Vivid pink flared around her deep-purple eyes, the only warning before her hand shot out with a hiss.

Fingernails as sharp as daggers pressed into his cheeks as Inga gripped his face and stared into his eyes. "Every moment you delay only does her greater harm."

It took too long to make the sounds form words he understood. The shattering had unleashed a roaring in his ears that he couldn't seem to silence.

Sachi was gone.

Zanya was hurt.

Sachi was *gone*.

Gone, gone, gone.

"Elevia!" Inga's relieved voice broke through the whirlwind, but it swept away whatever she said next. He could barely track what was happening, only that Elevia was suddenly *there*, the Huntress in all her immortal fury, and the pained sympathy in her eyes didn't stop her from grabbing him by the hair and hauling him away from Zanya.

They landed on the cold tile floor with a force that rattled his bones. He tried to move, but Elevia braced a hand on his chest. "You have to let her work, Ash."

"I just want to be able to see."

Elevia cast an assessing look between the table and Ash. Only then did she climb to her feet, and it was the Huntress who reached down to offer him a hand. "Take a few steps back, then, and give them space."

He didn't waste time on promises he was in no state of mind to keep, but he did accept her outstretched hand. Once on his feet, he could see that Aleksi had joined Inga at the table, disheveled from sleep but attentive as she placed seeds from one of her thousands of vials onto his palm.

Her murmured words reached Ash, their tone intense. "I need sufficient for every wound. Will there be enough?"

Aleksi touched the small, dark seeds. "I will make it work."

"They're old, Aleksi. Almost a thousand years."

"I will make it work," he said again, then closed his fingers over the seeds in his palm.

The Lover used the full scope of his powers so rarely that most people thought the old descriptions of him walking across blasted grounds with flowers growing in his footprints were mere stories. And it was true that Aleksi preferred to let the natural rhythms of nature take their course. But when he wanted, he could stand on barren ground, reach for the tiniest scraps of stubborn life within it, and coax it into vibrant, beautiful being.

Tiny shoots of green appeared from between his fingers, twining around them as they climbed and grew faster. A vine circled his wrist and climbed his arm, growing thicker as more offshoots flourished. And as those expanded, tiny midnight buds appeared. They dotted every vine, wrapping around his shoulders and sprawling across his chest. He held out his other arm, and the largest vine shot down it, spiraling and spiraling until the largest bud came to rest on his palm.

It opened, dark petals unfurling one by one to reveal something rather like a Witchwood rose, except for the colors that sent a shiver down Ash's spine. Instead of the vivid pinks and purples and teals the Witch favored, these petals had a glossy black sheen with deep blue and purple overtones, so dark they seemed to grab hungrily at any available light, as if to consume it.

Sweat beaded Aleksi's upper lip, the strain of exertion tightening his eyes and the corners of his usually lush mouth.

A familiar growl rattled the room, and Ulric rounded the table, his eyes glowing gold. "Are those what I think they are?"

"Void roses," Inga agreed, not looking at any of them. "And yes, I know that even having the seeds in my possession is a danger. But we're lucky I do."

Void roses did more than make them uncomfortable. Flowers that had been cultivated with power drawn from the Endless Void retained properties that made them outright dangerous to those with a strong connection to the Dream. Concentrated sufficiently, the scent alone could induce a mental fog that bordered on delirium. And the petals themselves . . .

Before Void roses had been all but obliterated from the Sheltered Lands, nearly a dozen of the youngest Dreamers had died from poisons distilled from those eerie blooms. If Sachi's family had managed to unearth their existence and provide her with access, she might well have been able to kill Ash on their bonding night with the single kiss they'd shared.

Inga murmured something to one of her assistants, who immediately began to pluck the full blooms from the vines that wound around Aleksi. With that taken care of, she turned back to Zanya and pulled out the knife once again. Then she hesitated, glancing at Ash. "You may not want to watch this. Threads of the Dream itself are trapped beneath her skin. I plan to cut them free."

He shook his head, rejecting the words. Rejecting this reality.

How had he fallen asleep with both of them and woken up in this nightmare? Sachi swept away, possibly into enemy hands, and Zanya sprawled on a table like death, ready to be sliced open.

He stumbled and fell to his knees, his panic and his rage churning so hard that the lamps in the room flared wildly. In the corner, the fire overflowed Inga's little hearth, causing another assistant to leap out of its path with a yelp of terror.

"Ash!"

He slammed his hands down onto the stone, begging for the grounding comfort of the earth. But the world trembled beneath him, as uncertain and anxious as he was. The whole room rattled.

where where where

But he couldn't answer the world. He'd lost their dream. He'd lost *the* Dream.

"Ulric!"

"I'm looking!"

"In the third drawer!"

Fire spilled over the lanterns like fountains overflowing. The castle shook, and Inga's voice rose shrilly. "Elevia!"

"Got it!"

Elevia was suddenly *there*, in front of him—blonde hair and golden skin but nothing like Sachi. She wasn't sunshine and smiles, but the implacable truth of the hunt. The truth, whether you wanted it or not.

"She's gone," Ash rasped. The full impact of it, previously blunted by Zanya's peril, slammed into him as he tasted that truth on his tongue. "Sachi's *gone*. He has her."

"You can't know that," Elevia cautioned.

But he did. He *knew* it. In the deepest part of him, the part that screamed for him to form wings and launch himself directly at the Empire. He didn't care how vast the lands were, or what awaited. He'd raze the place to dust if they tried to keep her from him.

"Elevia, I can't do this if he's shaking the tower."

Ash had prized his patience and his self-control for thousands of years. He'd sat above the humans, refusing to be drawn into their games, because his power was *too much* and their lives should be their own. But that control had been unraveling from the moment Sachi entered his life. She had been unraveling it, walking into his bedroom, into his *lair*, teasing and taunting the Dragon, begging for him to be exactly what he was and no less.

Zanya would expect him to act. Zanya, who'd held the power of a god in her hands for mere weeks and had almost shattered herself trying to go after Sachi. What would she do when she woke and found him still here?

"I have to go," he growled, jerking against Elevia's grip. The Huntress only tightened her hold on him. And then Ulric was there, too, both of them holding him down as he called fire to form wings that would carry him to his ancient enemy and end this once and for all.

"I'm sorry," one of them said. He didn't know which, because something sharp bit at his neck, and ice flooded beneath his skin as the world faded into darkness.

Chapter Fourteen
WITCHING MOON

Week Two, Day Four
Year 3000

Sachi woke with a pounding head, a dry mouth, and the deep and abiding sense that she was being *watched*.

"Good afternoon, Lady Sachielle."

She bolted upright in a large, luxurious bed in an equally large, luxurious room. The walls were covered with gilded paper, and ornately carved furniture filled the space. There were windows that glittered in the slanting afternoon sun, casting rays of jewel-toned light across the room.

But those windows were unreachably high, secured with delicately wrought metal bars. And of the two doors she could see, one was barred tight. This lovely room, with its expensive fabrics and furnishings, was nothing but a glorified prison cell.

A beautiful wingback chair upholstered in silk-embroidered brocade had been placed beside the bed. Her jailer sat in it, watching her as if he'd counted every breath while she slept.

For once in her life, Sachi didn't hold her tongue. "You *bastard*."

The Betrayer sighed gently, then inclined his head. "I expected you would be displeased. This is not the beginning I wanted for us, either. But I could not take the chance, you must understand. Bringing you to safety overrode every other concern."

"Safety?" Sachi echoed, her ire only growing. "You drugged me, and yet you talk of *safety*?"

"The drug is perfectly safe," he told her, his eyebrows sweeping up. "Something I designed with my healer centuries ago. It is a sedative that also numbs one's connection to the Dream. I couldn't risk having the Dragon pull you back into danger, Sachielle. Not without at least giving you a *chance* to choose."

No matter what he said or how he justified it, the lingering heaviness in her limbs and head told the real story. Sachi knew when she'd been sedated, and not just by magic. Memories and lingering trauma swirled up, as if blown aloft by a storm, and she had to close her eyes, swallow hard, and take a deep breath to quiet the rising panic.

Losing control would not help her navigate this situation.

When she was absolutely certain she could unclench her jaw without screaming, she opened her eyes. "I have very bad associations with being drugged. I would prefer you refrain."

He went from sunshine to stormy in a heartbeat. His brow furrowed, and his eyes seemed to darken. "What has my former brother done to you? Did he force you to drink the Dragon's Blood?"

He had, of course, as part of their traditional bonding ceremony. Or, at least, Ash hadn't warned her about it beforehand so she could decide whether to partake. But Sachi couldn't bring herself to say as much to the man—no, the *god*—sitting before her. "The experiences predate my time with Ash. Or did Nikkon not tell you?"

The Betrayer froze. "You say Nikkon did this to you?"

A tiny vulnerability, a crack in his smug authority. "Not always with his own two hands, but he directed every aspect of my training." Sachi paused. "And my torture."

That crack widened, even as the Betrayer hurried to cover it. "Surely *torture* is a strong word," he insisted. "Perhaps with the other one, harsh measures were necessary in an attempt to civilize her. But you would have needed no such guidance."

"Maybe not. But that didn't stop him from providing it." Her smile felt brittle. Honest. "I'd offer you details, but if you haven't eaten recently, I should warn you. Dry heaving is painful."

For a heartbeat, it seemed she'd rendered him literally speechless. Then he shifted his shoulders, as if shrugging away any responsibility, and his expression settled into smooth sympathy. "I regret any pain you may have suffered. To be perfectly honest with you, Nikkon was a disappointment. That he had you *and* your . . . counterpart under his direct supervision and failed to see what you truly were?" The Betrayer made a disapproving noise. "I suppose he deserved whatever inglorious end Ash provided."

Sachi inventoried what she'd learned. Her captor could be moved, but only so far before excusing himself from any blame or culpability. He held nothing but disdain for Zanya, to the point where it hadn't even occurred to him that *she* might have been the one to slay Nikkon.

And then there was his assumption that Ash had been the culprit. Always, *always*, the Betrayer would place the offending blade in Ash's hand. And that came from a place not of disdain, but of fear.

Interesting.

"I thank you for your regrets," Sachi allowed, "but where does that leave us? Do I have your word?"

"As much as I lament the painful associations, it simply doesn't seem practical." He even managed to look regretful, as if this were a mild inconvenience he hated to inflict upon her. "I have been preparing for your arrival for thousands of years. All you know of me are the ghost stories from mortals who have grown pettier and pettier over the centuries, not to mention whatever poison my former associates managed to fill your mind with. You *will* attempt to escape me."

"You may have prepared for my arrival, but you clearly do not know me." Sachi squared her shoulders and straightened her back. "I will not lie to you, even when you want me to do so. When I give you *my* word, you may rely on it absolutely. I will not attempt to escape this place. I will stay with you until our business is concluded."

He arched an eyebrow. "And what business do you imagine I have with you that will end so cleanly?"

"I claimed nothing of the sort."

Now both eyebrows swept up. "You expect me to believe an offer to stay here, at my side, indefinitely? Lady Sachielle, while I am quite devoted to the idea of you joining me here of your own free will, I am *not* a fool."

She had claimed nothing of *that* sort, either, but she could tell already that the Betrayer saw everything as clearly delineated. Right or wrong, necessary or unnecessary. *His or not.* "You aren't the first to doubt me, but that doubt never lasts long. Regardless, I have made my promises. And I always keep them."

"Understood. I will think on the matter." He rose and snapped his fingers. A wan young woman dressed in neat servants' livery stepped just inside the door and dropped a deep curtsy. "In the meantime, this is Lyssa. She has been trained to serve as your maid. She'll help you dress for dinner, if you would deign to join me."

The words sounded like an invitation, but his tone made their true nature clear. This was an order. But Sachi *was* hungry, and she doubted the Betrayer had gone to thousands of years of trouble just to poison her at their first meal.

No, the danger he represented—to her, to Ash and Zanya, to the *world*—was far less mundane.

I will obey you. The words dried up on her tongue like tiny drops of rain in the desert sun. For the time being, she might have to play this game, but there were some lines she could not cross.

Instead, she asked, "May I know your name?"

It was hard to evaluate the odd little smile that twisted his lips. Superiority, perhaps? Distaste? If there was sadness there, he certainly tried to hide it beneath his light tone. "They have erased me so completely, then?"

"No one mentioned you much to me, that's all."

He proudly squared his shoulders, exhibiting his full and considerable height. "I am His Imperial Majesty Under the Light, Undying Emperor of the Nine Kingdoms, Keeper of Dreams. But you may address me as Sorin."

Sorin. It echoed in Sachi's head as he turned for the door. In all likelihood, it was his real name, or the closest thing he had left, because what reason would he have to lie? Anything that kindled a measure of closeness, of *connection*, between them could only further his cause.

As the door swung wide, Sachi spotted a guard hovering in the hallway. And there were probably more, just out of her sight. She expected no less, but she was surprised to feel the walls thrum with familiar energy, as well. Sachi approached the wall, held her hand to it. Her eyes widened when she realized what it was.

The Dream. Somehow, the Betrayer had woven it through the walls, reinforcing them. Sachi had never imagined the Dream could be used as such, as a *cage*, and she drew her hand back as if burned. This went against everything she believed, everything she knew to be true. It was an ugly use of such beautiful power, and Sachi hated it even as she acknowledged its effectiveness.

It seemed that Sorin guarded his treasures well.

With a sigh, Sachi turned toward the only other person left in her cell. "Hello. Lyssa, is it?"

The woman still hadn't risen from her curtsy. A light-gray scarf covered most of her hair, revealing only a few strands of bright red. Her dress was of the same faded gray color, and even her voice seemed to match. "Yes, Your Excellency."

No matter how deferential she appeared to be, the woman was doubtless under orders to report to Sorin—assuming, of course, that she wasn't an outright spy. Sachi would have to tread very carefully not to give away more than she learned.

"You may stand," Sachi told her, "and bring your work."

"Thank you . . ." A hesitation. "Shall I call you Empress? Or would you prefer something else?"

"My name is Sachielle. Sachi."

Lyssa's head shot up, revealing a round, pale face with a dusting of freckles and panicked hazel eyes. "The Emperor would not tolerate such disrespect. Is—is Lady Sachielle acceptable?"

"If you like." Sachi took a seat at the expansive vanity while Lyssa searched through the ornate wardrobe in the corner.

She pulled out an elaborate sapphire gown and laid it across the bed, then returned to retrieve matching undergarments and shoes. Only then did she join Sachi at the vanity, opening the left-hand drawer to reveal an impressive array of fine silver combs and brushes. "If you have a preference as to style, my lady, I am happy to adapt. But if you'll allow, the Emperor requested I dress you for dinner at court."

"I am in your hands. Do what you will." Sachi watched in the mirror as Lyssa began to section and brush her hair. "How long have you served the—the Emperor?" She had barely managed to catch herself before calling him the Betrayer.

"Only a few weeks," was the soft reply. "But I'm very experienced. I was fortunate enough to apprentice to the Domestic Guild at age ten. The youngest apprentice in five hundred years."

"That *is* impressive. And do you enjoy working here?"

Lyssa ducked her head, focusing on the braids her quick fingers were weaving—and neatly hiding her expression from Sachi. "The Emperor has honored me with the most coveted position in all nine kingdoms. I only hope you find my service worthy, my lady."

She hadn't answered the question, but Sachi let it go. Pressing too hard would only show how desperate she was for information, and that wouldn't do at all. Instead, she focused on what Lyssa *had* said. "Nine kingdoms?"

"The nine kingdoms of the Empire," she confirmed. "We're in Kasther now. The first and most powerful of all kingdoms, as it is the Emperor's home. Though the other kingdoms can be quite beautiful, I'm told. I've only seen Vinke, where I was born."

"I see."

Lyssa finished twisting Sachi's hair into heavy, braided coils. It was more difficult for Sachi to continue her line of questioning as the woman helped her dress, since the process often involved sucking in her breath for corsets or pulling heavy lengths of fabric over her head.

Too soon, Sachi was fully dressed. Lyssa slid an exquisite pair of jeweled slippers with a low heel onto her feet, since the construction of Sachi's dress made it impossible for her to accomplish the task herself. The bodice wrapped around her in rigid, boned panels of an asymmetrical design. One panel rose to a point above her right shoulder, while another's top edge rested scandalously low on her left breast. Only the skirt flowed freely, a full length of gauzy silk that billowed behind her when she moved.

That left only her jewelry. Sachi stood as Lyssa clasped a delicate fall of sapphires to each earlobe. Then the maid lifted a heavy-looking sapphire and diamond tiara from its case. Sachi wanted to protest, but practicality stayed her tongue. The tiara had been fashioned into wickedly sharp points that, laden with jewels though they were, looked positively deadly.

Sachi tested her theory by prodding one of the points with her fingertip. It was sturdy, more like a dagger than an ornament, and she smiled. "This will do nicely."

Just in case.

Lyssa's brow furrowed in confusion, but she settled the tiara on Sachi's head. She spent a few moments fussing with her braids, smoothing them into place, then stepped back and gestured to the door. "If you're ready."

It didn't matter if she was or not, it was time. The door opened before Sachi, and she shivered as she stepped through. Walking through the open doorway felt the same as when she'd moved through the

Dream, like passing through cobwebs and feeling them break and linger, clinging to her skin.

There was not one guard outside, but two. They fell into step beside her, though they paid her little mind. Their gazes darted around, taking in all corners of the labyrinthine corridors, as if watching for threats. It was clear she was under guard not to prevent her escape, but to prevent others from mounting a rescue.

The guards didn't speak. Sachi counted their footsteps instead, memorized the turns and flights of stairs as they walked on. The knowledge would prove useful, should she manage to slip out of her cell later for a little exploration.

Her escorts stopped before an inordinately large set of doors. They were exquisitely carved, but easily ten times the necessary size. They opened silently, without a single creak, but instead of swinging either in or out, they retreated into hidden crevices in the walls.

Beyond lay a dining room, identifiable by the long table that occupied the space. The room was oddly shaped, oblong and rather narrow, ringed with windows all the way around. The windows slanted inward toward the bottom, as it appeared the ceiling was slightly larger than the floor. Sachi looked over as she walked past a window and almost stumbled.

They were suspended in the air, with nothing beneath them.

The Betrayer—*Sorin*—waited at the other end of the room, a broad smile curving his lips. "Perfection," he declared.

A man and a woman stood with him, dressed in noble finery rather than the leather armor and standards of a guard. Sorin turned to them and performed the necessary introductions.

"Lady Sachielle, may I present two trusted members of my court. Grand Duke Demir holds the kingdom of Rehcs for me, as well as serving as my personal guard when the need arises."

Sachi studied him. He had dark hair and a square jaw, and was handsome in a primal, hard sort of way, though the effect of his pleasant-looking face was somewhat chilled when he turned his gaze on her.

A shiver of warning scraped up Sachi's spine. His eyes should have been lovely, even beautiful, except that they held an unpleasant flatness that made Sachi think of a discordant musical note. Of biting on metal.

Instantly, she knew. This was a man who could break your neck and never stop grinning. In fact, it would make his grin a little wider.

As if he saw the realization in her eyes, his beautiful lips curled into a cruel smile. "Princess."

It wouldn't be appropriate for her to curtsy, which was lucky, because Sachi wasn't sure she was physically capable of taking her eyes off this man long enough to bow her head. She nodded instead. "Grand Duke."

As if oblivious to the undercurrents, Sorin waved a hand at the woman. "And this is Grand Duchess Varoka. She oversees the kingdom of Leighael, and also serves as one of my most valued advisors."

The woman made Sachi feel uneasy for an entirely different reason. She also had dark hair, though the majority of it had been intricately dyed in varying shades of pink and purple. It had been arranged on her head in swooping, rigid curls that never moved, even when she dropped a curtsy so low she was almost kneeling. Rather than being flat, her gaze nearly burned as she looked at Sachi with something uncomfortably close to jealousy—or perhaps simply a fascination so avid it could only be unsettling. The unnatural fervor carried through to her smile, gleaming and white, showing far too many teeth.

Sachi wasn't sure what to make of her almost aggressive demeanor. *Was* that jealousy? And if so, did it concern the Betrayer . . . or something else? "Grand Duchess."

"Please, call me Varoka." She rose, letting her dark skirts flutter around her. "I have waited so long for your arrival, my lady."

"You flatter me."

"Hardly. We have spent millennia—"

Dark irritation flashed across the Betrayer's face, and he flicked his fingers to one side. Varoka fell abruptly silent and dropped into an even deeper curtsy. Without another glance at her, Sorin put a hand at the small of Sachi's back and guided her toward the head of the table. "Shall we take our seats?"

Sachi had barely claimed her chair when the entire room shifted and swayed. Her stomach lurched, and she grabbed the edge of the table as they began to move.

"My apologies, Lady Sachielle." Sorin steadied her by laying his hands on her shoulders and pulling her gently back against the seat. "I sometimes forget how backward the Sheltered Lands truly are. This must be your first time flying."

Flying? Sachi glanced through one of the windows, where the spires of the castle were quickly receding into the distance. "All my experience *is* with more traditional modes of travel, Your Imperial Majesty." A tiny lie, yes, but literal torture could not have induced her to tell him about Zanya's ability to travel through shadows.

"Perhaps we sat too soon, then. Come, I will show you something." Again, the words held the cheerful cadence of an offer, but the hand he held out to her was nothing short of a stark command.

Sachi rose and allowed him to lead her through an open doorway, toward what turned out to be the front of the craft. Here, the glass made up not only expansive windows but part of the floor, as well. The world passed beneath her feet in a dizzying rush, and Sachi clung to Sorin's hand out of sheer necessity.

"Oh," was all she managed to say.

"This is Kasther," he said proudly as they glided over street after street of neatly organized buildings in a dozen shades of gold and tan. They rose in organized ranks with precisely intersecting streets, and on those streets people bustled about their daily work in shocking numbers. Every few blocks held a bright pop of green—a park of some sort, usually with a glittering pond at its heart. Wide, reflective panels dotted the roofs of the taller buildings, making the entire city glitter like a prism.

The city went on and on. "This is your capital?"

"This is the kingdom," he corrected. "We see no need to scatter people around in remote villages where they are cut off from the resources and pleasures the city provides. Do you see those silver tracks that cut through the city?"

She did. They were all a uniform distance apart, like the tracks for the rail carts that the dockworkers used to load and unload ships in Siren's Bay.

"Our high-speed rail cars can travel the distance from Siren's Bay to Dragon's Keep in a single day. Slower ones connect the various districts. Some nobles still keep horses, of course, but out of affection for the beasts themselves. Or for the exercise. If they've earned their way into the upper class, I allow them their affectations."

Allow them, indeed. "And how, exactly, do they do that? Earn their way into nobility? At Dalvish's court, very few were elevated through their own endeavors. They were mostly born into the privilege."

"A rather meaningless way of bestowing honor, in my opinion." Sorin lifted one hand to her shoulder and turned her toward the broad window. With his other arm, he reached past her to point toward a towering mansion in the distance.

It was the closest thing Sachi had seen so far to a country estate. But instead of being surrounded by fields and forests, metal buildings entirely encased in sparkling glass dotted the land. Each one was like a massive version of the conservatory at Castle Roquebarre, where they'd grown exotic flowers that would never survive the gardens outside.

"Lady Nezak's estate," Sorin murmured next to Sachi's ear. "Her great-great-many-times-great-grandmother invented the prototype of our rail system. That woman's noble lineage persists because her descendants continue to innovate. Each generation must further the achievements of their forebears if they wish to enjoy the rewards. If they don't, other bright and inventive minds will happily take their place and their comforts."

"Is that the only way? Industrial innovation?" Sachi turned to face him. "What about art? Music?"

"I am not barbaric, Lady Sachielle." He smiled as he gestured back to the table. "There are patronages for artists of all kinds. And, of course, the guilds find rare talents and elevate them. Those who achieve the highest levels of mastery in the guilds want for very little in life."

And what of everyone else? What do they want for in life?

Sachi quelled a shudder. She'd met people like Sorin before. They had often come to Dalvish, with their grand smiles and grander ideas, seeking his monetary contributions. Pretty faces and pretty words, all of it too good to be true.

But Sorin didn't need anyone's support. He had power, and he'd already realized his grand ideas. Which made him something else: dangerous. Because there was one thing Sachi had learned before *anything* else.

Nothing came without a cost.

Once they were again seated at the table, a parade of servants in that familiar neat gray livery streamed past, each depositing some fantastical dish to the growing feast. There were meats encased in delicately wrought pastries, and bowls piled high with steaming vegetables—no doubt courtesy of the massive greenhouses she'd glimpsed at the outer edges of the city.

Sorin sat back in his chair, his wineglass held loosely in one hand, looking pleased with himself and the entire world. "I imagine you'll be tired after dinner and wish to turn in. I've arranged quarters for you downstairs. We'll travel through the night and arrive at your palace tomorrow. I've already summoned the rest of the court to greet you."

Startled, Sachi met his eyes. "At *my* palace?"

"Of course. Did you imagine I would not build you one?" he huffed. "Then again, I suppose being married to the *Dragon* does tend to lower one's expectations. Did he even clean out the old consort's room before he gave it to you?"

Across the table, Demir chuckled, an ugly sound that made Sachi's fingers itch to creep toward her dinner knife. But she kept her gaze on the table as the first course began. It was clear that the Betrayer had plans for her, all based on his own ideas of an optimal outcome.

But he wasn't the only one who could make plans, and she had goals of her own. This wasn't a journey she would have chosen to undertake, but here she was, deep in enemy territory.

Back in the Sheltered Lands, at Dragon's Keep, she was limited to what she could learn from others or in her dreamwalks. Here, she had the chance to get closer to Sorin, to learn firsthand and from his own mouth why he'd turned the Mortal Lords against Ash—and what he planned to do next. If she managed to work her way into his full confidences, she might even be able to stop him without risking anyone else's safety.

It was an opportunity she couldn't waste. But she couldn't leave Ash and Zanya worrying about her, either, wondering where she'd gone but suspecting the worst. Before she could truly devote herself to gathering intelligence about the Empire—and figuring out how to earn the Betrayer's trust—she had to let her lovers know she was all right.

They were, and would always be, her first priority.

Chapter Fifteen
WITCHING MOON

Week Two, Day Four
Year 3000

Zanya floated in darkness.

"Where are you?" she whispered, extending her hands to her sides. There was no sense of movement, no way to walk through *nothingness*, but she still searched. She hunted the presence she'd felt once before, on the night she'd first manifested.

Herself. But . . . more.

Instead, she found darkness, then more darkness. Shadows caressed her as she reached out. Pleading. Calling. Demanding.

Screaming.

That *other* Zanya had helped her before. She'd told her how to break a curse, how to travel, how to unmake death itself. Surely the Void had the power to bring her to Sachi, no matter what lay in her path.

"Tell me!" Zanya was already growing hoarse. "Face me and *tell me how to save her!*"

"I told you last time," an irritated voice snapped behind her. Zanya whirled and saw the shadow version of herself standing there, arms crossed as if utterly exasperated. "I *am* you. I was always you."

"But you're the Void," Zanya protested.

"Yes," came the terse response. "And so are you."

"But you *know* things!" Zanya threw up her hands. "You taught me! I need you to keep teaching me!"

"You don't want me to," her shadow retorted. "Because I can only tell you what your instincts already know. And right now? You're shouting at me so you won't have to hear them."

It made no sense. If Zanya had any idea how to reach Sachi, she'd already have done it. "Is it something with the shadows? Or with Terrors? Could a Terror cut through whatever is stopping me?"

A sigh. "I don't know. I doubt it. You already know what you ran into."

Zanya looked down at her arms, and suddenly the glowing lines appeared, crisscrossing her body as if someone had laid a glittering web across her. But the web burned, its essence eating into her. Because it was the opposite of shadows. It was—"The Dream?"

"Pieces of it, yes." Her double's face twisted. "A perversion of how it should be used. But as long as it's woven into a barrier and a weapon, you can't pass from the Void there. It drapes across the place where the Dream and the Void touch the world like a trap."

"Then what am I supposed to know? What are my instincts telling me?"

The shadow version of Zanya reached up with strong fingers tipped with sharp black nails and cupped her face. "That the only person who could have stolen Sachi away is the Betrayer. And that you aren't meant to rescue her at all."

"No!" Zanya knocked the hands from her face and spun, rage and fear colliding with a force that made her glad she had no physical body here. Surely you couldn't be this angry and this scared and still *survive*.

"I told you I had nothing to say that you would want to hear," her alter ego said, already backing away. "But you know, Zanya. The two of you were born with the power to stop a god for a reason. You were simply sent to kill the wrong one."

Oh gods, no. *No.* They were meant to slay a god *together*. And no matter what Sachi might have planned, Zanya had always known the killing blow must fall on her shoulders. Sachi's heart was too soft for murder.

"Could you get close enough to kill him?" her own voice taunted from the shadows, hateful as it cut her rationalizations out from under her. "Could you fool him? Navigate his court? Sit at his table and smile while you plotted his downfall?"

No. No, she couldn't do any of those things.

An improbably light breeze whispered through the Void, carrying the scent of soft rain and Witchwood roses and sunlight.

Zanya's shadow-wreathed double stared at her, dark challenge in those achingly familiar eyes. "Can you trust Sachi to be everything that she is?"

If she didn't, was she any better than those soldiers who had tried to diminish her? Who had beaten her and hurt her and tried to drive her to her knees? The weapons Zanya wielded against Sachi had been different, of course—obsessive protectiveness. Love. Using her own heart as a hostage against Sachi's tendency toward self-sacrifice. But did it even matter if her intentions had been good?

Had she been so fixated on making Sachi *safe* that she'd also made her *small?*

The breeze wrapped around her, soft and caressing, whispering her name in Sachi's voice. Zanya's double smiled. "She's calling you."

The Void shattered.

Soft fingers touched her cheek, and Zanya leaned into them as the shards of darkness melted away, revealing their cozy little seaside cave with colorful blankets and bright candles —and Sachi, watching her anxiously.

"Wait for me," Sachi whispered. "I'm going to find Ash, as well."

Sachi drifted away, a sense of loss more than distance, before returning with a disoriented Ash in tow. He stumbled to his knees in the darkness of their little cave, his gaze flying around. "Where are we? Is this your hideout by the capital? Did Zanya find you?"

"It's a dream, my love." Sachi's nightdress drifted up around her as if submerged in water as she grasped both of Ash's hands. "Just a dream for now."

The sand beneath Zanya's feet felt as insubstantial as mist. She tried to step closer, but she couldn't move. This was nothing like the secret dream worlds Sachi used to build for them, and the implications terrified her. "What happened? Where *are* you?" *Please don't say—*

"In the heart of the Empire."

Zanya's stomach dropped, but it was Ash's snarl that almost shattered the dream. "I knew it. I *knew* it was him."

"Ash." Zanya reached for him, and at least *he* was solid. Her fingers found hot flesh, and she gripped his arm in warning. "Let her finish."

Sachi bit her lip. "I was walking the Dream, trying to reach Anikke . . . but I found the Betrayer instead." Her hair floated around her face as she shook her head. "I don't know yet how he did it, but he physically pulled me from the Dream."

"Sachi." Ash's expression was stricken. "Has he hurt you?"

She soothed him with a soft smile. "I'm fine, Ash."

There was something about her voice. The way she wasn't meeting Zanya's eyes, or even looking at her. Because Ash could be distracted with smiles and petting, but Zanya . . .

Zanya *knew* her. "Come back. If you felt him pull you through, then you can do it. It sounds like the same thing I do when I travel through the Void. You just need to concentrate."

"You're probably right. My expert in unorthodox travel." Sachi looked away, then finally met Zanya's gaze squarely. "But I can't stay here."

"Because you're staying with him," Zanya challenged, begging Sachi to disagree. To laugh or look shocked, the way Ash did.

But she didn't. "I gave my word. I swore I wouldn't try to escape."

"Your *word?*" Ash's roar blew Sachi's hair back. "He's the *fucking Betrayer.* No word is sacred to him."

"But it is to *me.*" A sudden warm breeze blew through the cave, and Sachi was standing only inches from Zanya. "He wants me to be his Empress. Think of what I could *do* with this, Zan. I have to make the most of it. Anything else would be criminal."

Odd. That breeze had turned the blood in Zanya's veins to ice. She stared into the familiar blue eyes she loved so much, and she knew there was no point in fighting. Sachi had found a wrong she was determined to right, and she would willingly and eagerly smash her own body and bones to dust if that was what the mission took.

She'd be smashing Zanya's and Ash's hearts into nothing at the same time, but she'd never see it that way. She had always underestimated her value to others. She'd plunged a knife into her own heart, under the delusional belief that Zanya's life could simply . . . go on without her.

Then again, if Zanya hadn't fought her every step of the way, maybe the curse wouldn't have come down to knives in the heart and battles to the death. Zanya's inability to trust had nearly brought them all to ruin. Maybe, this time, she had to trust Sachi to fight on the battleground for which she'd been trained.

Maybe she had to stop making Sachi small.

"Look at Zanya," Ash growled from behind them. "Do you know what this will do to her? To *me?*"

"Yes," Sachi whispered, the word seeming to echo even in the scant space between them. "I know."

Ash loomed beside them, fire and rage and the ghostly echo of dragon's wings flaring out behind him as if in dreamlike memory. "You can't, or you wouldn't be asking this of us."

Zanya lifted a hand to cup Sachi's cheek. "She knows."

Sachi grasped Zanya's hand and held it as she turned toward Ash. "I've watched the two of you ride off to battle. I've watched, and I've stayed behind, even though I wanted—no, *needed*—to come with you. No matter how much it hurt, I stayed behind because those weren't my fights. This one *is*."

"No." Ash's expression was pure denial. "Come back to me, Sachi. We'll fight him together, but I cannot lose you."

If the pain in his voice was shredding Zanya's heart, Sachi must be bleeding inside. But her expression was resolute.

"I have to do this, Ash." Her tone was equally decided. "He thinks that he knows me, that he can woo me, but he has no idea. *You* do. At least . . ." She swallowed hard. "I hope you do."

She'd rendered the Dragon speechless. Very well, Zanya would finish this dance. "Do what you must, Sachi." She used their hands on Sachi's cheek to pull her close. "But as soon as the Phoenix says the word, we *will* come for you."

"I'm counting on it." She closed the last of the distance between them and kissed Zanya, *hard*. "And when you do, we'll tear down his precious Empire."

"To the bedrock," Zanya promised.

That shattered Ash's silence. "You're going to let her do this, Zanya?"

Let. She almost pitied Ash, though the look she fixed on Sachi was chiding. "You really do have him fooled. I hope you're just a little ashamed of yourself."

"I am, but not for the reasons you imagine." Sachi finally went to Ash then, cupped his face between her hands and made him look at her. "You said I was the one from the prophecy, the one who can break the Builder's chains. Do you believe that?"

The *what*?

Ash covered Sachi's hands with his. His chest heaved. "He can chain the whole fucking world for all I care. I just want you safe."

"Liar." She kissed him gently, her lips lingering on his. "You have to believe in me, Ash. Give me just a handful of days. If I'm meant to break those chains, this might be exactly where I'm supposed to be."

"Sachi . . ." His arms wrapped around her as if he could hold her to him. "Be careful. I love you."

"I love you, too. You and Zanya both." She slipped out of his arms, *through* them, as if she'd become no more substantial than the mist shrouding the confines of the cave. "Take care of each other. Promise me."

Zanya opened her mouth to whisper the words, but Sachi vanished and the dream space fractured. She couldn't see Ash anymore. The sand beneath her feet was wet and gritty. Waves crashed outside of the cave.

A dragon roared overhead, loud enough to shatter the world.

The ground disappeared. Zanya fell, tumbling through shards of her own nightmares. Only that roar was constant, growing louder and angrier until even the slender fragments of shattered dreams trembled around her like leaves in a storm.

Zanya crashed into a shadow-strewn bed, so disoriented that an attempt to scramble to her knees sent her careening over the edge. Her back hit thick carpet over harsh stone, and that furious roar was in the real world, too. A dragon's keening cry of rage and denial, loud enough to shake the mountains.

With panic pounding through her and the only light coming from a bedside candle, it took Zanya a moment to recognize the consort's suite. Someone must have tucked her in to rest here after her thwarted attempt to rescue Sachi. They'd also dressed her in one of the thin, delicate shifts Camlia had ordered made for her. They mimicked the designs of Sachi's, but in midnight blues and glossy blacks, with barely there straps on the shoulders and lace fluttering at the hem where it brushed midthigh.

Zanya disliked how exposed she felt in them, so she rarely wore them. Now, staring at the thin white scars crisscrossing every inch of bared skin, she imagined it had been easier to care for her injuries in something like this.

Whatever had been done, the wounds had all but healed. She flexed her arms as she rose and felt nothing but strength. Only the ghostly memory of hitting something as flimsy as spiderwebs but strong as steel lingered—some protection woven around Sachi's prison. A protection that had to be rooted in the power of the Dream, twisted as it was, since *Sachi* had just walked blithely through it.

But not to return to them. No, not that. Sachi had walked straight back into her prison. And now Zanya would have to deal with the Dragon.

His betrayed shock still rattled the castle. Zanya could sense him coming closer, a wave of furious power that instinct demanded she meet on her feet. There was plenty of room to maneuver at the foot of Sachi's bed, and if she faced the door that opened onto the bridge to Ash's tower, it put easy escape routes at her back and side.

Even unarmed, clad in this ridiculous scrap of silk, she wasn't afraid. *She* was on solid ground, facing Sachi's latest stunt in a string of them going back to their shared childhood. Ash was the one out of his element now, a beast roaring at the surprised realization that being the biggest predator or a scary dragon or even a god didn't mean you could keep your precious mate safe.

Not when you loved someone with Sachi's impossible courage.

The doors to the consort's bedroom slammed open with a force that shattered their delicate glass windows. The Dragon swept in, clad in nothing but pants he'd clearly just shoved his legs into. The pulse of his rage was enough to cow any reasonable person. His hands formed fists at his sides as he stopped a dozen paces in front of Zanya, hurt and betrayal naked in his eyes.

"You didn't even fight her!" he roared.

"There wasn't any point," Zanya told him. "She'd made up her mind."

"She'd made up her—" His chest heaved. A curse escaped his lips as his gaze darted around the room, as if looking for something he could smash to vent his anger. "You were supposed to *convince* her."

"Was I?" Zanya took one step forward, letting her own anger slip free. "Then tell me something. What *prophecy* was she talking about?"

Ash froze.

Another step. Zanya hadn't realized how *angry* she was until she saw the tiny hints of guilt—his tightened jaw, the lines bracketing his eyes. He *knew*, gods damn him. "Is there a prophecy about her?" She bit off each word, as if faking calm might force its reality. "One you never bothered to mention to me in all this time?"

"Zanya—"

"*Tell me.*"

He took a shuddering breath and closed his eyes as he recited, "The Dragon's consort will break the Builder's chains, and the people will dream again."

It was Zanya's turn to close her eyes. She covered her face with her hands as she let the words sink in and tasted a terror she hadn't known possible. Because until a few weeks ago, Zanya had never really believed there was a future for her, just a mission she'd die to finish. Her happy ending would have been knowing that Sachi would live on.

Now, she had tasted hope. She'd taken that first terrifying step into trying to imagine a life where she and Sachi thrived. And this fool had told Sachi that it was her destiny to single-handedly save *the entire world* from the Betrayer.

Zanya flung her hands down and let out a frustrated scream. Ash stumbled back a step, and she struggled not to close that distance and lash out. But she couldn't stop the words. "What is *wrong* with you? You've lived with her. You've talked to her. You had her every emotion in your head for as long as that bond lasted. Do you not know her at *all?*"

Ash's hands formed fists. "I didn't think she'd do something like this. Who would walk out of their greatest enemy's cage and then just . . . walk back into it?"

"If she thinks she can save all of his victims? Save us? *Sachi.*" Zanya had never wanted so desperately to break something. A glass. A chair. A wall. Ash's stone-thick skull.

But kicking him now felt like kicking a puppy. He might be an ancient god with millennia of experience, but she felt an improbable prick of pity. For the first time in her life, perhaps, she wanted to shake Sachi for the selfishness wrapped inside her selflessness. She was always so quick to sacrifice herself, to step into the path of danger . . . and she gave so little thought to the hearts she left broken in her wake.

Zanya caught her temper in a tight grip. "This is who she is, Ash. She's the girl who steps in front of another child to take their beating. She's the woman who stabs a knife into her own heart to stop the people she loves from fighting."

Ash looked like a shattered man. Zanya sighed and tried to gentle her voice. "Maybe you couldn't have known. At first, she showed you the parts of herself that were safe and useful for the mission. Her sweetness. Her joy. Her love. Even her surrender. Those are all real, and they're all true."

Zanya stepped closer and stroked her thumb over his lips, the same way she'd seen Ash do to Sachi a thousand times. And Sachi would dimple, and smile, and part her lips and invite him to push that thumb deeper. She'd lick and she'd taste and she'd conjure the vision of her on her knees, lips parted in sweet submission, already eager for the masterful thrust of his cock.

Had he not realized yet where she'd learned those skills? *Why* she was so good at it?

"She seduced you," Zanya whispered. "And she enjoyed it. She loves the way you fuck her, there's no deception in that. But you see her on her knees, all sweet and yielding, and you don't realize that is her battleground. Seduction is *her* war. And she was trained every bit as thoroughly for hers as I was for mine."

Oh, she thought he'd been angry before. But the rage in his eyes now burned their soft-brown depths into embers. "I knew they had hurt her," he rasped, the words barely human. "That they hurt both of you."

Hurt was too small a word for what had been done to the pair of them. Snatched away as orphans, forced into brutal training as small children. The pain had been simple and straightforward for Zanya—beatings meant to toughen her, training meant to hone her ability to commit violence. But Sachi . . .

"They made us into weapons," Zanya corrected. Then she gripped Ash's face and forced him to meet her eyes. "And whatever you're thinking? It was probably worse. The High Priest would drug her, you know. Aphrodisiacs. Sedatives. Potions of war, meant to confuse the senses. To provoke hallucinations. To elicit truth. He tortured her mind so she would build the defenses necessary to lie to you even after you bonded her. Everything they did to my body, Nikkon did to her heart and soul."

"I'll kill them," Ash snarled, missing the point entirely. And as sweet as that protective rage was—as much as Zanya *thrilled* not to be alone in it anymore—it wouldn't do them any good now.

And he'd forgotten who he was dealing with.

The soft hand at his cheek became a vise as she gripped his chin in warning. He wasn't that much taller than she was, but she still dragged his face down so they were on eye level. "You still don't understand," she hissed. *"She is not a helpless damsel."*

He went rock still, the only movement the rise of his chest with his unsteady breaths, and the fire that danced in his wild eyes. Zanya held him there, not easing her grip. "They made us into weapons," she whispered. "The Betrayer thinks he kidnapped your consort, but he has *no idea* what he's brought into his home. She might get on her knees for you, but he'll be lucky if she doesn't bring his entire Empire to its knees before she's done with him."

Ash broke free of her grip with a snarl, only to snatch her wrist. The pointless little strap of the ridiculous chemise left her arm bare—and her newly won scars on display. "Don't pretend you're fine with this," he rumbled, rubbing his thumb over one of them. "You almost killed yourself trying to get to her. You almost killed *me* making me watch it."

Zanya shuddered, not wanting to remember that first moment when she'd awoken to sudden *nothingness* where there had been light, with the taste of Sachi's fear somehow bright and hot on her tongue. She'd flung herself into the Void on instinct, struggling to reach for that familiar presence. And she'd been there—just out of reach—

And *terrified*.

"That was different," Zanya muttered, jerking her arm from his grip. "I didn't know where she was. I didn't know if she was hurt or dying."

"And your instinct was to fight to get to her." Ash caught her wrist again. The thumb that touched the scar was gentler this time. "I understand the urge."

"Well, maybe it's the wrong urge." Zanya swallowed guilt and stared up at him. "We told her that we believe she's the Everlasting Dream, an elemental force of nature. And then we made her hide in a castle, because we're selfish and possessive and terrified of losing her."

"Zanya—"

She shook her head. "She doubted herself, and we made it worse. Whether we meant to or not, we made it worse. Think about it, Ash. Isn't that the basis of our whole world? That *believing* something can make it real, especially if you have the power of the Everlasting Dream behind you?"

"Yes," he admitted. "But—"

"She *is* the Dream," Zanya interrupted. "How powerful must her doubts be? Is it any wonder she feels driven to prove herself?"

"Alone."

"For now." Zanya covered his hand with hers. "I didn't fight her, because I know that look, Ash. I know when she's made up her mind. Nothing we could have said would have swayed her. And it's not because she made a promise to the Betrayer. It's because she's sure she's doing the right thing."

His voice dropped to a rough whisper. "Is she?"

The impossible question. Zanya had never been able to look past the panic that filled her when she thought of losing Sachi before. But perhaps that had been a disservice. "Maybe. You don't understand. This is what she trained for—to infiltrate the court of a god and bring him down from the inside."

She had hoped to alleviate his fears. If anything, he looked more haunted. "But I was never going to hurt her."

"We didn't know that," Zanya reminded him in a whisper. "And believe me, she's been trained to compensate."

He shuddered, and she almost regretted telling him. "How did you survive it?" he growled. "Thinking that I might hurt her? Watching me take her to bed?"

Zanya's heart beat faster. With a gentle tug, she freed her hand and rubbed at her wrist. "Do you really want to know?"

"Yes."

"Mostly, I imagined killing you."

His huff sounded almost like laughter. "That was no secret. It was in your eyes."

"You don't understand." Zanya turned her back on him, unable to stare into those gentle brown eyes while she conjured her darkest memories—not that the view of the consort's empty bed helped. She swallowed around shards of glass. "I was probably ten years old the first time High Priest Nikkon came to me and told me that one day, the Dragon would take Sachi away from me. That you were a monster who liked to hurt princesses, and that you would carry her off to your tower and torture her for days before you burned the flesh from her bones and devoured them."

His voice came from behind her, painfully gentle. "He trained you to fear me."

"He trained me to *hate* you." The sight of their bed sitting there without Sachi in it hurt too much, so she closed her eyes. "I was hardly sheltered at ten, but he kept the details sparse. By the time I was sixteen, though, his bedtime stories had become quite graphic. He put night-mares in my head that I still can't escape."

"And you called yourself a coward for not wanting to be vulnerable with me?"

The words were so close to her ear, she flinched. And she *did* feel vulnerable—off-balance, caught between grief and rage, between the present and the past. And alone. So terribly alone. All of her life, even when they'd kept Sachi from her, Zanya had known where she *was*.

There was no Sachi to run to now. No other half of her heart.

No home.

She wrapped her arms around herself, as if she could hold the weakness in. "Sachi went through worse," she said hoarsely. "And she didn't fear you."

"Sachi—"

"*Worse,*" she repeated, putting force behind the words as she spun to face him. "They trained me to hate you, but they trained her to seduce you. And that's a weapon she might have to use, Ash. Do you understand?"

His chest heaved, and she saw the horror in his eyes. The rejection. "No. She can't."

"She may not have a choice," Zanya said roughly. "And if you judge her for it—"

The shock that flared in his eyes eased that fear, at least. "How can you think that I would do that?"

"You'd be surprised." She couldn't keep the bitterness from her voice. "The people who made us never let us forget how deeply they judged us for being what we are. A murderer and a whore."

For long heartbeats, he simply breathed. But the floor trembled beneath them, and the candles flared higher, as if he struggled against impossible rage. "More and more," he ground out finally, "I see little reason not to fly to the capital and raze that palace to dirt."

From the god who had calmly lectured her against using dispropor-tionate force against mortals, it was a profound statement. Ash would never allow himself to actually do it, but the desire on his face was real. And the protectiveness surging beneath it sparked a tiny bit of warmth that fought the chill of loneliness.

"You should leave the castle standing," she said, forcing a light tone, "because more servants live there than nobles anyway. And they did nothing wrong. But if you expect me to discourage you from murdering the rest of them . . ."

He flexed his fingers, and she thought she saw claws shimmer at the tips of his fingers. But then they were gone, and he sighed. "I trust in Sachi's mind and heart, but if I knew where she was, I'd already be on my way to reclaim her."

He spoke the words like a confession. Like they were *his* vulnerability, one he was offering to her in this quiet moment of shared loss and painful intimacy. So she whispered her own confession back.

"So would I."

Ash reached out, but he didn't touch her face. His fingers found a lock of disheveled hair and freed it from the strap on her chemise. "The Phoenix will find a path to her. I believe in them."

Zanya was glad one of them did. "Soon?"

"I have to believe so."

Delusion or faith? There was such a fine line between the two, and Zanya had never been able to tell the difference. Sachi had a kind of faith that humbled even gods, but Zanya believed in only one thing.

One *person.*

Or maybe . . . maybe two people. Because she might not trust in the Phoenix, but she had no doubt that Ash would burn the world if necessary to reclaim his consort. "Okay. I'll try to believe, too."

He smiled, as if he understood how much that took. But his gaze drifted over her shoulder, to the rumpled, empty bed, and that smile faded. "I've never been this helpless before."

"It's not something you grow used to." The glass was back in her throat. She couldn't stand the idea of facing that empty bed. How many nights could a god go without sleep? But if she didn't sleep, Sachi wouldn't be able to find her in dreams if she needed her . . . "All we can do is keep busy."

"Doing what?"

Zanya flexed her fingers and choked back tears. Swallowing them hurt, but she'd had practice. A lifetime of it.

She'd also had a lifetime of keeping busy while Sachi faced peril she couldn't stop. "You can do whatever you want. I'm going to train with Ulric and Elevia. When the time comes to go to the Empire, I have to be ready."

Because Sachi might have been trained to infiltrate a god's court, but Zanya had always been meant to strike the killing blow.

Zanya *would* destroy the Betrayer. And if it broke the world . . .

So be it.

Chapter Sixteen
WITCHING MOON

Week Two, Day Five
Year 3000

Sachi woke slowly, confusion pounding through her as she shifted restlessly beneath the plush coverlet. So great was her desire not to leave Ash and Zanya that it had taken her what seemed like days to navigate her way back to the Empire. Back to the swaying bed in the Betrayer's flying machine.

Even now, she wasn't sure she'd managed it. She certainly wasn't moving. *Was* she in the Empire? Or was this her bed in the consort's tower, cold only because her lovers had already left it for the day?

She sat up, her gaze landing on the Betrayer.

There was a *throne* at the foot of her bed. From it, Sorin smiled as he watched her, turning over another of those blasted silver cylinders in his fingers.

"What are you doing?" she demanded hoarsely. She was barely dressed, in silk so thin it seemed more like a cloud than fabric, so she gathered the covers higher and held them beneath her chin. "I asked you a question."

"I was watching you. For signs that you'd betrayed me." That smile turned pointed. "Varoka tells me you walked the Dream last night."

So Varoka was the one with a talent for manipulating the Dream. That was useful information, though turning the woman's allegiance away from Sorin seemed unlikely. Judging from her resentful assessment the previous evening, she'd already declared herself. She could be won over, perhaps, but not by Sachi.

So Sachi shrugged one shoulder and mirrored her captor's brittle smile. "And what of it?"

"She told me that you were leaving me. Returning to them." His eyes narrowed as he caressed the metal cylinder. "She urged me to drug you before you could try."

She could confess that she wasn't certain how to physically return to Dragon's Keep through the Dream, or even if she *was able*. But a different truth would serve her better. "I told you I wouldn't leave, and I meant it."

"You told me," he agreed. "I almost drugged you anyway."

"And I'm surprised you didn't," she shot back. "So. Now we know where we stand."

"We do. If you're to be my Empress, I have to know if your word is good. You have passed the first test of not lying to me." He held up the cylinder, then tucked it into a pocket on his elaborate brocade robe. "I resisted the urge to take away your opportunity to do so."

"Yet you did not resist the urge to enter my private chambers." Sachi tilted her head. "Am I to expect this, going forward? I'd simply like to know."

He tapped his chin, as if the matter warranted grave thought. "It is a tad bit uncivilized, isn't it?" he mused. "At the same time, until I know you've come to understand your place here, these small violations may be necessary. Perhaps we can agree that if you continue to make no effort to flee, I will do my best to respect your privacy."

"I would appreciate it, Your Majesty."

"Very well, my lady." He smiled and stood. As soon as he'd gained his feet, the throne behind him vanished. A single clap of his hands brought Lyssa running to drop her customary curtsy. "A few members of the court will be waiting to greet her," he told the maid as he turned. "The blue gown, I think. See that she's prepared."

"Yes, Your Majesty."

Sorin left without another word, and Sachi raised her estimation of the danger he posed. It was easy to see why the rest of the High Court had loved him, once upon a time, and equally easy to see where and how that love had fractured. He was charming, so much so that a person could forget that every situation ended in selfishness, defined solely by what Sorin wanted.

Easy to forget, at least, for a while.

Sachi rose and accepted the robe her maid held for her. "Thank you, Lyssa."

"My lady." There was a numb sort of weariness to the smile she offered before moving to a cabinet to begin pulling out the outfit Sorin had ordered. "The Grand Duchess of Akeisa has already arrived. After serving you, working as her maid is the second most coveted posting in the Empire. She sets much of court style."

It was the most information the woman had freely offered in the short duration of their acquaintance, and Sachi finished brushing her teeth, then rewarded her with a smile of her own. "Then we'd best impress her, yes?"

That sad little smile brightened until it actually reached Lyssa's hazel eyes. "Oh, I have no doubt you will."

As she started on Sachi's hair, brushing and sectioning the locks, Sachi considered the girl's wan reflection in the mirror. Questioning her would be a delicate process, one requiring the utmost care.

Sachi started gently. "You've said that serving me is a prestigious position," she murmured. "But it didn't exist until very recently, did it?"

"Oh, no," Lyssa denied. "It's existed for hundreds of years. Thousands. There's always been a personal maid for the future Empress as part of the Emperor's household. Our duties are to oversee the wardrobes and jewels that travel with him, and to tend to the quarters built for you in each of the nine palaces." She hesitated. "Though I *am* new. The old maid was close to retirement when you arrived, and I believe the Emperor thought it best you have someone young and spry to care for your needs."

"I see." And Sachi did. All of this effort was as much about control as it was about her comfort. Sorin wanted to be certain that every aspect of her arrival that could be dictated by him was. "You're doing an excellent job."

"Thank you, my lady." Her quick fingers wove braids that spilled into others, forming a complex wreath around Sachi's head, the perfect resting place for another tiara. Thinner braids incorporated delicate silver chains dotted with sapphires and tiny bells that pealed softly with every tilt of her head.

More sapphires and crystals studded the dress Lyssa helped her don. Whereas the last dress had been highly structured, this one fell from thin jeweled straps on her shoulders to flow around her body. There were more chains and jewels that the maid began to attach to the straps, as well as delicately wrought cuffs that fastened around Sachi's wrists and upper arms. The whole thing was accompanied by another sapphire tiara, this one molded into intricate peaks that also dripped silver and jewels.

As Lyssa navigated the complicated accessories, she smiled. "Are you excited to see your palace, my lady? I admit I am. I've heard it's spectacular."

"You've never seen it?"

"Oh, no. The Emperor rarely visits, and no one else is allowed. Except Grand Duchess Varoka." A brief hesitation. Lyssa fussed with the fall of one of Sachi's skirts, not quite meeting her eyes, and her voice dropped to a whisper, as if she were conveying forbidden gossip. "Some call her the Dreamweaver."

Sachi remembered the odd sensation of moving through the Dream just before she encountered the Betrayer, like cobwebs on her face, not to mention the strange threads of energy shot through the walls of her initial chamber. The feeling was even more prevalent here, like fibers woven through the wood and metal, familiar, like—

Bits of the Dream. Of course.

"The Emperor already told me a little," Sachi confessed. "And I can sense some of her magic through my connection to the Dream."

Lyssa's wide-eyed gaze clashed with Sachi's for just a moment before she turned away to fetch Sachi's shoes. "That is a *very* special gift, my lady. But, you being the future Empress, that makes sense."

"Does it?"

"Of course. He would hardly choose someone unworthy to sit beside him." Then, as if afraid she'd gone too far, Lyssa sank her teeth into her lower lip. "No offense intended, my lady. It's not my place to gossip about the Emperor, under whose grace we all enjoy peace and prosperity."

Damn, Sachi had almost pushed too hard, too fast. "I'm not offended, Lyssa. Quite the contrary. I don't know much about the Empire, and I'd like to learn."

The maid seemed to consider that as she eased another pair of sapphire slippers with a firm heel onto Sachi's feet. Then she rose and began laying out the jewelry. "Part of my training was learning about the Imperial Court," she said casually. "In case I was called upon to serve one of the grand duchesses. Do you know who they are?"

Sachi didn't have to fake nervousness as she answered. "I've met Varoka, and you mentioned the Duchy of Akeisa."

"That would be Grand Duchess Gwynira." Lyssa picked up the tiara. "She holds the kingdom of Akeisa for the Emperor. It's an island off the northern shores of Kasther that is covered in snow and ice for much of the year. She has a nickname, too. The Ice Queen."

Sachi had no doubt the name fit the Grand Duchess, but had it been bestowed in honor of her frozen homeland, or her own demeanor? "Do all the others have less formal titles, as well?"

Lyssa began to list off a set of nicknames that made Sachi's blood run cold. The Stalker. The Shapechanger. The Seducer.

"And the Beast, of course." Lyssa fussed with Sachi's hair, smoothing the tiny braids around the tiara until it was situated perfectly. But her hands trembled, and her voice sounded strained. "But you've met Grand Duke Demir already."

"Yes, I have." Sachi recognized the sudden tension, knew it the way she knew an old trial she had overcome but would never forget. So she caught Lyssa's hand and held it until the startled woman met her gaze in the mirror. "You'll tell me, won't you? If he steps out of line? I can make it an order, but I'd rather it be a request."

Lyssa's fingers shook inside hers. "He's a Grand Duke, my lady," she said hoarsely.

"And it seems I'm meant to be the Empress." Sachi lowered her voice. "I *will* protect those in my care."

The maid swallowed hard and then eased her hand away, turning to retrieve a brilliant sapphire necklace. "It is not so bad. A Grand Duke's . . . attentions can keep others at bay."

As if that made the situation *better* instead of leagues worse. "Lyssa—"

An insistent bell cut off Sachi's words, and Lyssa hurried her from the vanity chair. "That's the summoning bell. You must go."

Sachi marched through the halls, once again flanked by guards who didn't acknowledge her existence. This time, instead of seamlessly moving between aircraft and castle, they exited the wide double doors onto a glittering expanse of stone so bright it hurt Sachi's eyes.

The Betrayer waited there, in a long brocade tunic belted over dark pants. He smiled at her arrival and took her hand. "The stone catches the light at sunrise," he said smugly. "Take a moment to let your eyes adjust. But I hope you appreciate its beauty."

Sachi refused to show weakness by shading her eyes against the glare. Slowly, the details of the palace resolved—swooping rooflines and gleaming glass, all supported by carved columns and flat expanses of stone like the one on which they stood. There were levels, each one rising toward a singular tower in the center of the palace, a delicate spire with a flat roof. Everything was white, the stone almost luminescent in the breaking sunlight.

Then Sachi saw the water. A huge lake surrounded the palace, much like the caldera in which Dragon's Keep had been built. However, this structure seemed to sit directly on the lake, with no landmass in sight. Huge, craggy mountains rose behind and around the palace. From the highest peak of the mountains, a torrential fall of water cascaded down into the lake.

So the falls fed the lake, but there were no mountains to form its opposite edge. Instead, the circle had been completed with the same ghostly white stone, damming the falls.

At the far edges of the water, Sachi could just make out the remnants of trees and other foliage. What had once been a valley gorge, teeming with old-growth forest and *life*, had been drowned long ago.

A knot formed in Sachi's throat, and she had to swallow past it to speak. "It truly is a marvel."

"I've been perfecting it for almost three thousand years," he replied, glancing at her. "Since I saw you at my lowest moment, a vision from the Dream itself. Such beauty in such darkness. I knew I had to build an Empire worthy of you if I wished for that promise from the Dream to come true."

What would he say if she told him what *her* experience of that moment had been? If she confessed that all her attention, all her concern, had been for Ash and the land he'd been desperately trying to protect?

If she told him the *truth* she saw, that he'd worked so hard to impose his own sense of order on everyone and everything, to tame and ultimately destroy the wilderness, only to turn around and try to approximate it with this hollow, meaningless, *empty* palace?

Sachi merely smiled and held out her hand. "I am to meet the rest of your court, yes?"

"Not everyone arrived on time." The words held a faint bite of disapproval. But he banished it with one of those tooth-baring smiles as he took her hand and tucked it into his arm. "But those who were timely await you eagerly."

He led her down a long stone walkway lined with planters laid out with geometric precision. The greenery was beautiful, but so utterly identical that Sachi reached out to touch one leaf, expecting to find it waxy and artificial. But it was real.

At least, as real as anything could be in a place like this. Even the weather was mild, drier than it should have been over this much water. As if it had been as carefully calibrated as everything else.

Sorin guided her to a set of broad stairs that led up. A strange vibration, unmuffled by her shoes, wound its way up through the stones and into Sachi's bones. She'd never felt anything like it before. She supposed it could have been caused by the lake lapping against the ramps' pillars beneath them, but to Sachi it felt more like the way the earth trembled when it reached out to Ash.

Was it this place, reacting to Sorin's presence?

Or even to hers?

Dozens of people, all dressed in matching servants' livery, waited for them at the top, spread out across a broad veranda that ended in two massive glass—or perhaps crystal—doors flung wide open. The moment Sachi's slipper touched the top step, the waiting crowd dropped to one knee in unison, their collective faces fixed to the floor.

Only two satisfied themselves with shallower obeisances. One was a handsome man dressed in fine velvets and silks—the Seducer that Lyssa had mentioned, no doubt. He studied Sachi with the same critical but approving eye one might use when appraising a lovely piece of furniture or a purebred pet. Something you fully intended to possess, but only if it met your exacting standards.

The woman next to him curtsied just deeply enough to warrant calling it a curtsy, but her back remained stiff, her dark eyes haughty. Even on a warm day, she was clad in a white fur cloak that fell to the stones and covered an equally flawless white dress. Diamonds studded her upswept black hair on either side of a tiara that looked like crystal shards of ice stabbing the sky. *Ice Queen, indeed.*

"The Grand Duke Enzi of Vinke," Sorin rumbled, waving a hand toward the pair. "And Grand Duchess Gwynira of Akeisa."

Sachi moved, a cross between a shallow curtsy and an indulgent nod. At least her time at Dalvish's court had taught her how to navigate the tricky waters of relative rank. "It is a pleasure to meet you both. You honor me with your presence." Formal, wholly false words that she was able to murmur with the ring of truth only because they had ceased to mean anything to her long ago.

Enzi stepped forward with a smile. For a moment, it reminded Sachi of the day she'd arrived at Dragon's Keep, how Aleksi had flowed in to fill the awkward silence, and she smiled at him.

The expression froze on her face when she met his eyes. There was a predatory gleam there, a vicious glint that elicited a shudder she barely managed to quell.

"Your Serene Highness," he murmured. "Empress Sachielle, Lady of the Dream." He bent to kiss her hand, and another shudder threatened. "Your glow is truly magnificent."

Another lump rose in Sachi's throat. "Grand Duke."

The Ice Queen stayed true to her name, flicking an assessing look over Sachi before dismissing her. "Sorin, you must be so pleased she agreed to play nicely. It would have been terribly embarrassing for you if you'd had to drag your bride to her castle in chains."

Sorin's smile remained fixed, but the depth of the rage in his hazel eyes made Sachi's heart thump painfully. "Jealousy doesn't become you, Gwynira. Be civil to your future Empress."

Or else. He didn't say it, but his meaning hung in the unnaturally pleasant air nonetheless. Gwynira stopped short of rolling her eyes, but her lips tightened.

They remained pressed together in a thin, angry line as she curtsied properly. "Welcome, my lady."

"I appreciate your gracious welcome, Grand Duchess."

The woman took the words as the chiding reminder they were meant to be. No matter what position or authority of hers she *thought* Sachi would be usurping, they were not dealing with a naive girl. She had been raised in the court of King Dalvish II, Divine Ruler of the Sheltered Lands.

Sachi had survived evil before. She would not be easily cowed.

Sorin took her arm. "Shall we?"

The interior of the palace was the simple inverse of its exterior. The vaulted ceilings had not been covered or altered with rafters or ceilings. They soared overhead, bare and stark. Tiled floors stretched out before them, in alternating patterns of white and palest gold. The wide, high windows let in a nearly blinding amount of sunlight, and Sachi turned her face away from the glass wall.

Which left her looking at Enzi, who oozed and smiled some more. He seemed so eager to deepen their acquaintance that Sachi considered whether it might be worth cultivating an attachment. He would be a more extensive, powerful source of intelligence than her maid, that was certain.

But what would he want in return? Judging from the way his gaze roved her body, the answer had the potential to turn Sachi's stomach. And nothing he could tell her would be worth obliterating her efforts to lull Sorin into fully trusting her.

No, then.

Enzi immediately confirmed that she'd made the right choice by licking his lips. "You really are lovely, my lady. I feel as if you've not heard this often enough."

"A thousand thanks, Grand Duke."

He waved a hand dismissively. "Please, call me Enzi. We shall be great friends, and friends don't stand on ceremony, do they?"

Sachi managed a vague smile that she held through sheer force of will when Enzi stepped closer, leaning in with a secretive, conspiratorial half-smile. She glanced at Sorin, but he seemed to be fully occupied with admiring the palace's sunlit corridor.

"Tell me," Enzi purred. "Is it true that the Dragon's bloodlust is literal?"

Taken aback, Sachi almost recoiled. "Pardon me?"

"That he whips his lovers until they bleed, and slakes his monstrous thirst by lapping the blood from their lacerated flesh?"

Sachi looked away, swallowing her revulsion. Gwynira rolled her eyes but said nothing.

"I confess, I myself am intrigued by the carnal possibilities, though you must be glad to have escaped such a fate." Enzi inhaled sharply, his eyes gleaming, his smile turning wicked. "Or are you? Does Princess Sachielle long for such things?"

He simply wanted a reaction from her, any reaction. He might not even give a damn whether she laughed or cried—though Sachi would have bet a truly prodigious amount of gold that he wanted her to be horrified. Scared. *Hurt.*

She stared at him for a moment, then turned her attention back to Sorin. He was speaking now, murmuring something about the windows.

"The glazing took decades to perfect, you understand. We had to fully automate the process. It's so difficult to create smooth, unblemished glass by hand . . ."

"Yes," Enzi whispered from just behind Sachi. "And it is *so very important* for things to be smooth and unblemished."

She jerked away as cold fingers, gentle but still somehow threatening, brushed the back of her bare shoulder. There was no way Sorin hadn't heard Enzi or seen Sachi's violent reaction, but he kept on blathering about glass as if nothing untoward had happened.

She realized, abruptly and with some horror, that this must be part of Enzi's powers. Somehow, he had the ability to harass and coerce in secrecy, with his foul words and deeds hidden from view.

Though perhaps not from everyone, because the Ice Queen grasped the Seducer's shoulder and hauled him away from Sachi. "Stop it. *Now.*"

Enzi bared his teeth. "Mind yourself, Gwynira. I do have a temper."

"You also have putty for brains. Shall we continue listing your many faults?"

Enzi looked as if he wanted nothing more than to press the argument until it turned into a physical altercation, but after a moment of trying to match Gwynira's flat, unblinking stare, he subsided with a growl and fell back several steps.

Sachi pitched her voice low. "Thank you, Grand Duchess."

The woman's jaw clenched. "Nothing I did was for your benefit. Only my own."

"Still, I appreciate your intervention."

Gwynira stopped, her cloak swirling around her as she turned suddenly to face Sachi. "Next time, you can help yourself by not cringing like a defenseless baby seal. It only encourages him."

Sachi kept her expression carefully neutral. "I did not—"

"Yes, you did. Enzi is a shark, *Princess*. Your soft feelings are simply blood in the water. And if you can't handle him? Eirika will eat you alive." Gwynira scoffed. "You think your time at your Mortal King's court prepared you for this? Nikkon was the least of us, and perhaps the kindest, as well. Remember that, Sachielle."

Sorin, who had drifted a bit farther down the hall, stopped and turned with an irritated frown. "Is there a problem, Gwynira?"

"Not at all, Your Majesty," she answered smoothly. "I was simply making Her Serene Highness's acquaintance."

"There will be plenty of time for that later." His frown deepened. "Leave us, the both of you. I would speak to Lady Sachielle alone."

"Of course." Gwynira took Enzi by the arm and dragged him away. The snappish sounds of their bickering lingered, tense and vicious.

Sorin didn't speak again until the noise had faded. "They can be challenging at first," he told Sachi softly. "But you will grow to love them, and they, in turn, will worship you."

Sachi had often had occasion to doubt the veracity of words spoken to her, whether muttered or bitterly shouted or breathed with the sincerity of a vow. But she'd never doubted anything as much as this. "As you say, Your Majesty."

He grasped her shoulders and smiled down at her. "It is important to have allies. And I've no doubt you will dazzle the entirety of my court."

His court was a twisted version of the one he'd left behind. Looking at them was like peering at the High Court through a plane of that blemished glass Sorin so despised. Warped, wrong. If you twisted the Lover's genuine, open affection, you could too easily find yourself with the Seducer, a man determined to dominate others. Pleased by nothing so much as his successful conquests, even if they happened by force.

The parallels were *all* there. The Dreamweaver worked the Dream just as the Phoenix did, but it was a sad, confining version that made Sachi's skin crawl. The Ice Queen ruled her watery realm just like Dianthe, only the whole damn thing had been frozen solid by disdain and unhappiness. Sachi could only imagine that the Stalker and the Shapechanger were versions of Elevia and Ulric, predatory creatures unfettered by the bonds of mercy or conscience.

And the Beast had to be a replacement for Ash, the most inaccurate reflection of them all. Demir lacked so many of Ash's better qualities— his intellect, his curiosity. His gentleness. No, the Beast was what Sorin had always imagined Ash to be, a true monster.

The realization sickened Sachi. Sorin had tried to recreate his lost family, but he'd failed. In his hubris, he'd gathered a handful of the vilest creatures she'd ever encountered to rule his kingdoms and enable his desires. It was the height of selfishness—and the absolute nadir of loneliness.

She hid her horror behind her practiced mask and gazed up at him solemnly. "I will endeavor to live up to your expectations of me, Sorin."

A slow smile curved his mouth. He pulled her closer, and his lips brushed her forehead beneath the ornate fall of silver and sapphires. "You will, Sachielle. I can feel it already."

Chapter Seventeen
WITCHING MOON

Ash found Elevia in her strategy room, which was expected.

What he didn't expect was to find her leaning over an unfamiliar three-dimensional map table. It was every bit as exquisite in detail as the one that featured the Sheltered Lands, only nearly twice the size. At its eastern edge, a familiar jut of land ended in an ocean and a string of jagged islands he knew well. They lay just to the west of this castle, and he stared down at them often.

The Western Wall.

Which meant the huge continent laid out in detailed miniature across the table must be the Empire.

He strode to Elevia's side and stared down at the heart of the continent. A massive city sprawled across an area that seemed *impossible*, the tiny buildings filling all the space between two large rivers. If the scale of the islands in the Western Wall held true, then this city alone was the width and breadth of the entire Burning Hills. It would take *days* to ride a horse from its northern tip to the southern one, even at top speed.

And it was just one of *eight* such cities.

He wouldn't insult her by questioning the map's accuracy. But he could hardly credit the work that must have gone into smuggling this much information about the Empire past its borders. "How long have you been watching him?"

Elevia glanced up at him, one eyebrow raised. "It's your job to defend the Western Wall, Ash. It's mine to know what lies beyond it." She gestured toward the center of the map. "Kasther, Sorin's personal stronghold. It's the only one of the Nine Kingdoms that he rules personally instead of by proxy."

Sorin. Was this the first time his name had been spoken in this keep? Perhaps not, but it was certainly the first time it had been spoken in Ash's presence. He had all but wiped the name from his memory. It was easier to think of the Betrayer. Easier not to remember that his great enemy had once shared the same intimacy with him as Elevia or Ulric.

Easier to keep his distance.

Ash ran his fingers over one of the cities, tracing the tiny bumps that represented what must be massively tall buildings. The Betrayer had always imagined building cities that reached the skies, but where was the room for nature in this? Where did the wild things roam, or the crops grow? Or had he provided for that, too, with buildings dedicated to raising beasts and cultivating food?

And how many people did it take to fill a place like this? "There must be millions of citizens. How is it even possible?"

"You forget what human lives are like, my friend. How quickly they pass. It's been at least thirty lifetimes for them, birth to death. Generations of families."

Ash supposed she had a point. Even though plenty of his retainers' children had left, moving on to seek their fortunes elsewhere in the Sheltered Lands, the amount of housing they needed had expanded with every generation. From a handful of brave followers who'd retreated with him into the mountains, Ash had grown a thriving keep.

And he *allowed* those children to leave as they wished. There was no guarantee that the Betrayer was so generous. He'd always hated losing access to resources.

Ash touched the city in Kasther again. "Do you think this is where he took her?"

"Probably," she admitted. "But I imagine they've already left."

"To where?" He skated his fingers over the map, walking the length of it. One city sprawled across an icy island far to the north. Others hugged inland rivers or coastlines. None looked particularly susceptible to invasion, especially if whatever treasure they held had been secreted somewhere in the center. Though if an angry dragon attacked by air . . .

The first thing the Betrayer would plan to thwart in any *city he built.*

"I've heard persistent rumors about a hidden stronghold for hundreds of years. I had always assumed it was where he planned to hole up if you ever sought him out in siege. But now I wonder." Elevia exhaled roughly. "Perhaps he was always building a place to put Sachielle."

Ash remembered the last time they'd stood around a map in this room, the blithe words Sachi had whispered. "Do you think he truly saw her during the War of the Gods?"

Elevia hesitated.

"Elevia."

"Yes," she answered softly. Carefully. "I think he must have."

It would explain the fervor in his eyes when he'd confronted them all at Seahold. The Betrayer hadn't acted like a man who had only recently discovered Sachi's existence. There had been too much proprietary interest there. Too much entitlement.

As if his old enemy had been waiting for her almost as long as Ash had.

Ash continued to circle the table. "Where?" he whispered just as softly. "Where would he take her?"

"I don't know. I've never been able to pin down the exact location. I'm working on it, but I'm getting nowhere, Ash." The Huntress swallowed hard. "We have to hope that Nyx knows."

"They told Sachi we had to wait." Ash found himself gripping the table and released it before he could shatter another precious map. "But it was easier to wait when Sachi was *here*. Zanya tells me we have to trust her, that she asked us for time . . ." He drew in a ragged breath and met Elevia's eyes. "Does it make me a monster if I want to fly over there and find her, no matter what she says?"

"Of course not," she said immediately. "You want to rescue her. But that's exactly why Zanya is *right*, Ash. You're thinking of Sachi in peril, not Sachi at war."

"At war against a power-mad god who almost killed *seven of us*," Ash growled. "How is that not peril?"

"It's *both*," she shot back. "We're gearing up for a battle that Sachi has been fighting for days already, and in a way that only she can. You have to *let* her. More than that, you have to respect what she's doing—warrior to warrior."

"I know. I *know*." He shoved away from the table and paced, trying to find a release for the anxious tension that curled inside him. "I just want her home, safe. She'd barely gotten a taste of a life without fear, and then my enemy and my war came for her. She never should have been forced into this fight at all."

"Even if she wanted to be?" Elevia pressed. "If I saw it, Ash, I know you did. She *hated* waiting here, doing nothing and feeling helpless."

Guilt stabbed through him, along with the memory of Zanya's words. *She doubted herself, and we made it worse.* "So now it's my turn." He sighed and scrubbed a hand over his hair. "To wait. To do nothing and feel helpless."

"Or you can make plans." Elevia touched his arm until he looked at her. "We're all going to get Sachi back. But you're the one who has to bring her home."

He heard the subtle distinction in her words, but the meaning eluded him. "How do you mean?"

Elevia turned and leaned against the edge of the massive table, her arms crossed over her chest. Her expression was thoughtful, but her eyes were almost haunted. "War is hell for all who fight," she began. "But there are different flavors of hell, aren't there? I would choose the clear brutality of the blade over the sort of covert work Sachi does any day of the week, Ash. Because my mind can still be my own."

Zanya's voice taunted him again, listing the tortures that had been visited on Sachi at her family's hands. Not for their own casual enjoyment, but specifically to send her to him. To his bonding ceremony.

Ash had taken the solitude of her own mind away from her, too. Had he simply been the latest torment, the latest test? A hell she had to survive?

No. No, Sachi had been honest with him about some things from the beginning. He could still remember the look in her eyes when she told him she'd left her own personal hell behind when she traveled to Dragon's Keep. She had never viewed *him* as a torment, only an impossible situation, because she'd never wanted to deceive him at all.

Would it be easier to play that game with the Betrayer because he deserved the deception? Or would it be worse, because it meant putting on a show for a monster who felt entitled to her in a way Ash never had? If she had to get close to a man she didn't care for, one she didn't *want?*

Worse. It would be so much worse.

He swallowed bile. "I've never had to lie, not like that. How do I help her?"

Elevia took his hand and squeezed it. "You watch her. You give her space to be wounded, but you never stop reminding her—that you and Zanya love her, that she's home. That the war is over."

Loving her would be as easy as breathing. Giving her space . . . Well, he could practice self-control when it was needed. But reminding her the war was over . . .

He turned back to the table, to the vast Empire that had grown on the other side of a wall he'd made impenetrable in his mind. He'd ignored what the Betrayer—what *Sorin*—was doing with a dedication that wasn't just reckless. He'd let danger grow to monstrous proportions to the west, and for the worst of reasons.

The war may have ended for everyone else, but it lived on in his blood and bones.

"*Will* it be over?" he asked hoarsely. "Can we beat him?"

"It will be over, one way or another. But, Ash?"

"What?"

Elevia's eyes were wide. "You know she's not going to be the same person who left this keep. And I'm not talking about the vagaries of war, either. Sachi will more than likely manifest her full powers before this is all over."

Part of him yearned for it, because the strength of the Dream could keep her safe, even from the Betrayer. Most of him dreaded it. Zanya's manifestation had been traumatic, and she wasn't alone in that. So many Dreamers had had to come close to death before the magic rose up in them. Some had faced moments that had nearly shattered them.

He didn't want that pain for her, even if it ultimately lent her power. But he couldn't lie to himself, not about this. Trapped as she was in the Betrayer's hands, Sachi's pain was almost inevitable. "It seems likely."

"She'll still be your consort. Still be *Sachi*. But she'll need you more than ever."

Just as Zanya had, except that her manifestation had been that of a warrior. Zanya had needed Ulric and Elevia more in some ways—teachers who would help her hone the weapons that came with her powers.

Somehow, Ash doubted that Sachi's would be the same. She would never long to truly master the weapons she had been trained to use in her own brand of warfare. She would need a safe place to be herself, and *only* herself. A place where she wouldn't have to lie, with the truth or otherwise. Where she needn't perform or put on a smile. Where she could rage or cry if she wished.

She needed him and Zanya to take care of her heart, the way she'd always so effortlessly sheltered theirs.

She needed a home.

"She *is* my consort," he told Elevia finally as resolve formed inside him. "You make sure we bring her out. And I'll make sure we bring her home."

Chapter Eighteen
WITCHING MOON

Week Two, Day Seven
Year 3000

The next morning, Sorin surprised Sachi with breakfast in her sitting room—eggs poached in sweet wine, bacon, and a saucer of sugared plums—along with an announcement.

"An event," he told her proudly. "To welcome you to your new home and celebrate your new status."

As prisoner of the realm? She held her tongue, but her head was already beginning to ache. "What sort of event? A party?"

"A tournament. Mostly jousting and swordplay, with a pageant to follow." He took one of the plum halves and waved it in the air. "I will be competing in your honor, of course."

"That *is* an honor, Your Majesty." A swordfight could happen anywhere, but Sachi had seen no area at the palace large enough to accommodate a list field—with one possible exception. "Is it to be held in the courtyard?"

Sorin threw back his head with a laugh. "And litter the place with horse shit? The Dragon might do such a thing, but I like to think the Empire is more civilized."

Sachi had to pull her hand away from her fork before she clenched her fingers around the handle like it was a weapon. "I appreciate your commitment to sanitation."

He braced one hand on the back of her chair and leaned closer, still grinning with something almost like affection. "The tournament field is near the overflow barracks on the other side of the mountains. There's a hidden path that leads there, but don't worry. I won't make you walk it with the soldiers and spectators."

Sachi held very still as Sorin pushed a lock of hair back from her temple, then brushed his thumb over her cheekbone. But he only turned to go, ignoring Lyssa's low curtsy as he breezed through the door.

Lyssa straightened and flashed Sachi an encouraging smile. "The Emperor is in a good mood this morning."

"Yes," she answered faintly, and with no small amount of dread. "He certainly is."

Sachi couldn't eat another bite, so she let Lyssa dress her, this time in a gown of ice-blue chiffon and darker brushed satin. A separate bodice embroidered with silver thread and adorned with chains went over it. The long sleeves were tight, fitted by corset-style lacing, with criss-crossing ribbons of pale blue marching up the backs of her arms.

The transportation of which Sorin had spoken turned out to be a floating litter held aloft much like the airship they'd traveled in before. It was luxurious, festooned with roses and silver-and-blue banners featuring a hammer and a crown.

"My sigil," Sorin told her, clasping her hand. "And now yours, as well."

The hair on Sachi's nape rose as she climbed in and settled on the plush pillows. She recognized Sorin's sigil; it hadn't changed from his time among the High Court, when he'd personally built Castle

Roquebarre, as well as most of the older section of the capital. It represented his goals, his life's work.

Whereas her symbol had nothing to do with *her*, with who she was or what she wanted. It had been reduced to what she represented for Sorin—a decoration, an Empress who existed only to look pretty and please him as he ruled his lands.

The litter rose until it floated higher than the tallest tower of the palace, high enough to clear the jagged peaks surrounding them. The air was appreciably thinner, thin enough to leave Sachi's head spinning as she peered out. Far below, a stream of people trudged along a path down from the palace and through a narrow pass.

Sachi made note of its location, just in case, and turned her attention back to Sorin. "How often do you do this sort of thing? Not here, of course, but back in Kasther?"

"Not often. Only on *very* special occasions."

His tone made it clear how grateful she should be, so Sachi affected mild shock. "You did all this just for me?"

His brow furrowed in irritation. "Didn't I say as much already?"

A slight miscalculation, then. Sachi immediately corrected course. "My apologies, Your Majesty. You did. It's only, I'm not accustomed to such consideration. Not after . . ." She trailed off and lowered her gaze.

He took the bait. "Shh. I know, my former brother must have treated you abominably. All is forgiven, my lady."

As predicted, Sorin couldn't pass up an opportunity to malign Ash—or to position himself as the superior god *and* consort. Sachi hated to hear it, but she couldn't deny that it was a valuable tool, capable of winning any hand, even when she was out of other cards to play.

The litter landed next to the tiltyard, behind an imposing box supported by artistically lathed wooden posts. It had been painted blue and silver, and more standards just like the ones on the litter flew above it. Other boxes surrounded it, ranging in extravagance from very plain to ones decorated almost as resplendently as Sachi's.

Almost.

Sorin helped her out of the litter and led her to a plush bench that overlooked the tiltyard. "I will return before the pageant begins," he promised before dropping a kiss to her cheek.

Then he was gone.

Sachi managed her first deep breath since before breakfast and studied the field. A long barrier had been set up on the bare earth of the yard. At each end, magnificent caparisoned horses with chanfrons guarding their faces stamped and snorted, awaiting their riders. In the distance, tents rippled in the breeze, and servants rushed between boxes with trays of glasses and tankards.

In the box beside Sachi's, the Ice Queen held court with a group of obviously rich, obviously important women, chatting with the nearest one behind a handheld fan. Lyssa *had* said that Gwynira was one of the more popular of Sorin's proxy rulers, an influential member of the court as well as a god.

Gwynira glanced over and caught her gaze. After a moment, she looked away and snapped her fan shut. After a few murmured words to her companions, she rose and made her way to Sachi's box.

She stopped in the doorway, her expression unreadable. "May I join you, Lady Sachielle?"

"Please do." It would offer both a distraction and an opportunity to find out more about the Empire. "I don't really know anyone else yet."

Gwynira arched one eyebrow as she rounded the bench and settled next to Sachi. "Why would that matter? You're to be the Empress. You could command anyone's attention or entertainment on a whim."

"I'd rather not *have* to command it."

The woman sighed and tilted her head back. "Please don't tell me my first impression was correct, and you really are this soft."

Genuine, uncomplicated amusement drifted through Sachi for the first time in days. "Yes, I suppose. *And* no."

Trumpets sounded, signaling the beginning of the event, and Sorin rode onto the field on a great white beast of a horse. It was bigger than any stallion Sachi had ever seen, fully armored in addition to his chanfron, and draped with more silver-and-blue cloth emblazoned with hammers and crowns.

The sheer size of the animal was stunning, but it was the way the horse moved that made her gasp. Despite his size, he moved with impossible grace, so light on his feet that she wouldn't have blinked if he'd spread wings and taken flight.

"A Rehes charger," Gwynira murmured. "Demir breeds them. They're stronger than any other mount you can find, but graceful and fleet as a hart."

Sorin rode forward, a long metal lance balanced upright at his side. He guided his horse to a stop in front of the box and slowly tipped the lance toward Sachi. "Will you honor me with your favor, Lady Sachielle?"

Lyssa had blushingly pressed a fluttering length of silver ribbon into her hand earlier. Sachi pulled it from her bodice now as she rose, then tied it around the end of Sorin's wicked-looking weapon with a shy smile.

Thunderous applause rang in her ears as she reclaimed her seat, but she couldn't stop thinking about the cold bite of metal. "I thought it was customary to tilt with a wooden lance. This seems . . ."

"Dangerous?" Gwynira supplied smoothly. "Deadly? A bit like cheating?" At Sachi's startled glance, she nodded. "Oh, yes. His opponents *will* be wielding those fragile wooden lances."

Sachi looked out at the field. For the first time, she saw that men were only lining up for the joust at one end of the list, and that Sorin was riding toward the other. Then she noticed the *expressions* on the men's faces. The ones who had not yet lowered their face shields were pale, their lips bloodless with fear and dread.

And no wonder, for none of them stood a fighting chance against the Emperor, and *they knew it.* What could have been a show of bravery and sportsmanship had been twisted into a series of challenges that Sorin could not lose. And Sachi was willing to bet that if anyone did prove to be a superior rider and manage to unseat him, the consequences would be grave, indeed.

Gwynira's murmuring voice broke the tense silence. "You play your role well. When you look at Sorin, I could almost believe that you want this. Him. But you don't, do you?"

Sachi met her gaze and found the other woman studying her—thoughtfully, a bit quizzically. As if she didn't quite know what to make of the future Empress's revulsion. Sachi swallowed hard and cast about for any appropriate reply.

But Gwynira stopped her with an upraised hand. "No, please. It isn't your performance; that is impeccable. But . . . What is it they call me? The Ice Queen?" She tilted her head, then lifted one shoulder in a shrug. "I understand what it is, that's all. To be frozen. And like recognizes like."

Sheer, absolute loathing for Sorin seeped from every pore of Gwynira's body, and Sachi spoke without thinking. "What did he *do* to you?"

But Gwynira turned away to face the field as a loud noise announced the start of the first match. Sorin dropped his lance and urged his horse forward, hurtling toward his opponent. The other rider's lance shattered, and he tumbled from his mount with a scream.

Sachi tried to watch, she really did. She made it through three matches before the first man went down with blood streaming out of his helmet, and she had to look away.

But still, the carnage went on.

"There used to be another member of Sorin's court, you know," Gwynira whispered.

The day was warm, but gooseflesh still rose on Sachi's arms, and she had to resist the urge to rub it away. "Yes, I suffered his acquaintance."

Gwynira made a soft sound of denial. "Not Nikkon. This was many, many years ago. Her name was Isa, and her power was like nothing any of us had ever seen. It was only a trickle, barely enough to summon an effect."

Sorin wasn't the sort of person who maintained allies who could not serve his purposes. He would jettison a weaker god in an instant and describe it as shedding deadweight. "Did he—?"

Gwynira went on, as if Sachi hadn't spoken. "The thing is, she could command the light of the Dream *and* the darkness of the Void. And when she used them together, she was strong, so strong. And magnificent." Her eyes glittered as she sucked in a sharp breath. "Do you understand, Princess?"

Yes, more than Gwynira could ever know. Together, Sachi and Zanya had survived abuses that could have killed them, even *should* have, a hundred times over. But staying together had saved them.

And she understood something else from Gwynira's rough voice and the frozen droplet trembling on her cheek. "You loved her."

"I worshipped Isa." It was a flat statement of fact. "And Sorin murdered her."

The pain in the matter-of-fact words hit Sachi like a blow, and her chest ached. "I'm sorry."

Gwynira stared at her in open confusion. "You truly *are*, aren't you?" Then she turned in her seat to face Sachi. "Can you do it? Stop him?"

"I don't know. But I'm going to try."

"Then take this." Gwynira pulled a slim bundle of dark-gray silk from her cloak and passed it to Sachi.

Pulling the silk aside revealed a plain dagger with a leather-wrapped handle. Hiding it within the voluminous folds of her skirt, Sachi eased it only a few inches from its scabbard. The blade was of folded steel in an intricate, swirling pattern, and it practically vibrated with an energy she recognized.

It was Void-steel, but not *just* Void-steel. This blade had been folded together with bits of the Dream, as well.

Gwynira's voice dropped, turned urgent. "The scabbard is enchanted and will keep the blade hidden from Sorin's senses. Do not draw it until you're ready to use it." The tear that hung on her cheek melted, slipped down her face. "You'll likely have only one chance, Lady Sachielle. Spend it wisely."

"I will." Sachi hurried to rewrap the silk and ease the dagger into her sleeve, where it could rest along the underside of her forearm, concealed by the gathered chiffon and the lacing. "I—"

But by the time she looked up, Gwynira was gone. She didn't return to her box, and no one came to take her place. Sachi was left alone, with her racing thoughts and the butchery on display before her.

She cast about for a distraction, *any* distraction, but there wasn't a single one that justified removing her full, pleased attention from a tournament held in her honor. So she watched as Sorin battered opponent after opponent, until the screams of men and horses alike echoed in her mind. Lyssa brought her a tray of food, which she could not bring herself to touch, and a bottle of wine that she dared not drink.

On today of all days, Sachi had to keep her wits fully about her.

Finally, the long barrier was dragged away from the field. The swords came out, and pages raked over the dirt to cover the dull puddles of blood. Sorin entered the field once more, armed with a beautiful blade that glinted in the slanting afternoon light.

He stood in the center of the field while other armed men streamed in after, taking up their positions surrounding him. Another trumpet, and the melee began. Steel rang, drowning out grunts of effort and cries of pain or triumph.

As Sachi watched, a man faced off with Sorin. He aimed a skillful blow at his Emperor, and Sorin barely managed to bring his sword up in time to block it. The swing should have been enough to drive Sorin back, or even disarm him. Instead, the blade shattered when it made contact with Sorin's, and the man fell to his knees.

More trickery, perhaps even magic this time. Sachi wouldn't be surprised if Sorin had had Varoka fortify his blade with the same sticky webs of the Dream that suffused his castle walls.

She couldn't watch any more. She stared ahead at the field, but saw none of it. She simply existed until the trumpets blew again, declaring

His Imperial Majesty the victor of the melee. She rose with everyone else, smiling and applauding as Sorin celebrated his victory.

Instead of raking the puddles, the pages simply left them this time, and Sachi understood why. It would have taken forever to uncover fresh, dry dirt. So they merely cleared the field of limbs, broken armor, and viscera before moving a wide stage in to conceal the blood-soaked patch of earth.

It seemed like an intermission of sorts. Spectators milled about, chatting and laughing, as Sachi sat, stone-still, her hands folded in her lap. Part of her considered that she might join the throng of people, attempt to glean something useful from their chatter, but she didn't have the heart.

Besides, she suspected that Sorin would want her to be waiting patiently for him when he returned.

He arrived half a candlemark later, dressed in fresh finery, his hair still curling wet over his collar. A wide, pleased smile curved his lips as he slid onto the bench beside her, and Sachi responded in kind.

"Did you enjoy the tournament?"

"Parts of it more than others." The truth, followed by a truth that would serve as a lie. "Your performance was stunning."

"All for you, my darling. As is this." He gestured toward the stage, where a frame had been erected and a curtain hung, hiding the bulk of it until the performance. "It's called *The Final Battle*. I wrote it myself. You might recognize some of the characters."

Sachi's toes went numb as music played and the curtain parted. A man with obviously dyed red hair stood against a group of four men and three women. Their costumes were lavish, and too on the nose to be mistaken for accidental resemblances.

The High Court.

The play began, a simplistic melodrama in which Sorin's character faced off against each member of the High Court in turn, delivering blistering monologues about their struggles against progress as he beat them down to the stage with a large war hammer.

The vague smile on Sachi's face almost slipped when she felt a light touch on her knee. The back of Sorin's hand, grazing her leg.

"I won't rush you," he whispered, his breath hot against her ear. "You needn't concern yourself on that count."

"You're too kind to me, Your Majesty." She heard the words, heard her own voice, placid and serene.

"But when you're ready . . ."

Sachi stared straight ahead as the actors dressed as her family pantomimed death. She stared as Sorin's hand crept from her knee to her thigh, then tightened, his fingertips digging into her flesh through all the layers of her clothes.

She stared straight ahead and let her mind wander. She went somewhere else, someplace where the only thing she had to be aware of was the comforting weight of her gifted dagger tucked up her sleeve.

Later, when she could come back to her own body, she'd make plans. Perhaps it was time to visit Ash and Zanya again. Sachi had hesitated because it was so hard to find her way back from them when she wanted so desperately to *stay*. But she'd learned so much, and some of it might be able to help them.

Yes. She would go see them tonight, when she'd managed to escape into the safe oblivion of sleep. It was the smart choice. The tactical choice.

And she *needed* it.

Chapter Nineteen
WITCHING MOON

Week Two, Day Eight
Year 3000

Zanya dreamt of Sachi.

It wasn't surprising. It had been several nights since Sachi had visited their dreams and told them she wasn't coming back. Every time Zanya closed her eyes, she whispered a prayer to the Everlasting Dream—*let me see her.*

Perhaps the Dream didn't answer prayers sent aloft by the manifestation of the Endless Void. Or perhaps her own gift of nightmares had taken control. Sachi appeared in the darkness each night, but it wasn't *Sachi.*

Every night, Zanya raced through dark mazes, chasing the scent of Witchwood roses. She caught glimpses of golden hair swirling through the mist. Sachi's voice called out to her, but no matter how fast Zanya ran, she could never find the source. It was as if Sachi were trapped behind whatever wall had barred Zanya from the Empire, and even her own mind couldn't conjure a gentle dream that bridged the gap.

So when Sachi finally appeared before her, Zanya braced herself for another agonizing night spent chasing a specter she could never catch.

"Zan." Nervous fingers curled into the image's gauzy white nightgown. "It's good to see you."

Zanya's heart leapt. "Sachi?" She took a step forward, then another. The figure didn't vanish into smoke. "Is it really you?"

She nodded, her breathing unsteady. "I—I thought I should check in."

Zanya lunged, dragging her lover close. "Tell me you're okay. If you need us to come—"

"I'm fine," Sachi whispered. "I just . . ."

The words were a lie, but if Zanya pressed, then Sachi would only be forced to fight two battles—whatever fight she'd left behind that had her looking so pale and drawn, and the fight to keep Zanya from overriding her will. So she choked back the need to save Sachi and simply held her. "It's hard. What you do is so hard."

"It's a softer life than most." But Sachi's voice broke on the last word.

Suddenly Ash was there in the darkness, spinning wildly until his gaze landed on them. "Sachi!"

He was at their side in a heartbeat, his chest pressed to Sachi's back as he wrapped his arms around them. He buried his face in Sachi's hair and dragged in a shuddering breath. "Thank you."

Sachi grasped his arm, clung to them both until her breathing began to even out and her trembling stilled. All the while, she whispered over and over that everything was fine, and that she was okay.

It could have been days, but it felt like mere moments until she pulled back. "I brought news. I think I have an ally in the Empire."

Zanya twined her fingers with Sachi's, refusing to let her go. "Who?"

"One of the gods who helps rule Sorin's kingdoms. Her name is Gwynira."

Ash's brow furrowed. "Did you get a sense of how strong she is? Or what her powers are?"

She shook her head. "They call her the Ice Queen. I don't know how literal that is, but I suspect very." She held out her hand. "She gave me this."

A dagger materialized on her palm, painfully simple in design, but redolent with *magic*.

Ash reached for it but froze with his fingers hovering above it. "That feels like . . ."

"Like me," Zanya whispered. She reached out to slide a finger over the flat of the blade, admiring the intricate pattern that must have come from folding the steel many times. But there were dark streaks and pale ones, starlight and the vast blackness that contained it. "It's of the Void. *And* the Dream?"

Ash's expression tightened. "Be careful, Sachi. The Betrayer would be furious if he knew you had such a thing. He hates the Void and anything touched by it."

"I know. It's well-hidden." Her jaw clenched. "But now I'm armed, and that's something, isn't it?"

Zanya laid her free hand over Sachi's, curling around the hilt. She hated the idea of Sachi being forced to defend herself, but she would *not* express doubt. Not again. She was through with making Sachi smaller. "And you know exactly how to use it if you must. Don't hesitate."

"When the time is right," Sachi agreed, and the dagger dissipated. "I've learned more."

She told them about the layout of the Empire, the vast cities she'd spied from the air. About the landscape surrounding the Empress's Palace, and the location's fortifications and troop numbers. She told them about the gods she'd met, every last one, and what she knew or suspected of them. She told them *everything*.

But she said nothing of the Betrayer.

She likely meant to spare Ash—gods knew the reminder that his ancient enemy held Sachi captive was weighing him down with a millennium's worth of guilt—but Zanya couldn't dispel the memory of Sachi's shaking hands and nervous eyes.

She was trapped in the heart of the Betrayer's Empire, bound as his future Empress, no doubt being forced to play the part in ways that Zanya didn't want to imagine. But she *could* imagine them, because she'd spent her life doing it. She'd just been imagining the Dragon as Sachi's cruel captor.

Ash had no such practice, no emotional armor. If Sachi wanted to spare him, Zanya wouldn't press.

Instead, she leaned her forehead against Sachi's temple and sighed. "I miss you."

"I know, my love." Sachi's breath stirred Zanya's hair. "But it won't be much longer."

"The castle isn't the same without you," Ash rumbled. "Camlia's in the worst mood. You're the only sensible person she's had to talk to in decades. If you don't come back, she'll never forgive me for losing you."

Sachi turned, cupped Ash's face in both her hands, and stared silently up at him. He covered her hands with his, his thumbs stroking her fingers, and Zanya ached for how lost he looked in that moment as he lowered his forehead to touch hers. "You're my heart, Sachielle. Take care of my heart."

"You have the bigger responsibility," she murmured against his lips. "My heart *and* Zanya's. Keep them safe for me, Ash."

Zanya huffed and swept Sachi's hair aside so she could brush a kiss to the spot beneath her ear. "Don't you trust me with my own heart?"

"No." Sachi tilted her head with a breathy noise of pleasure. "But only because it's ours now."

Ash rumbled as his lips drifted to Sachi's ear. "Maybe Zanya will let me cuddle her."

"If she does, I hope you're very sweet to her." Sachi's fingers curled, her nails scratching over Ash's cheek. "As sweet as I would be."

Heat flooded Zanya's cheeks, but Sachi's obvious delight made it hard to be too self-conscious, even if she still struggled with the idea of anyone other than Sachi seeing her vulnerable. She nuzzled Sachi's neck and closed her eyes, inhaling the scent of roses that somehow persisted even here, in her dreams. "He's not as soft as you."

"No, he isn't." Sachi laughed quietly, then sighed. "I will do everything in my power to come back to you. Everything. I promise."

It wasn't quite an ironclad reassurance, but it was a start. "We need you," Zanya whispered. "But we're not the only ones. You have to come back for all of us. The Siren may have thwarted the regents by stopping their travel by water, but it's only a matter of time until they start moving overland. We need you to deal with the Mortal Court."

"No, you don't," Sachi said firmly. "If I'm not there and it needs to be done, then you can do it, Zanya."

"What?" Zanya shook her head in immediate rejection. "No, even the ones who don't think I'm an assassin remember me as a maid. They'll never listen to me."

"You watched those people for just as long as I did. You *know* how their court functions." Sachi's encouraging smile glowed with literal light. "All you have to do is tell the truth, Zan. You're so good at that, you always have been."

It was hard to cling to her denials with Sachi gazing up at her with such naked, uncompromising *faith*. And then Ash made it worse by stroking Sachi's hair with a fond smile. "I thought you told me we're supposed to listen to the expert, Zanya."

"Just remember who you are, and *make* them hear you." Sachi touched Zanya's lower lip. "Tell Inga and Elevia that it's time. They'll know what it means."

Zanya opened her mouth to say *she* wanted to know what it meant, but Ash was already moving on. "I'd go with her, if I could. But I suspect my presence would cause more issues than it solved."

"Send Aleksi. No matter what, half the court is still in love with him." Sachi stretched up on her tiptoes and kissed Zanya. Once, twice, lingering the third time. "Be careful. It's no less dangerous in its own way than where I am right now. Never forget that."

Zanya sank her fingers into Sachi's hair and held her still for another, deeper kiss. "I never do," she promised against her lover's lips. "But I'm not promising to leave all of the regents alive."

"You'll do what you must. Isn't that what you always tell me?"

"It's easier to give the advice than to take it," Zanya retorted. It was so hard not to press closer to Sachi, to wrap an arm around her waist as if she could make this dream *real*. Perhaps, if she refused to let go, then the sheer, desperate *craving* that curled through her would perform whatever magic was required to pull Sachi back, and Zanya could wake with her in her arms.

Sachi's voice echoed around her, filling the darkness and whispering in Zanya's ears. "Tell me what you need."

"Stay," Zanya whispered back, closing her eyes as she buried her face in that silken, glorious hair. Ash was there, too, his arms around them both, and Zanya locked the feeling in her memory, even if it was as hazy as a dream. "For as long as you can. Let us hold you."

Sachi's lips grazed her cheek, then her jaw, soft as a promise. "I'm not going anywhere."

"Good." It was Ash, his voice a low rumble that came from everywhere and nowhere. The dream was twisting, becoming less solid, but Sachi stayed firm in Zanya's clutching arms as Ash went on. "What do *you* need, Sachi?"

"Tell us a story," she answered, dreamy and low. "Something from when you were a boy."

A chuckle curled around them like a warm embrace. "So long ago. I'm sure you know I was a terribly behaved lad. You *have* spoken with my grandmother, after all. And I was always fascinated with what lay deep beneath the earth. There were some caves in the hills near our village . . ."

Ash's words faded into a murmur, their meaning slipping past Zanya's sleepy brain. She focused on the body snuggled tight against hers, resting one hand on Sachi's chest, where her heart beat even in the Dream. Steady. Strong. Proof that she lived. The warm skin beneath her fingertips begged to be stroked, just as the cheek beneath her lips needed to be kissed.

She clung to Sachi, floating on the Dragon's words, never noticing when she slipped back into her own dreams. Because Sachi was still there, warm in her arms, a promise left behind by the woman whose heart *was* the Dream. There were no nightmares to chase Zanya through endless corridors, no shadows to steal this feeling away.

There was Sachi, and warmth, and the scent of Witchwood roses, and peace.

Chapter Twenty
WITCHING MOON

Week Two, Day Nine
Year 3000

After the third time Ash ignored a tentative knock on his tower door, he had to admit to himself the truth.

The Dragon was brooding.

He'd already sent both Inga and Aleksi away this evening. If there was an emergency, Elevia would break down his door no matter how studiously he ignored her, so he imagined whoever had come knocking only hoped to offer him support.

He didn't want support. He wanted to ignore the advice of every person he'd ever known and loved and fly directly into the Empire to face a battle he'd been avoiding for three thousand years.

But Sachi had asked them for more time. *More time.*

This was the fifth day he'd suffered without her. He didn't think he could survive a full week.

She'd been part of his life for so little time, and yet living already felt *wrong* without her. And it wasn't just the lack of her in his bed. A shroud had descended over Dragon's Keep, as if its inhabitants mourned the loss of their lady. Servants performed their tasks in tense silence. The laughter of children was too often shushed by those worried about respecting his grief. Even Camlia, his unshakable steward, seemed perpetually cross—though she stopped short of taking that anger out on *him* for losing Sachi.

The overall mood in the castle was not improved by Zanya's temperament. Ulric and Elevia had begun taking her on longer and longer training runs just to get her out of the castle. Left to her own devices, she paced the battlements like a shadow wraith, every movement that of a feral, penned creature waiting for a fracture in their cage.

Elevia still didn't know the location of the palace where Sachi was being held. All they had were the words Sachi had passed along to them from the Phoenix, words that soothed and enraged him in turn.

It's to be war. They must prepare. I'm coming for them as soon as I can.

There was nothing he could do but wait. And he *hated* the helplessness of it.

The shadows shifted in front of him with a tingle to which he'd become accustomed. So he didn't start when Zanya stepped out of them, her eyes alight with a feverish sort of energy. "Are you finished working for the day?"

"Unless Elevia has another task for me." He raised an eyebrow. "Did she send you?"

Zanya shrugged as if it didn't much matter and pulled two wooden practice swords from behind her back. "She doesn't have a task for you, but Ulric does."

"Oh, does he?"

She extended her hand. "Only if you're up for a little sparring."

Sparring was dangerous. With them, it usually led swiftly to either unchecked violence or unbridled arousal. The former might be a suitable outlet for his temper, but the latter would only sharpen it. Until Sachi was safely home, in the protective shelter of his arms, sex was the last thing on his mind. As if Zanya wouldn't stab him for the presumption in any case.

"I don't think it's a good idea," he rumbled, turning his gaze back to the fire. "Besides, Elevia and Ulric are training you now."

"Ulric says you've been holding back with me."

Then Ulric was clearly talking too much—a situation Ash would rectify with the Wolf the next time he took it upon himself to batter on his door. "I hold back with everyone," he said shortly. "Sparring is not deadly combat."

"It shouldn't be," she agreed softly. "But I'm not learning fast enough. We're going to rescue Sachi, and I have to be strong enough to keep her safe. Ulric said you're the only one who can teach me how to stop holding back."

Ash hesitated. All their previous sparring matches had been, if not polite, then at least following the gentle rules of human combat. While he'd always accepted the possibility that Zanya could very well kill him if she caught him by surprise, he knew in his bones that if it came down to a fight between gods—the kind that had once nearly shattered the world—she wasn't ready.

Which was undoubtedly Ulric's point. They could be called into the heart of the Empire, to war, at any moment. Zanya had too little time to become ready. In a perfect world, Ulric and Elevia would have led her to this point slowly, but *slow* wouldn't be good enough. Someone had to goad her into tapping into that primal part of her. Someone who knew just which buttons to press.

Someone with a personal enough connection to rile her.

It would be difficult for Ulric or Elevia to make her angry enough, but Ash certainly could . . . if he was willing to face whatever ancient power he provoked.

If he could *survive* facing it.

A dangerous game, and one Elevia never would have agreed to if she hadn't thought there was a chance that they'd need Zanya—*all* of her—when the time came to rescue Sachi and face the Empire.

So Ash had no choice, in the end. He had to do this. For Sachi *and* for Zanya.

Rising, he reached out a hand. Her fingers brushed his, barely making contact. Then the shadows curled around him, a caress that had become familiar. Her power felt of *her*—sharp edges and fierce protectiveness and a snarling dominance that held a precious, wobbling edge of uncertainty. When she found her confidence and truly embraced that part of herself, he expected most of the world would fall to their knees for her.

Ash certainly would.

He'd expected her to carry them down to the practice yard. But when the shadows receded, he found himself in a dusty training yard in the Witchwood, the circle lit by nothing but starlight and the glowing flowers on distant trees. He turned, getting his bearings, and recognized the shuttered campsite and the nearby stone cabin.

This was a stop along the consort's progress. Not just any stop, though. This was the one where he'd first coaxed her to spar with him. Where the sparks between them had first lit, and they'd ended their battle with her straddling him, any pleasure he'd taken in the fight swept away by the blade she'd held to his throat.

He turned to face Zanya and lifted a querying brow. "This is a long journey for a sparring match."

She stood in front of him, tense and wary. "Ulric said it should be far away from other people."

At least he'd told her that much. But how deep had the Wolf's warning run? Ash paced away from her before turning. "Do you know what this will mean? If I stop holding back?"

Zanya shrugged one shoulder, the forced casualness of it betraying her nervous anticipation. "I assume it would mean using all of your powers. Throwing fire at me, ripping up the ground underneath my feet. Pelting me with rocks and trying to slash me with your claws." She almost smiled. "Maybe you'd even turn into a giant dragon and try to eat me?"

That was a very short sampling of the many tactics he could—and had—deployed when the situation called for it. "And you want to face that?"

"Not particularly." Her stance widened, her chin drawing up. "But the Betrayer won't hold back. So I have to be ready."

A painful truth. More painful was the knowledge that she wouldn't thank him for what was about to happen. He'd have to peel away her layers of safety and truly make her believe her life was in peril. The one thing he'd hoped to avoid—but Zanya wouldn't thank him for coddling her. Not if it put Sachi's life at greater risk.

A test of the full breadth of her ability, then. He'd poke and he'd prod until she exploded into violent life. There was a shameful sort of thrill in knowing he'd be the first to glimpse the blazing dark star she would become.

He could only hope she wouldn't hate him for it.

Or kill him by mistake.

"All right," he said quietly. "We'll do this."

She exhaled roughly in relief and held out one of the practice swords. "Just don't let me kill you."

He ignored the statement as he plucked both solid practice swords from her hands. Before she could protest, he gripped them in both hands and reduced the pair of them to splinters with one brutal twist. "The first thing you must learn is this: this isn't a battle about weapons. We fight with weapons when we want to give mortals a chance on *their* battleground."

He brushed away the wood from his hands and paced a wide circle around her. As expected, Zanya watched him warily, pivoting with his movements to keep him in front of her. "Then what is this a battle about?" she demanded.

"You, Zanya." Fire danced at his fingertips, and he let her see his smile. The Dragon's smile, full of arrogance and fangs. "On the battle-fields of the gods, *you* are the weapon."

She parted her lips, undoubtedly to ask another question, but Ash didn't give her the chance. Flames pooled in his palm. With a lazy flick of his wrist, he sent the fire streaking toward her. Not the safe fire he toyed with in the bedroom, but true flames—the kind that would burn if they struck her.

He stood braced to extinguish them if necessary, but he shouldn't have worried. Zanya flung herself out of their path and came up in a defensive crouch. She said nothing, but her eyes were wide with surprise. No doubt she'd felt the deadly serious heat—and the threat.

Either way, best to make it explicit. "You told me not to hold back," he reminded her. Fire danced above his palm again, gathering into a sizable sphere. "You think you can kill me? *Try.*"

She lunged at him.

It was fast, and she did something with the shadows to make her body harder to see. But Ash had been fighting for millennia. A flick of his fingers raised columns of fire that burned through the darkness. A lazy twist of his wrist broke off smaller pieces that rained down on her, forcing her to abort her attack and focus on staying out of their way.

And she did. She moved with a grace any dancer would envy, twirling between the flames and twisting away with impossible speed. After the fifth attempt, he realized she was testing him, watching his hands for tells as she attempted to map a path through his defenses. She was *thinking*, still reacting like a human-trained assassin among mortals.

He needed to prick her temper and unleash the god.

With a silent apology, he summoned a gout of fire in front of her next advance. She'd expected it and was already spinning out of its path when he plunged his power deep into the earth.

The ground exploded beneath her feet, sending her flying twice his height in a cloud of dirt and pebbles. Her yelp of surprise melted into a curse as she hit the ground and tumbled, her chaotic flailing of limbs turning into a deadly precise roll that ended in another defensive crouch.

Fire erupted beneath her before she gained her balance. His instincts screamed at him to hold back, but he crushed them in a brutal grip.

And let her burn.

The heartbeat before she rolled across the dirt, extinguishing the flames, lasted forever. Her clothing had protected her from the worst of it, but her hands battered at the burning tip of her braid. The scent of burnt hair lingered on the night air as he stood, impassive, hiding the need to comfort her as she rolled to her knees.

Something vast and terrifying stirred behind her dark-brown eyes as she watched him, panting for breath. He could taste her frustration on the night breeze. His instincts screamed at him at the recklessness of poking at her, as if even the Dragon could sense a predator stirring beneath that golden skin.

He ignored it and let his lips curl into a small, mocking smile. "Let's worry less about whether or not you can kill me. Can you even lay a finger on me, Zanya?"

She growled and lunged. He let her get two steps before he punched his gift into the earth and sent her flying again.

Zanya hit the dirt on her back this time, seething. Ash gave her a moment to get to her knees before he warned her with a rumble beneath her feet. She flung herself into a tumble and came up with daggers in both hands, facing a wall of fire. The noise she made sounded like some unholy cross between a snarling beast and a teakettle about to explode.

The flush in her cheeks wasn't mere exertion. She was embarrassed, and Ash used his words as ruthlessly as he had his power. Folding his hands behind his back with a lack of concern that was a direct insult, he let the fire die and strolled around her. "Knives again. What do you think to do with those?"

She actually snarled at him. "Stab you in the face."

He could summon massive avalanches of flame. He could summon a single spark, too. It landed on the tip of one knife and circled it before rolling down, heating the metal until even the grip was so hot she had to spread her fingers with a hiss and let it clatter to the dirt.

"Stop playing with mortal toys," he instructed her. "You have better weapons at your disposal, if you'd simply start using them."

Her eyes didn't look brown anymore. Blackness swallowed the irises as she stabbed the second knife into the dirt and rose with a predatory slowness that sparked warning down his spine. Something ancient and unknowable stared at him from behind those dark, glorious eyes.

"There you are," he whispered.

Zanya laughed, dark and eager.

Then she lunged again.

It was faster than before. He barely had time to raise a wall of fire in front of her. Shadows exploded as flames swept across the spot where she'd been, and Ash only had time to think *finally* before a heavy weight slammed into him from above, driving him face down into the dirt.

Strong fingers grasped his hair and jerked his head back. Lips brushed his ear. "Here I am," she rasped, and the shivery echo beneath her voice was the closest he'd heard to that midnight choir from the night she'd first manifested.

He'd invited a god to the fight. It was time to see what she could do.

In a surge of muscle he rolled them, slamming her back into the ground. She responded with a punch to the jaw hard enough to rattle his teeth and both legs wrapping around him, denying him the leverage to rise.

So Ash called flames.

They slid over his skin in a protective coating of armor. A second later his back hit the dirt as Zanya vanished, reappearing a dozen paces away. He lunged to his feet as she vaulted toward him. The ground exploded in front of her, and she dove into a twisting vortex of shadows and slammed into him from behind.

He staggered, and her laughter cut through the night as he whirled to find those damnable shadows. A fist launched out of them, smashing into his face. Lightning-fast, he caught her wrist and flung her across the practice yard, but she learned *so swiftly*. In another surge of darkness she vanished, only to appear sweeping his feet out from under him with a force that crashed him back into the dirt.

She was on him in a heartbeat, her fingers tight around his throat. "Still think I can't lay hands on the Dragon?"

He formed claws and dragged them up her outer thighs, the prick all the warning he intended to give her before he swiped. But she was gone already, leaving only shadows, and this time he swore he *could* feel them, like a cool touch along his skin.

Ash rolled to his feet, breathing hard. The fabric of his shirt felt too confining, too *human*, so he stripped it off and tossed it aside. He sank his awareness into the earth, waiting for the vibrations that would tell him she'd come back.

There, just behind him. A tremor.

Ash let go of the lesson, let go of planning . . . and let the Dragon play.

They crashed together, and it was glorious. The more he turned earth or fire against her, the more refined her use of the shadows became. Sometimes she exploded out of them in daring attacks. Sometimes they whispered past him, carrying her away. She fell from the sky and crashed into him. She surged up from the earth at his feet in ways that defied logic.

She countered every attack, but there could be no frustration in defeat, not when the punishment was feeling her strength grow, feeling her *awaken*, her dark laughter curling around them both as her confidence soared and her hunger for victory deepened.

He tried everything against her. Walls of fire. Slashing claws. Explosions of dirt that catapulted her skyward and rents in the earth that tried to drag her down. He simply couldn't lay his hands on her unless she allowed him to.

Finally, when she landed on his back for the fourth time, he summoned fire—not to burn, but to transform. "Jump off or hold on," he told her, his only warning before the flames formed wings that swept out to either side in majestic fury.

And the Dragon exploded out of him.

He'd expected the cold bite of shadows, but he could feel her there at the base of his neck, strongly muscled legs squeezing tight at his shoulders. Then her hands pressed to his hide, fingers spread wide, and he almost forgot his purpose as she stroked wondering fingers over him. The whisper that the wind carried to him wasn't a midnight choir, but soft Zanya. "You're magnificent."

Yes, he was. And to show her just how much, he gathered himself and launched them both into the sky.

She shrieked into the night, the sound half outrage and half joy. But as he flapped his wings and carried her higher, it was the joy that lingered, bubbling up out of her in laughter that rang like glorious bells. He banked, giving her another moment to enjoy the wind whipping past them and the freedom of being high in the air with the world stretched before you in perfect miniature like Elevia's little wooden table.

But this night wasn't about play. So he warned her with another sharp turn that tipped one wing toward the ground. A drop from this height wouldn't injure a god, but it would certainly knock the wind out of her. A solid lesson learned.

So he gave her a chance to leap free. And when she didn't, he flipped.

She managed to cling to him for a few sweeps of his wings, but the buffeting air was too much. She slipped free with a yelp, spinning head over feet and clearly too disoriented to summon her shadows. The ancient wisdom of a teacher willing to let her learn a hard lesson vanished under a wave of protectiveness, and he folded his wings to dive after her, with every intention of catching her before she crashed into the earth.

The ground surged up too quickly. But just as he got his claws in place to catch her, shadows exploded through his talons and she vanished.

A heavy weight crashed into his back. Darkness spiraled wide, climbing up his arms and torso and wrapping him in midnight. Something inside him *jerked*, like Zanya was trying to pull the essence that was *him* into the Void, but the massive body of the Dragon simply wouldn't follow. The pressure intensified, tightening so much that he roared and spun, summoning his own flames.

Fire and darkness twisted around them as they fell. The Dragon burned away in an inky inferno, leaving Ash and Zanya fighting for supremacy as they crashed into the earth hard enough to leave a perfect crater in the center of the practice yard.

She was just stunned enough that he managed to roll her beneath him, pinning her hands as she snarled. Shadows immediately appeared, twining down their arms, but he leaned over her and clucked his tongue in a mockery he knew would stiffen her pride. "Running again?"

She hissed at him, but the shadows slowed.

Ash let his hands form claws, let the fire dance in his eyes as his fangs appeared. "Fight like a god, handmaid."

The dark brown of her eyes bled to black and expanded, until staring down into them was like staring into the Void itself. The shadows slid up his arms and around his body, and he *could* feel them—a touch every bit as tangible as his own flames, and *not* the ones he used in battle. A treacherously distracting tingle followed the path of those shadows, as if her hands were stroking over him.

Her lips curled in a dangerous smile. It was the only warning he got before those wisps of shadow clenched tight, like the fingers of a giant wrapped around his body. He was airborne in the next moment, slamming face down into the dirt hard enough to knock the breath from his lungs.

Zanya crouched a few paces away, that glorious black rainbow exploding around her. The breeze lifted her dark hair, and she stared at him as if studying a puzzle. She lifted her hand experimentally, and the shadows swirled around him jerked him upward. She twisted her wrist, and he tumbled over and slammed back into the dirt, this time on his back.

The shadows held him pinned in place. He bucked against them, using a force that would have shattered stone. His fingers barely scrabbled against the dirt. Summoning fire to burn through them did nothing—the shadows simply churned, drawing the fire into their depths, where it vanished as if snuffed out. Out of instinct he lashed out, tearing at the earth beneath her feet. She launched into the air, swirling away in a vortex of shadow.

All the air left his body when she landed on top of him, straddling his chest. Her hand shot for his throat, clenching so tightly he couldn't wheeze in another breath. For a heartbeat her eyes seethed fully black, and her nails dug into his skin deeply enough to draw blood. She tilted her head, and whatever was watching him from behind those dark eyes was pure predator.

The god of destruction, in human flesh.

And he couldn't do a godsdamned thing to stop her from strangling the life from him. Except rasp out her name with the last of his breath. "Zanya."

The shadows trapping him vanished abruptly. Her fingers loosened, and she rolled off him and sprawled in the dirt next to him. Her braid had mostly unraveled, and she lifted it, staring at the charred ends of her hair in silence punctuated only by their breathless pants.

He wanted to apologize for burning her, but he held his tongue. If a warrior wouldn't appreciate being coddled, he could only imagine how poorly an ancient, primal god would take it. And that was what she was—a trueborn warrior god, with instincts that would only sharpen with experience.

Elevia would be giddy. Zanya wasn't. She stroked her thumb over the singed ends of her hair, again and again. When she spoke, it wasn't of her hair.

"I burned the bread," she whispered softly. "At the orphanage. I don't think Sachi remembers, but that's what started it. Ma'am had one of her headaches—she was the one who ran the house for lost children—and the older girl had run away. I can't remember her name. She must have only been fourteen or fifteen but she seemed so old to us. The older girl used to make Ma'am her tonic and toast, but she was gone and it was just me and Sachi. I tried to make it, but I burned the bread, and she was *so mad at me* for wasting it. So she took out the strap, but Sachi got in the way. On purpose."

Ash dug his fingers into the earth, pulling on its strength to keep his voice even. "Is that when the Terrors came?"

"Not at that moment. I was so scared, I tried to put myself between them, but Ma'am was furious with Sachi, so she shoved me into the closet. In the dark. And I had to listen . . ." Zanya's voice hitched. "Sachi tried not to cry, but we were so little, and that bitch hit her *so hard.* The healer had to come, and the old woman glared at Ma'am the whole time . . . and I thought, *She'll take Sachi away. She won't leave her here, not with the woman that hurt her."*

"But she left you both."

"She left us both." He heard Zanya swallow. "Sachi was whimpering in her sleep because it still hurt. I couldn't even hold her. And I wasn't scared anymore. I was *angry*, because how could that healer look at Sachi and not take her away? How could anyone want to hurt her, when she only ever wanted to make people happy? And I don't think I even understood what death was, but I wanted them all to *stop being.* To go away. To never, ever, ever be able to hurt us again."

And so the Terrors had come. Ash turned his head to look at her profile, silvered by moonlight. "Elevia heard they destroyed the whole village."

"Everyone," Zanya said dully. "I regret some of it. There weren't many children in the village, but there were some. They were older than us, and I know now that they couldn't have done anything. But when you're five or six, a teenager seems like a god. So I hated them, too. I hated all of them, and I was *glad* they were dying. Until Sachi started crying."

Her voice cracked. The soft light of the double moons caught a tear glistening on her cheek. "She looked at me . . . and she *knew*. I don't know how, but she knew that I'd called the Terrors. And she looked at me like I was one of them. A nightmare. A *monster*."

The bitterness in that single word held a mortal lifetime of self-loathing. Ash swallowed the sympathy that she wasn't ready to hear and let her finish.

"So I shouted for them to stop," she whispered. "And they did. I didn't exactly mean to call them, but I did know they came from someplace inside me. I just didn't know that place was *wrong* until Sachi started begging for it all to stop. I didn't know I *was* a monster."

This time, he couldn't hold his tongue. "Do you still think Sachi sees you that way?"

Zanya's abrupt laugh was hoarse with tears. "No, of course not. She was young and scared and didn't mean it. Sachi loves me, and that's the end of it as far as she's concerned."

"But not as far as *you're* concerned?"

A huff. "Sachi has a big heart and a soft spot for unlovable monsters."

He'd thought he was beyond feeling the sting of that word, but his heart twinged at the truth of it. After all, what was Ash if not a monster the world had forgotten how to love? But Sachi had opened that fearless heart to him at once.

She'd had practice.

"Elevia wants me to learn how to summon the Terrors," Zanya whispered. "She's frustrated that I won't. She doesn't understand that nothing good has ever come of it. I slaughtered a village the first time. And the last . . ."

The last, she'd been planning to slaughter *him*. The arrival of the Terrors had stayed her hand, but it had also forced her to reveal her power to the High Court and the inhabitants of the Villa.

He could still see her in memory, stiff and proud, walking back through the darkness past dozens of terrified faces with the whispers of

Void-touched and *cursed* following in her wake. And he could remember well the instinctive reactions of the High Court—horror, mistrust, animosity.

They might not have said the word *monster*, but what screamed it more loudly than the fearful enmity of literal gods?

"I'll talk to Elevia," he promised. Not that Zanya could put it off forever. She *would* have to learn to control this power. But if the Huntress understood the traumatic origins of Zanya's resistance, she might be able to handle it with delicacy.

If they had time.

Zanya sighed softly. "Maybe it's foolish to still care. But I was so little the first time, Ash. And then Nikkon came and took us, and he told me Sachi was beautiful and would be a princess, but that I was an abomination. And that was all I felt like, for the longest time. Except when Sachi was there. Because she knew the worst part of me, and she knew it was wrong. But she still loved me."

More tears glistened on her cheeks, but Ash was afraid to move, afraid to do anything that might shatter this fragile moment of trust. "Zanya . . ."

"I *am* a monster without her," she whispered. "Don't you see that? I care about you, Ash. I care about Ulric, and Elevia. Even Aleksi and Inga. But some part of me is always going to be that little girl who summoned Terrors to destroy an entire village and was glad they died, because they hurt Sachi. If something happens to her—"

"Shh." Now he did roll onto his side, cupping her cheek with one hand. The tears spilled forth as fast as he could wipe them away. "Zanya, we *will* find her. We'll bring her home."

Zanya pressed a closed fist to her chest. "I can't live without her. Do you understand? I can't—" A gasp. "I can't—"

Ash sat up and hauled her into his lap. She stiffened, arms flailing, but when he only settled her across his legs with her head tucked against his throat, she shuddered and pressed her face to his chest, as if to hide her tears.

"She's too brave." The words trembled on the edge of a sob. "She'll take too many risks. I know I said we have to trust her, but I'm *terrified*. I can't protect her this time."

"I know," he whispered, stroking her back. The charred ends of her hair tangled around his fingers. "But you aren't trying to protect her alone anymore. Every last member of the High Court will lay down their lives for her. So would all of the Raven Guard. The new Dreamers who haven't earned titles or followings but still have power. *Me*." He spread his fingers wide when they reached the back of her head, cradling her gently. "I will never let you carry this burden alone, Zanya. Never again."

Another shudder rocked her body, and it was as if the tension inside her finally shattered. Her fingers came up, splayed against his bare shoulder, clinging to him as the first sob ripped through her.

The tears kept coming. A trickle. A wave. A river. His throat and collarbone were slick with them, but he ignored it just like he ignored the way her nails bit into his skin, staying rock steady beneath her. Only his hand moved, stroking down her hair and across her back in gentle, soothing circles as he whispered against her temple. "You've done so well," and, "You've kept her safe." Over and over, interspersed with other whispered promises.

You're safe, Zanya.

She'll be safe soon, too.

You're not alone.

I'm here.

We'll always come save her.

We'll always come save you.

That last only made her cry harder, and he knew these weren't just the tears of her grief and fear over Sachi. She'd unlocked something primal in herself tonight, something as elemental and feral as that tiny little girl who had destroyed a town in retribution for Sachi's pain.

That monster wasn't going away. It was as much a part of her as his dragon was of him. And people would fear her for it. They would revile her and flee from her, and no one knew better than he how the pain of that could calcify over the years. But he'd been a grown man with centuries of life behind him the first time he'd been called a monster.

She'd been little more than a baby.

So he stroked her hair until her sobs eased, then carefully wiped the tears from her cheeks. When she stared up at him self-consciously, he cupped her cheeks and pressed a tender kiss to her forehead.

"There's only one thing to remember," he said softly. "Sometimes the world needs monsters. Everything you learned today? You'll have it to use against the Betrayer."

She nodded, her eyes shadowed.

"He's a monster for the sake of being a monster. You?" He smiled. "You're *her* monster. And that makes all the difference."

He watched something shift in her. She didn't look young or lost or nervous anymore. She looked *ancient* and unfathomable, like those first moments when she'd stood before him in her newly awakened glory. An elemental force of the world stared up at him, and Ash knew that somewhere in the vastness of the Empire, its equal opposing force rested in the deceptively fragile body of a captive princess who might manifest her full power at any moment.

For the first time in many, many years, Ash almost pitied the Betrayer.

Chapter Twenty-One
WITCHING MOON

Week Two, Day Ten
Year 3000

Sachi was starting to dislike the color blue.

Which was unfortunate, because so many things she adored were varying shades of it. A clear summer sky. A robin's egg. Siren's Bay at midday. Hell, Sachi saw blue every time she looked in a mirror.

But, right now, staring down three partially finished dresses in helpless frustration, she couldn't bear to look at it. Not the gold-laced brocade of dark navy, or the periwinkle silk, or the royal-blue chiffon.

"I don't care, Lyssa," she said finally. "Just . . . pick whichever one you like best."

"Are you sure? This ball is in your honor, and the Emperor wants you to be pleased."

She would be *pleased* when she'd finished her work here and could go home. The previous day had been relatively uneventful. She'd taken the midday meal with Sorin, then been banished to her luxurious cell for the rest of the day. And since Sorin had finally stopped entering her chambers unannounced, Sachi had decided to explore the palace. Long after sunset, she'd attempted a full survey, only to be stubbornly turned back at the door by her guards.

Still, Sachi had other methods of exploration at her disposal. She'd entered the Dream, intent on mapping the palace's strengths and weaknesses. But where Sorin's home had walls suffused with webs of the Dream, this place had *layers* of it, so thick they were practically solid. Doors and windows were indistinguishable from walls. Sachi could move through them with ease, but she couldn't discern any of the corresponding structures in the real world.

So she'd retreated, but she had not given up. Because she'd felt it again—the strange vibrations coming up through the floors, as if some unknown force were reaching out to her. *Calling* for her.

The layout of the palace didn't matter. What Sachi really needed was to find the source of that power. She would get through this ball, and she would try again.

She shrugged at her maid as she eyed the unfinished dresses laid out on her bed. "I like all three of them equally well. So, you see, I *can't* decide."

Lyssa bit her lower lip, her fingers smoothing over the dark navy. "I don't want to presume too much, but . . . if it were me, my lady? I would choose this one."

Sachi eyed the dress. It was solidly, almost modestly, constructed, with long sleeves and a reasonably high neckline. The bodice and hem had been hand-embroidered with gold thread, with lovely, lacy patterns that reminded Sachi of the aged family portraits that had lined the gallery hall at Castle Roquebarre.

It was the least revealing, most armor-like of any of the dresses presented, which had no doubt prompted the maid's suggestion. But while Sachi appreciated Lyssa's concern, mere clothing wouldn't save her from the vagaries of Sorin's assembled Imperial Court.

Gwynira aside, Sachi had no allies here, even grudging ones. While the rest of Sorin's court displayed varying levels of curiosity about her, that was where their consideration appeared to end. If they thought of her at all, it was with either predatory interest or dismissive disdain. They showed no hint of awareness that she might be dangerous. Even Gwynira seemed to have offered her the dagger now hidden in her wardrobe because she lacked for other options, and had not so much as *looked* at Sachi since.

It had obviously never occurred to any of them that Sachi might harm them—the Betrayer included. Sorin treated her solicitously, had even shown her whispers of kindness. Mostly, he courted her, quite obviously biding his time until she let him touch her. He had finally stopped thinking she might run away or try to escape, because Sachi had mostly managed to convince him that she didn't hate him to the depths of her very soul.

It had never crossed his mind that she might try to murder him. A curious thing, since he, above all others, should have known how thoroughly she'd been trained to do just that. She'd learned how to administer poisons from Void-cultivated flowers, potent and quick enough to kill even a god. There were complicated explosives whose compositions and chemistry she had committed to memory. There was even the time-honored blade across the throat in the sticky, breathless aftermath of sex.

But Sorin didn't fear her. No one here did. Did she play the role of wide-eyed, sheltered princess a little *too* well? Were these strange gods just that lethal, in ways Sachi had yet to discover? Or had their instincts merely whispered the truth—that she didn't *want* to kill anyone, and never had?

In the end, the reasons didn't matter, only the outcome. If this court decided they wanted to hurt her, nothing as prosaic as a dress would stop them.

Still, it would not hurt to clothe herself purposefully, and with intent. "That's a splendid idea, Lyssa. Yes. Please have the seamstresses complete that one for tonight."

"Of course." Lyssa smiled as she began to pack away the other two partially constructed gowns. "The gossip in the servants' quarters this morning is that the Stalker has finally arrived—the Emperor was *most* displeased by her tardiness—but no one has heard a word about the Shapechanger in weeks. If he doesn't appear to honor you, the Emperor will be furious."

They were, to Sachi's knowledge, the last two members of the court she had yet to meet. "Surely Sorin must know where he is."

"I'm certain he does. I've heard he keeps a much closer watch on the court since the loss of Grand Duke Nikkon."

Hearing his name was still enough to raise the fine hairs on Sachi's nape. But his mention did present an opening, a chance to establish more intimacy with Lyssa, who heard *everything* and could tell her secrets perhaps even the gods didn't know.

It was a risk, but so was Sachi's very presence here in the Empire. So she told the truth. "Did you know that my previous maid is the one who killed him?"

Lyssa stilled, the periwinkle silk clutched tight to her chest. "A *maid* killed the Grand Duke?"

"A maid. An assassin. The embodiment of the Endless Void." Sachi met Lyssa's eyes. "My lover. Zanya is all those things, and so much more."

Lyssa paled until her freckles stood out starkly against her skin. "My lady, that sounds like blasphemy. You must not repeat such things where others can hear them." She hurried to tuck the dress away before returning to Sachi. "There is no Endless Void, and the Dream is simply another word for the Emperor's will to see us all strong and protected."

Perversely, Sachi almost laughed. It was a far cry from what Sorin had said to the High Court during his visit to Siren's Bay. He'd expressed disappointment in Nikkon for not realizing who Sachi was—insinuating, of course, that he believed her to be Zanya's counterpart, the Everlasting Dream. Just like the rest of them.

After the events of the past few weeks, Sachi had to admit she was a bit more open to the possibility, though she still wasn't fully convinced. So the fact that Sorin's lies rankled? That surprised her.

She gave voice to her irritation. "I haven't even agreed to be his Empress, and here he is, claiming I don't exist. How rude of him."

Lyssa somehow went even paler, dropping to one knee with her eyes fixed on the floor. "Forgive me, my lady, I must have misspoken. The Emperor would never diminish you. It is for the priests to understand the nature of such things, not foolish maids."

Remorse flooded Sachi. Her sharp words had cut, but not the person who deserved it. "No, Lyssa. I'm sorry. Please." She reached for the other woman to pull her to her feet. "You said nothing wrong. I just . . ." From this vantage point, Sachi could see under the high, starched collar of Lyssa's uniform. And bruises ringed her neck.

Bruises in the shape of fingers.

"My lady?" Lyssa scrambled to her feet, her face tight with self-consciousness. "Please, pay me no mind. Sit, and I will help you ready for breakfast."

"Who was it?" Sachi's voice was amazingly calm, considering the fury bubbling through her veins. "Was it Demir? Is he the one who choked you?"

Color flooded the girl's cheeks. But it was the resignation in her eyes and the helpless slump of her shoulders that truly hurt. "He could make trouble for me with my guild, my lady. Being tradeless in the Empire is a terrible fate."

"No, Demir will disturb you no longer." Sachi turned and, heedless of her bare feet, unbrushed hair, and dressing gown, left the room.

Her guards jumped to follow her, though they didn't try to stop her, incandescent as she was with rage. Perhaps her temper startled them. More likely, they only had orders to contain Sorin's poor, sad little captive princess when she wasn't allowed to be out.

And right now, she was due at breakfast.

Her anger carried her to the dining hall, where she pushed through the doors with no announcement, no servants rushing before her to prepare. "Where is he?"

Sorin sat at the head of the table, his teacup frozen halfway to his lips. His gaze swept over her disarray, lingering in places she had no patience for, especially when his slow smile was so patronizing. "Who would that be, my dear?"

She gritted her teeth. "Demir. He has injured my maid, left bruises on her body. I would see him answer for it."

"If that is your desire, we will get to the truth of the matter." Sorin set down his cup and gestured to one of the guards. "Fetch Demir at once. And bring my lady's breakfast." He pointed to the chair on his left. "Join me, Sachielle."

She had no choice. She sat. "I am not ignorant, Sorin. I grew up in Dalvish's court. I know how these things work. You will ask him, and he will deny it or say that she enjoyed herself. And you will take his word, because he is one of your nobles and she is a servant."

"Is it so impossible that she did enjoy herself? I agree that leaving bruises is gauche, but consider how many fools throw themselves into the Dragon's bed. There's no accounting for taste."

Sachi clenched her hands into fists beneath the table. "I am not innocent, either. I know what sorts of activities people can enjoy together. This was *not* that."

Sorin studied her, his expression unreadable. He was still watching her when the guard returned with Grand Duke Demir striding behind him, clearly irritated by the summons. "What is it?"

"My lady says you have touched her maid in an inappropriate fashion and left bruises behind."

Demir cast a glare at Sachi, one that left her in no doubt of how much he'd like to choke *her*. "So now it's a crime to bed a girl properly?"

"Was the girl willing?" Sorin pressed.

Demir actually laughed. "Willing enough to use my name to discourage other suitors, wasn't she?"

"Such odd notions you have," Sachi said evenly. "You say these words—*willing, properly, suitors*—and yet I don't believe you know what any of them truly mean."

The Beast took an angry step forward, his mouth opening . . . and shutting again after a cautious look at Sorin, who was neatly folding his napkin.

"You say the girl was willing." Sorin pushed his chair back and rose. "My lady says she was not. I'm sure you can see where this leaves you."

It left Demir furious, judging by the look in his eyes—but not reckless enough to challenge the Emperor to his face. "Fine, I'll leave her be. She was starting to bore me anyway."

His eyes still burned with thwarted ire, so Sachi added, "And there will be no retaliation. From you, from her guild. From anyone."

"Of course not." Sorin undid his cuff links and set them above his plate. "I'll see to it."

"And I'll stay away from the bitch," Demir growled.

"While that is an admirable sentiment, Demir, the fact remains that you were reckless. You injured a member of the future Empress's household." Sorin began to meticulously roll up his sleeves as he stepped from behind the table. "Restitution is due, I'm afraid."

Demir dropped to one knee, his anger melting into panic with a chilling speed that confused Sachi. "Your Majesty, I'm sorry—"

"You will be," Sorin said gently.

Then he hauled back his fist and drove it down into Demir's face so hard that Sachi heard his cheekbone shatter. She recoiled, closing her eyes and turning her head as another blow landed, then another.

"Stop," she whispered.

Instead, she heard the distinctive crack of breaking ribs. Memory assailed her, the ghosts of beatings too much like this one, delivered with a straight face and pragmatic cruelty. Her hands and feet grew cold, and she heard herself breathing too fast. Heard, as if she were already outside herself, drifting away.

"Please, Sorin, stop." She forced her eyes open, because whatever carnage was taking place before her, it was better than drowning in her memories.

Or was it? The beating continued, and Sachi's vision narrowed and darkened at the edges, tunneled until she could see only bits of the scene before her. Split skin. Flecks of blood landing on the pristine tile. Sorin's determined fists.

Stop.

At last, it did. Demir lay curled on the floor with Sorin standing over him, his head tilted in assessment, as if he were trying to determine whether a few more punches or kicks were warranted. Apparently decided, he walked back toward the table.

Sachi flinched, but he only retrieved a napkin and began to methodically clean the blood from his hands. "You see?" he told her brightly. "You shouldn't assume things must always go badly. I trusted your word, did I not?"

Sachi couldn't feel her lips, and her hands were shaking so hard they rattled the silverware when she bumped the table. "You did, Your Majesty."

Several guards came in to drag away a groaning Demir. A maid dodged past them, carrying a tray with Sachi's breakfast. Sympathy filled the young woman's eyes as she hurriedly placed a plate full of eggs and toast in front of her, but any concern she felt for Sachi didn't stop her from fleeing the room as soon as she could.

Next to Sachi, Sorin picked up his fork and took a bite of his eggs. "These eggs are from your own coops, you know. Specially bred for your table. You'll never taste finer."

Sachi couldn't cry or scream, so she shut down. She took all her terror and gut-wrenching panic and balled it up into a little corner of her mind. Just tucked it away, where it would keep until she could deal with it later. So she was able to smile and nod, but her attention kept drifting to the center of the room.

One of Demir's teeth still lay on the floor, in a pool of blood.

And finally, Sachi thought she understood what the Ice Queen had truly meant, and why no one here was afraid of her.

Chapter Twenty-Two
WITCHING MOON

Week Two, Day Ten
Year 3000

By the time word came that the queen's soldiers were on the move, Zanya was almost grateful for an interruption.

Ulric and Elevia had been as ruthless in the training of her newly discovered ability to manifest physically tangible shadows as they had been with her traveling. Over the course of a grueling morning, they had forced Zanya to answer dozens of questions.

Could she lift something heavier than a person? (Yes.) Could she lift inanimate objects? (Heaving boulders indicated yes.) Could she deploy it at long distances? (Flinging those boulders at the distant peaks across from Dragon's Keep seemed promising.) Could she use it as a weapon of blunt destruction? (Easily.) In place of her own hands? (With some concentration.) With delicate precision? (Not without much more training.) Could she form the shadows into a blade? (Yes.) Did it do the same damage as Void-steel?

Zanya had balked at that test, but Ulric had simply held out his arm in implacable demand, and Zanya had given in, scoring him lightly across the forearm. His golden eyes had flared and a hiss of pain had answered the question, but all three of them had watched the blood seep from the thin cut long after it should have healed.

"She needs to train with this," Ulric said finally, wiping away the blood. "Not with the Raven Guard."

Elevia was already there, with one of Inga's special bandages that had been steeped in healing salves. "Only us, and we'll take care. But it has to happen soon."

Her implication hung in the air: they could be called to the heart of the Empire at any moment, and Zanya was still far from ready.

A chill struck her, as if a cloud had passed in front of the sun. But when she looked up, the shadow was cast by Kardox, who'd been manning the walls. "One of your messengers is on the last switchback, Huntress. Riding fast."

Zanya followed the pair as they strode through the gates and across the causeway to meet the messenger. Neither rider nor horse looked particularly calm after taking the switchback up the mountain at speed, but the young woman still dismounted and clasped a hand over her heart.

"Huntress, you were right. With the rivers closed to them, the queen's soldiers tried to cut south around the Burning Hills to march on Vienda's Hollow. Malindra's regiment turned them back, but it's her opinion that the next confrontation could result in significant bloodshed."

Zanya barely heard the words as Elevia questioned the messenger further, getting details on troop sizes and tactics. Sachi had been determined to go to the capital and put a stop to this by confronting Anikke. She would care deeply about the villages and towns currently under threat. She'd even care about the citizens of the Mortal Court. Not the wealthy and powerful ones, but the ones Zanya had known as she moved through the servants' quarters. The ones now at the mercy of regents who wanted to play foolish games with gods.

But Sachi wasn't here . . . and she'd asked Zanya to go in her place. In fact, it was the only thing Sachi had ever asked of her—to do this in her stead while she was trapped in the Empire.

The rest of the High Court who were in residence had joined them in a tight cluster on the causeway, everyone discussing in low voices what the best move would be. Zanya stepped forward. "I should go. Now. That's what Sachi wants. I can deal with it."

Inga tilted her head. "What do you consider *dealing with it?*"

"Just what Sachi said. We tell the truth. King Dalvish II broke faith with the High Court, nullifying the ancient treaty. One of you can come with me and make it official. Then we find out what's really going on. If Anikke is truly not responsible for what has been done in her name, she can ask for protection." Zanya squared her shoulders. "I won't be able to do this as elegantly as Sachi might, but I still know where most of the bodies are buried. And if all else fails, I'll murder the regents."

"I like the sound of that part," Ulric murmured.

Inga winced. "It's a touch blunt, but they haven't exactly earned our subtlety. If Sachi thinks you can handle it, I see no reason to doubt her."

"Aleksi is supposed to go with me," Zanya added, turning to face the Lover with an apologetic look. "Sorry, but that's what Sachi said. That everyone at the court still reveres you. And it's true."

"The curse of being lovable," Aleksi said with a heavy sigh. "A burden I bear."

"Then you'll come with me?" Zanya asked.

"Yes. But I will need to change into something a little more appropriate." He glanced at her. "In fact, I think we both should. Ash?"

Ash nodded to Zanya. "Tell them what Sachi said."

What Sachi . . . ? Oh. Turning, she found Inga. "She said it's time."

Inga linked her arm through Zanya's and led her back toward the castle. "Excellent. Come with me."

"What is it time for?"

Inga smiled mysteriously. "Just a little something to help you make an impression. It was Sachi's idea, but we all wanted to help with it. Consider it a reward for how hard you've been working with Elevia and Ulric."

Since there seemed nothing to do but follow them—and trust Sachi—Zanya let them lead her inside the castle.

Then, for the first time in her life, she learned what it must have been like in Sachi's shoes for all those years.

As soon as they stepped into the odd little parlor, a young man appeared wielding a brush and a smile. The seamstress bustled into the room trailing two attendants, and the armorer strode in chivvying four in front of her. Dark fabrics and leather overflowed arms and spilled onto the floor. They spoke over Zanya as if she weren't there, while the man's fingers twisted her hair into intricate braids that drew the locks away from her face and wound around her head before twining together to cascade down her back in one thick tail.

He didn't even blink at the charred ends of her hair, which told Zanya more than she wanted to know about the High Court and the people who lived there.

Someone brought her sturdy black pants constructed of a rare fabric she recognized only from the Raven Guard's battle armor. Somehow tough but flexible, it could deflect a glancing knife blow and yet still moved with her body. The long-sleeved shirt she donned did the same, clinging to her skin without hampering her movement.

The armor was another matter.

"Inga provided most of this to the leatherworkers," Ulric said as he and Elevia helped her into the stiff leather brigandine. It was stained a midnight black with shiny silver buckles, but it was the studding that stole her breath—dozens and dozens of steel rivets that glittered with an impossible darkness she could taste in the air. One brush of her fingers whispered the truth to her.

"Void-steel?"

"Mmm." Ulric tightened a buckle at her side. "Trust Inga to be sitting on a cache of the stuff, even knowing it could kill her."

An impressive cache, apparently. Bracers followed, along with greaves, both studded in the same glimmering darkness. So was the sword belt, which already had a heavy sheath strapped to it. The sword it contained was Void-steel, as well—a curved blade with a single cutting edge and the inky waves that indicated death to the Dreamers, and a humbling level of trust when they placed it in her hands.

Finally, the crowd of helpers dispersed. Only the High Court remained, all of them studying her in silence that dragged on just long enough to make Zanya feel self-conscious. How did she appear to them? Like a child playing dress-up? A little girl with pretensions of godhood?

She stared at her own reflection in the full mirror, trying to see herself through new eyes. Through *their* eyes. Glorious dark hair braided for battle like the barbarian clans Malindra called home. Proud, bold features. Brown eyes ringed with a hint of shadows. Sleek black leather armor that shimmered like an oil slick in sunlight, an impossible shadow rainbow that danced when she moved. She was tall, well-muscled. She wore her sword and her knives with easy assurance.

It didn't matter what the rest of the High Court thought. *She* knew she looked powerful.

"She's ready," Elevia murmured.

"Yes," Ulric agreed.

"Ready." Aleksi smiled. "And terrifyingly gorgeous."

"I have the finishing touch," Inga said from behind her, and Zanya turned to face her. The Witch eased the knife from Zanya's belt and tossed it to the table. Then she flipped her wrist, and the Void-knife appeared in her palm. Inga tucked it gently into the sheath and gave it a pat. "It belongs with you."

"Thank you," Zanya whispered.

"Of course." Inga's violet eyes lit with mischief. "Would you like to add a little drama, my love?"

"Drama?"

"Close your eyes."

Zanya obeyed. Inga's thumbs ghosted over her eyelids as she whispered something unintelligible. Then she gripped Zanya's shoulders gently and turned her back to the mirror. "Look."

It was still her face. But a bold black line outlined each eye, sweeping out from the corner toward her brow in a point sharp enough to cut. And dark pigment shimmered on her eyelids, as if the colors of her armor had been crushed to a powder and smoothed across her skin. Over her shoulder, Inga watched her study the makeup, looking almost . . . nervous.

Without warning, the world turned on its head. She stared at the gift they'd so painstakingly constructed for her—clothing tailored to her measurements in secret. Armor pulled from ancient caches and resized to fit her, even though the mere presence of it must scrape their collective nerves raw.

Sachi had been right all along. Zanya didn't have to earn her place among them. She was the manifestation of an elemental power they feared and worshipped. *They* were uncertain about earning acceptance from *her*.

"Do you like it?" Inga asked. "If you don't—"

Zanya clasped her hand. "I love it," she said firmly. "It's perfect."

"It's her," rumbled Ash's voice. Inga moved aside, letting him step up behind her. His fingers ghosted over her braid, evoking a soft shiver, and he lowered his voice. "Sachi didn't want us to give this to you until you were ready. But she has always seen you so clearly. A protector."

The pain of missing her was cut by the pleasure of feeling her loving touch in every inch of this outfit. Sachi believed in her. That was power enough. "I love it," she said again. "I'm ready."

"You are," he agreed, and now the look he gave her in the mirror was pure Dragon. "It's time for the Mortal Lords to meet their newest god."

Chapter Twenty-Three
WITCHING MOON

Week Two, Day Ten
Year 3000

They made an entrance.

As much as she had loathed King Dalvish's court, Zanya knew its rhythms like the beat of her own heart. The court would be well into its weekly afternoon of audiences by now, with every lord and lady who had pretensions of power clustered into the massive hall, awaiting the queen's judgment on their petty disputes.

Zanya wrapped Aleksi in her shadows and carried them both directly to the hallway outside the grand doors.

Curses erupted, along with the clang of metal as the guards drew their swords. The herald at the door nearly choked, his gaze darting wildly between them as if he couldn't decide what was worse—that someone had just appeared by magic, or that he didn't know their proper titles and lineage in order to construct a formal introduction.

"It's her," one of the guards hissed, whipping his sword toward Zanya. "That traitorous handmaid!"

Without looking away from the herald, Zanya held up her arm and braced herself against the force of the blow. The sword blade threw sparks as it slammed into the Void-steel that swirled up her forearm in intricate studs. With a single thought, she sent shadows cascading back down the sword's length and tore it from the guard's hands. The hilt sailed into her grip, and she rammed the blade point down into the pristine marble floor, using her full strength to embed it halfway to the pommel.

Shocked silence filled the hallway.

Still holding the herald's gaze, she said, "You have the rare honor of being in the presence of a member of the High Court of Dreamers. The Lover wishes to address the Mortal Queen. Please announce his arrival."

The herald's desperate dedication to protocol and tradition won out over his shock—or any recent declarations about the High Court's traitorous status. He scrambled through the open doors and shoved an inconvenient chair out of the way. The ceremonial gong sat behind it, dusty with misuse. The last time Zanya had heard it sound had been for a visit from Dianthe on the occasion of Anikke's birth.

His thin face red with embarrassment, the herald wiped away the dust with one sleeve and hurriedly picked up the mallet. A few low-ranking courtiers at the back of the room had started to turn at the commotion, but everyone else remained focused on the dais at the far end of the hall, where a young lord currently held sway.

The loud clang of the gong changed that.

Confusion rippled through the crowd, moving slowly at the back and then racing through the front as the gong sounded again. Then silence fell, and the only sound was the rustling of fabric as hundreds of decadently clad nobles turned as one to face the wide doors.

"Chin up, love," Aleksi whispered. "Remember who you are."

The herald drew in a breath that Zanya feared would pop the buttons on his vest, and his deep voice rolled through the hall. "On this day, as on the first of days, the Mortal Court cries welcome to one of our protectors. The Lover walks among us. Give thanks for his bounty, and pray for his blessings upon your land and your line."

Zanya hid nerves behind a huffing laugh. "Well, that's to the point."

Aleksi laughed. "Yes, but if he tried to elaborate, we might be here all day."

She was suddenly desperately glad of his presence as she took her first step into the hall. Sachi might be used to bearing this many eyes upon her, but Zanya felt each individual gaze like a prick at the base of her spine, warning of an enemy that her instincts screamed for her to confront. The collective weight of it might have sent her screaming into the shadows not so long ago, but with Aleksi walking easily beside her, Zanya managed to block it all out and focus on her target.

The dais.

She'd expected a throne. Instead there were *three*. Queen Anikke sat in the center, painfully young and fragile in spite of her rigidly perfect posture. Her gaze was the only one that jumped back and forth between Aleksi and Zanya, her brow somewhat furrowed, as if she were trying to remember why Zanya looked familiar. They were only halfway down the endless walk when those blue eyes widened in recognition. Her gaze immediately dropped to her lap, where she'd folded her hands together so tightly her knuckles stood out white against her skin.

The thrones on either side of her held King Dalvish's next youngest siblings. Princess-Regent Tislaina sat on the left, her fancifully curled hair a mixture of gold and silver. She was just over fifty, a famed beauty, and utterly ruthless. She had been a willing accomplice in Dalvish's plan to destroy the Dragon—not to mention personally responsible for some of Sachi's cruelest training.

Tislaina watched Aleksi approach with reluctant reverence, as if struggling to remember that her family had declared war on the High Court. Perhaps she'd thought she could disparage the Dragon and burn the Witch's followers without drawing the ire of the Lover.

A tactical error.

Prince-Regent Doven sat in the throne on the left, his golden hair equally dusted with silver but his pose far more relaxed. Though only a few years younger than Tislaina, Zanya honestly couldn't say if he'd been a part of his elder sibling's schemes. His dedication to hunting and horsemanship had kept him rotating between the royal family's various country estates, and Zanya had seen him no more than a dozen times in her entire life.

His dedication to pleasure should have had him watching Aleksi with the same fervor as his elder sister, but his gaze was fixed on Zanya, his head tilted in curiosity. She did her best to stare past him.

King Dalvish's youngest brother stood on the steps at the base of the dais, dressed in full armor. Prince-Regent Bodin had known the family secret, too. And he had *hated* it. He'd hated the dishonor of breaking their ancient contract and had loathed the distasteful tasks involved in Sachi's and Zanya's training.

Perhaps that should have made him feel like an ally, but some days, Zanya had hated him most of all. Of all the powerful adults around them, he'd been the only one who seemed to realize that what they were doing was fundamentally wrong. It had haunted him, she thought. Enough to make him avoid Zanya and Sachi as much as he could.

But not enough to help them.

The murmur of the court finally broke through Zanya's silent assessment of the powerful quartet in front of them. A brief glance around her showed the lords and ladies whispering in excitement and jostling for a prime spot and the best chance at a smile of greeting from the Lover.

Under better circumstances, Zanya might have laughed. The current regents, and High Priest Nikkon before them, had done their best to turn the sensibilities of the capital against the High Court, but the Lover remained a favorite. They still sought his blessings for their unions and their babies. They thanked him for the bounty the farmers enjoyed. He'd served as muse for generations of storytellers and poets, who rendered him as charismatic and desirable, benevolent and joyous.

And he was the god of lust as well as love, the winking encouragement to give in to your carnal urges and call it worship, the walking epitome of everything sensual and luxurious.

It didn't hurt that he was handsome enough to weaken anyone's knees, especially when he actually *tried* to be charming. One or two of those whose eyes he met in the crowd actually swooned, and nervous laughter and excited chatter followed him and Zanya as they approached the throne.

Before they reached the base of the dais, Prince-Regent Bodin stepped into their path. Reluctance stiffened his shoulders and lines of stress aged his face—he looked a decade older than either of his siblings instead of nearly ten years their junior.

"The herald has forgotten that we no longer offer welcome to the traitorous High Court. They violated any pact between us when they allowed this *assassin*"—he flung out a hand to point directly at Zanya— "to murder our beloved brother and king, Dalvish II. If you have come to submit the so-called handmaid to justice, perhaps the relationship between our courts can be repaired."

"I'm afraid not, my prince," Aleksi said smoothly. "Rather, I'm here to inform you that the ancient contract between the High Court and your Mortal Lords was broken when King Dalvish II sent an impostor as the Dragon's proffered consort instead of his true heir. Therefore, we have come to reclaim the land that was, at that time, given in trust." He paused, then smiled the most dazzling smile Zanya had ever witnessed. "Unless, of course, you wish to negotiate a new contract."

Stunned silence greeted the words.

Anikke's head snapped up, honest confusion in every line of her expression. Something in Zanya relaxed—the girl still didn't know. There was hope for her yet.

The same couldn't be said of the regents. Doven might be lounging in his throne with the air of one watching an engaging sports match, but Bodin's gaze was stunned, as if he'd never considered he might be forced to answer publicly for the family's dirty secret. And Tislaina . . .

She was *enraged*.

The crowd began to murmur, mostly whispers confined to the edges of the room. Those with the most to lose—or gain, if House Roquebarre should fall—crowded near the front, hanging silently on every word.

Finally, Anikke spoke. "What do you mean, an impostor? Do you claim that my sister, the Princess Sachielle, is not truly of noble blood?"

"It's a lie, Your Majesty," Tislaina said swiftly. "They seek to confuse you to cover their own crimes. See how brazenly they bring your father's murderer to face you? They have no decency."

Long-buried anger stirred inside Zanya, and she took a single step forward. Tislaina's bright-blue eyes flitted anxiously toward her, and Zanya captured her gaze, holding it through sheer force of rage. "Decency?" she demanded, finally breaking her silence. "Why don't you tell your niece your definition of *decency*? Tell her about the drugs you provided to torture Sachielle. Tell her about the men you brought in to *test* her."

Tislaina gripped the arms of her throne, her face ghostly pale. "We should have cut out your tongue," she hissed. "A handmaid has no need of one."

"And neither does an assassin," Zanya countered, caressing the hilt of her dagger. The Void-steel sang to her now, an eager hum every time she touched it. It wanted what she wanted—the blood of those who had wounded Sachi's heart and body. *Vengeance*, righteous and bloody vengeance.

But that wasn't what Sachi desired from this confrontation. She wanted the truth told, the people of the Sheltered Lands protected. So Zanya eased her hand away from the knife and turned her back on the dais. The court faced her, hundreds of pairs of eyes eager for her words. Eager for drama and gossip, for the chance that whatever she revealed today would topple their enemies and allow them to climb.

"The Lover speaks the truth," she announced, raising her voice to carry to the far reaches of the audience hall. "Almost twenty years ago,

High Priest Nikkon took Sachielle from the orphanage where she had lived since birth. I know because he took me, as well."

Someone in the crowd gasped. Murmurs started, whispers flying around the edges of the room like a quiet rumble. Zanya only lifted her voice again.

"The queen allowed the deception because she had recently lost a child. She didn't want the next one born of her body to be sacrificed to the Dragon. Sachielle was raised as a princess but trained as an assassin. King Dalvish II intended to break faith with the High Court not just by refusing to send them his blood to bind to the land, but by slaying the Dragon."

She turned back to face Anikke, who stared at her, stricken. Given what Zanya knew of the royal family, it was possible that Sachielle's absent-minded kindness had been the closest thing to affection this girl had truly known. And Zanya was about to rip away the only family member who had ever treated her well.

"I'm sorry, Anikke," she said softly. "Sachielle still thinks fondly of you, blood or no. She was the one who wanted to come here. She was sure you couldn't be responsible for the horrors they've committed in your name."

"Where is she?" Anikke asked just as softly.

"Held captive in the Empire. The Empire your father collaborated with—"

"Outrageous!" Tislaina shrieked, cutting her off. "You expect this court to listen to the ravings of some power-mad maid? Look at her—"

"We are all looking at her, sister," Doven interjected mildly. "Can you not see the way the shadows around her consume the light? Can you not *feel* what she is in your very bones?"

"Evil!" Tislaina retorted.

"Yes, rather." Doven sounded more curious than outraged, though. "My Lord Lover, might I ask how you find yourself traveling so willingly with a murderer who was clearly born of the Endless Void?"

Aleksi's brilliant smile didn't fade, but it took on an edge sharper than Zanya's Void-steel blade. "Such things you say about my sister. I thought you were smarter than that, Doven."

"Clearly not."

"Very well." Aleksi focused his attention on Queen Anikke as he spoke, his words ringing with *truth*. "The Void has its place in creation, as do we all. Without it, we could not exist, for there are no beginnings without an end. And evil? Your Majesty must know that evil can easily be the dominion of those who have been touched by the Dream." He looked pointedly at Doven. "Your family proves that."

Tislaina sputtered. "Why are we discussing this at all? Bodin, *arrest—*"

"No."

The gentle, clear voice cut through the muttering of the court and the bickering of the regents. Queen Anikke rose from her chair, drew herself up to her full height, and stared directly at Aleksi. "My Lord, it appears I am ignorant of some of the choices made by my predecessors. Will you, as a representative of the High Court of Dreamers, grant me leave to seek the truth before you revoke your protection?"

Could Aleksi hear the plea inside those careful words? Could he see the terrified girl beneath the proud young queen? Sachi had been right all along—whatever had happened here, it had not been at Anikke's behest. She was just the latest victim of House Roquebarre, and perhaps its cruelest because *she* truly shared their blood.

Aleksi stepped forward, heedless of Bodin's threatening posture and Tislaina's protests. He took Anikke's face between his hands and smiled down at her. "I know what your heart wants, my child, just as I know these others'. Yours is a loving soul, and I don't see as many of those as I would like. So yes, I give you leave."

Anikke smiled, and the regents shifted uncomfortably.

"What's more, I offer you my blessing of protection." He touched the young queen's forehead. "For as long as your soul seeks truth and love, no harm will come to you. Upon my word and power as a Dreamer of the High Court."

This was too much for the court. They exploded into shouts of religious fervor and pleas for further blessings. Someone shouted Anikke's name. A particularly overwhelmed noblewoman sank to her knees at the front of the crowd. "Long reign to Anikke the Blessed!"

Another courtier dropped to their knee, and then another, until it was a wave of rustling fabrics behind Zanya, and cry after cry filled the air. "Anikke the Blessed!" and "Our Blessed Queen!"

Emboldened by the cheers of her court and Aleksi's promised protection, a flush-cheeked Anikke turned to Zanya. "I wish to speak to you about Princess Sachielle. Will you dine with me at the high table tonight?"

Tislaina drew in a breath that almost popped her bodice. "Absolutely *out* of the quest—"

Anikke held up a hand without looking around. Her aunt's gaze flew to Aleksi, who arched one eyebrow. Her teeth snapped together.

The young queen didn't bother to hide her small smile of triumph. "My sister's old rooms are available for your comfort. I trust no one needs show you to them. We still dine after the fifth bell. I look forward to renewing our acquaintance, Zanya."

Because reinforcing her status to the court mattered, Zanya bowed to her. And lied cheerfully. "I look forward to it, Your Majesty."

As Anikke held out a hand and invited Aleksi to adjourn to her private library to begin negotiations, Zanya assessed the three regents.

Prince Bodin seemed at a loss for what to do. Defiance against the High Court had never come naturally to him, and it appeared that direct defiance in the face of a god was simply beyond him. He melted to the side and fell in behind Anikke and Aleksi like a relieved guard dog.

Disappointing, really. Having an excuse to kill him would have been helpful. But it would be best for Anikke if at least *one* member of her family proved loyal to her in the end.

Princess Tislaina more than made up for it. She remained sitting in her duplicate throne, beringed hands gripping the arms so tightly Zanya was amazed she hadn't left dents in them. Her hate-filled eyes followed the progression out of the room before swinging back to Zanya.

She didn't have to speak the words. Zanya saw her own death in those icy blue eyes, and only prayed the woman was reckless enough to attempt it on her own. Zanya would take true pleasure in ending her life, but it would be easier to explain it away if it was a legitimate case of self-defense.

Not that an inability to explain herself would stop Zanya. Anikke would never sit firmly on that throne while Tislaina lived.

As Zanya turned toward the exit, the final regent caught her eye. Prince Doven had slipped from his throne swiftly enough, but he loitered near the door that held the swiftest path to Sachi's rooms. He assessed her openly as she approached, gaze dragging from her new boots up her body, lingering on her Void-steel studded armor before sweeping over her face.

"It's a pity I didn't visit more," he murmured as Zanya reached the door. "I heard stories about you, of course, but they left out a few things. What fun we could have had."

Zanya flicked her eyes down to the sword belted at his waist. It was pristine, almost untouched, the scabbard encrusted with jewels that dotted the hilt, as well. A rich man's show-toy, not a warrior's weapon. "I don't think you would have enjoyed it any more than the rest of them did," she said, not slowing her step.

She was past him and out the door when his final words drifted back to her, and the eagerness in them prickled warning down her spine. "I suppose we'll find out."

So Zanya would be killing *two* regents before she left this castle.

Hopefully, Sachi wouldn't be too angry with her.

Chapter Twenty-Four
WITCHING MOON

Week Two, Day Ten
Year 3000

The rest of the day almost made Sachi appreciate the years of practice she'd had in smiling through her pain and horror back at Dalvish's court. How many times had she spent her afternoons being drugged and beaten, only to be expected to charm a cadre of diplomats through a state dinner that same evening?

She could do this. After growing up in Castle Roquebarre, she could do anything. She could dress in heavy, embroidered brocade and a fortune's worth of jewels. She could walk down the hallways toward the grand ballroom with her head held high, smile vaguely as she was announced as the guest of honor. Nod regally to Sorin's guests.

She could even allow Sorin to take her hand and lead her through the ballroom, which had been lavishly decorated in shades of silver and blue, to the raised platform at one end. It was nothing as simple or functional as a dais, but rather three tiered levels, each one higher and smaller than the last. An ornate throne sat on the top tier, while a more delicate one encrusted with sapphires sat just below it, on the second.

The overall effect was that of a particularly gaudy wedding cake, and Sachi had to bite the inside of her cheek until it bled to keep from laughing hysterically.

She also took a measure of morbid amusement in the fact that her education at Dalvish's court would likely be the thing that carried her through her time in the Empire and helped her survive it—*if* she managed to survive it. According to Nikkon and the others who had overseen her training, they'd been preparing her to face the dangers of Dragon's Keep—and its master's nonexistent mercies.

Hilarious. Ash had treasured her from the very beginning, even when he thought her fear would remain, a permanent and insurmountable wall between them. He'd even treated her kindly after he realized she'd been sent to end his life. Cherished her. *Loved* her.

But now? She was most certainly in the court of a madman whose capricious whims had the potential to ruin or end lives. And here, her training would *shine*.

"You are not dancing," Sorin observed from his perch. "I would like to know why."

Looking up at him felt ridiculous, but what choice had she, when he so obviously put himself above her? "Because I don't feel like it, Your Majesty."

"Then what *do* you feel?"

Alone. She came so close to saying it aloud that she could taste each cold, acrid syllable on her tongue.

When she'd left the capital, bound for Dragon's Keep, she'd had Zanya with her—not only as a companion but as a co-conspirator, another soul to bear the burden of the secrets she carried. Before that, when she'd suffered in isolation at Nikkon's hands, Sachi had always known that Zanya was *with her* in all the ways that mattered.

Now, she was truly on her own for the first time in her life, and she hadn't been prepared for how lonely it would be. The Empire was a vicious place, with sharp words and condescension and *violence* at every turn. The closest things Sachi had to friends here were her maid—a woman who thought she was ignorant at best, and blasphemous at worst—and a god who was obviously using Sachi to further her own ends.

Ash and Zanya weren't here. And though she missed them desperately, Sachi was glad. She only enjoyed a modicum of safety because Sorin wanted her here, had some grand, imagined use for her. But the two of them? The only things Sorin had planned for them were pain and eventual death.

No.

Sachi's vision blurred into a haze of white. The throne beneath her rattled, and she clenched her hands on the arms until the sapphires bit into her skin. She breathed in deeply as the room began to spin, and bit by bit, the haze cleared.

Almost. Here and there, an afterimage lingered—golden ribbons of light that trailed behind some of the people in the ballroom, servants and partygoers alike. Sachi blinked to clear her vision, but the ribbons remained until they slowly faded.

Across the ballroom, Enzi spoke with Varoka and a willowy blonde that Sachi recognized from her formal introduction—Grand Duchess Eirika of Kelann. The Stalker. She was fashionably dressed, impeccably styled, and she eyed Sachi with a mixture of brutal pragmatism and contempt. Trying to decide if she was useful, perhaps, or if she truly had the ear of the Emperor.

Sachi wasn't sure herself. She knew that, whether Sorin truly trusted them or not, he leaned heavily on his court. They held his kingdoms, lent him their strength and support when needed. And when Ash and the others arrived to fight the war the Phoenix had predicted, the Grand Dukes and Duchesses—with the possible exception of Gwynira—would stand and fight for Sorin. Sachi still didn't know what sorts of damage they could wreak, but she suspected it would be significant. Deadly.

The smart plan would be to sow discord between Sorin and his court. Any wedges she could manage to drive between him and his closest allies could only serve Sachi's purposes. She had already considered but then discarded the notion, deeming it too soon to attempt anything of the sort. But that was a rational analysis, wasn't it? It was based on weighing her acquaintance with Sorin against the centuries of dubiously loyal service he'd enjoyed from his court. But Sorin wasn't rational, and Sachi wasn't just the woman he'd chosen to be his future Empress.

She was irreplaceable.

More so than his court?

There was only one way to find out.

"I am unhappy, Sorin." The words held the full weight of her truth. "Lonely. Your court does not care for me."

"What?"

She met his bewildered gaze. "They do not want me here."

He dismissed her words with a wave of his hand. "Nonsense."

"Look at them, Your Majesty," Sachi urged. "Truly *look*, and then tell me I'm wrong."

He left his throne and dropped down to Sachi's tier. His hand fell to her shoulder as he looked around the ballroom, studying the assembled members of his court. Their posture, their faces.

Finally, his jaw tightened in silent confirmation, and he pulled Sachi from her seat to stand beside him. "They do not decide," he whispered fiercely. "They will feel as I instruct them to feel and do as I command. Does that satisfy you, Sachielle?"

She squeezed his fingers and allowed a carefully calibrated blend of gratitude and admiration to shine from her eyes. "Thank you, Your Majesty."

"Now . . ." He lifted her hand and pressed a lingering kiss to the back of it. "Let's have a demonstration, shall we?"

"As you wish."

Sorin clapped sharply, and the music stopped. He surveyed the crowd for a moment, the silence broken only by the gentle rustle of elegant fabrics and the clinking of glass stemware. Then he raised his arm, where a goblet full of shimmering liquid had appeared in his hand.

"A toast," he boomed. "To Lady Sachielle, Queen of Dreams, the future Empress of the Nine Kingdoms." As the assembly echoed his words, he cast pointed looks at his court.

But his inclusion of all their holdings in her title served its purpose. They shifted uncomfortably or even seethed at the reminder that Sorin intended to give her precedence over them, in name if not in practice. His meaning was perfectly clear, and if anyone doubted it, they had only to look at Demir's battered face and blood-filled eyes.

To anger Sachi was to anger the Emperor himself.

Enzi approached the dais. He stopped at the base of it, bowed low, and held out his hand. "I seek the blessing of a dance, my lady."

Placing herself within Enzi's reach was very nearly the last thing Sachi wanted to do, but to reject his overture would cause a scene—or, leagues worse, show fear. So she joined him on the ballroom floor, braced for all manner of ugly remarks and disgusting advances.

None came. Enzi smiled politely, inquired after her enjoyment of the ball, wished her well, and then fled the moment the dance was over. Baffled, Sachi stared after him until Varoka approached with the enthusiastic offer of a drink, specially concocted by the palace chefs to celebrate the occasion.

And so it went. Gwynira pulled her into a conversation with an artist, an architect who had always longed to see the Builder's ancient work and had a million questions about the capital of the Sheltered Lands and Castle Roquebarre. Even Demir was pleasant, making small talk as if his brutal beating from that morning had never happened.

So when the Stalker approached to beg a dance with a smile, Sachi anticipated more of the same.

"You honor me, Grand Duchess."

The woman scoffed as she took Sachi's hand in hers and placed the other on Sachi's hip. "You must call me Eirika. May I call you Sachielle?"

"Of course."

Eirika hummed and cast a glance at the dais, where Sorin had retaken his throne and watched their dance with avid interest. "I'm rather impressed, you know. The Emperor loathes sharing power, yet you've already tricked him into declaring for you. And publicly, no less. Oh, but I underestimated you."

This was more like what Sachi had expected from Sorin's court. She steeled her spine and smiled vaguely. "Sorin appreciates what I have to offer."

"I'm sure he does." The corner of Eirika's mouth ticked up. "Or he would, if you ever planned on giving him a single precious drop of your power."

"He has power enough of his own."

Eirika threw back her head and laughed. "Does he? Charming. And not wholly accurate, I would say."

Sachi almost faltered. The words felt like a harder version of Lyssa's whispered revelations, a tiny bit of substance wrapped in the shell of an offhand remark. "What do you mean?"

"Ask him. I dare you." Eirika's dark eyes glittered, and she laughed again. "You could likely find a way to do it that reeks of earnest honesty yet allows you to keep your secrets. I see you, Princess Sachielle. Dragon's consort. You always tell the truth, but oh, you are *so careful* about how you tell it. Did Nikkon teach you that?"

"Nikkon taught me many things," Sachi told her flatly. "Would you like an exhaustive list?"

"Hardly. He wasn't exactly my favorite person in the world." Eirika paused. "But you could be."

Sachi stared at her in disbelief. "I can't imagine what use you would have for me."

"Ugh, false modesty." The tempo of the music changed slightly, and Eirika pulled Sachi closer. "Can you not see? You can continue to perform your magic act on Sorin, promising him the Dream and all your affections, yet never quite delivering. I'm sure it will work for at least a few centuries. Meanwhile . . ."

"I further your interests while I whisper sweet nothings to the Emperor," Sachi finished.

"I *knew* I liked you," Eirika whispered fiercely.

"And in return?"

Eirika's dark eyes flashed red. "In return? Why, I make sure you survive long enough to fully enjoy being Empress of the Nine Kingdoms. So many things can happen at court. Allegiances change, my lady. And fortunes rise and fall."

Faster than the tides, Sachi suspected. Whether the offer was genuine or some sort of test, it mattered not. Her answer would be the same. "Wherever did Sorin *find* all of you?"

"Find us?" Eirika blinked, then lit up like a child with a brandnew puppy. "You think he found us? Oh, that's priceless. I want this moment encased in amber." She leaned in, close to Sachi's face, vicious red flashing in her eyes once more. "He only found poor little Varoka. The rest of us . . . *he made.*"

The words were impossible, unthinkable . . . but again, they tasted of truth. "What?"

"Mmm. Pulled us straight from the Dream like good little toy soldiers." Eirika giggled and spun Sachi in a dizzy circle. "Oh, you didn't know. I love it."

Sachi shuddered. If Sorin had truly done what Eirika claimed, that meant he was more powerful than any of the others. Stronger than the High Court. Stronger even than *Zanya*, in all her glory.

And if the war that the Phoenix had predicted did come to bloody fruition, it wouldn't simply be Ash and his friends against Sorin. They'd be facing their own worst mirror images . . . and a god-emperor mad enough to have pulled them from his will and dreams.

Chapter Twenty-Five
WITCHING MOON

Week Two, Day Ten
Year 3000

Zanya was still staring out the windows of Sachi's old chambers when the fifth bell rang.

There wasn't much to do to prepare for dinner. Nothing could entice her to remove one scrap of her armor until she was quit of this place. She needed it to help insulate her against the memories of being small and vulnerable and *hurt* by the people who called this beautiful palace home.

She was as prepared for dining with the queen as she could possibly be. She simply didn't want to.

No one had touched Sachi's quarters since they'd left a few moons ago. It was jarring to stand here, where nothing had changed, as if she hadn't been remade into an entirely new person over those scant weeks.

The view out the window held no answers. Siren's Bay churned uneasily, as if it had caught the mood from the capital. Whitecaps broke against each other as waves swelled to the height of a grown man before crashing against the shore. In the distance, Zanya could barely make out the island where the Siren's keep perched high on a cliff.

Seahold. Where she'd fought Ash, and almost killed him. Where Sachi had plunged a dagger into her own heart to save them both.

Where Zanya had manifested, tearing open the power of godhood.

"Are you not coming to dinner?"

The low, rumbling voice behind her was familiar, but unexpected. Zanya glanced back, surprised to see Ulric crossing the room toward her. "What are you doing here? Is something wrong?"

"No, quite the opposite. It seems like you've done a wonderful job turning the court against itself." He huffed his amusement. "They're like little sheep running in all directions. It's tempting to bite a few."

Something about the words wasn't quite right. Neither was the bright golden glow in Ulric's eyes as he came closer, stopping well within her personal space. His chest brushed against her back. His breath smelled of whisky, and something sharper. Raw liquor? "Have you been drinking?"

"Only a bit." He nuzzled her temple. "I missed you."

Zanya froze, her instincts screaming. Power prickled over her, but this wasn't the seductive darkness she associated with Ulric. This challenge roared up from someplace endlessly cruel, where *playing* wasn't a game, but something you did with your prey before you slaughtered them. The fingertips suddenly sliding up her arm weren't the soothing touch of family, but someone testing her boundaries. Seeing how far he could go.

She snatched at the shadows and vanished into them, appearing on the other side of the room with her hand gripping the hilt of her knife. "Who are you?"

Ulric's perfect eyebrows swept up above Ulric's golden eyes. "It's me, pretty shadow girl. Your Wolf." He prowled toward her, but there was nothing of Ulric's predatory glide in his movements. Too much arrogance. Too much swagger. And his smile was all teeth. "Don't tell me you haven't felt our connection. I knew the moment I laid eyes on you that you like a little monster in your man."

Zanya tightened her grip on her knife. "You're nothing like him. You might as well give up now."

"Ahh, well. A pity. In my defense, I only had descriptions to go on, and my source does have his prejudices." The man's face *rippled*, a confusing play of shadows and light that spilled down to swirl around his body. His hunting leathers vanished, replaced by familiar court finery. The face settled into the haughty smile she'd stared up at in the audience chamber.

"Better?" Prince-Regent Doven asked, smoothing one hand over his embroidered tunic. "Though it's a bit boring, if you ask me. These Roquebarres are so washed out. Pale skin, pale hair, pale eyes. Their features are as generic as dirt. Between you and me, I suspect their bloodlines haven't branched sufficiently in recent years."

"You're—" No, whatever this was, he clearly wasn't a member of the royal family. And now that he wasn't trying to hide it, power seethed from him the same way it seethed from the High Court.

The same way it had seethed from High Priest Nikkon.

"Of course, I mean that as no reflection on your beloved Princess Sachielle," he continued, as if she hadn't spoken. "Now, I've heard she's quite an eyeful. Even better than the portraits they have hanging around here. Lush and sweet, ripe for the plucking. I'm supposed to be meeting her tonight, you know. Before your theatrics, I had arranged to absent myself to one of my estates. No one at court knows where I *really* go, of course."

Ice flooded her veins, but she refused to react. Every word he uttered was that of a child with a stick poking at an animal, seeking a vulnerable spot. "You're from the Empire. Part of the Betrayer's . . . court."

"See? You're not nearly as stupid as Nikkon made you sound. I was worried I'd have to spell it out." His face rippled again, revealing a handsome man with a strong jaw, reddish-brown hair, and green eyes that might have been beautiful if they hadn't been so chillingly *hard*.

"You have the honor of addressing Grand Duke Hinrick, Guardian of the Kingdom of Inavihs. And occasional spy."

An invaluable spy, with a power like that. Though his faulty impression of Ulric would not have held up to the close scrutiny of anyone who knew him, Prince Doven was a much wiser target. Aside from his well-known reputation for hunting and horses, who at court truly knew the absent prince? "Did you kill Doven?"

"Mmm. He went on a final hunt, where he found prey intent on hunting *him*." Hinrick smiled and edged closer, his gaze flicking to her hand wrapped around the hilt of the Void-blade. "Between us, it wasn't much of a challenge. He was a lackluster hunter, at best. Far more accomplished at hunting pleasure in bed, and even that he usually paid for in lieu of earning."

He edged another step closer, testing her response, and it felt the same as when he'd stroked her arms. Pushing her boundaries again, creeping over them to see how far was too far. He liked the idea of playing with her. *Scaring* her.

He also enjoyed the sound of his own voice. Zanya gave him what he wanted to see—a nervous woman taking a step back—and kept asking questions. "How long ago did you replace him?"

"Oh, not long. After you killed Nikkon." He bared his teeth in a sudden smile. "That *was* you, wasn't it? They said a mistress saw you slaughter the king. But I figured Nikkon would have groveled once he got a proper look at you. You shine with the power of the Void."

"He groveled," Zanya agreed. "It wasn't enough."

"Brutal girl." He sounded delighted. "Poor old Nikkon. You probably gave him mercy, you know. The Emperor was *very* upset with him for not realizing he'd found the future Empress. Though I suppose he might be in a forgiving mood, now that he has her. Tell me, was the Dragon *very* angry? Did he moan and brood and break things?"

Ice would be warmer than what flooded her now. The frozen midnight *nothingness* of the Void wrapped around her as she studied her prey. The foolish inconsequential verbal sticks could only shatter on her armor. It wasn't worth getting upset over the words of a dead man. The only question was how she would reveal his nature to the Mortal Court before she did away with him.

So she smiled at him.

In the space between heartbeats, Hinrick crossed the remaining space between them and slammed her back against the wall. Only that protective layer of black ice kept Zanya from stabbing him in the gut when he reached out to touch her face. "Look at you, so freshly made you still shine. Like a wobbly baby colt who doesn't know her own strength."

"Is that what you like?" Zanya asked conversationally. "Easy prey?"

Her words seemed to sting. Rage tightened his eyes, and he bashed a hand against the wall next to her head. "No, I like them with some fight. That's what's going to make you so much fun. You'll be the best hunt of my life, little deer."

The menacing threat rolled off his tongue, and it took everything in Zanya not to laugh. How could they *all* be like this? The guards who'd tried to put her in her place out of fear, the nobles who'd thought their power over a mere maid made them strong, even a god—all of them so pathetic, so *worthless*. Give them a scrap of power, and all they wanted to do was use it against someone else to make themselves feel bigger.

How small they must be inside. How ruined. And then she *did* laugh, letting the pity show on her face. "Is that it? Your best material? We can keep going if you have more. I can help. Are you going to teach me my place?"

"Someone should," he snarled.

"I can guess where you think it is," Zanya taunted him. "Go on. Put me there."

His hand flew back too fast for a mortal to see, but Zanya had to wait forever for his knuckles to crack across her face. The backhand would have shattered the cheekbone of a human, sent them flying. Zanya absorbed it by turning her head, then looked back at him, implacable and unimpressed, as she lifted a finger to her split lip. It had already begun to heal, but she wiped away the blood and smiled. "Feel better?"

Hinrick recoiled in surprise, but Zanya caught him by the throat before he could retreat, gripping hard enough to choke him. She forced him to his knees and bent over him, lowering her voice to an intimate whisper. "This is the part where I fight back," she murmured. "I hope it's everything you dreamed."

Then she kicked him through the wall.

Stone that had stood for thousands of years shattered at the force of his body smashing through it. Outside, someone screamed. Zanya ignored the clatter of silver—probably a servant abandoning a tray to flee—and lunged after Hinrick.

He was already shaking off the blow, climbing to his feet with blood dripping down the side of his face. "Beginner's luck," he snarled, then lunged for her. Zanya let the shadows take her just long enough to let him hit the wall face-first, then reappeared behind him. Fisting her hand in his hair, she crashed his face into stone again. She *heard* the crunch of bone this time, and he howled in pain.

"Enjoying the hunt?" she demanded.

"You're an abomination."

"So I've heard." She ground his shattered cheek into the stone. "Do you want to make this easy on both of us and come to dinner with me? You can explain who you really are to the court and queen, and perhaps I'll let you live."

"*Let* me live?" he scoffed. "I have chess games older than you, brat. I *will* go to dinner, just for the pleasure of spitting that child queen on my knife, and then—"

Zanya hauled him back and knocked his face into the wall again—only to watch in horror as the hair wrapped around her fist turned to waves of shimmering gold. Sachi's cute, upturned nose bled, and her full, perfect lower lip split as her face crashed into stone.

"Please," Sachi's voice begged, blood and tears running down her face. "Please stop hurting me—"

Zanya's brain screeched a warning, but she was already recoiling, horror flooding her in a wave so vast it shattered her protective shell. For a shuddering moment, all she could do was stare at Sachi's bloody face twisted into an expression of shocked betrayal. The tangy metallic scent of blood mixed with the salt of tears, and she choked on it as she stumbled back.

Not real! It's not real!

It took a heartbeat too long for Zanya's body to catch up, and a heartbeat was all he needed. In a clatter of footsteps he was gone, his form melting back into that of Prince Doven as he raced toward the grand dining room.

Cursing under her breath, Zanya sped after him. Shadows tickled her fingertips, offering her the promise of a shortcut. She could step through them and be at Anikke's side in the blink of an eye—but bursting from the Endless Void in a swirl of shadows in front of the entire court seemed unlikely to de-escalate tensions.

So she ran.

The palace was a maze of hallways that haunted her nightmares. She flew past doors leading to rooms full of terrible memories, each one fueling her rage as she sprinted after her prey. But as fast as she was, he was faster. She skidded around the final turn to see him disappearing into the grand dining room past two guards.

"Move!" she screamed, barreling toward them. Both unsheathed their swords, steel flashing in the torchlight as they attempted to block her. They'd be easy to kill, but they'd steal precious moments she didn't have.

Fuck de-escalation.

Reaching for the shadows, Zanya *stepped*.

She exploded from the Void in the middle of the room, near where performers played to entertain the court. Long tables flanked her on either side, and ahead of her, raised on a slight dais, the high table stretched the length of the room with Anikke at its center. Tislaina had claimed the seat to her left, but sliding into the empty chair on her right—

"*Anikke!*" she screamed as Doven lunged, the flash of silver damning Zanya for her caution. She should have traveled sooner, she should have—

The knife arced toward Anikke, then froze, mere inches from her heart.

Anikke stumbled back, pale with shock, knocking over her chair as screams filled the hall. Guards rushed toward the dais, only to stop short when they realized that Doven still wasn't moving. He stood, dagger in mid-swing, his face fixed in the rictus of a war cry.

Zanya started forward, only for Aleksi's voice to stop her. "I would appreciate it if you left him for me, love."

Zanya started as Aleksi strolled into the hall. He was the picture of relaxed ease, but she felt a strange sort of vibration when he passed her, almost like the tension that rolled through a room when Sachi was furious over some wrong or injustice. A protective rage, born not of darkness but of light.

Aleksi approached the dais, then stopped and studied Doven's immobile features. "Who are you? You are not Prince Doven, though you wear his face."

The disguised Hinrick just managed to mutter something.

"No, thank you. I'm not in the mood." Aleksi's brow furrowed. "Zanya?"

"Grand Duke Hinrick," she told him. "From the Empire."

"I should have guessed." Aleksi shook his head. "Such violence in your heart. Magenta streaked with rust red. But no matter. You will answer for your crimes."

He grabbed Hinrick by the shoulders and threw him over the high table. Still held immobile by Aleksi's magic, he was not able to break his fall, and the man hit the floor at the musicians' feet with a thud and a muffled, pained moan.

Aleksi rounded the table and addressed the lute player. He touched the musician's cheek gently, then smiled. "You know how much I adore and support your work, but I need the space to deal with a matter of some importance. If you would?"

The other musicians scattered immediately, though the lute player lingered a little longer, his eyes shining. "As my lord commands."

"Many thanks, love." Aleksi turned to the nearest guard. "I require two swords."

The guard paused, confused. "Two, my lord?"

"Two." Aleksi addressed the crowd. "Grand Duke Hinrick has made an attempt on Queen Anikke's life. In doing so, he has violated my blessing of safety. This offends me. Still, you all know me to be a fair man. I will not strike him down where he lies, but seek redress in combat."

Zanya barely managed to keep the grimace from her face as the guards fetched the weapons. Hinrick had proven himself to be a brutal fighter, and Aleksi was . . .

Aleksi.

He caught her gaze—and winked. "Don't worry about me, sweet Zanya." He hefted his sword as the magic prison melted away from Hinrick's growling form behind him. "Love is stronger than you think."

Hinrick rushed Aleksi's unguarded back, his blade raised. Aleksi spun, blocking the blow with a languor that belied his speed. Then he struck in return, delivering a quick slice to Hinrick's sword arm.

She saw the moment Hinrick decided to flee. He dropped his sword and turned, his form already melting into that of a servant in nondescript clothing. If he managed to evade their sight for even a moment, he could turn into anyone. *Be* anyone. He would escape.

The cry of warning caught in her throat as Hinrick rebounded off an invisible barrier. By the time he hit the floor, he wore the visage he had presented to Zanya as his own. Gasps filled the hall as he turned and tried again in a different direction, but with the same results.

Aleksi had retrieved Hinrick's discarded sword. He held it out to him now. "You will need this."

"I won't fight you," Hinrick spat.

Aleksi simply waited.

Hinrick shook his head. By the time he stilled, he looked like Zanya, and her gut roiled to see such a cruel beast wearing *her* face.

"I won't fight you," he said again, Zanya's shaking voice pouring from his lips in a desperate rasp. "Please."

It made for a pitiful sight, a terrified woman begging for her life. But seeing *herself* brought so low, made so pathetic—her grip on her knife tightened, the temptation to end this farce nearly overwhelming her.

But Aleksi only sighed. "I will not be moved by your games, and I don't care what face you wear. I see your heart, remember? Magenta streaked with rust red."

"Fine." Zanya's features melted away, and Hinrick glared at Aleksi with fury twisting his lips into a snarl. "Suit yourself."

Zanya's breath rushed out as he snatched the sword from Aleksi's hand and immediately attacked. He didn't hesitate as he rained Aleksi with a flurry of slices and stabs.

But Aleksi countered or parried every one, and with a grace that stunned not only the crowd, but Zanya, as well. He flowed across the floor like he was dancing instead of fighting. Every line of his body was beauty and pure elegance.

"People make assumptions, you see," Aleksi said conversationally as Hinrick charged him. He stepped aside, and Hinrick skidded to a stop just before hitting the unseen boundary of their dueling ground. "Love is soft, a tender emotion meant for moonlight and babies' blankets and a mother's kiss. They forget."

Hinrick had already fought Zanya, and his desperation grew as he began to tire. He started to make mistakes, allowing Aleksi to get past his guard.

And Aleksi struck.

"Love can be a blade." A slice across Hinrick's cheek. "A cudgel or a shield, harder than tempered steel."

Hinrick feinted and lunged. Aleksi bashed him in the head with the pommel of his sword, driving him back.

"Love can heal," he murmured. "But it can also wound. And it can be a fury that no one who has not yet loved another to the very depths of their soul could ever hope to comprehend."

Hinrick rushed Aleksi with a scream—and met the end of a blade. He and Aleksi both stared down at it, Hinrick in dumbfounded horror, and Aleksi with something almost like resignation.

"Love protects," he whispered gently, then dragged Hinrick closer, running the blade through his body. "It can even avenge."

After a gurgling moment, Hinrick slipped off the blade and fell to his knees. His face *bubbled*, shifting through features so fast he barely looked solid as Aleksi stepped back, raised his sword, and cleanly struck the fallen god's head from his body.

Chaos.

The room erupted, people scattering and guards rushing around. Aleksi handed his bloodied blade to one, as if depositing an empty wine goblet on a server's tray, and approached Zanya.

He pitched his voice low, so no one else would hear. "I don't like it. There was something odd about him."

"Odd how?"

"I don't know. Something almost . . . familiar."

A sudden wind whipped through the hall, blasting open windows. Thunder rattled the castle. A few new cries rose over the crowd as panic mounted, but a haunting hum vibrated through the room, growing louder as the notes twined with the rumble of thunder.

The ghostly song vibrated in Zanya's bones, scraping her nerves raw. But it swiftly became clear it was having the opposite effect on the crowd. Their shoving subsided. Shouts faded. A path opened up down the center of the room as if a gentle hand had decided to part them.

Framed by torchlight, Dianthe stood in the center of the double doorway. Her gown flowed around her, midnight blue at the base brightening up through the colors of the ocean until a high collar the white of cresting waves framed the dark skin of her face. Her black curls flowed unbound down her back. Behind her, two of the most beautiful men Zanya had ever seen proved to be the source of that unearthly hum.

The Siren stepped through the door, and people scrambled from their chairs and sank into deep bows as she passed.

At the high table, Tislaina's heavy makeup stood out garishly on her deathly pale face. Prince Bodin actually trembled. Aleksi, with his easygoing reputation as a devotee of love and peace, might have been popular, but for those who had lived their entire lives on Siren's Bay, always at the mercy of the sea, the Siren was not simply joy and blessings and crops and babies.

She was also the wrath of storms and the cold judgment of the unfathomable deep. After years of Nikkon urging disrespect, the regents had grown complacent. The High Court rarely left their keeps, after all. Many in the capital could go their whole lives without encountering one of them. How easy it must have seemed to wage war against the gods when you sent orphan girls and disposable soldiers in your stead.

It was different when the gods came to *you*.

Dianthe stopped next to the body of the Shapechanger and raised one eyebrow at Aleksi. "He must have angered you greatly. I haven't seen you so much as draw a blade in a hundred years."

"I take my blessings of safety seriously, sister."

Queen Anikke stepped forward and inclined her head. "My lady Siren. You are welcome in my home."

"Thank you, child." Dianthe's gaze swept across the table, lingering briefly on the two regents. "The last time I visited was at your birth. I see much has changed . . . and much has not."

Anikke swallowed, but lifted her chin. "Much *will* change in the days ahead. I have given my vow to the Lover that my kingdom will honor the High Court and protect *all* of your people."

"Then perhaps you will allow me to serve as your advisor at this transitional time in your reign. The rest of the High Court will be busy addressing other matters, but I suspect in the days ahead we will wish to strike a new accord with the Mortal Lords."

The young queen's eyes widened. "I would be honored, my lady."

Whatever spell had been cast over the crowd seemed to shatter. Murmurs immediately erupted, and Zanya hurried to Dianthe's side. "This wasn't part of the plan, was it? Did I do something wrong?"

"Plans change, little sister." Dianthe beckoned to Aleksi as she turned to fully face Zanya. "Word has just reached me that the Phoenix rides the waves with the Kraken. They sail for Dragon's Keep, where you and Aleksi must go. The time has come to bring Ash's consort home. I will hold the Sheltered Lands safe until you return."

Finally. She touched Dianthe's hand in thanks. As she turned to Aleksi, Anikke's voice rose behind her. "Is Sachi in danger? Can I help?"

The true concern in the words halted Zanya. She retraced her steps, climbed the dais, and stopped in front of Anikke. The girl had King Dalvish's eyes. His cheekbones, his hair. But the soft worry in her expression looked so much like Sachi. So did the stubborn set of her chin, and her determined posture—too young to carry such burdens, but standing proud in spite of them.

She might not be Sachi's sister by blood, but there was more than one way to be family, so Zanya gripped Anikke's hand. "Your job is to keep the people of the Sheltered Lands safe," she said firmly. "The Siren will help you. I'll bring your sister home."

"And I can see her?"

Such hope in her eyes. She didn't care if Sachi was her older sister by blood. It was clear that the scraps of kindness Sachi had bestowed upon her loomed large in a childhood otherwise barren of affection.

Sachi might never be able to look on the girl without a bittersweet ache, but Zanya knew that wouldn't stop her. "I know she'll want to see you."

"Thank you," Anikke whispered, releasing her hand.

Zanya nodded and reached for Aleksi. "Ready?"

"Never, my love. But let us go."

Zanya seized the shadows, and even the weight of carrying Aleksi didn't bother her. Not when she was traveling toward Sachi.

Chapter Twenty-Six
WITCHING MOON

Week Two, Day Ten
Year 3000

That night, Sachi escaped into the Dream.

She couldn't call it wandering this time. Instead, she moved between the gossamer layers of blinding white with desperate precision, and with only one goal—to warn the High Court of what she'd learned. She searched the places that felt most like them, determined to touch just one mind. Ash. Zanya. Elevia, Ulric, Inga. Naia, along with the entirety of the Raven Guard. She even looked for Camlia, just in case.

But she could find none of them in sleep, and she screamed her frustration to the vast emptiness of the Dream.

No, she refused to suffer defeat, not when the stakes were this high. The others had to have the truth before they invaded the Empire—that Sorin was no longer the god they had known. His power had grown so great that Sachi wasn't sure *what* he was anymore, only that if Ash and the others came here, unprepared, it could end in pure slaughter.

And it would be entirely her fault.

Think, Sachi. There had to be a way. Perhaps she should simply try to *go* to them, in life instead of in sleep. Wasn't that what she'd done when she'd finally found the Phoenix? Her heart *yearned* for Ash and Zanya, pulled her toward them both with an inexorable hunger that gnawed at her insides. If longing to be with them again was enough, she could make the trip in the span of a single heartbeat. And if there was ever a time or a reason to break her vow not to flee Sorin's custody, this was most certainly it.

She could find them. She could do this.

Sachi faced the full-length mirror in the corner of her bedchamber. Her own reflection stared back at her—pale and frantic, all clenched fists and gritted teeth—but she forced herself to breathe and look past the curves of her own face, past all the abstract lines and colors that came together to create an image.

To look deeper.

To look with *love.*

The room began to shift, moving around her in swoops and whirls that picked up speed until reality itself merely flashed by, skipping past in Sachi's peripheral vision. She kept her focus pinned on the mirror. On her goal.

Her feet lifted from the floor as the spinning intensified. As the room fell away.

She found Zanya first, standing in the courtyard at Dragon's Keep, her gaze fixed to the southwest. Toward the Empire.

"We're coming for you, Sachi," she whispered. "Just hold on."

Belatedly, Sachi realized that the courtyard was brimming with activity, with people rushing back and forth, preparing—

Preparing for battle.

The true import of Zanya's words sank in, and Sachi's desperation cranked even tighter. She moved closer, reaching for Zanya, but the same shimmering veil that had separated her from the Phoenix in those Imperial caverns was here, too. Thicker, so thick that she couldn't seem to break through it.

Kit Rocha

But she had to. Sachi strained, reaching for Zanya, pushing harder, until the veil pulsed and faltered.

Please, let this work.

But it did not fall. Sachi sagged, a cry of frustration and helplessness rising in her chest. What good was this ability if she couldn't use it when it mattered? To save the people she loved?

Abruptly, Zanya straightened and turned, her wild gaze flitting around the courtyard.

"What is it?" Ash asked in alarm.

"Witchwood roses," she whispered. "Sachi."

"Can you hear me?" Sachi gasped. "Please, Zan, you have to hear me. *Don't do it.* Don't come here—"

The world began to spin again, ripping her away. Sachi shrieked a denial, her pain and frustration shaking the very air around her. She reached for a stone wall, for the line of a fence, anything to halt her movement. If she could just touch something solid, something real . . .

Her last glimpse of that reality was of Zanya's stricken face, and Ash's voice followed her as she was swept away.

"Sachi!"

When the spinning stopped, she was back in her luxurious room in her luxurious palace, staring at her own tear-streaked reflection. A prisoner in a gilded cage.

Sachi squeezed her burning eyes tight, willing the tears of isolation and failure to stop. When they did, she went to the small room that housed her wardrobe, all the way to the ornate chest in the back that held her delicates. In the second drawer, she'd stowed two things: a gauzy, exquisite nightdress embroidered with delicate roses, and the dagger that Gwynira had given her.

She'd tucked them away in anticipation of the right moment, which was apparently now. Because she'd run out of time. If Zanya and Ash and the others were on their way, she had to act quickly.

Even if her destiny was to fall here, at Sorin's merciless hands, then she would at least take him with her.

266

And Ash and Zanya would be *safe*.

Sachi slipped into the nightdress and tied the dagger along her arm. Most people preferred low light in their bedchambers, and with some careful maneuvering, she should be able to stow the hidden blade beneath the mattress or a pillow before . . .

Before.

She brushed her hair and opened her chamber door in her bare feet. The guards blocked her way, but she beckoned them before her.

"I wish to see the Emperor," she told them haughtily. "You will take me to him."

Sorin must have given them standing orders that this request was not to be denied, because they immediately turned and began to march down the darkened hall. Sachi followed, lagging behind until they had to slow their steps.

A future Empress would not hurry to catch them. *They* would have to wait for *her*.

Sorin answered the door to his chamber himself and blinked when he saw her. "Lady Sachielle."

"Your Majesty." She curtsied, low and deferential. "I was too excited to sleep."

It took only a moment for anticipation to bleed into his gaze. "Leave us," he ordered the guards, then gestured her in. "Please."

He stood on her unarmed side, so she lingered as she brushed past him. "Thank you."

His bedchamber was nothing like what she'd imagined. The light *was* low, and the decor was impeccable, but it was a sparse, soulless place that felt cold despite its warm temperature. There were no objects or furnishings dedicated only to comfort. Even the art was technically perfect but pedestrian, just realistic depictions of cityscapes and his castle in Kasther.

"It's beautiful," Sachi told him even as she quelled a shiver.

He hummed in agreement and lifted an exquisite, empty wineglass. "Would you like a drink?"

"Yes, please." She would not drink it, but the glass itself could serve as a weapon in a pinch. "I hope I'm not disturbing you."

He smiled as he splashed blood-red wine into her glass. "No need to be coy, Sachielle. We both know why you're here."

Do we? She lowered her lashes as she accepted the glass. "My singular goal is to please you, my lord." *And then.*

"Oh, you do." He tipped her face up with his hand beneath her chin. "You were brilliant tonight. Beyond my wildest expectations. I thought for sure I would have to rescue you at least once, but you handled them all flawlessly."

Looking away would be the absolute wrong choice, and Sachi almost did it anyway. "Your faith in me does not go unnoticed."

"Or unappreciated, I hope." He leaned closer and brushed a soft, open-mouthed kiss over her lips. "I wish to show you something."

Sachi glanced over at his bed. "But . . ."

"Eager minx. There's plenty of time for that." Sorin laughed and took her hand. "Varoka thinks it too soon, but I had already decided."

"Decided what?"

"That when you were ready to offer yourself to me, you'd be ready to see this."

The sudden, eager quality of his voice scraped over Sachi's nerves like metal against metal, and the air was thick and heavy with warning. Something was about to happen, something momentous.

And inescapable.

She barely had time to set her glass down as Sorin dragged her back toward the door and then through it, nearly slamming her shoulder against the frame in his haste.

The guards were long gone, and the hallway was empty as Sorin led her to a rounded stone column inset with a completely smooth set of metal doors and stopped before it.

There were no handles, but Sorin spoke a single word. "Open."

The metal doors slid apart, revealing a small box lined with mirrors and the same gilded wallpaper that decorated Sachi's bedchamber. "What is this?"

"A conveyor. It will take us down beneath the palace."

Before she could ask any more questions, Sorin pushed her into the enclosure, stepped in after her, and pressed a large button on the wall. Immediately, Sachi's stomach lurched as they began to descend rapidly. She tried to stumble away from Sorin in favor of clinging to one of the rails along the wall, but he held her arm tight.

Thank the *Dream* it wasn't the one where she'd hidden her dagger.

"Everything will make sense once you know," he muttered, but with only a fraction of his attention. "You'll see."

The conveyor stopped, and he dragged her out and into a—

Sachi stared, her heart galloping. It was a room of sorts, positively cavernous, with curving walls made of sheer panes of glass, reinforced only with thin strips of metal. The delicate nature of the construction frankly terrified her because they were *under water*, beneath not only the palace but the lake, as well.

"It's wondrous, isn't it?"

In the center of all this precarious beauty hovered a huge glowing ball of light. It swirled with a familiar warmth, and equally familiar golden ribbons. They wrapped around but also revealed little sparkling prisms just like the ones she'd seen floating above Ash's bed.

It felt like the vibrations she'd sensed since her arrival.

It felt like the Dream.

It felt like *her*.

Sachi drew in a ragged breath. "What *is* this?"

"The Heart of the Empire." Sorin gazed up at it with naked pride. "The secret to our bounty, our power."

The longer Sachi stared at it, the more it seemed to unravel before her eyes. It wasn't solid at all, wrapped in a few ribbons of golden light. It was *millions* of them, spun together in a pulsing nexus of power.

"Varoka was the key," he murmured as he lifted his hand. His fingers trailed through the threads, and the light reacted to him, crawling over his skin. "I'd been here five hundred years already. There had been progress, of course. My stronghold at Kasther was well underway, but I needed *more*. Then one of my priests brought her to me. Such an odd child, with one foot always in the Dream. Some days, she barely saw the mortal world."

One ribbon unfurled, reaching toward Sachi, and she saw that it wasn't a ribbon at all.

It was a chain, like the ones she'd glimpsed earlier in the ballroom.

A sick suspicion took root in her gut, one she could barely fathom, much less verbalize. "Where did all this come from?"

"Varoka could do the most amazing things. But the most astounding was that she'd figured out how to take the power of someone else's wasted dreams into herself, feeding on them to make her own dreams come true."

A cold chill that had nothing to do with her thin, mostly decorative nightgown rattled Sachi. "Sorin, *where did it come from?*"

He didn't even look at her. His gaze was still riveted to the dancing light. "It isn't everyone in the Empire, of course, though not for lack of trying. Most see the benefits of being born in a hospital under the care of well-trained healers. And the only way to receive the mark of citizenship is to have a child blessed by the priests at birth. Varoka personally trained them all. Just a simple web woven around the newborn . . ."

Sachi's mind screamed, not only at the revelations but at Sorin's mild tone. This was how he'd manifested the rest of his court, how he'd constructed soaring marvels of architecture and industry. How he maintained his iron grip on control.

"You take it from them," she whispered, then whirled on him, furious. "How much? How much do you steal from them?"

"I don't *steal*." He threw his arms wide. "Sachi, don't you see? Most of them wouldn't know what to dream for in the first place. It's power that would otherwise go to waste because they don't have the capacity to imagine a better world."

As if that was *his* determination to make. "They were born from the Dream. You have no right to separate them from it. These people—*your* people. You're supposed to protect them, Sorin, *that's* what a ruler does."

"This *is* protection!" He waved at the spinning ball of light. "It powers everything we do! The transportation that eases their lives. The innovations. Small people have such petty dreams, Sachielle. You must know that. You've *seen* them. Now they needn't dream of soft beds or food or shelter, because I provide that. And I take so little in return."

"No, you take everything," she countered. "If they volunteered, if you *asked*, maybe it would be different." Her head and heart both pounded with the force of her anger. "But you would never do that, would you, Sorin? Because you're a coward. They might say no, and then where would you be?"

He stared at her with such shocked hurt, as if he'd held out a prized gift and she'd slapped it from his hands. "If they said no, it would only be because they lacked the vision to understand—"

Sachi cut him off. "No, it would be because they know exactly who you are. You aren't giving them opportunity and largesse, you're giving them *your* rigid, narrow idea of it. You're so absolutely certain that your way is the right one. It has never occurred to you that any single one of these lost, violated souls could have more beautiful dreams than you. Because you're a tyrant." Tears streamed down her face. "The Betrayer."

He recoiled as if she'd slapped him. But, just as fast, his pain gave way to rage. "How dare you? I built this *for you*. Once you manifest your full gifts, and with the power I've collected for you, there will be *nothing* we cannot build together. We could remake the face of the world if it pleased us." He scoffed. "You were supposed to be better than those backward fools squatting in their hovels. You're the spirit of *creation* itself. Don't you yearn to build something astounding?"

All that concerned him was what he wanted. His plans, his power. Despite his words, Sachi was no different to him than the people he'd robbed over the centuries. She only existed to serve his needs.

Could he even hear that? Would he understand, or did it simply not matter to him at all?

"You don't love me," she said. "You feel entitled to me."

He stared at her in blank incomprehension. "What does that have to do with anything?"

"You want to possess me," she went on. "And you don't care how I feel about it or what I want."

"I saw you," he snarled. "Three thousand years ago. I could taste what you were even then. I knew what you would become. You were *promised* to me by the Dream itself. What is love compared to destiny?"

"You saw me," she agreed, "but I wasn't there for you. I was there for *Ash*."

"Liar," he spat.

"It's the truth." Some of Sachi's anger ebbed, replaced by sadness and a loneliness that made her very bones ache. "Surely you remember what it feels like, having him love you? You must, or you wouldn't have spent thousands of years trying to replace what you threw away."

Sorin's face went chillingly blank. "I would not pursue this line of discussion, if I were you."

This was the man she'd watched rain violence on his own people under the auspices of a celebration. The one who had drugged her, and who had calmly thrashed the Beast half to death before sitting down to enjoy his breakfast. A cold, trembling knot formed in Sachi's stomach, but she squared her shoulders.

Perhaps she *should* continue to provoke him. Here she stood, armed for the first time since her arrival in the Empire, surrounded by thousands of threads of the Dream. If she didn't manage to cut Sorin's throat, surely those bits of the Dream would respond to her in a time of true crisis. Stories of the Dreamers' awakenings often involved injuries near or even unto death.

At least here, in this isolated space, it would only be her life at risk.

So she stepped forward. "You're a small man, made smaller by his fear. And I am not afraid of you."

He stared down at her with utter disdain that finally settled into disappointment. "You speak those words so forcefully, as if you ever had anything to fear. I see now that Varoka was correct, and you're too young and frivolous to understand."

"Oh, I understand perfectly," she taunted. "You're not a god at all. You're so weak you have to steal your power from humans."

A thunderous scowl twisted his features. "Silence."

"Ash always said he was afraid another war with you would break the world—"

"Silence!"

"—but I think he just felt *sorry* for you—"

He advanced on her so quickly she barely saw him move. He wrapped his hand around her throat and lifted her. "I said *be silent!*"

Sachi's toes barely scraped the floor, and Sorin was gripping her neck so tightly she wouldn't have time to run out of air. She would lose consciousness from lack of blood flow first.

She had to act quickly.

She reached into her fluttering sleeve, drew the dagger, and positioned it to strike in a few fluid movements. But Sorin must have sensed its magic the moment it cleared the scabbard, because he flinched violently, and the blade skated harmlessly across his ribs in a shallow slice.

He wrenched the dagger from Sachi's hand with a cry more of anger than pain and threw her to the floor. She landed on her shoulder, and a white-hot bolt of sheer agony shook her entire body.

Sorin stared at the dagger with a bewilderment that slowly changed to rage. "Gwynira," he growled. "Treacherous, sentimental *bitch*. I should have known."

Sachi tried to scramble back, but Sorin grasped her injured arm and dragged her to her feet. She cried out, and the writhing ball of Dreams in the center of the room pulsed brighter than ever. Seeking.

Reaching for *her*.

"No. I've come too far to harm you, Sachielle. But we can't have *that*. Not yet." His hand dipped into his pocket and returned with one of those hated silver cylinders.

"That won't help. I will *never* stop fighting you. And Ash will come for me—"

"Of course he will. He's little more than an animal, but he's a possessive one." His fingers closed even tighter around her arm, and he jerked her close. "Do you think I didn't plan for that?"

Sachi struggled, but she couldn't break free. Sorin brought the injector down forcefully on her bruised neck, and more pain mixed with her fear as the room began to swim in darkness. Not fear for herself, but for Zanya and for Ash.

Especially when Sorin's next words followed her down into oblivion. "He'll come for you, sweet Sachielle. And then I'll be rid of him, once and for all."

Chapter Twenty-Seven
WITCHING MOON

Week Three, Day One
Year 3000

Naia was the one who felt the Kraken coming.

The chaos in the courtyard cut off abruptly as Naia gasped and swayed. Zanya barely reached her in time to keep her from going to her knees on the cobblestone path to the main gates, and even with support the young water nymph hauled in gasping breaths. "Something's happening. Something—"

A roar sounded on the other side of the keep walls, followed by the mighty crash of water being violently displaced.

Ash instructed the guards to open the gates. "It's time. Make sure you have what you need for the fight ahead."

"I don't understand." Zanya gently handed Naia off to Inga. "What's happening?"

"The Kraken." He tried to hide his exasperation as he gestured to the walkway that led across the vast caldera lake. After all, the man was about to risk a great deal to help them fight the Betrayer and retrieve Sachi. "He likes to make an entrance."

Still looking confused, Zanya strode past him. Ulric followed with an unapologetic shrug. "It *is* fun to watch," he reminded Ash.

Everyone else clearly agreed with him. The Raven Guard streamed past him, followed by Elevia. Only Aleksi and Inga remained, both steadying Naia as her color returned.

Ash moved to her side. "Feeling better?"

"Yes, thank you." Naia's cheeks had flushed, and it didn't look entirely like embarrassment. "What *was* that? It felt like the water . . . *welcomed* someone."

No doubt it had. Einar might not hold the Siren's sway over water wherever it rested, but the element certainly seemed almost as fond of its pirate prince as it was of its queen. "It's easier to show you. Come." He ushered her through the gates and onto the stone walkway over his usually placid lake.

Not so placid at the moment. A massive ship took up most of the space between shore and island, water still cascading off its sides and down its sails. The entire deck stood ominously empty of crew, drawing every eye to the lone figure at the wheel.

Einar. Once a mortal sailor and now a younger god who shared the title of *The Kraken* with the ship that currently floated, impossibly, in Ash's caldera lake.

When Ash reached Zanya's side, she was staring at the ship, her eyes narrowed. "Ulric and Elevia said everyone else they know who can travel long distances does it through water."

"That has always been the case," Ash agreed.

Her focus only tightened as hatches on the ship's deck popped open, revealing crew who began to bustle along the side, preparing rope ladders. "But Ulric said—" She broke off with a frown. "No, I asked him if the Siren could take people with her."

"She cannot." Even now, after so many years, the brief memory of Dianthe's attempt to transport him made Ash shudder. "But there's something about the ship. As long as the crew and passengers stay belowdecks while he makes the passage through the heart of the ocean, they are safe."

"If that's how we're going to get to wherever this bastard is keeping Sachi, it must be close to water."

"The Betrayer's pride will be his downfall," a familiar voice called from the side of the ship, and Ash's heart leapt when he saw the Phoenix throw back their hood. "Come aboard, and I'll explain everything."

The sailors had swung a small rowboat over the side and were lowering it toward the water when Naia stepped up. "There's an easier way. Allow me."

She bent and began to slowly raise both arms. Water bubbled up from the lake and stretched out in a graceful, obliging arc, forming a pathway onto the deck of the ship. Einar, who still stood at the wheel, fixed an almost irritated look on the young nymph, as if a whimsical bridge that sparkled like sea glass was far too frivolous for his dangerous ship.

She answered his irritation with a cheerful smile. "Less work for your crew, Captain."

As many times as Dianthe had made a water bridge for him, Ash had never quite grown used to it. He stared straight ahead at his destination as he crossed the expanse of the caldera, then hopped onto the ship's deck with a relief he didn't bother to hide.

He was even more relieved to see the Phoenix. Opening both arms, Ash wrapped them in an embrace. "It has been too long, my friend. What do you go by these days?"

"Nyx is fine." The Phoenix was watching Zanya drop lightly onto the deck. "Is that her? The Void-born?"

"It is. Hold on." Ash waved Zanya over, feeling oddly nervous. He supposed this was like introducing the last of his family to a new lover . . . except that the Phoenix was inextricably tied to the Dream, while Zanya embodied the very opposite. Protectiveness drove him to settle a hand at the small of her back as he made the introductions.

"Nyx, this is Zanya. Zanya, the Phoenix. You can call . . ." He raised an eyebrow. "Is it still *them*?"

"For now," Nyx confirmed.

"You can call them Nyx."

"Nyx." Zanya inclined her head. "Thank you for helping us rescue Sachi."

"Best save your gratitude for when the job's done," Nyx advised. "Is this everyone?"

"It is." And enough power to make Ash uneasy. In three thousand years, they'd all grown in their gifts. How much worse would this clash be, even without the unknown entities of Zanya and Sachi?

"Then it's time." Nyx called out, "Einar! The briefing."

Einar passed the wheel off to a short sailor with bright-blue hair shaved along the sides and tromped down the stairs. "This way."

The cabin he led them to was beneath the first deck, toward the rear of the ship, and surprisingly spacious. A massive wooden table large enough for everyone to gather around stood in its center, heaped with scraps of paper and large maps. A wide, blank parchment sat on top of everything, the corners pinned down by massive conch shells.

A young, dark-eyed woman with a brilliant blue headscarf covering all but her face stood at the head of the table, a handful of sketches in one hand. As Ash watched, she upended a jar of ink and touched her finger to the edge of the parchment. Her eyes closed, and the ink began to spiral out from the central splash, twisting into intricate patterns with increasing speed until it seemed like it was racing across the parchment, and the lines began to form a clear picture.

Mountains. An artificial lake at their heart. A castle, built on stone slabs held up on pillars.

"The Empress's Palace," Nyx explained. "Sorin has been building it for centuries. Remote, inaccessible except by air, and the architecture is deceptive. It looks purely decorative, but it's built like a fortress." They looked up and met Ash's gaze. "It's where he plans to house his most precious jewel."

"Sachi," Ash growled.

Elevia peered down at the sketch. "It's clearly accessible by water, as well. At least, by some definitions." She raised both eyebrows. "He may not know what Einar can do, but he surely remembers Dianthe's gifts. What else surrounds this place?"

"The Dream," Nyx answered softly. "Webs and webs of it. The strands encase the entire palace. They're even woven into its structure. I've never seen anything like it."

Elevia looked up. "So it's a trap."

Aleksi tilted his head. "Or we can view it as a special invitation to the sort of party he undoubtedly has planned."

Ulric nodded at the table. "How well defended is it?"

"The palace houses a small force of five thousand soldiers."

The number was high enough to stagger Ash. "You call that *small*?"

"I do," Nyx shot back. "Since his main seat has a standing army of two hundred and fifty thousand. Ash, he's spent the last three thousand years building his Empire—and encouraging his people to populate it with strong bodies." They rubbed the back of their neck and sighed. "But his military might isn't the true danger here."

Zanya was the one who murmured the words. "His court." She glanced at Ash. "You knew he called Nikkon a member of his court, but we never really had any indication about his power, other than the fact that he didn't age normally. But the one Aleksi and I fought at the palace? Hinrick, the Shapechanger? He was *strong.*"

"Because they're also gods, or something close. As powerful in their own ways as we are in ours." Nyx hesitated, their lips pressed together in a tight line. "Sorin created most of them."

Aleksi barked out a rough laugh. "Excuse me, but *what?*"

Nyx's smooth, ageless face suddenly looked *old.* "He pulled them from the Dream. I haven't been able to ascertain how, and I don't know if he snatched them from some other plane of existence, or if he *made* them."

Ash had thought himself long since inured to miracles. Inga performed gentle tricks that seemed like pure magic. He held regular conversations with the world itself. Ulric spoke to animals more willingly than people, and Dianthe could soothe a storm or marshal a tempest with a snap of her fingers. Nyx could summon flames that would restore and remake the land itself or the people who walked through it.

But *creating* people? Creating *gods*?

"That must be what felt familiar to me about Hinrick," Aleksi said. "It wasn't Sorin's essence, not exactly, but . . ."

"Like a child resembling a distant relative?" Elevia finished.

"Yes, precisely like that."

"How does he have the power?" Ash asked.

"*He* doesn't." The Phoenix's eyes flashed fiery blue. "He's chained them, Ash. His entire Empire, nearly everyone in it, for generations. He steals their dreams, their hopes. Their belief in anything but what he dictates. It all flows to Sorin." They shoved a hand through their disheveled hair. "I've managed to free a few at a time over the years, but it's a strenuous, difficult process. I needed to find the source of the magic, you see, so I could end it all at once, even if it took everything in me. But I couldn't, because he almost never went there."

"The Empress's Palace," Aleksi breathed.

Nyx didn't respond. Instead, they closed their eyes and touched the edge of the sketch. The lines began to glow, and when they lifted their hand, the lines shimmered up to follow.

The ink solidified in midair, forming a three-dimensional image of the sketch of the palace. But this rendering included a pulsing golden glow beneath the structure, situated so that it would be fully underwater.

"He started constructing this palace thousands of years ago, but he rarely visited. And he only opened it during the last Dragon's Moon."

When he knew Sachi had arrived.

Elevia eyed the three-dimensional diagram critically. "Practically speaking, we'll have the element of surprise on our side. And a force only five thousand strong shouldn't pose too much of a problem. His court? That's a wild card. We don't know exactly how powerful they are or what they can do, so it's best to assume the worst."

Aleksi sighed. "Are we ever allowed to do anything *else* when you're in charge?"

But Elevia didn't laugh. "We won't prevail, not while Sorin has access to all that stolen power. Nyx was right. It's imperative that we cut him off from it."

Ash took a deep, bracing breath. "Then Zanya and I will do our best to find Sachi while Nyx tries to take down this power source. And everyone else . . ."

"Kill everything in our path?" Inga asked wryly. "A task to which some of us are more well suited than others."

Einar grunted. "Let us break them up first. I'll bring the boat up here." He jabbed his finger at the place where the barracks were marked. "A few rounds of cannon fire will rattle them."

"We've fought together enough times to know how to defend," Ulric rumbled. "We'll buy time for the real fights."

"Then if you're all ready . . ." Einar knocked his fingers against the table. "The crew'll be shutting the doors and locking everything down. Whatever you see or think, do *not* try to come above decks or open that door until one of us comes for you."

Both of Zanya's eyebrows shot up as Einar left. The young woman with the blue headscarf smiled at them all before swinging the door shut. Something scraped on the other side—a latch locking into place.

"What's going to happen?" Zanya asked.

"Most find it best not to ask," Inga replied, still studying the map. "I must say, I much prefer your method of travel. It's less jarring."

A bell began to ring somewhere above them. It tolled in warning as the ship swayed violently. Ash, who'd been ready, caught Zanya around the waist before reaching up to brace one hand on the beams above them. "Careful. Like Inga said, this can get rough."

Water churned outside, splashing up over the portholes of thick glass. Something *thumped* against the hull, and the entire ship rocked again, as if in the grip of something far larger than itself. Zanya turned to peer out the nearest window, only to recoil when a massive tentacle slammed against it, shimmering purple and teal like an oil slick.

The boat lurched again and began to dive.

Zanya's wide-eyed gaze remained fixed on the porthole. "Is he—is he *actually* . . . ?"

"No one knows for sure," Ash admitted. "His crew, maybe. But they hold his secrets. This is as close as any of us ever come to seeing . . . whatever he might be."

She stared at the Kraken's very real tentacles as the boat plunged deeper. The lanterns swaying from the ceiling fought the gloom outside the portholes, as the water grew darker and darker.

Zanya sucked in a hoarse breath and doubled over just as Naia let out a soft exclamation of surprise. "He's taking us through the Heart of the Ocean!"

Outside, the darkness had been replaced by a wonderland of vibrant colors and iridescent shine worthy of the depths of the Witchwood. Fantastical fish darted past the windows, glowing from within with their own light. Seaweed swayed with the current, shifting color with its mood.

Zanya braced her hands on her knees and struggled to breathe. "Are we—" Her voice sounded small. "Are we *in* the Dream?"

Fuck. He hadn't even considered what it might do to her. Panic flooded him, and he knelt and cupped her face with both hands. "Look at me. Are you all right?"

"I think so." She shuddered and closed her eyes. When she opened them again, her breathing steadied. "I don't have any power right now. But other than the shock of losing my connection to the Void, I feel fine." She rubbed at her chest with one hand. "Like something's protecting me."

Something probably was. *Sachi.* But he didn't get a chance to tell her. The ship spun again, and Ash felt the loss of the Dream even as

Zanya slumped in his arms with a relieved sigh that quickly turned into a hiss.

"What is it?"

"Can't you feel it?" She summoned shadows, then flinched. "It's *everywhere*."

Ash couldn't. But when he closed his eyes and entered the half-trance that let him reach into the Everlasting Dream with his soul, he shuddered immediately at the sensation of cobwebs sliding over his skin. Pressing forward hardened their clinging filaments to forbidding steel.

The Dreamweaver's traps. So the battlefield was to be well and truly rigged.

He opened his eyes and met the gazes of his friends, one by one. He saw the same resignation there that he felt in his own heart. It didn't matter how skewed the battle was, they couldn't turn back and wait for a more opportune time. The Betrayer hadn't only imprisoned Sachi. Hundreds of thousands or maybe even millions of souls were caught in webs that were slowly destabilizing the very bedrock of their world.

No wonder Sachi and Zanya had been born now, at this time. Someone had to stop the Betrayer before he wrenched their world apart.

Someone had to break the chains.

And the rest of them had to make it possible, one way or another.

The water outside the portholes grew lighter. Ash drew Zanya to him, savoring the way she came to him willingly as much as he reveled in the fierce savagery of her hug. When she pulled back, her eyes held deadly anticipation.

"Welcome to the Empire," Zanya murmured. "Let's tear it down."

Chapter Twenty-Eight
WITCHING MOON

Week Three, Day One
Year 3000

"Wake up."

Sachi drifted in the darkness, her limbs and her mind heavy. Her throat hurt, and her arm throbbed. Sorin had drugged her, she remembered that, though she couldn't quite recall why.

"Sachi, you have to wake up." Silence, followed by a far-too-familiar sigh. "I don't want to do this, truly I don't. But I have no choice."

The sharp crack of a palm across her cheek jerked Sachi from her stupor. She rolled away from the blow and fell off the bed, hitting the floor with a painful thud.

Except . . . no, she didn't. She hovered just above the hardwood and expensive carpets, and when she looked up—

Her own face leaned over the side of the bed and peered down at her. "Well. *That* didn't work, did it?"

Sachi's tongue felt clumsy, and she tried to stand but slipped on nothing and fell again. "What is this? What's happening to me?"

In the next moment, she was back in her bed, beneath the covers. But the mirror image of her still sat on the edge of the bed, watching her.

"I'd prefer to do this gently," Other Sachi said, "but there's no time. They're almost here, and you have to be ready. So *wake up*."

The strangest sensation overtook Sachi. She was sitting upright, wide awake, and yet she had the feeling that she was also lying right where she'd slept, eyes closed, dead to the world. "I can't," she said finally. "Sorin—he drugged me again—"

"The Betrayer?" Other Sachi shook her head. "How could he, when he has no dominion over us? We are the Dream, Sachi. Creation itself." The words began to echo, as if her double's voice was beginning to slip away. "Reality is ours to shape. All you have to do is open your eyes."

Sachi tried, she *did*, but her lids were so heavy they wouldn't budge.

"Ash and Zanya need you, Sachi."

She sucked in a rough breath that turned into a sob.

"Open your eyes."

This time, she did. She was alone on the bed, but not in the room. Lyssa sat in the corner, hunched in on herself, her eyes red and puffy. Golden chains encircled her, magical bonds that glowed and pulsed like a heartbeat.

Sorin's chains.

When Sachi sat up, Lyssa lunged for the bed. "My lady! Thank the Light, you're alive."

"Of course I am." Sachi gripped the girl's hands.

She shook her head, her red hair flying wildly around her pale face. "You don't understand. The Emperor said he had to sedate you, then he locked us both in here and left. I've been watching, but—but you were barely breathing. I wasn't sure you'd wake up at all."

"I'm fine. I'm—" Suddenly, alarm bells split the air, so loud they rattled Sachi's teeth. She covered her ears, trying to block out the noise. "What in the world?"

Lyssa's eyes had gone wide. "That's the alarm that signals an invasion, my lady. Someone has crossed our borders!"

Could it be? Sachi rushed to the tower's wide window, pressed her feverish hands to the glass, and looked down into the lake. There, with water still rushing off its deck, as if it had just breached the surface like a giant sea creature, was the Kraken's ship.

Sachi wanted to laugh and cry at the same time as she sagged against the pane in sheer, helpless relief. At that moment, nothing—*nothing*—could have kept Sachi away. Ash and Zanya were down there, and she had to go find them, even if it meant walking into the middle of a fight.

Staying away was more than unthinkable. It was impossible.

She turned and grabbed Lyssa by the shoulders. "My friends have come, so we have to go out and *help them*, all right?"

The girl started shaking her head before Sachi finished speaking. "We can't, my lady. It isn't safe. Besides, we're locked in."

That *did* present a problem, but not an insurmountable one. Sachi would tunnel through the wall if she had to, or use one of those endless diamond and sapphire tiaras to scratch a hole in the window and jump.

She'd set fire to the whole godsdamned palace if that was what it took.

"We'll find a way out," Sachi reassured her. "And then we'll run like the Void."

But Lyssa was unmoved. "I *can't*. You don't understand, the Emperor . . . He ordered me to stay here." Her hands moved wildly as her agitation grew. "I can't disobey him!"

Because he was the Emperor . . . or because she wore his chains?

"Lyssa." Sachi waited until the woman took a breath and met her gaze. "Listen to me. You do not have to obey him."

"But I do!"

"Sorin has no power over you." A strange plucking sensation thrummed under Sachi's hands, where the golden chains wrapped around Lyssa, trapping her arms. "You are free to do what you want."

Lyssa gasped, jerked, and one of the chains popped, as if it had been grasped by two giant hands and pulled apart.

Oh, gods. Could it be . . . ?

"You're free," Sachi said again.

Magic whipped through the room, and Lyssa cried out.

"You are *free*."

Lyssa screamed and slumped to the floor as the remaining chains vanished. Sachi dove after her, but the woman hurried back to the corner and pressed her back to the wall. Her eyes were wild, and her breath came in short, uncontrolled pants.

Sachi moved toward her—slowly. "Lyssa . . ."

The lock on the door creaked, then shattered, and Demir pushed the door open.

No, not Demir. This was *the Beast* standing before Sachi, alert and ready for the hunt.

"The Emperor sent me to fetch you," he told her. "He wants you with him when the battle begins. *And* when it ends."

Sachi didn't move.

"Of course . . ." The Beast smiled in anticipation. "He only said you had to be alive and conscious, and you and I? Have a little unfinished business." He stepped aside, leaving the door wide open, and tilted his head.

"Run."

Chapter Twenty-Nine
WITCHING MOON

Week Three, Day One
Year 3000

The battle started flawlessly.

By the time Zanya and the rest of the High Court made their way above deck, the ship had already opened fire on the endless ranks of guards scrambling to form up. Einar's crew loaded bulky cylinders into the cannons and lit the fuses, and the cylinders exploded out the other end as dozens of tiny, deadly projectiles that slammed into the front ranks and sent bodies flying.

Ash's touch on Zanya's cheek drew her attention away from the carnage. "Can you feel Sachi yet?"

Bracing herself against the disorienting sensation of the Dream webs, she summoned shadows. They came swiftly enough, swirling around her. But when she closed her eyes and *reached* for Sachi, delicate filaments as strong as steel caged her in. Somewhere on the other side of the webbed barrier, Sachi's bright presence flared like a beacon. "She's in the castle somewhere," Zanya said as she released her shadows.

"But I can't get to her. I can't move at all. The whole place is riddled with those webs."

"Then you take the low way, and I'll take the high way. One of us will reach her."

Zanya dragged him down into a rough, abrupt kiss. She broke off just as abruptly and pushed him toward the open stretch of deck. "Don't get killed."

"I wouldn't dare."

Two steps back, and his flames erupted. Zanya watched Ash's fiery wings flare out on either side of his body as the Dragon burst from his human form. He took flight with one powerful sweep of his wings, the wind of his passage whipping past her. His roar of challenge echoed across the valley.

Zanya hoped the Betrayer could hear his own death in it.

As soon as Ash was clear, the Raven Guard made their own transformation. A massive swarm of dark, beautiful birds burst from the ship's deck and sailed over the confused mass of guards to land behind their lines. When the ravens swirled again, reforming as warriors, they hit the Imperial forces *hard*, further collapsing any hope of their officers gaining control.

Zanya had planned to use her shadows to get past the guards and head for the palace, but thankfully she had a fallback plan. "Naia!"

The sweet-faced young god appeared, pausing only to point one slender finger at an archer who'd taken aim at the ship with a fire-arrow. Water fountained out of the lake in front of him and crashed down, extinguishing the fire and driving him onto the stone platform hard enough to stun him.

Apparently Zanya wasn't the only one who'd been practicing.

"What do you need?" Naia asked when she turned back. Her eyes were bright, her cheeks flushed. "A ride?"

"Can you get me behind the Raven Guard?"

She gestured to the railing of the ship. "Jump up and take a deep breath."

Unsure exactly what to expect, Zanya stepped up and sucked in air. A moment later, water shot up around her, catching her on the tip of a wave that rose impossibly high. The wave twisted, and Zanya tumbled inside it, temporarily losing all sense of direction.

Just when panic was about to set in, the ground loomed in front of her. The water hit first, cushioning her landing. Once her boots found traction, the water spilled away, dragging every drop of moisture with it as it cascaded down her body and retreated toward Naia. Zanya's hair and clothes weren't even damp.

The two guards standing watch over the outer gate gaped at her. Zanya shot both hands forward, letting shadows explode from her with enough force to blast them both back against the wall. They hit and slumped down, and she used a second blast of shadows like a battering ram. The gates burst open, revealing another long stone pathway framed by sad little gardens. At the far end, stairs led up to the palace.

Between her and the castle's entrance, reinforcements scrambled to form a defense. Behind her, the howl of a wolf rose, triumphant and furious, a promise that the High Court was coming to assist her.

Smiling, Zanya drew her sword and ran toward that bright presence inside the castle.

Toward Sachi.

Chapter Thirty
WITCHING MOON

The aerial view of the castle the Betrayer had built for Sachi felt like staring into the broken pieces of his old friend's heart.

Did he know how much he revealed with its construction? This false caldera lake, so like Ash's own—except created by use of a dam that had flooded the valley. The waterfalls spilling down behind it that framed its spires, so precisely formed from diverted rivers to mimic the falls that greeted you upon arrival to Witchwood Castle.

Those elegant spires were stolen from Blade's Rest. The endless, carefully reconstructed gardens were a hollow recreation of the bounty at the Villa. Even the tower at the castle's heart, with its glorious panoramic view of surrounding territory, had been taken directly from Seahold.

He'd taken the best features of all of their homes and crafted them into something breathtaking—no one could deny that. His buildings had always been art in and of themselves. But art told a story, and the story this palace told was of a man trying to recreate what he'd lost.

Was that how he'd come to create his own court, as well? Drunk on power, yearning for a family, but one that wouldn't judge him for his acquisitive instincts and less generous tendencies. A family that would obey and enable, help him achieve his vision instead of standing in his way.

Ash might have found a thread of sympathy, if the man hadn't bloated himself on the stolen hopes of dozens of successive generations. Millions of people had been born to lives where they might never know *what* was missing, only that *something* was, cursed to endure without hope or peace.

The throb of that stolen power was a storm beneath him, more vast than Ash could fathom. The entire High Court together couldn't face that kind of strength head-on. Zanya might have had a chance, if she'd had more time to prepare.

And Sachi? If she was down there, Ash couldn't feel her. Her presence was lost in the terrifying swirl of the Betrayer's magic.

Sudden screams rising from the battlefield prompted Ash to bank sharply and glide back toward the fight. Beneath him, a single dark-haired woman clad in a billowing white fur cloak strode through the gates.

The ground froze beneath her with every step she took, ice racing out in all directions. Anyone unfortunate enough to be standing on a bit of frozen ground swiftly found ice climbing their limbs, and the shrieks made it sound painful. The ice rolled out in all directions, oblivious to friend or foe, spiraling down the pillars toward the lake until its surface began to freeze.

Below Ash, the twins erupted into ravens just ahead of a blast of cold. Kardox swore and dove out of the way, dropping his sword in the process. Most of the Raven Guard and the High Court knew how to dodge elemental attacks—Ash had certainly trained with them enough using fire.

Just like Naia was currently using water. But the first blast she sent at the fur-clad woman exploded into tiny icicles, which flew back into their lines. Ambrial barely rolled clear of one. Ulric cursed as he took an icy spike in the thigh.

Enough of this. Diving, Ash exhaled fire. It melted the burning ground that endangered his friends, then carried on toward the fur-clad woman. She threw up both hands in response, summoning a swirling blizzard of ice as a shield. The two collided with a sizzle, the heat of his flames evaporating the water.

The ice withdrew, cracking on the lake's surface. She could defend against him, but not while she continued to attack. Flipping over in midair, he plummeted back toward her, sending another burst of flames that she barely managed to hold off. The iced-over ground continued to thaw.

And a too-familiar voice boomed out over the battlefield.

"Now, now, Ash. Leave Gwynira alone. I have someone more your size for you to play with."

Something massive flashed past him in the sky, giving only the impression of shimmering blue scales. Ash banked on instinct, pumping his wings to give him enough altitude to assess the latest threat.

The wrong move. Lightning crackled through the sky. He tucked his wings and rolled, barely avoiding a direct hit. When he pulled out of his dive and turned, he found a second dragon with a dark-green hide and eyes that burned bright yellow.

Both were larger than Ash. And both possessed an otherworldly aura, as if their physical forms were immaterial, simply vessels meant to contain the power of the dream that had manifested them. They existed only to bring that dream to fruition.

The Betrayer's dream of seeing Ash beaten, broken, and humiliated.

Lightning cracked the sky again. Spreading his wings wide, Ash met it with a roar of defiance.

And fire.

Chapter Thirty-One
WITCHING MOON

Week Three, Day One
Year 3000

The Beast roared, and Sachi ran.

Somehow, she was faster than him. It was her only advantage as she hurtled down the unfamiliar hallways and around corners. At first, she thought to hide, but beasts were beasts for a reason. This one would find her, and then—

Fear threatened to close her throat at the vicious snarls that dogged her steps. If Demir caught her, he would *savage* her, and there might not even be enough of her left for Sorin to chain.

One volley of growls sounded even closer, and Sachi chanced a look back to find him gaining on her.

Help me.

A brick flew out of the wall, crashing through the plaster, and slammed into Demir's head. He stumbled and went down with an animal howl.

Sachi almost stumbled as well, before she managed to skid to a stop. Was it possible that the palace could physically respond to her pleas? As she watched, another brick, and then a third, sailed through the air toward Demir.

He dodged these and climbed to his feet with a rumble that shook the entire corridor. His eyes glowed a sickly green, and dark, mottled fur sprouted from his skin as the bulk of his body began to shift . . .

And grow.

"No," she whispered, but it was happening anyway.

The Beast was becoming literal before her very eyes.

He launched himself at her, this massive creature who had to be eight feet tall, and it was no use. Sachi could not outrun him like this, and he was on her in moments, snatching her up in one massive, furry arm. His claws dug mercilessly through her thin gown and into her midsection, drawing bright spots of pain and blood.

The bricks didn't stop him, nor did the carpet jerking from beneath his feet. He batted away the suits of armor that stepped out to intervene, even crushed one poor stone archer beneath his enormous foot as he hauled her up the endless stairs . . .

To the open, flat top of the tallest tower.

On a clear day, the view would be unimaginably majestic. Right now, all Sachi could see was the carnage below.

Sorin stood at the edge of the tower, watching the battle rage with apparent delight, as if it were nothing more to him than a play or the tournament he'd staged. Varoka—no, *the Dreamweaver*—circled him, restless and attentive. Bits of those golden chains flashed from her fingertips, ready to lash out. To entrap.

"Took you long enough," Sorin observed.

The Beast threw Sachi to the stone. The wind whipped her hair as she rushed forward to cling to the ornately carved ledge on the parapet wall.

Beneath her, the world had exploded into blood and violence. A tiny figure that had to be Zanya fought alongside three others she only recognized when they moved—Elevia, Ulric, and Aleksi. The Raven Guard swirled around the field, breaking apart and reforming with the grace of a single unit.

Naia and the Kraken fought from his ship, sending cannonballs and cascades of water into the field. But every volley was turned against them as the Ice Queen exploited their advances, turning them into weapons of her own. Sachi watched in horror as they fell back to regroup.

Then a massive, almost metallic screech surrounded her, and she looked up to see Ash engaged in combat but outnumbered by two hellish-looking dragons. "No!"

Sorin glanced up and smiled. "Ah, yes. Do you know how long it took to perfect them? The first few I tried to pull from the Dream were disappointing, to say the least. But it was ultimately worth the effort. Ash needs playmates who want to bite and claw, and I decided to spare myself the discomfort this time."

"Stop this, Sorin," Sachi choked. "You can stop this before it goes too far."

"They came to *my* castle and began killing *my* soldiers," he pointed out, the righteous indignation of his tone undercut by the way he leaned over the parapet and stared down into the vast courtyard. "Rather efficiently, too. I suppose I can see why Nikkon and his pet king were so distracted by your little handmaid. She is relentlessly brutal."

Below, Zanya spun, her blades flashing, neatly cutting down a wide arc of Imperial soldiers. Above, Ash's pained roar split the sky.

Sachi flinched. "What do you want?"

"Truthfully?" He tilted his head. "I want them to know what it's like to lose everything. Would it be callous of us to place bets on who lasts the longest?" At her shocked silence, he only smiled. "Wait, it *would* be unfair to let you wager before you know what Varoka can do."

The Dreamweaver stepped forward. "Your Majesty?"

Sorin favored her with a smile. "She's been working on this little trick for almost as long as it took me to perfect my dragons." He gestured to her encouragingly.

Varoka studied the courtyard below, then tilted her head. "Gwynira is on the field. She will also be adversely affected."

"What are you going to do?" Sachi breathed. A million possibilities flitted through her brain, each more horrific and deadly than the last.

Sorin ignored her. "Sacrifices are necessary for all great work, Varoka." Then he grimaced and clutched his side, where his bloody, sliced shirt gaped open to reveal the gash over his ribs. "Besides, I'd say she's earned a spot of punishment. Now get to it."

Varoka stepped back, closing her eyes and raising her hands, which spat out pieces of the Dream, sharp and lashing. It was the same magic that Sachi had seen in the ballroom, and in the underwater heart of the palace. Wrapped around Lyssa, chaining her, body and soul.

She hadn't been able to do anything about the first two, but she'd freed Lyssa. Unraveled her bindings in an instant, without even really trying.

Sachi would have to try now.

She took a deep breath and slipped into the space between, the line between the world and the Dream. This way, she could see both. She could see everything.

Varoka *glowed*. Sachi had never seen anything like it, not even during her visions. Not even in the Dream itself. But when she peered deeper, it was the same as the nexus of energy beneath them—a hollow core, wrapped in a shell made of the others' dreams.

Sachi left her body behind, frozen in stasis, slipped through that liminal space, and seized the Dreamweaver. Around her, they weren't chains, but soft ribbons of wool or silk that would warm and soothe in turn.

But the moment Sachi touched her, those ribbons hardened to armor, a *literal* shell. Sachi pounded on it with her fists, determined to stop her from gathering the power to cast whatever infernal spell she had planned.

More chains slithered up around Sachi's ankles, locked on to her upper arms. *Fool.* The voice came from everywhere. Nowhere. *If I chain you here, you'll never escape. You'll linger, even after your body dies.*

It was far from an idle threat. Sachi could feel the truth of it, the disconnect from her physical form growing with each passing moment.

But she couldn't think about that right now.

Everyone felt different in the Dream. Zanya was dark, luscious, like the spiced cider she adored. Ash felt like a warm hearth, stone and fire, the perfect combination of comfort and safety.

Varoka was a pit, yawning and ravenous. Empty, never able to be filled. She drew in the power of the Dream, had learned to wield it, but it was not hers. No wonder she'd been able to set up this spell, to steal so much power for Sorin.

It was what she'd been doing all her life.

Slowly, carefully, Sachi began to lock her away. It was no different from the boxes she'd built for herself over the years when she needed to hide. It was a lengthy process, but that was all right. Time had no meaning here. This was existence, the root of it all, a single moment and an eternity.

She managed three full sides and most of a fourth by the time Varoka caught on. *You think you can imprison me?* the voice demanded. *And with such weak walls as these?* A burst of the Dream hit Sachi like a blow, and she knew only pain. The power wasn't Varoka's, of course, but any child could pick up a hammer and swing it.

It slammed Sachi back into her body, and she found herself kneeling on the cold stone, her hair wrapped around Varoka's fist.

"And he said you were *special,*" she hissed, then dragged Sachi up by her hair. "Watch. Look at what real power can do."

Down in the courtyard, one by one, the gods began to fall.

Chapter Thirty-Two
WITCHING MOON

Week Three, Day One
Year 3000

They'd fought their way to the inner courtyard and the final rank of terrified guards when everything went wrong.

One moment, Zanya was dancing through the battle with Elevia and Malindra, the three of them forming a wedge to eviscerate everything in their path. In the next, Zanya stood alone as Elevia stumbled and crashed into a disoriented Malindra.

Both went down. A few paces behind them, a group of ravens abruptly converged into Ambrial, who tumbled out of the sky and hit the stone on her back.

A howl of rage twisted into a human scream of denial as Ulric's wolf form collapsed in on him. He hit the ground, too, next to Aleksi, who had simply stopped.

"It's gone," Aleksi whispered as his knees buckled. Zanya lunged to catch him—and barely brought her sword up in time to block the blow that an opportunistic soldier aimed at the Lover's unguarded throat.

"What's gone?" Zanya let Aleksi slump to the ground so she could dispatch the next attacker. A full circuit showed her the rest of the Raven Guard in various states of shock, some flat on their backs and some struggling to their knees.

"All the love. *All of it.*" Aleksi curled over his knees, burying his face in his hands, as if the pain was so crushing he couldn't breathe.

"Our powers," Elevia ground out as she regained her feet. She picked up her sword and swung around, effortlessly beheading someone who'd charged at a recovering Kardox. "Our connection to the Dream. Something has severed it."

Horror flooded Zanya as she gazed across the battlefield. Their trail of destruction was obvious, the number of guards left willing and able to fight down to a scant handful. The stranger in white fur keeping Naia and the Kraken penned in had been the only enemy of note left—and even she was on her knees, clutching at her head as the ice immobilizing the ship fractured.

The Betrayer wouldn't have deployed this weapon *now* unless something worse was coming.

Instinct pulled her gaze to the castle gates, and *worse* appeared. There were two of them, a tall, handsome man and a blonde woman, both dressed in battle-blooded leather armor. They moved with the easy assurance of trained predators—and the hot anticipation of people who didn't just savor victory, but the kill itself.

And they pulsed with power.

"Go, Zanya." Elevia dragged Ulric to his feet. "The top of the tower, that's where Sorin will be. He'll want to watch us be cut down."

"And he'll have Sachi with him," Ulric growled. "So she has to witness what happens to Ash."

The reminder pulled Zanya's attention to the darkening clouds above. She could only see flashes of scales as the three dragons dove through smoke and mist, exploding out of terrifying cloud banks to spit fire and lightning and rake each other with talons longer than her entire hand.

Ash, stay alive. Stay alive, please.

Elevia gripped her arm and shook her. "Climb, Zanya. You have to end this."

"I can't leave you! You're practically helpless!"

Elevia arched an imperious eyebrow. "Darling, I was deadly before I ever became a god, and that was thousands of years ago. I'm not about to learn what defeat tastes like now."

Zanya wavered, torn between conflicting duties. It would have been so easy before, bolting away and leaving them to near certain death if it meant saving Sachi. Frustrated tears stung her eyes. Why had she made herself so vulnerable and weak? *Why* had she split her purpose?

In the next heartbeat, Zanya rejected the notion. This terrible ache in her chest was the price she'd paid for opening herself to loving more than a single person. But the rewards had been beyond anything she could have imagined.

Elevia's and Ulric's friendship hadn't made her weaker. It had made *her* deadly, too.

She gripped the other woman's shoulder in return, trying to say with her eyes what she knew she could never put into words. Instead, she echoed the silent command she'd given Ash. "Stay alive."

Elevia nodded, her eyes shining. "Or die with glory."

Zanya spared her friends one last look. They were all on their feet again except Aleksi. Naia stood with him, her arms wrapped tight around him as she whispered something in his ear. The Kraken hovered over them both, his bloodied trident lashing out in defense.

They were strong. They were smart. They had thousands of years of experience. They *would* survive.

Zanya chanted the entire litany to herself over and over as she made it to the base of the tower and pulled two daggers. Slamming one into the rock, she hauled herself up high enough to smash a second hand-hold into place.

One furious thrust at a time, hand over hand, Zanya climbed.

Chapter Thirty-Three
WITCHING MOON

Week Three, Day One
Year 3000

The world was screaming.

Ash twisted into a dive, ignoring the fiery agony of ragged claw marks on his shoulder, even though the wound turned every movement of his left wing into sheer torture. A jagged mountain peak spun up at him, and he longed to alight on that rocky outcropping and thrust his power deep into the earth, to soothe it and promise that everything would be fine.

Nothing was fine.

The storm of power around the castle tower had become a veritable whirlpool, dragging hope and color and *life* from the land in all directions. Instead, the maelstrom funneled it toward the familiar enemy who stood atop his stolen tower, triumphant in anticipation of his impending victory.

The Betrayer didn't care that whatever he'd done had rent asunder the natural rhythms of the world. That the dark clouds gathering above them were unnatural, that the winds buffeting Ash as he flared his wings wide at the last moment and flung himself skyward were growing more and more destructive.

Behind him, the blue dragon that had been tailing him missed the turn and crashed into the mountain peak. Ash hoped for a moment to catch his breath, but lightning crashed out of the sky and arced toward him. He tucked his wings close and turned, feeling the forked heat crackle over his back.

Too close. He didn't know if the attack had come from the other dragon or the furious sky. Dianthe wasn't here to calm the storms. He'd have to hope the wind held some fondness for the Siren's oldest friend, even this far from her touch.

Ash broke free of a dark cloud and soared over the tower. A roar tore out of him at the sight below—a cruel-looking woman holding Sachi on her knees with a punishing grip on her hair. Every instinct in his body screamed at him to dive for the tower, to shred her captor into tiny pieces and burn the Betrayer where he stood.

No no no no no.

Even without his feet touching the ground, the howl of the earth's fear rose through Ash. The mountains rumbled in warning. Ash and the Betrayer had almost destroyed the world before, and there had only been a fraction of this much power in play.

A direct confrontation between gods could not be the solution. That was why Sachi and Zanya were here, wasn't it? The Everlasting Dream and the Endless Void, powers that transcended even those of the High Court. They could fight the Betrayer in a different way. They had to.

Talons shredded Ash's back. He folded his wings and nosedived again, but the blue dragon was on his back, barely visible out of the corners of his eyes. Claws dug deeper, into muscle, and Ash couldn't reach him to bellow fire at him.

But he was the *Lord* of Fire. It answered wherever he called. It cascaded from him in a wave, and the dragon clinging to his back screeched as the scent of scorched flesh filled the air. With the other dragon's weight suddenly gone, Ash checked his dive and turned on one wing.

There, nearing the top of the tower, was a small figure in familiar black armor. Zanya clung to the stone as the entire valley shook again, then continued her determined climb.

Ash flared his wings wide and vaulted skyward, drawing the other dragon's attention before it could see the small figure making her way up the wall. If anything could hope to contain that bloated power stolen from the Dream, it was the touch of someone born of the Void. And if anyone could find a way to undo what the Betrayer had done, surely it was the Dream herself.

The Dragon's consort will break the Builder's chains, and the people will dream again.

This was the moment he'd waited three thousand years for, but it wasn't his battle. His duty was to give them time, to trust them to be what they were—strong, fierce. Glorious.

Heroes.

Roaring his challenge to both dragons, Ash spiraled upward, leaving his heart behind on a trembling tower with the power-mad enemy he'd once called brother.

And he believed.

Chapter Thirty-Four
WITCHING MOON

Week Three, Day One
Year 3000

Sachi sobbed.

It wasn't the turn of the battle below, or the blood that dripped from Ash's torn hide as he flew by to crash into one of Sorin's dragons. It was the trembling vibrations that made the top of the tower shake with barely contained power.

Because she *felt* it. Varoka had not simply severed the other gods' ties to the Dream.

She'd *stolen* them.

Things were about to get so much worse.

Then Zanya vaulted over the edge of the tower roof, and Sachi's sobs turned to relief tinged with a strange mixture of joy and dread. She still wasn't sure what would happen, but at least she and Zanya would be together, as they always had been.

As they were meant to be.

Zanya lunged toward her, only to stop abruptly when Varoka used the fist still tangled in Sachi's hair to jerk her head back. A knife appeared in Varoka's hand, the blade kissing Sachi's throat.

Varoka hissed his name. "Sorin—"

"Yes, I see her." Sorin flicked his fingers. "Bring the future Empress to me."

Zanya watched, unblinking, as Varoka dragged Sachi across the tower. "Just like old times, Sachi."

The words may have been flippant, but Sachi understood. They'd been in this position so many times, with a prodding knife at Sachi's throat, a blade meant to keep Zanya in line. "You do dance so beautifully."

"Enough," Sorin snapped. He grabbed Sachi's upper arm hard enough to bruise and hauled her against his chest. "I had hoped Ulric would be smart enough to put a knife in your back while you slept, *Zanya*, but he is nauseatingly loyal to Ash. Fortunately, I'm sure Demir will enjoy breaking someone Sachi loves in half."

Through the smoke and the rain that had just begun pelting down in huge, punishing drops, Sachi saw a slow, terrible smile curve Demir's lips. His eyes flashed with glee and rage, and she knew, if given the chance, he would tear Zanya limb from limb . . . and relish every moment of the carnage.

Sachi struggled against Sorin's grip. "Let her go. Let them all go, and I'll stay. I'll *stay*." She had trained to murder a god, after all. She'd infiltrated Sorin's court as more than a prisoner, seduced him into spilling his secrets.

She could stay. And, one day, when he'd stopped expecting it, she could finally kill him.

"You'll stay," Sorin murmured, his lips against her temple in a perverse mockery of a kiss. "But they'll never let us be happy if they live. No, a clean cut is best, my dear. I know you won't see it that way today. Your grief will take time to ebb. But I've waited thousands of years already. I can wait a few more."

No.

Shadows shot from the stones behind Demir, smashing into the backs of his legs and curling around his throat. He lurched forward a step before crashing to his knees, and Zanya was on him in a blur, her foot flashing out to kick him in the jaw. Blood sprayed as he bowed backward. Zanya twisted again, a blade of shadows forming in her hand, already headed for his throat. It had just kissed his skin when one of Varoka's chains lashed out, circled Zanya's wrist, and jerked her away.

Silence reigned for a tense moment, punctuated only by the roars of the battles above and below. Then Sorin made an irritated noise. "Two thousand years old, and that child almost gutted you before you could lift a finger. I thought I'd reached the depths of my disillusionment with you, Demir, but somehow you continue to shock and dismay me."

Demir staggered to his feet, spitting blood and teeth. "I wasn't ready."

"An understatement. You are woefully ill-equipped for this fight. Varoka, my dear. Do something about that."

Varoka smiled and wove her fingers together. Sachi watched in revulsion as spikes of the Dream shot out at Demir and burrowed into him. He howled as the spikes moved, their glow just bright enough to track through his skin. Then the light seeped out of him, coalescing on his skin like a custom-fitted suit of armor.

Then Varoka twisted her hands, and Demir threw back his head in a pained scream as the light solidified. When Sachi caught a glimpse of his eyes once more, they were oddly blank, as if Varoka had thrust so much power into him that he'd lost consciousness.

But still, he stood. He launched himself at Zanya with a roar, and as fast as she moved, he was faster. He caught her by the back of her armor and slammed her face down into the tower hard enough to crack the stone. She groaned and tried to roll away, only to receive a kick in the gut that sent her skittering across the tower.

"She can't use her little tricks here, you know," Sorin told Sachi conversationally. "No traveling away in shadows. No *cheating*. Varoka was well prepared for her."

Zanya struggled to her knees. She swung and managed to land a glancing blow on the Beast's scowling face, but he didn't even seem to feel it. He charged, knocking her to her back on the bloody stones. Her arms fell limply by her sides as Demir closed his massive hands around her throat—and squeezed.

"Zanya!" Sachi finally broke free of Sorin, tearing out of his hands in her desperation.

Only one thought filled her, head and heart—to get to Zanya. To *help* her. Her bare feet slipped on the slick stone, and she fell, but she didn't care. She crawled toward Zanya, and she'd almost reached her outstretched hand when Sorin snatched her up again.

"No," he told Sachi firmly. "No interfering, and no getting yourself killed by accident. You will *not* throw my plans into further disarray."

Across the roof, the door to the never-ending staircase swung open. Lyssa walked out slowly, as if in a daze, her wide, vague stare drifting over the scene before her.

Sorin didn't see her, but Sachi did. Sachi *saw* her, perhaps for the first time. Not bowed under the Dreamweaver's caging magic or drained by the Betrayer's thirst for power, but as a powerful creature in her own right.

It spilled from her in waves, not of light or even shadow, but of *rage*. Her eyes went dark as the most unspeakably gorgeous set of sparkling black wings unfurled behind her. As they lifted her into the air, her gaze found and fixed on the Beast.

Then she opened her mouth and screamed.

Chapter Thirty-Five
WITCHING MOON

Week Three, Day One
Year 3000

With fingers locked around her throat in a brutal grip and her air running out, Zanya closed her eyes and cataloged the weapons at her disposal.

Shadows: useless. The webs kept her from escaping into them, and whatever shimmering gloss of power coated the Beast like armor made even her most brutal shadow attacks slide off harmlessly.

Weapons: gone. She'd lost every one of them by this point, and Demir had been too savvy an opponent to leave them within reach.

Brute strength: meaningless. He was every bit as strong, and bloated with the power the Dreamweaver had fed him, besides.

Experience: pitiful. Zanya *was* the wobbly-legged baby deer the Shapechanger had called her, thinking her scant weeks of practice could stand up against thousands of years of brutal combat.

Brains: well, she had those. Because this idiot was still straddling her, slowly strangling her, when the smart move would have been to snap her neck and move on. No doubt Sachi's pained cries of her name were the point—she had enraged this monster somehow, and Zanya's pointlessly slow death was his revenge.

A foolish move, because every moment she lived was a moment she could still turn the tide. She just needed a weapon. Just needed . . .

The scream ripped across the tower like a physical wave, and the weight on top of Zanya vanished as the Beast went flying. Gasping in a shuddering breath, she rolled away and forced herself to her knees. Bright little spots of light still dotted her vision, and she shook them away.

Another scream tore across the tower, its source a young woman with a gray scarf slipping free of her disheveled red hair. Bruises circled her throat and her wrists, but it was the bruises in her eyes that Zanya recognized on a gut level.

She'd seen enough girls in servants' livery with those eyes to know exactly why she screamed.

Zanya couldn't tear her gaze from the girl's wings. Black and shimmering, they swept back from her shoulders like fairy wings that spat glittering shadows. She hovered above the tower on a wind that tasted of familiar power, and the scream that wrenched from her throat again slipped past Zanya like a caress before slamming into the Beast, as if the pain was a tangible repayment for some deeply personal agony.

Rage and destruction. Dark, beautiful power.

Mine, Zanya's heart whispered. The High Court might have been born of the Dream, but this fantastic creature, held aloft by righteous rage and vengeance . . . She belonged to the Void.

And her scream was a weapon flaying the Beast from the inside out.

Time on the tower seemed to slow. The Betrayer tilted his head and watched his ally writhe in agony. "Fascinating," he murmured, flicking his eyes from the Beast to the screeching girl and back again. His grip on Sachi's arm tightened as he pulled her more firmly in front of him, like a human shield. "A pity we don't have time to see what else Lyssa can do. Contain her, Varoka."

He gestured to the final person standing on the tower. The Dreamweaver, the one whose magic riddled this whole place. She perverted the Dream, wove traps to close people in, to take and steal. The Dreams she wielded had gone sour, selfish and greedy and always turned inward. If Zanya had struggled to understand that the Void wasn't always bad, surely this was her proof that the Dream wasn't always good.

But she was too strong. She had thousands of years' worth of stolen power penning Zanya in. And she was reaching out even now, magic twirling at her fingertips, no doubt intending to weave a cage to contain this glorious dark power newly born from the Void.

Protective rage tore through Zanya and ripped open memory. One of her earliest, a trauma so deep it had taken root and made her who she was. A belt that had been meant for her striking Sachi instead. They'd been so small, little children no more than five or six. The cruelty it must have taken to strike any child, but especially *Sachi*—sunny, friendly Sachi . . .

Zanya could hear the belt cracking across Sachi's face. Hear her friend's pained whimper. Taste her own blood as she tried to stand, to take the beating—but she couldn't. She was trapped, unable to save Sachi.

Trapped, but not helpless. Never helpless. Because there was one weapon she hadn't reached for. The first one she'd ever seized, the one she'd run from for most of her life because she hadn't been ready to stare what she truly was in the face.

Nightmares came when she called, and surely a castle like this must be rife with fears that had never been allowed to find expression in dreams.

Planting both hands on the cold castle stones, Zanya screamed for help, shoving her power out in wave after wave. Much of it tangled with the weaver's traps, Void against Dream. But they called the Void endless for a reason. Zanya let it pour from her as some pieces began to break through. More and more tendrils spiraled out, bait for the nightmares she could almost taste now as her power found the staff trapped in this castle, ghosting through minds that didn't know *how* to dream.

But they knew how to fear. And they feared one thing above all else.

The Dreamweaver laughed as she lifted both hands high, her fingers still twisting complicated patterns. "I've spent centuries making this place my own," she taunted. "You're a powerful child throwing a tantrum. You cannot defeat me."

No, probably not. But drawing Varoka's attention would give Lyssa time to flee.

Zanya bared her teeth in a grin, keeping the other woman's focus on *her* as shadows began to gather behind her. "Are you so certain?"

But Lyssa didn't flee. She had a kill to claim. So she dove at the Beast instead, clawed fingers digging into his flesh as she lifted him and flew over the edge of the tower. Once there, she dropped him. Her triumphant screech rose to join his panicked scream, both echoing as she followed him down.

Varoka's jaw clenched, and reckless confidence filled her eyes. She must have been brilliant once. So skilled with the Dream that she could work such magic . . . and so callous that she didn't see how wrong it was.

She didn't sense the shadows gathering behind her, either, spinning in bits of broken stone and shattered glass. The Terror took the form of the nightmares that had given it life, a furiously handsome, devastatingly cruel shadow version of the Betrayer who loomed half again the Dreamweaver's height.

Even the Betrayer himself seemed stunned by its sudden appearance. He grabbed Sachi to his chest and backed away, abandoning the Dreamweaver as swiftly as he had the Beast. Only then did she realize something was wrong.

The Dreamweaver spun, stared up into the brutal, monstrous face of the Terror. "You can't—" she whispered, but the words choked off as a hand made of shadows and stone and nightmares shot forward to grip her throat. It lifted her, oblivious to her flailing arms and sputtered threats, immune to the wisps of the Dream she attempted to lash around it.

Then it tore the Dreamweaver in half.

The light went out from her eyes, and the entire castle shuddered. Blood rained across the Tower, splattering Zanya's face—but she didn't care. The weight on her chest released so abruptly, she gasped in her first full breath since they'd come out of the heart of the ocean.

The Terror turned to stare at Zanya. For a heartbeat, time froze as she faced the monster that she'd created from the nightmares of the people here.

Nightmares.

They'd been part of her all her life. She could call them to her or spark them in others. She danced in the shadows others feared, and called to the Terrors given form by their nightmares. The shame of that had always curled deep in her, as if the affinity meant she was twisted. *Evil.*

But nightmares weren't evil. They were the mind's way of purging fears, of giving them an outlet, however imperfect. They had a thankless job to do and no gratitude for accomplishing it, just more hate and loathing. More fear.

Dreams were easy to love. But maybe this had always been Zanya's job—to love the unlovable. So she met the eyes of that terrifying shadow emperor and loved him for doing his job—for freeing the people who'd created him from Varoka's tyranny.

Then she whispered for him to be free.

Time resumed its march as the Terror crumbled into dust—and an inarticulate sound of rage shattered the sudden silence, nearly stealing the air from her lungs again.

Zanya stumbled under the force of it, her hands slipping on the bloody stones as she tried to regain her footing. She raised her head to see Sachi sprawled in a discarded heap on the other side of the tower.

That was all she had time to take in before the Betrayer's hand closed around her throat.

313

"You *foul abomination*," he spat, his fingers clenching tight enough to choke. Her boots kicked helplessly above the ground as he hoisted her up and leapt onto the edge of the tower. "I'll do to you what none of them had the courage. Send you back to the *nothingness* from which you came!"

And then he jumped.

Faintly, in the distance, Zanya thought she heard Sachi scream. It was impossible to tell over the rush of wind as she and the Betrayer plummeted toward the battlefield below. Her fingers spasmed as she clawed for the familiar brush of shadows, but even when they curled around her, they couldn't take her anywhere.

And they couldn't protect her when she hit the ground.

On the night she'd almost killed him, Zanya had stolen Ash's nightmare of what it had felt like to plummet to the earth at the hands of the Betrayer with enough force to create a lake bed. The pain of it hadn't seemed real.

It did now.

Stone shattered on impact. Maybe something inside her shattered, too. Zanya lay in a perfect circle of destruction, her body on fire, her lungs screaming because those fingers were still wrapped so tightly around her throat that she couldn't drag in even the tiniest breath.

The Betrayer leaned down, his beautiful hazel eyes glowing with the fury of an exploding star. "You think you've won because you killed my soldiers?" he hissed, raising his free hand. It slashed through the air, and something *wrenched* around them. He did it again, and again, as Zanya tried to regain enough control of her limbs to do more than scratch at his wrist and kick her feet.

A new yet familiar sound rose all around them. Battle cries. The sounds of hundreds, thousands of boots pounding against the stone. The first clangs of steel against steel.

Rolling her head to one side, Zanya caught sight of a . . . a *tear* in the world. As if he'd simply ripped open reality in order to pull something from the other side. Except that *something* was thousands of soldiers spilling forth, their weapons raised as they charged the blood-ied, weary remnants of the High Court and the Raven Guard.

Even if Varoka's death had returned the High Court's powers, it might not be enough. Especially when Zanya heard the same noises coming from every side.

They'd fight. They'd lose.

"Yes," the Betrayer whispered, as if he could hear every thought. "The High Court will fall today. But don't fret. You won't be around to see it." The fingers at her throat tightened. Zanya groped for a discarded sword nearby, but he slapped her hand away, crushing it against the stone. "Almost there."

Darkness rose up, as if to embrace her. At least there was comfort in that.

She'd always loved the shadows.

Chapter Thirty-Six
WITCHING MOON

Week Three, Day One
Year 3000

Sachi knew all the different tastes of fear.

Sometimes, it was cold and bitter, like a draught poured down your throat against your will. Other times, it was hot and metallic, the rush of blood over your tongue. And sometimes fear was silent, still. Waiting for the secret door in your chamber to swing open in the dead of night.

Sachi *had thought* she knew all the different tastes of fear.

Now, alone on top of this bloody, windswept tower, she learned a new one: Zanya's name, shredding its way out of Sachi's very soul.

She stared at the empty space where Zanya had *just* been standing, then screamed again and rushed to lean over the low edge of the tower wall. Down, down, so far down below, she saw a veritable *crater* in the stone.

Zanya lay half-buried in the neat, mocking circle of shattered stone, with Sorin looming over her. Panic threatened to choke Sachi as an unholy sound ripped through the air. At first, she thought it might be

Ash's aerial battle—but then the world *tore open*, and hundreds more soldiers poured from the rifts.

Thousands.

The edges of Sachi's eyesight wavered, turned white, collapsed in until her actual sight was occluded. What she saw then was hazy, a gauzy curtain draped over her. It unfurled like an endless carpet, black as death, and she knew in an instant what it was.

A vision of what would happen if Sorin won.

She saw it all in minute, abhorrent detail, and *oh gods*, how she wished she didn't have to, but the scenes flashed through her mind in paralyzing slow motion.

More soldiers than she'd ever seen, hacking and slashing until blood drenched the courtyard.

Inga, battered and unrecognizable.

Aleksi's flesh flayed from his bones.

Leather and steel and glossy black feathers, crushed beneath bloody boots.

Naia screaming with helpless fury as Einar was torn apart.

Elevia's twisted neck and sightless eyes, one hand still outstretched toward where Ulric lay, eviscerated.

Zanya's broken, lifeless body.

Ash, with his wings ripped away, dying slowly as he was forced to watch it all happen.

And, finally—alone—Sachi. Shackled and numb with grief.

The next million years passed in a heartbeat. Sorin drained Sachi until the Dream deserted her, then started in on the *world*, drawing its magic through her until the earth itself began to shake apart. Sachi lived its dying decades in a breath, whispering her apologies to the flailing world even as she drowned in sheer relief.

Because she wouldn't be alone anymore. She could finally join Ash and Zanya.

As quickly as it had descended upon her, the vision swirled away from her sight like eddies of bloody water. Sachi stood, every limb shaking, one thought consuming her until there was nothing else. No fear, no intention. No choice.

She had to get to Zanya.

She climbed onto the wall, swayed there for the duration of one painful thump of her heart, and jumped. Her ruined nightdress rippled around her as she fell, her hair whipping her tear-streaked face.

Halfway down, the Dream took her.

Chapter Thirty-Seven
WITCHING MOON

Week Three, Day One
Year 3000

Blood loss and pain had begun to take their toll when Ash tore out the blue dragon's throat. The hot blood tasted bitter on his tongue, and he didn't have a chance to savor victory. A roar of rage just beneath him warned that an attempt at revenge would be swift.

Good.

Dark clouds obscured everything up here. Only the occasional crack of lightning helped. But Ash's power flooded before him, seeking the bones of the earth. Seeking stone and rocks and dirt, all as much a part of his nature as his fire.

The jagged mountain peaks rose dangerously high south of the castle. Some of the rocks slicing upward were sharper than any dagger.

And the roar behind him meant his pursuer was close enough for this.

Folding his wings as close to his body as possible, Ash fell into a spinning dive. A few handspans too far to the left or the right, and he'd be regretting this maneuver for however long it took a dragon to bleed out.

But he didn't misjudge. Not when it came to the sweet caress of earth.

He dove between the jagged peaks of the mountain so close that the wind from his passage flicked pebbles at his tail. As soon as he was clear he unfurled his wings and rocketed upward, grazing the sharp mountain rocks. His power smoothed out, sharpening the towering peak as he passed, leaving a sword-edge a dozen paces tall in his wake.

The slick, sick sound of stone slicing through hide and guts was swiftly drowned out by the pained shrieks of an enraged dragon. In the dark clouds below, Ash saw the helpless flutter of wings as his foe sought to fight free of his impalement.

A mistake. Without the rock blocking the wound, blood gushed free.

And the dragon fell.

Ash felt a moment's grief as he cleared the dark clouds and saw the broken body on the rocks below, the dragon's green scales still shimmering in the light. But only a moment. Because when he turned back to the nearly empty battlefield . . .

It wasn't empty, not anymore. Thousands of soldiers had appeared from somewhere, their mass surrounding a pitiful circle of defense. The High Court and the Raven Guard held their own, but they were weary and wounded. Slowing.

And on the tower above them . . .

The sight nearly dropped Ash from the sky. Sachi, her golden hair blood-streaked and wild, fluttering on the wind. She balanced on the parapet, swaying for only a moment.

And then she jumped.

A roar of denial tore free of him. Folding his wings, he launched into a dive, speeding toward her. He knew the distance was too great, but if he could reach her, if he could—

Her plummeting body vanished.

Ash's human heart almost vanished with it. He flared his wings, checking his dive so abruptly that the slashes across his back screamed in agony. But when he spiraled higher, he saw that the Betrayer had vanished, too.

The world pulsed around him. Fear for Sachi vanished under a sudden wave of giddy anticipation that flooded him from all directions. He didn't need the earth beneath his feet to heed *this* message—every element whispered it. Sang it. *Screamed* it.

SHE WALKS THE DREAM

SHE WALKS THE DREAM

SHE WALKS THE DREAM

The Dragon's consort had gone to war where the Dragon could not follow. But she'd left part of her heart—part of *their* heart—behind. Below him, the endless wave of soldiers tightened around the High Court. Zanya lay at the center, with Inga bent over her.

Fight well, my love. He whispered the words into his heart and released them into the Dream, where Sachi did battle.

Then he turned toward the force that threatened his family and let the Lord of Fire reign.

Chapter Thirty-Eight
WITCHING MOON

Week Three, Day One
Year 3000

Sachi stood on the dark, empty battlefield.

The sky roiled overhead, red and troubled, as shadows moved around her. Winds buffeted her, seeking her touch, and she calmed them with a fond wave of her fingers. They murmured a warning, and she looked up.

Sorin stood in front of her, his confusion no match for his rage. He *seethed* with it, and Sachi could see the angry, jagged lashes of his temper bite at the air around him like serpents.

But she wasn't afraid.

When she opened her mouth, her voice was a hurricane, the protective snarl of a mother bear guarding her cubs. A chorus of righteous, indignant *power*.

"You wanted my attention," she whispered. Thundered. "You have it."

Chapter Thirty-Nine
WITCHING MOON

Week Three, Day One
Year 3000

Cool hands on her cheeks coaxed Zanya from the shadows.

She didn't want to leave. It was safe in the darkness. Her body didn't *hurt* in the darkness. Battle raged around her, a terrible song made of steel and flesh and cries of pain, but there was no death in the darkness.

Or maybe there was *only* death.

Was she dead?

She couldn't be. Because bit by bit, those cool fingers stroked away her protective cocoon, luring her back to a world that stank of blood and fire.

Her body returned first. Aching, but whole again. She flexed her fingers and groaned, and a familiar voice whispered her name. "That's it, Zanya. Almost there."

Soft power washed through her, like a cool breeze on a hot day, pushing those aches ahead of it until they seemed to tumble past her toes. She had toes again, and she wiggled them in her boots.

Her body wasn't broken.

So she opened her eyes.

Inga stared down at her, her dark braids tangled around her blood-streaked face. Her eyes flared pink, a sure sign her magic had returned. But Zanya's newly healed body was proof enough of that.

Zanya lifted herself on one elbow with a groan. "What's happening?"

"We're being overrun." Inga helped Zanya sit. The clash of steel was so close she flinched. "They bought me time to heal you, because we're hoping you can take us out of here."

Zanya reached instinctively for the shadows as she rose to her knees. Directly behind Inga, the familiar form of the Lover loomed, a sword gripped expertly in one hand. But there was nothing familiar about the way he moved—no courtly swordplay or controlled grace. He moved like a feral creature, grabbing one opponent by the hair as his sword sliced effortlessly through his neck. The body dropped, and Aleksi flung the decapitated head at an oncoming opponent with a force that snapped the soldier's neck. He didn't even wait to see him fall, just spun to take on the next fighter as a massive wolf surged to hamstring someone approaching his back.

Elevia and the Raven Guard stood their ground to the north. The twins protected Naia, who stood with both hands above her head and a look of pained concentration on her face as waves crashed down on the back lines, washing away dozens of soldiers at a time. The Kraken closed the circle, raising his trident in time to stab the man Aleksi flung toward him. A flick of his wrist sent the body smashing into the oncoming mob, scattering their line again.

Even with their full power, the numbers would have been impossible. But they weren't fighting at full strength—Zanya could see wounds bleeding sluggishly when they should have been closing. Enough of those would slow down even a god.

Shadows consumed her, and she tried to move. But though the Dreamweaver had died, the webs remained. Zanya battered against them, trying to flood them with her power the way she had created the Terror.

Her power slipped between the webs. But *she* couldn't.

Frustrated, she let the shadows fade and shook her head. Inga squeezed her eyes shut. "Then we fight—"

A monstrous roar shattered the sky, and a furious dragon dove perilously close. Fire exploded from his jaws, burning a path through the screaming soldiers. The main line shrank back, affording Elevia time to drag Ulric away after a particularly bad hit. Earth surged up in a circle around them, throwing their attackers aside as Ash swooped down to burn another screaming trail through them.

Inga forced herself to her feet, her hands trembling. "Ash is the only reason we're still alive. But even he can't hold them off forever."

Zanya's blood ran cold. "What about Sachi?" Her gaze shot to the top of the tower, but all she could see from this angle was the edge of the wall. "Has anyone seen her?"

"It looked like the Betrayer was killing you," Inga whispered. "Sachi climbed onto the wall—"

"No," Zanya rasped. Not again. Not *again.* "*No.*"

"She jumped," Inga said in a rush, but her hands flew to Zanya's face. "She didn't land. She vanished halfway down. Nobody knows where she is, but we can guess, because the Betrayer disappeared a moment later. She must have pulled him into the Dream."

The clash of swords sounded behind them. Elevia's shout of warning rose as someone broke through the Raven Guard's line. Zanya snatched up the nearest fallen sword and raced to back them up.

Sachi had disappeared, not fallen. Wherever she was, she was still fighting her battle. Zanya had to believe it, because she was the only one left with a chance of winning.

The Dragon and the High Court would fight as long as they could to give her time. But only the Everlasting Dream had the power to end this.

Fortunately, Zanya was used to having faith in Sachi.

Chapter Forty
WITCHING MOON

Sorin fought.

Anyone would. Sachi had expected it, might even have found a shred of sympathy for him, if she hadn't just lived through a million years of his cursed reign in a handful of moments. She knew what the stakes truly were, what would become of a world chained by this man.

The battle raged around them, ghostly fighters slipping between and through them as they stood. Some were brighter than others, more strongly present in the world of the Dream. Still others *glowed*—the Dreamers on the field, who were slowly recovering the power that Varoka had siphoned away.

But some were dim, dimmer still where Sorin's chains ensnared them. Sachi reached out to touch the trailing end of one chain as a man—one of Sorin's soldiers—ran past. It dissolved beneath her hand, and the man stumbled and fell. Stunned, much as Lyssa had been.

"Stop this at once." Sorin loomed over Sachi, reduced to using his height and broad shoulders as physical intimidation. The look in his eyes promised pain. "I have given you a great deal of leeway—"

"You have given me nothing."

"I have given you *mercy*." His hands flew out, flashing gold from the tips of his fingers.

The chain slammed into Sachi and tried to slither around her. She brushed it aside and stepped forward, where moving through the dozens of bindings stretched across her path shattered them all.

"I should have kept you sedated," Sorin hissed. "I should not have given you my trust."

"You didn't. I flattered your vanity, that's all. Just as Nikkon taught me."

More chains, harder this time. More vicious. "I let myself get distracted by a viper with a passably pretty face."

His anger battered at her like rough seas, salt and stinging. But Sachi could not help but remember—this was a man that Ash had *loved*. Beneath this rage, before he'd lost his way, there had been good in him. Sachi could taste it in the Dream.

So she gave *him* mercy. The mercy of truth.

"You have such a brilliant mind, Sorin. So much drive, so much will to create. And you used to make such beautiful things." Her voice caught on a sob, and she almost thought she could remember some of them—hand-shaped cradles for new parents, toy horses for the village children. Boats for the fishermen who plied their trade in Siren's Bay. "But you've hardened your heart, until you can't even hear the earth or your people screaming for mercy. You've hardened it so much that I wonder if you can be redeemed . . . or if you're too broken."

He stared at her in outrage. "Redeemed? You seek to judge me? I brought civilization to this world. How *dare* you?"

"You brought exploitation. Imprisonment. Even now, you're reacting with violence instead of understanding that you might have been wrong."

Sorin roared his wrath and threw another chain at her, this one barbed and white-hot. Sachi caught it, let it wrap around her hand and arm until she knew the feel of it. The weight.

Then she reached for the center of Sorin's power—the glowing nexus beneath their feet. If she looked down, she could see it, star-bright and pulsing. She'd once gone diving in Siren's Bay and found an anemone. Its tentacles had undulated in the clear blue water just like the millions of chains that spilled out of the nexus.

She could break them, but the chaos would be *unimaginable*. Millions of people waking up to the Dream at once. Some would manifest powers, as Lyssa had. Perhaps even more than usual, due to the inherently traumatic nature of what Sorin had done to them.

Sachi tried to take them instead. It was a violence she could barely countenance, keeping the people leashed like this, but what choice did she have? It was the kindest option. She would not take from them the way Sorin had, and she could dissolve the chains in a controlled manner. Their imprisonment would last longer, but it *would* end, and she could make sure that people were *safe*.

She pulled the magic close, but when she tried to take it in, she couldn't. Her stomach churned, as if everything in her was physically rejecting such a construct. She tried again, struggling to push past the waves of nausea and pain that seemed to sear her very soul.

There had to be a way—there was always a way—but it could take years, decades, to uncover. And time was running short.

But there was one thing left that she could try.

"You won't win," she told Sorin. "The question is, are you willing to learn from this? Will you let them go? Give *me* their bonds?"

"Of course I'll learn from this." His face hardened. "Next time, I'll make certain there's no one who can stop me."

Sachi's heart broke. She would do what she had to do, and could only hope the guilt wouldn't crush her. "So be it."

She reached for the nexus again. It danced at her touch, and she smoothed its chains, coaxing forth the bits of the Dream that held them together until she was surrounded by a jumble of magic.

Go, she whispered. *Be free.*

And when another, larger piece of the Dream came to her, the same question vibrating through it, she told it the same thing.

Chapter Forty-One
WITCHING MOON

Zanya had been born for this battle.

No holding back, no hiding. She danced through armed men as if this were a ballroom and she the most coveted heiress they'd ever seen. A gentle knife across one throat. A sword through the gut. Bow to slice a hamstring, spin to take off a head. She floated through the carnage, barely even missing the power that would have come from her shadows. If there had been gods from the Betrayer's court out here, they had fled when he vanished. Only mortals faced her blade.

But for every one she cut down, a dozen crushed in to take their place.

And Zanya's energy might feel endless, but those who had suffered under the Dreamweaver's magic were beginning to falter. Ulric had already melted back to his human form. Elevia bore a dozen wounds that weren't healing as they should have. Inga, always pale, looked like a ghost as she hunched over Ambrial, trying to save her savaged leg. The rest of the Raven Guard protected her with exhausted fury, but they were bleeding, too.

If Zanya summoned more Terrors, could she control them? Would they recognize friend or foe on a battleground this messy? There would be no second chances out here, not with the High Court's power fading.

But if she didn't do something soon, they would die either way.

"Einar!" Zanya dispatched her current enemy by depriving him of his sword arm along with his sword. "Cover me!"

The Kraken whirled, indicating his consent with a grunt as he spun his trident around over his head. When he slammed the staff down, the ground shuddered, spiderweb cracks flowing out as stone buckled and tossed Zanya's opponents to the ground. He was on them before she'd fully turned, the deadly weapon skewering anyone who dared rise.

Inga knelt in the middle of the protected space, still working on Ambrial. Zanya dropped next to her. "I'm going to try to summon Terrors."

It was a sign of the Witch's exhaustion that she didn't even flinch. "If you think it best."

Zanya pressed her hands against the bloody stone, her fingers splayed wide, and sank her power down. Webs snagged at it, just like before, glittering little traps made of corrupted bits of the Dream that stubbornly lingered after their creator's death. It took so much power to sink past them, to flood into the earth and spread out, searching for nightmares . . .

Instead, she found dreams.

The Dream.

Light.

It surged from somewhere beneath them, a wave sweeping away everything before it. The razor-sharp webs snapped under the force of it, their power consumed by the brilliance that spiraled up, carrying Zanya with it. Brightness that fierce should have shredded her shadows to ribbons, but they twined together like lovers, the caress so familiar, so *beloved*—

"Sachi."

Her numb lips formed the name. The warning. Inga jerked up, as if she sensed something, but there was no time to prepare her for the glory to come. Zanya lifted her hands and tilted her head back, a cry of relief bubbling up from deep inside her as the joyous light carried her back to her body.

Then it exploded from the earth, an incandescent pillar of light as wide as the battlefield. It washed away the world in its brightness, and Zanya's wild cry was abruptly the only sound to be heard.

No clash of swords. No grunts of pain. Even the Dragon fell silent as that pure sunlight glow swept over the assembled soldiers, sparkling like diamonds.

Then it faded, and the soldiers began to drop.

It happened slowly at first. One fell to his knees and clutched his head. A second stumbled and slumped to the ground. Then two more. Four. Ten. A dozen.

They went down in near silence, a sea of gasps followed by the soft sound of falling bodies sweeping outward in an ever-speeding wave. Zanya scrambled to the first one and saw dark-brown eyes open wide, staring skyward. Her fingers at his throat found a pulse. Thready, too fast, but there.

Elevia caught Aleksi by the arm before he could drive his blade down into a prone body. But before she could speak, a flame erupted a few paces in front of them. Fire curled skyward, all shades of blue and teal and green, and then Nyx stood there, their face ecstatic.

"Sachielle broke the Builder's chains," they said in a reverent voice. In the eerie silence, the words carried across the battlefield. "The people dream again."

Zanya's gaze swept over the thousands of fallen soldiers. Was this the response to Sachi shattering whatever magic held them? Was it happening to *every* citizen of the Empire? Her mind could barely grasp the implications. Millions of people dropping where they stood without warning . . .

A roar above them drew Zanya's attention skyward. Ash still circled warily, his angry rumbles vibrating the ground deep beneath them. His large head flew up suddenly, as if scenting the breeze. A moment later, the wind slid across Zanya's face, tugging teasingly at her hair and bringing with it the scent of Witchwood roses.

"Sachi," she whispered.

"She comes!" Nyx shouted.

A dozen paces away, Sachi appeared, glowing like a newborn star.

In the moment before the light overwhelmed her, Zanya realized the Betrayer had appeared, too, in a weeping huddle at Sachi's feet. But the light overpowered him. Transcended him. Sachi stood at its heart, glittering like diamonds, her usual glow magnified ten thousand times.

Was this how Zanya had looked to Ash in that moment when she had returned from her own private war, bloody but *awake*? A newborn god fresh from victory? Sachi had no blood on her hands, but her enemy still knelt, vanquished, at her feet.

And her power shone, incandescent. The Everlasting Dream, finally free of the chains that had bound it.

Nyx took a single step toward her, then fell to their knees. Inga followed. Ulric, Elevia, Aleksi, Naia, the Raven Guard . . . Even the Kraken bent his knee and his head in reverence to the elemental force that had granted them all life and power and eventual godhood.

Maybe Zanya should have knelt, too, or at least held back. But she couldn't. Ignoring the kneeling gods and the brilliant glow and the weeping emperor at Sachi's feet, she sprinted across the empty space between them and swept Sachi up into a hug that lifted her from the ground.

"Zanya." It was all Sachi had time to say before Zanya's mouth descended on hers. She kissed Sachi as if they'd been separated a thousand years instead of a handful of days, pouring the loss and the love and her gratitude and her *pride* into it, and when Sachi's arms closed around her in return, her hands gripped Zanya's arms tight enough to bruise.

A god's strength. Sachi didn't understand it yet. But she would, because there would be time to figure it out.

There would be time for *everything*.

Reluctantly, Zanya pulled back and pushed a lock of Sachi's hair from her forehead. "You did it."

Sachi just shook her head and beamed up at Zanya. "I missed you."

"*We* missed you." She started to set Sachi down and realized the Betrayer was *still* kneeling there, his face hidden in his hands, his shoulders shaking. "What did you do to him?"

"Nothing." Sachi looked down at the Betrayer sadly. "The Dream has deserted him. He used it viciously, and now he pays for his crimes."

Zanya frowned down at the huddled body. Not that there would be much satisfaction in sticking a knife through the back of his neck at this point, but she didn't love the thought of him remaining alive. "Does this mean I'm not allowed to kill him?"

"*Zanya.*"

"Are you telling me he doesn't deserve it?"

Sachi didn't get a chance to answer. A massive body streaked past them, its roar loud enough to shake the foundations of the castle. Or maybe that was the earth, obeying its enraged master. The Dragon crashed to the ground in front of them, oblivious to the dead bodies beneath his feet, and reared back, his wings spread wide, roaring a challenge that blew their hair back.

Flames spiraled high, engulfing the beast. Ash strode out of them, bloody and bruised but *alive*, his gaze fixed on Sachi.

Three paces from them, he dropped to his knees.

On a blasted battlefield littered with the dead and dying, the Dragon bent his head to the Endless Void and the Everlasting Dream.

Sachi went to him, her tattered gown fluttering behind her. But instead of pulling Ash to his feet, she knelt in front of him, heedless of the blood staining the cracked stone, and wrapped her arms around his neck.

"Sachi—" His voice broke as he buried his face in her hair, inhaling deeply.

"It's done," she murmured. "It's over, Ash."

He lifted his head, his gaze finding Zanya for only a moment before skipping to the man huddled at her feet. Flames danced in Ash's eyes as he glared at his ancient enemy. Zanya tensed, half expecting Ash to release Sachi and lunge toward the fallen god, to take his long-craved vengeance and victory.

Instead, Ash turned his attention back to Sachi. "You took his power?"

"No." Sachi shuddered. "No, that he did to himself."

"So be it." Ash rose, drawing Sachi up with him. "If that's—"

He never finished. Sachi's eyes fluttered shut, and she went limp in Ash's arms.

Zanya's heart lurched as shadows erupted around her. And whatever Sachi had done must have shattered the last of the Dreamweaver's barriers, because Zanya burst from the shadows at their side a heartbeat later, pressing a hand to Sachi's cheek.

Ash roared, *"Inga!"*

The Witch arrived in a swirl of torn skirts. She laid a pale, blood-streaked hand on Sachi's forehead, and power rose in a wave that prickled over them all as Inga's eyes flared pink. "All I sense is exhaustion."

"It would have taken a vast deal of power to break the chains." The Phoenix's face held a mixture of awe and grief. "She'll probably have to sleep for some time. The backlash of what she did ripples through the Dream."

"Will it hurt her?" Zanya demanded.

"No." At least the Phoenix's answer was firm. "But much will change. We'll all learn the true weight of her choice in the days to come. For now . . ." They gazed around at the dazed Imperial soldiers. "I suggest we remove ourselves as quickly as we can."

Ash stiffened as he stared at the messy aftermath of the battle, and Zanya could sense the struggle within him—his duty to his people warring with his need to carry Sachi away to safety.

Zanya felt no such conflict. "Elevia?"

"I'll handle it," she assured them, without waiting for the question. Then she laid a comforting hand on Zanya's shoulder. "Take them home."

Home. How odd for that word to suddenly *mean* something. For years, *home* had meant stolen moments in Sachi's arms, a fragile, ephemeral place with walls always under threat of being demolished.

But as she wrapped her arms around Ash and Sachi, Zanya longed for the peaceful quiet of Dragon's Keep. For the sharp bite of cool air and the ancient stones that ached of magic, for the fire that danced a little more coyly in the house of its Lord. She wanted nights in front of the hearth with Sachi and beds too vast and soft to imagine and even the quiet, mundane sounds of them breathing next to her. She yearned for the comfort of knowing that Sachi was safe, and that Zanya was no longer the only person determined to keep her that way.

The shadows swept up around them in a joyous, dizzying swirl, and some long-broken part of Zanya's heart healed as her shadows took them home.

Chapter Forty-Two
WITCHING MOON

Week Three, Day Three
Year 3000

Sachi woke up screaming.

Chains bit into her wrists, wrapped around her midsection, and squeezed until she couldn't breathe. The world seethed in shades of sickly green and bruised purple, twisted and warped by magic.

In front of her, Sorin tilted her chin up with exquisite gentleness and smiled. "My Empress."

"Sachi!" Warm fingers closed around her hands, and a deep voice rumbled directly over her, shattering Sorin's face. "Sachi, you're safe."

Sachi struck out blindly and rolled away, tangling in the covers in her panic. The room exploded with the sounds of splintering wood and breaking glass, and Sachi gasped for breath, her pulse pounding in her ears.

"Shh, Sachi." Someone tore the sheets away, freeing her legs. The hands that touched her this time were cool and achingly familiar. "It's me, it's Zanya. You're home, Sachi. You're safe."

Zanya. Sachi reached for her, her gasps turning to sobs as she found the unbound length of Zanya's hair and wove her fingers through it.

"That's it." Zanya pulled her closer, stroking soothing hands down her back. "Come back to us, love. We're here."

Sachi shut her eyes tight and breathed in Zanya's scent as she slowly regained control over herself. The dream—*the memory*—started to fade, to slide back into the recesses of her mind, where it would remain, crouched and waiting like a hungry lion.

Finally, when her arms and legs still shook but she knew where she was, she opened her eyes. Her gaze landed on the other side of the room, where bits of her shattered vanity littered the floor. Her heart began to gallop again when she saw Ash, brushing splinters and glass from his clothes and plucking at his soaked shirt.

Her lips were numb, but she licked them and tried to speak. "I—I'm sorry."

Ash smiled gently at her. "*I'm* sorry," he replied, his voice muffled as he hauled the shirt over his head. "I know too much about both nightmares and newly awakened gods to have been so reckless."

Zanya pressed her lips to Sachi's temple. "You broke your first piece of furniture. I wish I could tell you it will be the last."

The words were meant as reassurance, and Sachi felt horrible for not being able to smile in return. But the reminder stung, and she slowly disengaged herself from Zanya's embrace. "I'll replace it."

Zanya opened her mouth, no doubt to promise it wasn't necessary. But Ash merely held Sachi's gaze. "If that's what you want."

Someone had bathed her, washing away the blood and dirt that had clung to her hair and skin. Only the bruises lingered, secreted away beneath a frilly white gown. Sachi tugged at the sheets, pulling them back over her legs, and was suddenly glad the nightgown had short, puffy sleeves.

She wasn't sure she wanted to see what her shoulder looked like.

The miserable silence stretched on, and she had to *say* something. That was what she did, who she was. Cheerful, open Sachi, who never let an awkward moment stand or a lull in the conversation to languish. Her job was to make everyone feel better, no matter the circumstances.

But nothing would come, so she sat and stared at the coverlet instead.

It was Ash who broke the silence, coming to perch on the edge of the bed but not reaching out to touch her. "If you want to talk about it, we're here. If you don't, we're still here."

It wasn't funny, but Sachi started to laugh. *How* could she possibly explain it to them? How could she make them understand that the Sachi they had loved was gone, swallowed not by an awakening to the Dream, but by lifetimes of torture?

She had to start small. Somewhere. *Anywhere.* "I don't understand what happened to me. Not all of it. There are some bits that don't even feel *real.*"

Zanya settled cross-legged next to her, her elbows resting on her knees, her body canted toward Sachi and all of her attention focused on her—the same way they'd sat a hundred times. "Tell us," she whispered.

This was how she and Zanya had always shared their confessions and their pain—side by side, in a rush because they wouldn't come out any other way. If they hesitated, if they stuttered, they would keep it all inside, after all.

So Sachi spoke. "It's my fault that I wound up trapped in the Empire."

Ash made a pained noise.

Zanya toyed with the ends of her hair. "You think he found you because you were searching in the Dream?"

Sachi knew he had—or, at least, that Sorin never would have been able to reach her if she hadn't been so determined. So rash. "You think I'm so noble, so good. But I didn't walk the Dreams because I'm *good*, and I didn't stay in the Empire because I'm brave." She couldn't look at either of them. "I did it because I was trying to be . . . enough."

The bed dipped, and she felt Ash's massive warmth on her other side. But he didn't touch her, just sat next to her, the same way Zanya had. "Enough for what?"

"You're both gods." Sachi's throat tightened with tears that spilled down her cheeks. "And I wasn't even strong enough to stand next to you in battle. I was helpless, and *useless*—"

"Sachi—" Zanya's voice cracked. Her fingers found Sachi's knee, her touch tentative. "If I *ever* made you feel that way . . ."

Sachi grabbed her hand, desperate for her next words not to drive Zanya away. "Of course you did, but how could you not? It was all true. I had no business being here. You couldn't even make love to me because I was so godsdamned *weak*."

"No, *I* was the weak one," Zanya protested. "I didn't trust myself, but I should have tried harder."

"It wasn't just that," Ash rumbled from the other side. "You told me as much yourself, Zanya. We may not have chained the Dream, but we did lock her up in a castle tower."

"What else could you have done?" Sachi demanded. "One lucky arrow, and I'd be—"

The room fell away in a spinning motion, smoother and softer than the mad whirl Sachi usually experienced, but she knew what it was—a trip to the Dream.

But when the lazy spin halted, Sachi was not in the empty white expanse she'd come to know and recognize. She was in—

Paradise. It was a garden, peaceful and serene, but teeming with life. Stone archways dotted the landscape, each one covered with vines of night-blooming flowers in every shade imaginable. A violet sky unfurled above them, sprinkled with stars that twinkled like the distant, welcoming lights of home. A fountain burbled musically, water flowing over moss and stone.

Sachi turned in a slow circle. All around her, tiny spheres of pure golden light drifted up from the grass and stone to hover near her fingers.

"What is this place?" she breathed.

"The Heart of the Dream," Ash said behind her. "Have you never seen it before?"

Sachi turned to answer, but caught sight of Zanya's face, eyes wide, alight with wonderment. The tiny lights floated up to her, as well, bumping into her hands like a cat in anticipation of being scratched behind the ears.

Sachi could sense that they were deep in the Dream now, nestled beneath its breast, whereas the places she'd been before had felt thin, almost hollow. Reflected light in a puddle of rain.

Sachi had been thin and hollow, too—because of Sorin. She'd never had a chance to discover what she was, much less the most glorious depths of what she could become. She could have believed in the Dream, in *herself*, with all her might, and it wouldn't have mattered.

Zanya might have sensed the destruction inside her and turned away from it, but Sachi had been chained long before her birth. Any connection she'd felt to her true self had been accidental, because the Dream was simply too large to fully contain, no matter how many bonds you locked around it.

She'd known trickles of power. Hints of belief, of memory. The rest had been stolen from her. Sachi dropped to the ground, sank her fingers into the grass. No wonder it had been so easy for Sorin to drag her out of her bed.

He'd chained so much of her already.

"The Dream has never been like this for me," Sachi explained. "When I go there, it's always white, barren. At least until I find someone or something."

Ash knelt beside her, his expression haunted. "This is the first place most of us learn to come. The only place some of us can visit. I didn't realize that you . . ." His voice actually broke, and his eyes darkened. "I should kill him for this alone."

Someday, when it didn't hurt as much, or when they needed to know why she still hadn't stopped waking from her nightmares with desperate screams caught in her throat, she would tell them about her vision atop the tower. They would understand the hell she'd lived alone, a hell no one else would ever know.

For now, she had another confession to make. A more difficult one, but Ash and Zanya both deserved the truth. "I liked being in the Empire. Not the place, or Sorin, or being separated from the two of you." Sachi finally looked up from her fingers, still tangled in the grass. "But it was something only *I* could do. And maybe . . ."

They watched her expectantly, under the violet canopy of the nighttime Dream. This was no place for such ugly things as guilt and sorrow, but Sachi had to get this *out*, just say it and hope they understood.

"I needed it," she whispered finally. "Something that was mine, that was valuable to the High Court. A way for me to *mean* something to you that wasn't about smiling or being sweet or pretending to be something I'm fucking *not*."

It was Zanya who nodded, her dark eyes soft. "I think I understand. They made us into weapons, and I hate them for it. But it still feels good to use that power for my own purposes."

She understood now, in what she saw as the successful aftermath of the war. But at the time, she'd been wounded to her very soul by Sachi's actions, just as Ash had been.

"I'm sorry I hurt you," Sachi told them.

Zanya reached out to touch her cheek. "I was scared for you, Sachi, that's all. I wanted to be there to protect you. And now I know what it must have been like for you, all this time, watching me go off to wars you couldn't fight."

No, that part of Sachi's life was over. She was no longer a fragile human who had to be kept out of harm's way. She would go with them now. Even if she never raised a hand in combat, she would find other ways to support them—healing, defense. She'd funnel her own power into their bodies if she had occasion to do it.

How she had dreaded being left behind. Now, she feared just one thing even more.

"I'm not her anymore." Sheer terror dimmed the lights that surrounded her. "Sachielle, your impostor princess. I don't know *who* I am, but I worry that I might be someone . . ." Her voice failed her, and she tried again. "Someone you may not be able to love."

"That's not how love works." Ash pulled Sachi closer. "Falling in love can happen in an instant or over a lifetime, and you're always falling in love with the person you know on the day love blooms. But people change. We uncover secret facets of one another. Even Elevia and Ulric still surprise me sometimes." His fingers smoothed her hair back from her forehead. "Change is no reason not to *try*. Let us learn you, Sachi. Let us love whoever you want to become."

Sachi turned to Zanya, who watched them as bits of the Dream danced around her like fireflies. "Is that how you feel?"

Zanya actually laughed. "I'm standing in the Everlasting Dream. *Me.*" Her gaze followed the giddy dance of shimmering lights, her smile full of awe. "You love me so much that the Dream welcomed the Endless Void into its Heart. That's all I need to know."

"You protected her before," Ash added. "When you weren't even there. The Kraken's ship took us through the Heart of the Ocean, and I thought it might hurt her. But she said she felt protected. Safe."

Sachi pulled her down beside them. "Because we're not opposites, Zanya. Two forces destined for conflict. We're two halves of the same whole." She framed Zanya's face with her hands, then slid her fingers back to tangle in her hair. "I would not exist without you. I *could* not."

Zanya pressed her forehead to Sachi's, her voice dropping to a whisper. "I've always known I couldn't live without you. You're my light."

Sachi wanted to stay there with Ash and Zanya. It was where they belonged, after all—in her heart.

But leaving was fine, too. This wasn't an end, it was a beginning. Now was their chance to make good on every breathless, heartfelt promise they'd ever made to one another. It wouldn't be easy, especially as they faced down the mess Sorin's terrible misdeeds had left behind in the Empire.

But they would be together. And that was enough.

"Do you want to stay here?" she asked. "Or should we go home?"

Ash pulled them both into his arms and sprawled back in the soft grass in a tangle of limbs. "We *are* home."

Chapter Forty-Three
WITCHING MOON

Week Three, Day Five
Year 3000

Ash had hoped that asking Aleksi for help with a small project would shake his old friend out of the dark mood that had descended upon him. Everyone had been worried about him since they'd returned from the Empire, and Ash's predicament was the first thing that had sparked any interest in Aleksi's eyes.

Ash had forgotten how uncomfortable it could be to have the Lover's undivided attention when romance and sex were the topics at hand.

"Have you considered whether you might need to build a nursery?" Aleksi surveyed the open space of Ash's bedchamber. "It's an indelicate question, I grant you, and I wouldn't normally ask a member of the High Court." He paused. "But then, most of us aren't fucking Creation."

Ash pinched the bridge of his nose and exhaled slowly. At least Aleksi was invested in something again. "We'll face that challenge if it becomes an issue. I don't want to overwhelm either of them."

"Of course not." Aleksi finished his critical review of the room. "You've done well. I approve. Nice touch, putting the swing near the bathing pool."

Ash was nearly four thousand years old. Given the things he had done with *and* to Aleksi, he certainly was past the point of blushing. But a nervous flush filled him anyway as his gaze swept from the swing to the new hooks on the wall next to it. Three bathrobes hung there instead of the usual one. Piles of fluffy towels were stacked on the floor beneath them. The edges of the pool had been lined with dozens of new vials and bottles and jars filled with mysterious things Aleksi had insisted he include.

The Dragon's den needed more than Ash's single container of soap if it was meant to be a home for both of his lovers.

"Are you sure it's not too soon?" Ash asked, not quite meeting his friend's eyes. "I know Sachi has always wanted to live with me, but Zanya . . . Two predators don't always share space well."

"They do when they can find common ground. Besides"—Aleksi wrapped an arm around Ash's shoulders and pulled him close—"I suspect that our snarly shadow queen is fonder of you than you realize."

Ash was gambling a great deal on the truth of that. He slid his arm around Aleksi's waist and held his friend as his gaze swept over the changes they'd spent the afternoon making. Not so many that this wasn't still recognizable as his home—his *den*—but the subtle alterations still added up to a quiet statement.

A double vanity built to replace the one Sachi had unceremoniously tossed him through had been installed. It was flanked by twin wardrobes that held some of the more casual outfits Camlia had commissioned for Zanya and Sachi. Folding screens painted with exotic Witchwood flowers partitioned off a changing area lined with shelves meant for Sachi's everyday accessories and Zanya's weapons.

There were other touches, too. Three chairs by the hearth, as well as a far plusher rug covered in cushions spread out directly in front of the fire, comfortable for lounging. A couch large enough for three framed the sitting area, and new bookshelves full of Sachi's books lined the wall.

Ash hadn't tried to think of everything, since he wanted them to feel free to add their own touches to make the room *theirs*. But he'd done enough to make it clear he was ending his centuries of isolation. The consort's tower would exist for Sachi and Zanya to use if they wished.

But the Dragon's Tower would be home.

"Thank you for doing this," Ash said softly. "I know things haven't been easy for you since—"

Aleksi cut him off with a low growl of warning.

"No," Ash insisted. "I need to say this, Aleksi. What you do with my words is up to you, but I have to say them." *Even if you hate me for it.*

His friend pulled away, crossing his arms over his chest in a defensive posture, but he didn't argue, and he didn't leave. "Go ahead, then."

Ash took a deep, bracing breath. "What happened to you was wrong. And I know how hard it must be—"

"No, Ash. Truly, you don't. You weren't on that field." Aleksi's eyes flashed—with anger, sadness. Hopelessness. "What would you do? Not if you lost your fire, but if you reached for the earth and felt *nothing*? Not a Void-cursed thing. If you were *alone*, with nothing and no one."

The thought chilled him. Even now, instinctively, he felt himself reaching out. The implacable stability of their world pushed back, gentle and silent, a vast strength that had always been offered to him freely. What would it be like, to have that suddenly and violently ripped away?

"I'm sorry," Ash whispered.

"Don't worry about me." Aleksi clapped him on the shoulder and smiled just a bit too broadly. "Because you're about to have your hands full, old friend."

Ash let it go . . . for now. He squeezed his friend's shoulder and smiled back. "If you're looking for entertainment, I heard the Raven Guard has taken over Ulric's courtyard and are about to have a drinking contest—with his ale, of course."

"Another time," Aleksi promised. "But I'd better go anyway. I don't want to ruin your surprise. If you need me—which you won't—I'll be in my tower on the Godwalk."

A moment later, Ash heard what Aleksi must have sensed—the quiet murmur of voices on the bridge from the consort's tower. Aleksi had already reached the exterior door. "I'd wish you luck," he called out over his shoulder, "but you don't need it."

And then he was gone, and Ash was facing the door that led to the consort's tower, strangling any second thoughts as he waited for Zanya's knock. As usual, it rattled the massive door, but this time he didn't move to open it. Taking a firm grip on his territorial instincts, he raised his voice. "Come in!"

The door swung open, and Sachi entered first, looking behind her and laughing at something Zanya had said. But when she turned around, the laughter died as she gazed around his room, drinking in the changes.

She inhaled when she saw the chairs arranged near the fireplace. Her eyes lit up at the sight of the vanity, and she smiled when she spotted the three bathrobes hanging by the pool.

"You've been busy," she noted.

The pleasure in her eyes soothed his deep, lingering nervousness. Only the Dragon's curious assessment remained, sharpened by Zanya's furrowed brow as she examined the changes. Her response was quieter—a slight widening of her eyes as she examined the wardrobes and chairs, and a tiny smile when she saw the shelves on the wall that would hold her knives.

When her gaze swung back to him, there was a question there, so he answered it. "The consort's tower will remain open for you, to use as you will. But it would please me if the two of you made your home here. With me."

"Ash . . ." Sachi hesitated, seeming to struggle for words before she finally found them. "Are you certain this is what you want? You have nothing to prove—to *either* of us."

He closed the distance between them, and he didn't try to hide his predatory stalk or the hunger that rose in him. Not hunger for sex—not *just* that—but the hunger to have her safely wrapped in his arms. To have both of them here, in the heart of the monster's lair, boldly unafraid and *his*.

He held up his hand and exhaled when Sachi eagerly rested her cheek against his palm. "You told me you were no longer the princess they sent to me. But I was never truly the well-mannered god who received you. If you're brave enough to grow into who you were meant to be, then I will be brave enough to show you who I always was. If you want me like this."

Sachi laughed softly, but there were tears in her eyes, too. "I can't believe you think that flying away every time I spoke to you was *well-mannered*."

His own laughter rumbled up like gentle thunder. "It seemed marginally more polite than dragging you to the ground and fucking you until you screamed right there in Elevia's courtyard."

"Well, now you know better." She grasped his wrists and held them tight. "I love you, whether you're Ash or Sevastyan or the Dragon, Lord of Earth and Fire. You will always be mine."

Primal satisfaction roared through him, and nothing on earth could have stopped him from kissing her. She tasted sweet and bright, like Sachi but *more*, as if the gentle glow that had always trembled beneath her skin had been unleashed. It was heady, and the only reason he didn't fall into it was because one bit of business remained unresolved.

Gently releasing Sachi, he turned to Zanya. She wore her usual simple black tunic and pants, but one of the personal maids had finally gotten after her hair with the scissors to remove the charred ends. It fell just below her shoulders now, in dark waves that framed her face as well as the wild intensity of her deep-brown eyes.

She was wary. Insecure. He'd seen that look before, whenever her power evinced itself too strongly and she had to gather herself tightly inward to brace for rejection. "You don't have to invite us both," Zanya said softly. "She's your consort—"

"Zanya."

She fell silent, still standing stiffly. He approached with careful respect for a fellow predator, stopping only when they stood toe to toe, her head tilted back just far enough to meet his eyes. "She is my consort," he agreed. "And you are our shadow queen, our warrior with the heart of a dragon. I love you differently. But I love you both."

The words made her shudder. Her cool, protective shell cracked, and Ash touched her cheek, but only to catch a stray strand of hair and guide it gently away from her face. "You don't have to love me back yet," he told her. "I know it takes time."

Her gaze jumped to Sachi, as if grounding herself in that familiar support. "*Love* was always just the way I felt about Sachi." Instead of looking at him, she reached for his hand and turned his arm over. Her fingers ghosted over the scar left by a Terror, and he knew she was thinking about the night she'd told him about her own childhood scars. "I didn't think I had it in me for anyone else. What I feel for you is big and confusing. But I trust you with my life." She finally looked up at him, her brown eyes shimmering with unshed tears. "I trust you with *her* life."

For Zanya, it was a statement more profound than a declaration of love. She might as well have torn out her own heart and placed it into his hands. Humbled by that, he caught her hand, lifted it to his lips, and pressed a kiss to her palm. "I will never let you down."

Sachi slipped an arm around Zanya's waist and rested her forehead against her back in almost reverent silence. Zanya hesitated for the span of a heartbeat, then swayed forward, letting the space between the three of them dwindle to nothingness. She turned her head and rested her cheek on Ash's shoulder, and he wrapped an arm around them both.

He let the dragon revel in the moment, in the soft warmth of Zanya's breath against his throat and the silken fall of Sachi's hair over his fingers. Of the way they fit together, their chests rising and falling together, their hearts beating as one.

They were here. They were *his*.

And he was theirs.

"Come," he said finally. "Let me show you our home."

Chapter Forty-Four
WITCHING MOON

Week Three, Day Six
Year 3000

Zanya had expected to sleep restlessly the first night in the Dragon's bed. But the restlessness that dragged her from unusually peaceful dreams wasn't her own, but Sachi's.

She had thrown back the covers, pushing them off of Zanya and Ash, as well. She kicked and shifted position fitfully, her breathing heavy. Her cheeks were flushed, but Zanya didn't think it was a nightmare that plagued her. Still, she lifted her hand to Sachi's shoulder carefully, ready to lunge out of the way if she lashed out. "Sachi? Are you all right?"

Sachi's eyes fluttered open, and she laid her hand on her own cheek. "I think I might need a bath," she rasped. "A *cold* one."

Ash made a sleepy rumbling noise behind Sachi and rolled, flinging one heavy arm across her waist. Then he inhaled sharply, and his eyes drifted open. "Someone was having *very* good dreams."

"Not dreams, just . . . I feel . . ." Her words trailed off as her gaze fixed on Zanya's mouth.

Dark hunger surged up, bucking against the restraints Zanya had put on it. She of all people knew how confusing it was to wake up in a body that reacted differently than it had before. She'd promised herself she would be as patient as Sachi had, would give Sachi *time*.

But she could not deny that ardent, longing look, either. She cupped Sachi's cheek and brushed a thumb over her lower lip. "You don't need a cold bath. Just tell us what you want."

"The moons are full." Sachi's eyes flared gold. "Can you feel them?"

"Union Day," Ash murmured. "The day we celebrate the lovers who created our world. Creation and Destruction."

Satisfaction spiraled up as Zanya gazed into Sachi's glowing eyes. "Is that what we're doing? Creating a new world?"

Sachi's fingers drifted up Zanya's arm, then twisted in the front of her tunic. "Say yes."

It was the easiest word she'd ever uttered. *"Yes."*

"And you, Dragon." Sachi scratched her fingernails across the arm he'd draped over her. "Do you also say yes?"

His fingers bunched in her flimsy chemise, pulling the fabric tight against her breasts. Even in the dim light from the low-burning fire, Zanya could see the tight outlines of her nipples. Her fingers ached to touch them.

Ash lowered his mouth to Sachi's ear. "Yes to anything you can dream up, my sweet sunshine god."

"Careful with your offers, Lord of Earth and Fire." Sachi arched, rubbing her ass against him as she rolled to her knees on the bed. "You don't know *what* I can Dream."

Zanya's heart pounded harder as Sachi rose above her. Those sweet blue eyes glittered with a hunger both familiar and vast beyond imagining. As if an ancient force of creation had been chained within her all this time and only now prowled free, playful and demanding.

Sachi reached for the hem of Zanya's tunic, slipping her hand beneath the fabric as she leaned over her. She caressed Zanya's stomach as their lips met, retreated, then fused in an open, hungry kiss. And she still *tasted* the same, like coming home. Zanya twined her fingers into silken strands of hair and moaned into the kiss, her arousal rising with unnatural speed.

It went on forever, Sachi's tongue gliding over hers as her fingers drifted to Zanya's rib cage. She slipped one leg between Zanya's, higher, harder, until every instinctive rock of Zanya's hips left her grinding against Sachi's thigh.

"I missed this," Sachi murmured. "Feeling your skin get so hot when I touch you." She lifted her head as her fingers finally grazed the lower curve of Zanya's breast. "You're the reason I always knew what it was like to burn."

Zanya shuddered and tilted her head back, lost for a moment in the pleasure rising in her body. It was happening so fast that Sachi's thigh between her legs threatened to tip her over the edge before she'd even gotten her shirt off. But there was something intoxicating about Sachi tonight. Her boldness, her assertive hunger . . .

"Nothing held back," Ash said, as if he could hear her every thought. His fingers stroked down Sachi's back, loving and wondering. "You're glorious."

"Free, that's what I am. For the first time." She leaned back, gathered her gown, and stripped it over her head. It floated away, hanging in the air longer than it should have before drifting to the floor. "Do you want to be naked with us, Zanya?"

"Yes." Zanya grasped Sachi's hands and pulled them to her shirt. "You're a god now. You know what to do."

"What to do? There are so *many* things I want to do to you." She jerked at the fabric, and it fell apart in her hands, as if yielding to her will. Cool air washed over Zanya's skin, followed by the heat of Sachi's breath. "So many ways I want to make you come."

Zanya barely bit back a moan as she arched toward those beloved lips. She reached for Sachi's head only to have her hand intercepted.

Ash's fingers twined with hers as he guided her hand to the mattress and pinned it there. "I helped hold Sachi down so you could do wicked things to her," he told Zanya, his tone undeniably mischievous. "Turnabout is only fair."

"Nothing about this will be fair, Ash," Sachi corrected. "But it will be so, so good."

Her fingers traced over Zanya's chest—the line of a rib, the dip above her collarbone, the valley between her breasts. Every gentle glide left behind a tingling sensation followed by a spreading warmth.

"W-what—?" The warmth sank deeper, turned languid and hot. Every place Sachi touched became as sensitive as any erogenous zone. Even Ash's teasing fingertip following the path between Zanya's breasts felt like a hot tongue stealing over her clit.

She gasped and jerked, her entire body pulsing. "Oh *gods*—"

"Ash has his fire." Sachi's glowing touch finally reached Zanya's nipples, and the first brush of her fingertips was bliss. "You have shadows." Sachi lingered, pinching and toying with the hard peaks, and Zanya bit back a scream. "I have . . . this."

She flicked her tongue over one of Zanya's nipples, then sucked it into her mouth.

This time, there was no holding it back. Zanya's nipples felt a hundred times more sensitive, turning the gentle flick of Sachi's tongue into a pleasure that almost hurt. Her hips bucked, searching for the friction that would carry her over the edge—

But Sachi slipped away and settled beside Zanya on the mattress. She rubbed her thumb over Zanya's cheek until she eased back from the precipice. "Not yet, love. I've just begun, and Ash hasn't even joined us yet. Not properly, anyway." She leaned close again, licked Zanya's ear. "Shall he?"

The darkness stirred again. The urge to challenge him, to lunge and roll him onto his back, to pin him to the bed and make *him* whimper as the edge crept up on him—it rose on a wave of demanding desire, only to crash against the wall of Sachi's giddy eagerness.

No scenario she could dream up could stoke her passion as quick and hot as fulfilling Sachi's most debauched fantasies.

Zanya turned to face Ash and wet her lips. "It's her night," she rasped. Making it an order soothed her inner wildness. "Do whatever she tells you."

Ash leaned so close that his lips brushed Zanya's. "Even the Dragon bows to creation," he rumbled, the words both a kiss and a promise.

Sachi hummed her approval as she bent her head to Zanya's breast again, this time with slow, light licks that dragged gasps from Zanya's throat.

The words she murmured against Zanya's wet, burning skin were anything but light. They *demanded*, every bit as determined as the darkness within. "Your nipples get so hard in my mouth. I want to suck them while Ash fucks me. I want to suck them while Ash fucks *you*."

Both scenarios shimmered into being in Zanya's imagination. Sachi, kneeling over her, with her busy mouth and tormenting fingers, as Ash gripped her hips and thrust into her from behind. Every gasping moan he drove from Sachi would become a torturous vibration on Zanya's aching nipples.

How would *Zanya* fuck him? Astride him, with Sachi straddling his mouth, like that night at the Villa? Or would Sachi insist that she roll to her hands and knees and let him take her slowly, the endless thrust intoxicating Zanya even before Sachi brushed her lips over her nipples?

And how were these fantasies so *vivid*, as if Sachi had conjured waking dreams that let her feel *every* lick and touch and *thrust*?

Zanya groaned, fighting Ash's grip on her hands as Sachi eased her pants down her legs. It remained implacable, the squeeze of his fingers a reminder not to fight him in earnest, or he would let go.

Zanya shuddered. "Is this revenge for all the times I did this to you?"

"Revenge?" Sachi beckoned Ash closer and placed his hand low on Zanya's hip. "This is a gift, my love. One that we're all going to share."

Ash brushed a thumb over the sensitive skin at her hip, his touch blazing hot. Sachi stroked past his hand, lower, until Zanya instinctively parted her legs. Their fingers clashed as they moved—Ash's grazing Zanya's clit, Sachi's sliding down to push inside her.

Ecstasy tightened around her like a vise. At first she thought it was an orgasm, but there was no release in it, no *relief*. Just a tension that wound tighter as Sachi's fingers twisted inside her, every place she touched becoming sensitive enough to steal Zanya's breath. Even Ash's rough fingertips ghosting over her clit couldn't match the reckless need sparked by Sachi withdrawing her fingers and thrusting them deep again. "Sachi—your . . . your *fingers*—"

"Shh. Open up for us, love." Her lips drifted from Zanya's ear to the vulnerable curve of her neck, back down to her sensitive, aching nipple. "Let us be inside you."

Sachi's fingers eased out. The ones that replaced them were broad and so wide that the friction against her magically sensitized flesh made her breath seize. "Oh—*oh*—"

"Shh." It was Ash this time. His other hand still gripped her wrists, keeping them gently pinned above her head. But his lips found her other nipple, closing around it with a heat that intensified the sensation of his fingers curled inside her.

Zanya moved her hips mindlessly, and he soothed her as he lifted his head. "You can take us."

She didn't know what he meant. Not until his broad fingers withdrew and returned . . . along with Sachi's.

The stretch bordered on pain. Maybe it would have easily crossed that line, except for the glittering bliss sparked by every touch. They filled her impossibly, until Zanya whimpered, balanced on the edge. "Please—*please*—"

"Let her feel you, Ash." Sachi's stardust fingers touched her clit, followed by the slow, wet glide of her tongue.

Release barreled toward Zanya like a landslide—massive, impossible to escape, utterly overwhelming. And just when she thought she understood the mind-blowing scope of it, fire kindled in the darkness. It raced down Ash's arm, danced around his hand—

—and surged into Zanya, hot and prickling and wild, tiny shocks of pleasurable pain that cranked everything tighter.

Then the orgasm hit her, and she exploded.

Her hips bucked wildly, barely restrained by Sachi's firm hand. One of her own hands broke free of Ash's grip, and she buried it in Sachi's hair as she screamed, a moaning keen that barely sounded like her name. Fire consumed her, washing through her body in pulsing waves that made everything shake.

And just when Zanya thought she might claw free of the pleasure, Ash thrust their fingers in deeper and Sachi swirled her tongue, and the tension shattered again. Or maybe it only continued. Surely she couldn't be coming this many times, surely it was one endless fall coaxed on by their encouraging voices and their thrusting fingers and that clever tongue that knew all the ways to caress, to lick . . .

She was half-conscious when their fingers slipped away. Her body clenched around nothing, and she shivered through the aftershocks as Sachi and Ash climbed up to cradle her on either side, petting her and whispering soothing words.

Even those touches sparked hunger, as the warmth of Sachi's touch lingered. "Gods," Zanya whispered finally, her voice breaking. "Sachi's fingers are dangerous now."

Sachi laughed, a sound full of joy and love. "Dangerous . . . or magnificent?"

"Definitely magnificent," Ash murmured, brushing the hair back from Zanya's sweaty brow. "That was one of the most beautiful things I've ever seen."

Zanya's limbs still felt shaky, but there was nothing unsteady about her power. Shadows came at her call—not to carry her away, but to curl around Ash and flip him onto his back as he yelped in surprise. Loops of them wound up his arms to circle his wrists in solid cuffs, dragging his arms above his head. More curled around his ankles, trapping his legs. "I warned you I'd chain you to the bed," she rasped.

Ash's dark laughter filled the room as he tested his bonds. "Was that a warning? I hoped it was a promise."

"Then consider it both." Zanya turned to Sachi with a wicked smile. "I learned a new trick while you were gone."

"So I see." Sachi nipped at Zanya's lower lip. "What do you have in mind for him, my love?"

Zanya rolled onto her side, facing Ash, and propped her head up on her hand. "If he got a beautiful show, I think I deserve one, too." She traced a finger down his chest. His muscles jumped under her touch, especially when she teased a line over his hip. His erection already stood hard and proud, begging to be touched. "He should learn what your magnificent fingers can do."

Sachi crawled to Ash, stalking like a cat. Then she knelt over his thigh and ran a hand down her neck and over her breast as she stared down at him. "Just like the first time I touched you," she noted. "With a few *slight* differences."

Her graceful fingers fisted around him and slowly stroked the length of his cock.

Zanya's hunger should have been sated, but the sight sparked it anew, a craving that only intensified when Ash sucked in a breath, his muscles flexing and bunching as he strained against the shadows. His hips bucked hard enough to almost dislodge Sachi, so Zanya circled his waist with shadows, holding him in place.

His defiant growl turned into a shattered moan when Sachi dragged those glorious fingers over him. Zanya watched their slow path, her own breathing unsteady, and swore she could *see* the stardust left in their wake. "So? Are her fingers magnificent or dangerous?"

Ash hissed, and when he opened his eyes, fire danced there. "Magnificent. *And* dangerous."

Sachi stroked him again, rocking gently against his leg as she moved. "What does it feel like?" she asked curiously.

He gritted his teeth. "Like—" He shuddered. "Like every nerve is a thousand times more sensitive, but there's no pain. Only pleasure."

"And it's warm." Zanya trailed her fingers lower. "And once she's touched you, it's not only her touch that feels good."

Zanya dragged a finger up his length, marveling at the silky smoothness of skin over rigid steel. She'd never quite understood the fascination before, but if he was going to make *those* noises every time she traced a fingertip around the crown . . .

"Not the most useful ability where brand-new god powers are concerned, but right now?" Sachi licked Zanya's mouth and squeezed her fingers tight around Ash's erection. "I'll take it."

"*Fuck*—" Ash strained against the shadows again, and Zanya almost took pity on him. Almost. The Dragon, bound to his own bed, tormented and teased by *two* merciless young gods united in single-minded pursuit of his pleasure . . .

Actually, she imagined very few people would pity him at the moment.

A new craving blossomed, a delight brought on by his string of curses as they stroked upward without breaking the kiss. If her fingers drove him this wild, what could her tongue do?

She glanced at Ash and waited until she had that fiery gaze. And then she smiled. "Show me what to do with my mouth, Sachi."

Sachi settled down beside her with an answering smile. "Start slow," she instructed. "You have all night, if you want it. This spot here . . ." She rubbed her thumb over a delicate ridge of flesh. "Lick it."

Zanya lowered her mouth and parted her lips. Then she stared up Ash's body.

He growled.

She licked him.

He was salty with the liquid already gathered at the tip, the taste nothing like she'd expected but not unpleasant. His growling roar was better, a sound of unrestrained need that nearly shattered the night. Or maybe that rumbling was the castle itself, trembling on its foundations as Zanya rasped her tongue over skin sensitized by Sachi's touch.

No wonder Sachi liked doing this so much. It was heady to know you held the power to make the earth itself tremble.

Sachi's tongue met hers. She sank a hand into Zanya's hair and guided her up just a little, until their mouths met and fused around the head of Ash's cock.

Zanya swirled her tongue, licking Sachi, licking Ash, drowning in the taste of her lovers as the walls shook and Ash growled something that didn't even sound like it was in the common tongue.

Sachi broke away with a gasp. "When he's nice and wet, you can take him in your mouth and suck. It doesn't have to be deep. You can hold him in your mouth and fuck him with your hand." She wrapped both their hands around Ash's shaft, then guided Zanya down with the hand still in her hair.

It could have been awkward, but Sachi didn't let it be. Her fingers guided Zanya's in slow, determined strokes, even as the hand in her hair tugged her gently up and then pushed her back down. The rhythm was easy to catch, a different dance than one Zanya might perform in the practice yard, but—judging by the noises coming from the Dragon— every bit as deadly.

He began to growl words, threats that were all silken promise. "When I get my hands on you, you wicked girl . . ."

"You're just jealous," Sachi purred in response, "that I have such an impeccable view. I can see *exactly* how good she looks, sucking your cock."

Another snarl. "I changed my mind. I'm not letting Zanya spank you the first time. I'll get you across my lap and make you come from that alone."

"Thank you, my lord, for the reminder." Sachi's lips touched Zanya's ear. "Do you want him to come in your mouth? Or on your breasts?

You can hold him captive with your shadows, and he can watch while I lick you clean and make you come over and over."

Zanya whimpered around him. Remembering the way he'd responded to seeing his seed splattered across Sachi's skin, she raised her head so her lips barely grazed the tip of his cock. "If I let him come on me, he'll be so smug. The beast, marking his claim."

Ash's chest heaved, his eyes wild. But he didn't deny it.

She didn't need Sachi's direction for this. Without looking away from Ash, Zanya dragged their joined fingers up and down, faster. *Harder.* She followed those panting breaths, chasing his pleasure until his muscles tensed, his head dug back into the bed, and his cock jumped beneath their hands.

His roar accompanied the feel of hot seed splashing against Zanya's skin. It painted her breasts and spilled over their laced fingers. She shuddered at the way Ash watched her, the predator caged by her shadows but never cowed.

Zanya knew exactly what he wanted to do. She could *feel* it in the way he resisted her shadows. Lunge at her. Roll her beneath him. Drag his fingers across the proof of his release, rub it into her skin, taste it on her. Revel in his claim.

She would let him claim her, but only if he remembered that claim would always be shared. She lifted her fingers to Sachi's parted lips, edged one inside, and moaned at the gentle caress of Sachi's tongue.

"Poor Ash," Sachi murmured finally. "Should we have mercy on our Dragon?"

Zanya glanced at Ash again and couldn't stop her low laugh. "Get any mischief you want to do out of the way before I release him, love. Because the Dragon isn't going to have any mercy on *you.*"

"Fair enough." Sachi pulled her closer, until Zanya's side was flush with her body and she was practically riding Zanya's thigh. Her fingers slipped low, between Zanya's thighs, as she drew her tongue over the curve of one breast.

Desire flashed from languid to hot in an instant, whatever relief Zanya had had from Sachi's stardust touch blown away as her lover's fingers rubbed over sensitive flesh and her tongue slicked over her skin. Zanya thrust her fingers into Sachi's golden hair, holding her close as she sank back onto the bed. Sachi came with her, three fingers curled inside Zanya and her mouth locked on one of her nipples.

Pleasure spiraled outward in a dizzying whirl, shattering Zanya's self-control. She didn't even remember there was something she *should* be controlling until Ash reared up behind Sachi, his hands sliding to her hips.

Sachi lifted her head and stretched like a cat. "Are his eyes aflame yet?" she asked Zanya.

Zanya laughed as Ash bent down. "I can't tell, he's—"

"*Oh!*" Sachi's entire body jerked. The movement thrust her fingers deeper into Zanya, who also gasped, her eyes nearly rolling back in her head.

Too much. It was *too much*. She caught Sachi by the wrist and pulled her fingers away. Then Zanya caught Sachi's other hand as well, dragged them both up until Sachi's body was stretched out over hers, her hands braced on either side of Zanya's head.

"You had your fun," Zanya rasped. "Now it's our turn."

Sachi pressed against her with a low, tortured, *approving* moan.

Whatever Ash was doing with his tongue was clearly mind-blowing. Zanya thought she'd understood, having been on the receiving end of that fierce concentration once, when Sachi had shown him how to drive her mad with a slow, devastating build.

But there was nothing slow about what he was doing to Sachi now. She squirmed until Zanya had to free one hand just to wrap an arm around her body and hold her in place. "What do you feel?"

"The Dragon's tongue," Sachi whispered. "So hot, even without his fire. So *hungry*—" The last word dissolved into a whimper.

Ash's ravenous growl was audible, and the effects of it shuddered through Sachi's entire body. Then he was rising up behind her again, his large hands sliding over the curve of her ass.

"Such a wicked tease," he rumbled. "What should I do with her, Zanya?"

Zanya wrapped a hand in the wild strands of Sachi's hair and tugged her head up until she could look into those glazed blue eyes. "I'd tell you to make her wait for it, but I would never make Sachi beg. Not for this. Tell him what you want, my love."

"I want you inside me." Sachi arched into Ash's touch. "I want you to fuck me the way you haven't let yourself, not yet. I want you to *let go.*"

The flames danced in Ash's eyes as he stroked a reverent hand over the small of Sachi's back on his way to gripping her hips. Watching Sachi's face, Zanya knew the moment he pushed into her. Her blue eyes went wide, and her lips parted on a gasp.

"Not slow," Zanya ordered him. "Not this time. She's in your bed, Dragon. Caught, helpless, wet and waiting for you. *Fuck her.*"

The Dragon's growl filled the room, and Zanya braced herself, all her focus on Sachi's face as the final chains broke on Ash's self-control.

He drove into Sachi. *Hard.* She closed her eyes, sheer bliss overtaking her features as she shuddered and shook from the force of the thrust. Even with Ash's fingers digging into Sachi's hips, Zanya had to steady her as Ash drew back and slammed forward again.

And again.

And *again.*

The room filled with the sound of it—Sachi's helpless moans, the slick sound of him driving into her, the low, guttural groans that seemed torn from him every time he fucked into her only to find her gasping and grinding eagerly back against him.

Zanya abandoned Sachi's hair in favor of holding her in her arms to brace her for those unbridled thrusts. But then one of Ash's hands stole up Sachi's body, his fingers tangling in her loose hair as he pulled her head back.

"Touch her," Ash growled.

Any other command, Zanya might have resisted. But there was nothing she wanted as much as to lick over the pulse pounding in Sachi's throat and mark her with her teeth.

Sachi's breathing hitched. *"More."*

Ash gave it to her, his strength let loose. The flames in his eyes flared, and then it was all around him, a halo of prickling power that slid down his body and drove a scream from Sachi as it washed over her.

The room lit up with glowing bits of light as she came for the first time. They were pieces of the Dream, floating above the bed, gilding Sachi's skin as she pulled Zanya closer and urged her lower.

Zanya didn't need her silent plea. She drew her tongue over one tight nipple, savoring Sachi's hitching gasp. Then she switched to the other, giving Sachi a hint of teeth as her post-orgasm haze banked sharply toward another release.

Pleasure shone so bright in her. The room glittered with it, those tiny dancing sparks flaring when Zanya caught Sachi's nipple and pinched it just as Ash drove home. She screamed again, a sound of pure joy, and the glow expanded until it felt like they were fucking inside a star.

The ecstasy of it even claimed the Dragon. Ash's head fell back on a roar as he dragged Sachi's hips back toward him. He slammed into her once, twice, and when her body shook with release this time, he joined her, their entwined moans almost enough to send Zanya rocketing over the edge.

Almost.

Ash eased back and collapsed to the bed, carrying Sachi with him. The two of them panted as the dancing bits of light faded, but Sachi didn't look exhausted. Restless energy still seethed inside her.

The Dream had been chained for thousands of years. Zanya supposed the euphoria of so much life, so much *creation*, could not be fucked away so easily, especially at a time meant to celebrate unions.

Pleasuring Sachi until that restless energy vanished under a wave of sleepy languor appealed to every darkly possessive instinct in Zanya's body. And the Dragon's den of debauchery offered so many options.

Slipping from the bed, Zanya moved to the shelves he'd shown her the first time she'd stood in his bedroom. There were half a dozen of those long boxes she'd originally thought held weapons. After opening several, she found the one she wanted—a thick glass rod with spiraling ridges that flared at both ends. She'd imagined pleasuring Sachi with this so many times since Ash had shown it to her that she could already taste Sachi's gasps and moans, could feel the way she would tremble and writhe and *come.*

She lifted it from the box and returned to the bed, offering Sachi a slow smile. "You wore out the Dragon, but I think you're still needy."

Sachi slowly rubbed her legs against Ash's, looked at the item in Zanya's hand, and licked her lips.

Ash chuckled and tugged Sachi onto her back. "Excellent choice."

"It was memorable," Zanya admitted as she stretched out on Sachi's other side and slid the cool glass down the flushed skin of her lover's body. "It looked like it would feel . . . intense." Gliding it lower, she pushed the first twirling ridge between Sachi's thighs. Sachi moaned and parted her legs in invitation, so Zanya turned the toy as she moved it, covering it in the slickness of Sachi's arousal.

Zanya swooped down to catch Sachi's mouth in one blistering kiss, then moved on to the sweet curve of her throat. The flushed slope of her breast. Those tight, sensitive nipples, a caress that made Sachi arch and gasp. Lower, across the softness of Sachi's belly and the flare of her hips.

With a gentle hand, she eased Sachi's thighs wider, lifting one leg to hook over Zanya's shoulder. Then she settled in to savor the taste of her lover as she slowly, teasingly, worked that flared tip into her.

Sachi drove both hands into Zanya's hair, pulling almost hard enough to hurt. *"Yes."*

Zanya could have teased her, but she knew the agony of that restless energy. She also knew Sachi. She knew the rhythms that drove her mad, the pressure she needed for every kind of orgasm. Those fiendish ridges on the glass toy were a secret weapon that drove Sachi wild as Zanya worked it deeper, tilting it to hit every maddening spot inside her. The girth of it surely challenged Ash himself, filling Sachi until only Ash and Zanya's combined grip held her still.

She teetered on the edge, and Zanya smiled up her body at Ash. "Lord of Fire, we need a little magic."

Flames danced around his fingertips, then crept toward Sachi's nipples as Zanya lowered her head and drew Sachi's clit between her lips.

Sachi bucked, riding the toy and Zanya's mouth. She keened their names, then less intelligible words, and finally went silent as pleasure overwhelmed her. She clenched and shuddered, scratching them both in her ardor.

Lights exploded above them and danced through the room, but Zanya didn't relent. She pushed Sachi up and over the edge again and again, using everything she knew about Sachi's desires to wring pleasure from her body. A body that no longer tired the same way, that was *strong*, so strong that Zanya had to nip the inside of her thigh in warning and murmur, "Stay open for me," in a tone of dark command.

Sachi obeyed, moaning. Zanya fucked her harder and used the flat of her tongue to send her spiraling into another release, this one enhanced by Ash's fiery fingers on one nipple as his fangs scraped the other.

"Fuck—" Sachi sobbed. Screamed. *"Fuck!"*

Zanya rode the release, prolonging it until Sachi's sobbing cries turned into whimpers and she slumped to the bed. "Almost there," Zanya promised, turning to kiss her soft inner thigh. The glass toy was still buried deep inside Sachi, and pulling it free would send Sachi reeling.

Zanya met Ash's eyes and tilted her head. He slid his flame-wreathed fingers down and settled the intoxicating shock of his magic directly over Sachi's clit.

She jerked. The strangled noise she made wasn't even a word, just a desperate cry as Zanya began to pull the rod from her body, each ridge no doubt hitting every swollen, sensitive spot on Sachi's inner walls. Ash's fingers moved, almost vibrating, and Sachi shattered as Zanya finally eased the wide head free. Light filled the room, so bright that Zanya had to close her eyes against the first wild flare.

Tossing the toy aside, she kissed her way back up Sachi's body before opening her eyes to stare down into that beloved, pleasure-dazed face. "Feeling better?"

Sachi's chest heaved, and she raked her nails up Zanya's sides. "Better." Her gaze sharpened again with that predatory gleam. "But not finished."

Zanya laughed and nuzzled her cheek. "I hate to disagree with the god of creation, but I doubt your knees could hold you for another round."

"No," Sachi agreed with a hoarse chuckle. She shifted her leg, and Ash inhaled sharply as her thigh brushed his cock, which had once again hardened. "But I'm not the only one in this bed. Would you like to have him, Zanya?"

Zanya shivered. There'd been a time when she couldn't imagine wanting such a thing. When the *vulnerability* of it would have terrified her. But Ash had seen her more vulnerable than this already. He'd held her while her heart shattered, while she cried out the tears from a lifetime of pain. He'd comforted her during Sachi's terrible absence.

And he'd been patient with her. Breathtakingly patient, his ego unbothered by her need to challenge him, by her obsession with *defeating* him. Even when she'd pinned him, helpless and unguarded, he had not wavered in his trust.

She was finally brave enough to face the need inside her, the dark desire to let the simmering tension between them explode into something terrifying and wonderful.

"Yes," she whispered. Though the words were also meant for Ash, she didn't look away from Sachi. "Yes. I want him. Just like this. Caught between the two of you."

Sachi held her gaze as she reached for Ash and brushed the backs of her fingers over his lips. "Our lover needs you, my lord, if you please."

The bed shifted as Ash slowly rose to his knees. "As my lady commands."

"Gently," Sachi warned as she held Zanya. "Remember how she likes to be fucked."

"I remember." It was a low rumble directly behind her, and Zanya shivered again. Sachi's hands stroked soothingly over her shoulders as Ash's found her hips, his fingers large but achingly gentle as he traced the curve of her ass and dipped lower.

She gasped when he worked two fingers into her, the slick sound of them plunging deep almost as erotic as the sensation. Without Sachi's lingering magic sparking everything into instant bliss, Zanya could *feel* the breadth of his fingers more intensely, the slow friction intoxicating without overwhelming.

He pumped them once, twice, then slowly thrust a third finger inside her, as well. When Zanya snarled her impatience, he used his other hand to stroke her lower back. "I'm just making sure you're ready for me."

"I had your fingers *and* hers in me already," Zanya growled as she rocked back against him. "I'm not fragile."

"Not fragile," he agreed, fucking those three fingers deeper. The stretch of it made Zanya's hips jerk as tension curled through her. "Just different. Do you think she's ready, Sachi?"

Sachi traced Zanya's lips, then stroked her hand down Zanya's body until it clashed with Ash's. "I think she's *eager*. Perhaps too eager to wait any longer. Reward her courage, Ash."

Tingles raced down Zanya's body in the wake of that touch, distracting her from Sachi's ultimate goal. By the time Zanya's brain caught up, Sachi's fingers had found her clit. Her hips jerked, driving her back into Ash's touch, and Zanya muffled her moan against Sachi's shoulder.

Then Ash's fingers were gone, and something broader and harder pressed against her. Into her. Already drunk from the stardust dance of Sachi's fingers over her clit, Zanya could barely process the sweet friction of Ash's cock.

She'd known he was big. She'd watched him take his time working his cock deep into Sachi's body. But watching wasn't *feeling*, and the slow, maddening advance had her groaning and rocking, unsure if she wanted to pull away or push back to take *more* and *faster*.

Sachi kissed her softly and stroked her hair. "This is all for you, Zanya. You're in control, so you decide."

She captured Sachi's lips, drowning in her soulmate's kiss as she took Ash deeper. Pleasure was already wending its way through her, and Zanya was glad. After so much teasing, the soft burn and slow rise she usually preferred would be intolerable.

Tearing her mouth from Sachi's, she snarled. "Then I want all of him. *Now.*"

Ash tightened his grip on her hips and gave her exactly what she'd asked for. One long, merciless stroke, filling her and filling her until she thought it would be too much, and then sliding that final bit home while Zanya gasped against Sachi's cheek.

Then Ash was bending over her, too, his chest blazing hot against her back, his rumbled words a tease against her ear. "Is that what you wanted?"

She tried to say *yes*, but all that came out was a shuddering moan, especially when the pressure of his body pushed her hips down onto Sachi's searching fingers. They slipped across her clit again, sparking heat as well as pleasure. Zanya writhed between them, the tension inside her so tight she almost called shadows so she could flee from it.

But she didn't. She stayed. She *whimpered*, fingers tangling in the bedspread as she rocked her hips in the tiniest movement, and almost flew apart.

"I can't—" She gasped. "I can't hold on—"

"Then don't," Sachi urged. "You're so beautiful, love. So ready to come all over us."

"Tight and wet and hot and *perfect*," Ash growled. The words vibrated through Zanya. "Use me. Take what you need to get off."

Still so careful not to take anything she hadn't offered, not to challenge her for control. Zanya twisted her head and parted her lips, finding that strong, beautiful jaw—and biting it. "Don't be lazy," she gasped. "Fuck me, Dragon."

He made a single growling sound of dark pleasure that might have been a laugh and nipped her shoulder in return. "Hold on, shadow queen."

She clung to Sachi as Ash began to move. Not the long, hard rhythm Zanya expected, but short, grinding thrusts that kept his chest against her back. Without a full withdrawal there was no end to the pleasure, no chance to feel anything but the overwhelming *heat* of him as he rocked into her again and again, fucking her with his entire being.

Sachi wrapped her legs around them, her hands roaming Zanya's body and clenching in Ash's hair as she arched up against Zanya in counterpoint to every rocking thrust. "Harder," she rasped.

He obeyed, grunting with every movement, until Zanya's world was nothing but the slide of slick flesh and aching friction and those guttural noises—growling and deep from above, throaty and encouraging from below.

Hands touched her everywhere.

Mouths touched her everywhere.

The world spun into shadows. Zanya thought she'd summoned them, only to realize she'd merely squeezed her eyes shut, bracing against the wave that barreled toward her, unsure if she could survive it.

Then it crashed over her, and her world spiraled into throbbing, blissful release.

"That's it," Ash murmured against the back of her neck. "That's it, love. Take us. Take *everything*."

Zanya did, shuddering as pleasure turned her limbs to liquid and her bones to dust. *She* was dust, the stardust of the universe, remade in the arms of Creation with the fire of the Dragon, pulsing with the heat of distant stars.

She was losing her mind.

Vaguely, from wherever she still existed, still *trembled,* Zanya felt her lips part. Her tongue tasted salt and pleasure on Sachi's skin. She groaned and felt the vibrations of it. Sachi whispered her name, happiness and desire and *love* swelling through her, emotions that Zanya could feel as surely as she heard Sachi's voice hoarsely chanting every syllable. As surely as she could feel the dark, feral satisfaction that roared up from somewhere inside her, so like her own darkness and yet *different—*

Ash.

He groaned, thrusting into her again, and the three of them cried out in unison. Shock flooded Zanya, then understanding, all in a dizzying rush before he drove into her one final time.

Release exploded through her. His? Her own? *Sachi's?* Zanya couldn't tell anymore, couldn't separate the sensations flooding her— the tightness of her body around Ash's cock. The way her lips felt against Sachi's throat. The tug of someone's hands in her hair.

Release. Blissful, unimaginable release.

Creation and destruction.

They toppled to one side. Zanya panted and felt the tickle of her own breath against Sachi's shoulder even as Ash's heated the back of her neck. Every sensation still felt mirrored, giving her the drunken impression that she had three bodies.

"It's a bond," Ash managed hoarsely. "But I didn't do it. I couldn't have, not without the blood and ritual."

Sachi smiled, but she didn't open her eyes as her fingers combed through Zanya's damp hair. "Couldn't, he says, while he's in bed with *us.* The audacity."

Zanya nudged Ash back with an elbow and rolled onto her back. "Is this what it always felt like?" she demanded, closing her eyes. The *love* twining through her own tangled emotions felt like twin suns had taken up residence somewhere beneath her heart. She rubbed at her chest. "How did you get anything done?"

"It's overwhelming at first," Ash said with sympathy. "But that usually fades, except in times of . . . intense emotion."

"Who knows? With us? It might just remain like this." Sachi rolled until she was draped across both of them, her hair tickling their bare skin. "Would that bother you?"

Zanya was almost too tired to laugh, but she managed as she stroked Sachi's hair back. "You're saying you *want* both of us to come screaming across the castle in a protective whirlwind every time you so much as stub your toe? Because you know that's going to happen now."

"You'd do that anyway." Sachi rubbed her cheek against Ash's chest, and her hand over Zanya's hip. "You've always belonged in my heart, and I like having you here."

The physical sensations were fading a little, leaving more of a vague awareness behind. But the *love* was still there, overwhelming but comforting in a way words couldn't be.

Even more comforting was the fact that whatever they felt from her seemed to please both of them just as much. Maybe she hadn't been able to say the words to Ash, but whatever she felt for him had put a dark pleasure in his eyes that only deepened as he touched Zanya's cheek. "So many lifetimes ago, the world promised me that I would never be alone again. I waited three thousand years for that promise to come true. And it was worth it."

Sachi bit the spot right next to his nipple. "Just remember that when we're driving you to distraction. Because we will."

"Frequently." Zanya tugged on a lock of Sachi's hair. "Especially if her restlessness is going to manifest as an insatiable sexual appetite."

Ash caught Sachi's chin before she could bite him again and pressed his thumb to her lips. "Somehow, I suspect I'll carry on."

She snuggled closer and closed her eyes. "You had better."

They'd wrecked the bedsheets and probably needed a bath, but for one precious moment Sachi was nestled between them, sleepy-eyed and content. Zanya met Ash's gaze over her head and felt the swelling emotions—tenderness and affection for Sachi, and that love twined with recognition for her.

They were the same in more ways than they were different—both monsters in other people's eyes. Both warriors, sometimes easier with death than they were with life. But they had each other now, someone who could share that burden.

And they had Sachi. Sunlight and joy.

The world might be falling apart beyond the Western Wall, but here, in Zanya's corner of it, the future had never looked more hopeful.

Chapter Forty-Five
WITCHING MOON

Week Three, Day Eight
Year 3000

Dinner in the garden had been a wonderful idea.

The High Court, along with a select few others, had already gathered at Dragon's Keep for practical purposes. Sachi had meant to offer them respite from their strategy meetings. A bit of peace after their grim task.

So she'd asked Camlia to have a long table moved into the consort's garden. Ash had indulged her with torches, and their light blazed merrily around the party, lighting *and* warming the cool spring night. Sachi had asked the cook for little specialties from every corner of the Sheltered Lands, so everyone could feel at home.

And now, looking at their smiling faces and hearing their laughter ring through her garden like bells, it was so, so worth it.

Because the meeting had been grim, indeed. Elevia and Nyx had received their first reports out of Sorin's former Empire, and the place was in *shambles*. With their despotic ruler removed, the kingdoms had broken apart.

The Ice Queen had withdrawn to her fortified island kingdom in the north. No one knew what was happening in the lands farthest away, to the west. The Seducer had fled the battle and was presumably still alive. He might have retreated to Vinke, but no one had seen or heard of him in the days since. And with the deaths of both the Shapechanger and the Beast, the Stalker now controlled all territory between Kasther and the Sheltered Lands.

All of these disparate situations had the potential to be dangerous, but it was the state of Kasther that truly worried Sachi. The city had splintered into warring factions, some led by former generals of Sorin's army, still others by newly awakened Dreamers and Void-born. By all accounts, the huge city-state had fallen into chaos and violent confusion.

Because Sachi had broken their chains. She could not imagine waking up like that, with no idea of what was happening to her. Even the ones not suddenly flooded with the full power of the Dream or the Void would have felt *different*, their eyes opened for the first time. So much turmoil. Fear. So many of them must have thought they were going mad.

And Sachi had done that to them. That she'd had no other choice would be cold comfort to many, and who could blame them?

But they would make it right. The High Court had already decided on clear, actionable steps to address the issue.

First, they would send an envoy to Gwynira. She had allied herself to their cause once, in order to help stop Sorin. Perhaps she would be willing to do it again, if it meant saving the Empire's people.

Second, the rest of the High Court would travel into the war-torn kingdoms, their mission threefold: to calm the chaos, find the newborn gods, and—hopefully—eliminate what was left of Sorin's dark court.

But those fights were for tomorrow. Tonight was reserved for celebration, for being close to one another, for friendship and love. Sachi looked around, studying each face at the table.

Ash sat on Sachi's left, carrying on an intense conversation with Dianthe. She had brought guests—the Kraken and Naia, the godling who had accompanied Sachi and Zanya on their initial voyage to Dragon's Keep.

They sat beside her, bickering over a shared platter of oysters.

"Water shouldn't *sparkle*," Einar grumbled. "You'll make people think the sea isn't to be respected."

Naia just laughed. "Well, if they're going to think silly things like that, they can kiss my ass."

Farther down, Elevia sat with Ulric, their heads bent together over a map from her archives. The Eastern Waste, if Sachi wasn't mistaken. Elevia had proclaimed it as good a place as any to stage a thorough survey of the former Empire.

She'd also refused to stop strategizing long enough for dinner.

"It's the only place there might be actual wildlife left," Ulric muttered, running his finger over the map. "From what I can tell, every other place on this damn continent has either been built on or stripped for resources."

"We'll add it to our list of priorities," Elevia promised.

The Raven Guard had taken up the opposite end of the table and were currently debating who had won their drinking contest. Next to them, Aleksi sat, quietly pushing his food around his plate and sipping his wine. Sachi watched him until he looked up and caught her gaze. He attempted a smile, then tilted his head when she raised an eyebrow.

He hadn't been the same since the battle in the Empire, when Varoka had robbed him of his powers. Because she hadn't simply taken his strength, she'd temporarily severed his connection—to the world, to the Dream, to love itself.

Ash had tried to talk to him about that horrible battle, but Aleksi had thus far refused his overtures. Sachi wasn't surprised. She knew wh it was like to be cut off from a part of yourself. She was learning to move past it, and so would Aleksi.

In time. And until he was ready to open up, they would help him in other ways—with silent support, and a friendship so warm and fathomless he would always remember that they were there for him.

Beside Aleksi, Inga and Zanya flanked a somewhat abashed-looking Lyssa. They had both hovered over her since her arrival at the keep, Zanya especially. A fierce protectiveness for the woman burned in her chest, one that Sachi understood.

Before Lyssa, Zanya had only known two things born of the Void: herself, and her Terrors. Lyssa's manifestation was a very real indication that, despite the harsh words of Nikkon and the other priests in the capital, Zanya was not alone.

Sachi smiled. Zanya would march back into the fallen Empire, gather every Void-born godling she could find, and tuck them under her wing like a mother hen.

I love you, Sachi whispered.

Zanya looked up, her gaze swinging unerringly to Sachi. A surge of love flooded back at her, clearer than any words.

Ash leaned into Sachi, his lips brushing her ear. "You were right. This was just what we needed."

At the other end of the table, Isolde groaned and glared at her brother. "Remi ate all the fire grapes," she announced. "The special ones from Aleksi's vineyard."

Sachi placed her finger on Ash's lips. "Hold that thought, just for a moment."

Then she reached through the Dream and asked the world for a favor. Just a small one, but it was such a new sensation that it took the span of several heartbeats for Sachi to wordlessly explain what she needed.

A large bunch of fire grapes, fiery red and still attached to their stems, fell out of the night sky to land on Isolde's plate.

At first, everyone simply stared at the grapes. Then Isolde laughed, seized one, and popped it into her mouth. "Perfect!" she exclaimed. "Thank you, my lady."

Inga rested her chin in her palm and stared at Sachi. "You get more fascinating by the day. Ash certainly did well by us."

"I was rather selfishly only trying to do well by myself," Ash retorted. "But I am pleased that you are pleased, darling."

Inga smiled and turned back to Zanya, and Ash tilted Sachi's face up to his. "She's right, you know," he murmured. "You get more amazing by the day."

"What a lovely thing to say." But she didn't need the words when she could feel it all, simmering in her breast like a fire in a hearth. "I think you should kiss me."

He did. Sachi felt the darkness and heat of his love, and the silken, shadowy press of Zanya's emotions, as well. They swirled together, a concoction headier than any wine, and Sachi sighed into Ash's mouth.

Tomorrow, they would fight. Tonight, they needed to remind themselves what they were fighting for.

Chapter Forty-Six
WITCHING MOON

Week Three, Day Ten
Year 3000

Ash had never asked Dianthe why she'd built cells deep in the heart of her beautiful seaside fortress. Perhaps the dreams of superstitious sailors sometimes manifested things that required containment, or perhaps she had simply imagined a day when their fallen brother would return to them in chains.

That day had finally come, but they had not brought back the Betrayer.

This was Sorin.

Though the man's new home existed deep beneath the castle, Ash would hesitate to call it a dungeon. The reinforced door, guarded by a young man whose rich voice could sing sailors from their ships, opened into a surprisingly well-lit room. Large globes made of sea glass blazed from the center of the ceiling, their wicks floating in the distinctive blend of oils used only at Seahold—a blend that combined the stony smell of fresh rain with the salty depths of the sea. A richly woven blue carpet covered the stone floor, and a neat wooden table sat on top of it, surrounded by four comfortable padded chairs.

The door occupied one wall. Each of the three remaining walls was dominated by simple iron bars that peered into comfortable but modest rooms. A decent-size bed had been draped with enough warm quilts to fight the damp chill, a bookshelf had been stacked with books, and a comfortable reading chair sat close enough to the bars to take advantage of the light. A screen portioned off a part of the cell meant for more personal affairs, a nod to privacy that could not truly exist, no matter how many woven rugs and bright quilts you added.

It might not look like a dungeon, but it *was* one.

Sorin sprawled on the bed to Ash's left, his back against the stone wall and his legs crossed at the ankles. An open book rested on his chest, but his hopeful expression sank when Ash pulled one of the chairs up to the bars.

"And here I was, hoping for some decent conversation."

As a jab, it was somewhat weak. Sorin had been making snide remarks about Ash's lack of intellect for so long that any possible sting had faded. If Sorin was so much smarter than Ash, after all, he should have been able to come up with some new insults. "You'll have to settle for me."

"Well, what is it these sailors say? Any port in a storm?"

"Don't worry. I won't bother you for long." Ash hesitated a beat, then let himself be petty in return. "Sachi is waiting for me at home, after all."

Rage broke through Sorin's placid expression for a heartbeat before he managed to wrest his features into something more like boredom. He looked away. And lied. "I don't want her anymore. She's nothing like I dreamed she'd be."

"Odd. She's everything I dreamed she'd be."

Sorin made a rude noise. "Well, then, congratulations, Ash. You've won again."

"I never wanted to win."

"You could have fooled me."

Ash finally sank into the chair and leaned forward, bracing his arms against the bars of the cell. "I never wanted to *fight*. You forced us to it."

"Because you wouldn't listen to me," Sorin snapped. "And then you got the Phoenix all riled up and they destroyed everything I'd worked for without even giving me a chance to explain how much *good* I could do with it."

Ash hesitated. During the dark nights since the truth about the Empire had been revealed, he'd been forced to admit there was some validity in Sorin's claims. So much of what Sachi had revealed about life under Sorin's rule had been straight from a nightmare . . .

But not all of it.

In the midst of all those horrors, Ash had recognized echoes of the young man Sorin had once been. The one who had argued that it was their responsibility to ensure no one went hungry or homeless. That no one suffered illness untreated, or lacked the education that would allow a young mind to thrive. Sorin had argued that progress was the only path to equality, to a world where mortals could taste the wonders known only to the Dreamers.

"You can fly, Ash. What about those who can't? Is it fair to leave their feet forever bound to earth, just because they weren't born with the power you have?"

"You're right," Ash said finally.

Sorin's gaze flew to his, shock warring with suspicion as he slowly sat up. "What did you say?"

"I said you were right," Ash repeated. "Not in the end, when you were doing things too swiftly and too recklessly. But in the beginning. You had dreams, and some of them were good. Maybe if I hadn't been so resistant to *how* you wanted to achieve them, we could have found common ground on *why*."

Those cunning hazel eyes narrowed. "At least you realize that you're the one to blame."

Typical. "No, Sorin. I'll take my share of it, but I'm finished letting you dodge yours. The pain you caused in your Empire is your burden to shoulder. You lost your way, brother."

"I'm not your brother," Sorin spat.

Ash ignored the bitterness. "You lost your way. You forgot your own *why*. That you wanted to help people find their own power and achieve their own dreams, not strip away everything they could be and take it for yourself."

Agitated, Sorin swung his legs over the side of the bed and rose. "That's not how it worked—"

"No," Ash cut him off. "I don't want to hear your excuses. Not about that." Even now, thinking about the reality of what Sorin had done was enough to stir incendiary rage. Ash had watched Lyssa struggle against the numbness, the fog that still seemed to drown her mind some days. He'd heard her shrieks of terror as nightmares chased her from sleep. She was trying to remember how to feel, how to want, how to *be*.

Rising, Ash gripped the bars of the cage. "What you did was an abomination. You stole their hopes, their dreams. Their chance to be anything more than what you saw as their most efficient use in *your* grand plan. Generation after generation after generation. That is *your* shame. Your sin." He exhaled roughly, fighting to keep his tone steady. "So is every cruelty your court inflicted upon them. And all the atrocities they'll continue to commit, until we find a way to stop them."

"They're their own people who make their own choices," Sorin snapped, pacing away.

"And you *made* them." Could he not admit it, even now? "You made them because you wanted your family back, just not one that would judge and fight you. You wanted one that would enable your worst impulses and do your dirty work, so you could maintain the illusion that you'd built a paradise instead of a nightmare. You let them do things to people that should haunt you to your dying day."

Perhaps he *did* understand on some level, because Sorin stiffened and looked away. The accusation hung there between them in the tense, miserable silence. When it became clear the Betrayer would not answer, Ash sighed and sank back into his chair. "Do you know what my greatest sin was, Sorin?"

"Must I pick only one?"

"I think you'll like this one."

"By all means, entertain me."

Ash sighed and stared up at the ceiling. "Complacency. That was my greatest sin."

Sorin's chuckle sounded forced, as if he was trying to regain control of the conversation. "Not the one I would have chosen, but I certainly can't argue with it."

"Who could?" Ash agreed. "I let you wreak havoc and sow terror for three thousand years."

That hit Sorin's pride. He whipped around with a scowl. "*Let* me?"

"I let you turn your Empire into a playground for the perversion of everything good, because as long as I could stay in my castle, I didn't care. I thought that was how I would keep the world safe—by avoiding you. By making sure we never came to blows again. Instead, I almost let you destroy us all."

Sorin opened his mouth, but Ash leaned forward and cut him off. "And do you know what the worst part is? The prophecy. The promise from the world that my consort would break the Builder's chains. The world whispered that to me when our blood on the dirt was barely dry. Hundreds of years before you forged those first chains. Because it knew. It knew I wouldn't stop you. That I would fail it so deeply, so profoundly. The world *knew*, somehow."

Sorin's chill hazel eyes held only hatred. "And yet you still got your prize."

Ash shook his head. "Sachi was never a prize. That's what you can't understand. She and Zanya aren't here to reward us for being good or punish us for being bad. They're here to set this world to rights. All I can hope is that someday *I* will be worthy of being *their* reward for a job well done."

Sorin surged toward the bars of the cell and grabbed them. Fists that once would have been able to bend or crush the metal closed helplessly around the bars—mortal hands, stripped of their capacity to do terrible harm.

"What job is left?" Sorin hissed. "Your witch robbed me of the power that was my birthright. She took everything from me. She should have killed me."

Ash laughed. "If you wanted that kind of mercy, you should have appealed to Zanya. She'd happily water the dirt of what's left of your Empire with your blood. Sachi is a more demanding woman. *She* expects you to help us."

"Help you do *what?*"

"Save your people." Ash stood up. "Your Empire crumbles, Sorin. You stole their dreams and left them with nothing but fear and nightmares. The chains have broken, and new gods manifest every day. Some are born from the Everlasting Dream, and some from the Endless Void. All have powers we've never seen. They're scared and traumatized and angry, and they're tearing what remains of your cities apart. Terrors stalk your borders, too. Hundreds of them, born of nightmares given fresh power."

Ash wrapped his hands over Sorin's and leaned down, meeting his gaze with nothing but the scant space between the bars separating them. "God or no, you have valuable knowledge. You can help us. Or you can rot down here. The choice is yours."

For a moment, Ash thought it might be that easy. That the fragile *spark* of his old brother that was threaded through everything he did might burst into glorious being. He could have his family back, if not his powers. He could do what he'd always wanted and help people.

Sorin ripped his hands free of Ash's and staggered back. "You call that a choice?"

"It's more than you gave your people."

Sorin shot him a final withering glare. Then he strolled back to the bed, reclaimed his spot propped against the wall, and picked up his book. Pointedly, he turned the page and focused his entire attention on it.

Ash was dismissed.

Sighing, he picked up the chair and placed it back at the table. He nodded to the guard on his way past. His heart beat with each spiraling stair he climbed—rage and frustration and grief and his own guilt tangled into a ball that might take centuries to undo.

He had failed Sorin, just as he'd failed the world beyond his castle. But every day was a chance to make a different choice. To try again, to do better. Ash knew what his choice would be—to use everything he was to protect the people he had harmed with his complacency. To be worthy of the gift he'd been given when the world entrusted him with the power to see his dreams made real.

Maybe someday Sorin would make that choice, too. Until he did . . .

The rest of them had an empire to save.

ACKNOWLEDGMENTS

Every book is a journey, and this one was no different. For the past few years, these acknowledgment sections have turned into a snapshot of where our lives were at the time we finished a given book, because it feels like the more life swirls chaotically around us, the more people we have to thank for helping us keep our course steady.

We dealt with a health crisis during this book that would have broken us without the support (both emotional and, at times, financial) of our community. We are deeply grateful to every person in our lives who reached out to comment, to help, to send good thoughts and warm wishes. That energy kept us going, and we hope to pay it back and forward in years to come.

As always, our most profound thanks go to our team: our agent, Sarah Younger, and all her compatriots at NYLA who protect our interests and throw life preservers into the choppy ocean when needed. Our unbelievably supportive and excited editor, Lauren Plude, who once again worked with Sasha Knight to land this horny dragon. Our longtime last-defense readers Lillie Applegarth and Sharon Muha, who have been with us for decades, and our new behind-the-scenes cheerleader, Seher, who literally read parts of this book a paragraph or two at a time to encourage us to keep going.

Thank you to everyone who volunteered your names once again for our evil purposes. Many of you ended up becoming kingdoms in the Empire. Please don't go to war with each other—it will make the map messy.

Zero thanks to Amazon Prime for dropping *Wheel of Time* Season Two right when Bree was supposed to be focusing on the end of this book. Please coordinate future seasons more carefully with Amazon Publishing so that she can be a proper fangirl! Also drop the name of Lanfear's tailor. Thanks.

(What, did you think these acknowledgments were going to get less bananapants as the years went on?)

Thank you to our families and friends who patiently did not ask *how's the book going?* and instead threw support and occasionally cookies at us and picked up the slack so we could get the job done.

And of course, always and forever, thank you to our readers. Whether you are just joining us now, or you've been here for the last sixteen years, you are the reason we get to do this magical, strange, impossible job of telling stories. We write the words, but they only live when they meet your imagination.

Thanks for keeping *our* dreams alive.

REFERENCE GUIDE

Instead of alphabetically, this reference guide is laid out by location, to give you a history of certain places and families.

While this glossary is more or less safe to read before you have read Queen of Dreams, *it does contain spoilers for the events in* Consort of Fire.

General Information

The Sheltered Lands' current calendar was developed three thousand years ago. It is made up of eight moons/months with five weeks each. Each week has ten days. Weeks are marked by one full ten-day rotation of the larger moon, known as the Creator's Moon. Moons are marked by one full fifty-day rotation of the smaller moon, known as the Destroyer's Moon.

Both weeks and months start on the dark of the moon. Days on which both moons are full at the same time are known as Joining or Union Days, and are often celebrated with new marriages, betrothals, and attempts to have children.

Because of the powers the High Court hold over the natural world, and the world's own response to the near-breaking three thousand years ago, the continents have some odd geographical formations that did not occur naturally. Because of the nature of the dual moons, they also have *very* odd tides.

The Sheltered Lands

The Sheltered Lands were officially founded three thousand years ago, along with the start of the new calendar, by the pact between the Mortal Lords and the High Court of Dreamers. The Mortal Lords were given stewardship of the lands and rule over other mortals, so long as they agreed to care for both. They are also obligated to provide the Dragon with a royal heir as consort every one hundred years. That heir is bonded to the Dragon, with their family's fortunes thus tied to the health and prosperity of the land and its guardians.

The Capital

The main seat of the Mortal Lords sits where the country's main river spills into Siren's Bay. The only true city in the Sheltered Lands, it holds the royal palace and the great estates of all of the various lords.

Currently, House Roquebarre sits on the throne, and has for several generations.

House Roquebarre

House Roquebarre was the original ruling family of the Sheltered Lands. They have held the throne continuously since 2875, when King Bodilaine reclaimed it after the death of the final heir of House Montanne. While custom dictated that House Montanne be spared, Bodilaine nonetheless removed his old enemies from court, suppressing their fortunes. They fell out of favor and became a minor house. King Bodilaine married a daughter of the powerful House Sandrake, and they had two children:

Prince Tislaine (b. 2881): The eldest son and heir, sent to the Dragon as consort in 2900. He served a short and miserable span of years in the role, each year punctuated by a plea to be brought home. Tislaine eventually died at the hands of a Terror manifested by his own fear, though his family believes the Dragon murdered him. This belief soured the royal family on their obligation to provide consorts.

King Dalvish I (b. 2886): The second son, Dalvish I, ascended the throne due to his elder brother's sacrificial duty to serve as the Dragon's consort. The harsh strictures that prevented him from profiting on trade with the Empire—coupled with his mounting disdain for the High Court—prompted him to reach out to the Betrayer for help in breaking the High Court's control. He died before a plan could be enacted, leaving the throne to the eldest of his three daughters, Agatine. (Other daughters: *Ceilia, born 2926; Myshela, born 2929*)

Queen Agatine (b. 2922): Queen Agatine, while sympathetic to her father's ambitions and frustrated by the limitations set upon her family by the High Court, balked at the Betrayer's initially suggested solutions. She did, however, accept a member of the Betrayer's court into her house. High Priest Nikkon took personal responsibility for raising her heir, Dalvish II. (Other children: *Tislaina, born 2949; Doven, born 2953; Bodin, born 2950*)

King Dalvish II (b. 2947): Raised under the influence of High Priest Nikkon, King Dalvish II was the mastermind behind the plot to break his family's fealty to the High Court of Dreamers. After Nikkon uncovered a pair of orphans—one with the coloring to easily pass as Dalvish's own child, the other possessing dangerous Void magic—Dalvish took them into his household. He adopted Sachielle as his heir, and appointed Zanya to be her handmaid. Both were secretly trained in the arts of assassination. Upon Sachielle's offering to the Dragon in the year 3000, her lack of blood relation to Dalvish would free him of any retributory backlash if he violated the High Court's strictures . . . and there was always the chance Zanya would succeed in actually slaying the Dragon. Upon his death at Zanya's hand, Dalvish II was succeeded by his only blood child, Princess Anikke (b. 2085).

Princess Sachielle and Zanya: No one knows Sachielle's exact date of birth, only that she and Zanya were found at an orphanage when they were five to seven years old. An incident where the matr beat Sachielle resulted in Zanya summoning Terrors that savaged the entire village and left only the two girls alive. When High Priest Nikkon arrived, he recognized Zanya's connection to the Void as well as Sachielle's resemblance to the royal family. The decision was made to foster them, train them both as weapons, and unleash them upon the High Court. Things did not go as planned, instead resulting in the revelation that they were, in fact, the manifestations of the elemental powers of the Everlasting Dream and the Endless Void.

Queen Anikke (b. 2085): Only fifteen years old upon her ascension to the throne, Anikke is guided by her two uncles and her aunt, who serve as her regents. Little is known about the new young queen, though it is suspected she remains ignorant and innocent of her family's many lies and deceptions.

High Priest Nikkon (dead): Nikkon was sent by the Betrayer to raise Dalvish II and to guide him into making plans for the Dragon's downfall. While Nikkon recognized Zanya's potential, he overlooked Sachi's magical nature completely. As a result, he sent the Dragon two powerful weapons. His death at Zanya's hands might have been a mercy, since the Betrayer was very, very angry about this misstep.

Captain Arman Melwin (dead): Arman was one of Zanya's trainers during her time in the capital. Though he was fierce and rough, he grew sympathetic to Zanya's plight over the years and became protective of her. Because of this, he counseled her to hide her full strength so that the king would never know how powerful she truly was. His fondness for her was eventually uncovered. In a stark lesson to Zanya, Nikkon used him to perfect the curse he eventually laid on Sachi.

Seahold

Seahold is the Siren's ancient seat, perched on an island of the same name. It guards the mouth of Siren's Bay, ensuring any ship that wishes to reach the capital must pass through waters controlled by the Siren and her people.

The Siren (Dianthe): One of the oldest members of the High Court of Dreamers, Dianthe is also one of the strongest. This comes from her strong connection to both the sea and the sky, ensuring that water and air answer her call. Though she was born human, she has been a Dreamer for nearly four thousand years. She fought in the War of the Gods at the Dragon's side, helping him to hold the world together when it began to fracture.

Naia: Naia is a newly born god, and a rare kind. While most Dreamers were born mortal and manifested their powers in a time of crisis, Naia was born directly from the Dream. Usually, when a Dreamer comes into being like this, it means the world needed something only they can offer. Sometimes referred to as a nymph, she has an affinity for water.

The Kraken (Einar): Einar was born mortal, but became a god over two thousand years ago, during the last large-scale invasion by the Betrayer. A bold fishing captain, he outfitted his ship for war and became a legendary pirate captain who sank hundreds of enemy ships. He still patrols the Western Wall with his dedicated crew, letting no one pass.

Dragon's Keep

Dragon's Keep is the Dragon's seat, which sits high in the mountain range that guards the western coast. The keep itself is built on an island in a vast caldera lake, and is so inaccessible as to discourage visitors. In spite of this, a strong, mostly self-sustaining community has grown up here over the years, and traders brave enough to make the climb to offer their wares can turn a rich profit. Because the Dragon is considered the leader of the High Court of Dreamers, he built six grand estates along the path leading to the castle proper, one for each of the remaining Dreamers. This is called the Godwalk. While only Ulric and Elevia are frequently in residence, all the gods keep a household there.

The Dragon (Ash): The exact year of the Dragon's birth has faded from memory, but most people agree he was probably born somewhere between five hundred and eight hundred years before the War of the Gods. He manifested during a wildfire, showing a strong connection to both earth and fire, but he heard the whispers of the Dream from a young age and has always been the Dreamer with the firmest connection to the world.

After nearly dying to defeat the Betrayer in the War of the Gods, he struck an accord with the Mortal Lords and agreed to defend the borders if they sheltered the land and protected the people. Due to prompting from a prophecy heard in the aftermath of the War, he demanded that they provide him a consort every one hundred years—the current heir to the ruling family. The prophecy promises that one of the Dragon's consorts will be the key to ultimately defeating the Betrayer.

Camlia: Camlia is the steward of Dragon's Keep. It is a position she inherited. Her family has served the keep in various capacities for every generation since its founding, and have a somewhat proprietary interest in both the castle, the surrounding keep, and its lord. Because of this long service, they are granted a great deal of authority and trust.

Danika: Danika is currently the high priest of the Dragon. In practice, this means she performs all important ceremonies at the keep, and also travels to enclaves that hold faith with the Dragon to speak in his name and to draw his attention to those who need his aid.

The Raven Guard: The Raven Guard is a band of ferocious warriors dedicated to both the Dragon and the Dragon's consort. All five were fierce fighters in life who died in legendary battles while committing extraordinary acts of bravery and skill. Each rose from their funeral pyre as a group of ravens that resumed human form—-now stronger, faster, and unaging. The Raven Guard retains the ability to shift at will into an unkindness of ravens. The five current members include:

Malindra: Malindra tends to dress in the rough leathers and furs common among the tribes who reside on Dead Man Shoals. Those tribes are reportedly the descendants of those left for dead or ship-wrecked during the Betrayer's last invasion over two thousand years ago. She fights with two short swords.

Remi and Isolde: The twins dress in lighter leather armor and are thought to have come from the islands to the south of the Sheltered Lands. Remi is a huge bear of a man who wields two hand-axes. Isolde is a tall, dark-eyed beauty who carries a massive double-headed axe.

Kardox: One of the oldest members of the Guard, Kardox has a scarred face, intense eyes, and a wicked smile. He has trained many of the great warriors of past generations, including Arman, who went on to train Zanya. He is an expert with multiple kinds of weapons, and skilled at hand-to-hand combat.

Ambrial: Ambrial is a delicate, almost waiflike soldier with a deceptive strength. She tends to wear silver chainmail and wields a longsword with both skill and terrifying grace. She usually serves as the personal guard of the Dragon's consort.

The Den

The Den is the seat of the Wolf. It is a small hunting lodge situated in the northwestern part of the Midnight Forest, within a few days' ride of both Blade's Rest and Dragon's Keep. Ulric spends about half of his time at the Den, and the rest in his home at Dragon's Keep.

The Wolf (Ulric): The early life of the Wolf is shrouded in secret. Some legends say he was not born human at all, while others say he was orphaned and raised by a wolf pack. What is known for certain is that he was already strong in his powers when the War of the Gods took place. Ulric holds domain over the wild places and can speak to all creatures. He also can transform into a massive wolf.

Justav and Andra: Justav and Andra are the current caretakers of the Den, and rule it absolutely in the Wolf's absence.

Blade's Rest

Blade's Rest is the seat of the Huntress. It sits at the southwest edge of the Blasted Plains, and is home to the Huntress's formidable information network, which consists of finely trained riders on exquisitely bred horses who can travel vast distances to carry news.

The Huntress (Elevia): Elevia served as the High Court's general during the War of the Gods, and is considered by most to be the Dragon's second-in-command. While she is most popularly associated with hunting, military strategy, and victory in war, her true power is information. Her followers go everywhere and tell her everything, and her priests have even developed ways to pass information through the Dream when necessary.

The Villa

The Villa sits in the midst of the Lover's Lakes, on the northern edge of the Sheltered Lands. It is the beginning of a vast range of fertile farmland that stretches to Siren's Bay and provides most of the food for the country. It is popularly believed that the Lover's vitality is part of what helps the crops to grow, though mythology also says that the lakes are the remnants of a great battle between the Dragon and the Betrayer, and the blood they shed nurtures the earth still.

The Lover (Aleksi): Aleksi is the most revered of all of the High Court. While the passing years have changed the Dragon's reputation into something monstrous and eroded that of the Witch and even the Wolf, the Lover is still worshipped throughout the Sheltered Lands. This is no doubt in part due to the fact that the Villa has long been a sanctuary for artists, poets, and musicians, who have immortalized Aleksi as the height of desirability and godlike glory.

Witchwood Castle

Witchwood Castle sits in the heart of the Witchwood, an odd magical forest that dominates the southernmost point of the Sheltered Lands. Unlike the massive pines that grow in the Midnight Forest, the Witchwood is dominated by foliage and fauna of vibrant colors and frequent bioluminescence. Many luxuries, such as teas, spices, and even chocolate, can only be found within the confines of this forest. Stories of the fey-like creatures you might encounter keep all but the bravest away.

The Witch (Inga): Inga is a younger member of the High Court of Dreamers, having been only a few hundred years old when the War of the Gods occurred. She was already a powerful healer, though, and has only grown in skill during the intervening years. She is the only member of the High Court who is as fascinated with the Endless Void as she is the Everlasting Dream. She has a habit of cultivating both healing tonics and poisons, as she believes life and death walk hand in hand.

The Executioner (Livia): A younger god who manifested in the past few hundred years, Livia lives at the Witch's court and studies her passion—poisons. In this, she has already swiftly outstripped Inga, giving her a reputation for being the person to come to if death is the only path to justice.

The Burning Hills

The Burning Hills are an ancient and sacred row of hills that cut across the middle of the Sheltered Lands, dividing north from south. They are known for their hot springs, which are said to have healing properties. The entire area is under the protection of the Phoenix, who ha built a tower on the highest bluff, where their priesthood maintains t

Phoenix's Flame for those willing to travel into the Hills to face—or become—their truest self.

The Phoenix (currently going by Nyx): The Phoenix is the youngest of the High Court of Dreamers, but the most powerful when it comes to their connection to the Dream. They are gender-fluid, living a frequent cycle of rebirth and renewal. Sometimes they prefer to present themselves to the world as a nonbinary god, and sometimes they claim a gender and a new name for a span of time. Those who feel they have outgrown or have never fit their current bodies can walk through the Phoenix's flames to be reborn. Those flames of rebirth can also erase construction and even corruption from the land, making the Phoenix the one person the Betrayer truly fears.

The Empire

Three thousand years ago, the Betrayer's followers fled the field of battle in order to carry his injured body to safety. After the sundering of continents, they were left on a vast new expanse of land populated only by small communities living peaceful agrarian lives. As soon as he had recovered, the Betrayer moved inland to the center of the continent and claimed it as his own, beginning several millennia of conquest and intense construction.

Thus, he became the Emperor.

While the modern Empire is made up of multiple "kingdoms" overseen in trust for the Emperor, the kingdoms are actually massive, industrialized megacities that sit in the heart of each given territory. While a few people may live at remote outposts where resources are mined or processed, the vast majority of the population lives in ever-expanding and ruthlessly organized city-states.

The cities have much more advanced technology than the Sheltered Lands, with food coming from vast hydroponics factories or livestock complexes. Travel is possible via trolley within neighborhoods and high-speed rail between neighborhoods. While an upper class of nobility exists, most have earned their way to this position via technological innovation and will lose their status if their family doesn't continue to innovate. Because productivity is so valued, every trade has its own guild. Without guild status, the only work available is menial at best.

The Betrayer

The Betrayer was once the eighth member of the High Court of Dreamers. Named Sorin and formerly known as the Builder, he was famous for his architecture and progress. In the thousand years leading up to the War of the Gods, he began to disagree with the rest of the High Court regarding the scope of their technological progress and how much they should impact the world in its pursuit. When Sorin went too far and built a factory that poisoned the land itself, the Phoenix destroyed his entire operation with their own flames, renewing the earth and erasing any trace of it. This was the first strike in what became the War of the Gods.

After his defeat, the Builder was all but erased from the history of the Sheltered Lands. There is only the Betrayer, whose long moon during the dark of winter represents the terrible dark days after the war. The Dragon's Moon being the first of the new year in the calendar represents how the Dragon drove the Betrayer and his darkness from the land and offered them all a fresh start.

The Nine Kingdoms

Eight of the kingdoms are named for the great generals who stood by the Emperor's side as he conquered this new land. While the largest and grandest kingdom houses the Emperor's seat, the rest are administered in his name by an Imperial Court with godlike powers. Each is styled as a Grand Duke or Duchess, and all have their own title based on their skills or personalities—an affectation one might assume the Emperor stole from the High Court, if one were uncharitable.

A ninth kingdom once thrived in the area of the Eastern Waste. It has since fallen into ruin and bears no name.

Kasther

Ruled by: The Emperor
The largest kingdom in the Empire, and the seat of the Emperor. It is situated in the center of the continent.

Akeisa

Ruled by: Grand Duchess Gwynira / The Ice Queen
The only island kingdom in the Empire, Akeisa is far to the north and sits between two frigid ocean currents that render the winters brutal and even the height of summer unusually chilly.

Leighael

Ruled by: Grand Duchess Varoka / The Dreamweaver
Leighael sits on the far western shore of the Empire, cut off from Kasther by an impressive mountain range. While there is one high-speed rail connection through the mountain, much of the travel between Leighael and the rest of the Empire happens by air.

Linzen

Ruled by: A steward
Linzen, the northwestern coastal kingdom in the Empire, was previously ruled by Grand Duke Nikkon, also popularly known as the Priest. It has been under stewardship for the past generation as Nikkon worked undercover for the Emperor in the Sheltered Lands. It remains in stewardship, as Nikkon's untimely death has left the land up for grabs by anyone who can draw the Emperor's approval.

Vinke

Ruled by: Grand Duke Enzi / The Seducer

Vinke is the southernmost kingdom, with a strong harbor and good river access to Kasther. With an appealing climate and beautiful ocean and river views, it should be a coveted place to live. The Grand Duke's personal proclivities have seeped down into the culture, however, making it feel less safe for the vulnerable of every successive generation.

Rehes

Ruled by: Grand Duke Demir / The Beast

Rehes is a northeastern kingdom, sharing (artificial) lake access with the eastern side of Kasther and river access to the North Sea. While it could be a very solid city, given its resources and access to water, Demir is a negligent ruler who lets his lower nobility run wild.

Kelann

Ruled by: Grand Duchess Eirika / The Stalker

Inavihs

Ruled by: Grand Duke Hinrick / The Shapechanger

Kelann and Inavihs sit across from each other on a river in the southeast corner of the Empire. Their rulers are close, with Hinrick often acting as Eirika's subordinate, meaning that while these two kingdoms remain separate entities in theory, in reality they behave as one.

ABOUT THE AUTHOR

Kit Rocha is the pseudonym for cowriting team Donna Herren and Bree Bridges. After penning dozens of paranormal novels, novellas, and stories as Moira Rogers, they reinvented themselves by writing the nine-book, multiple award–winning Beyond series, which became an instant cult favorite. They followed it up with two spin-off series, including the popular Mercenary Librarians trilogy, as well as *Consort of Fire* in the Bound to Fire and Steel series. Their favorite stories are about messy worlds, strong women, and falling in love with the people who love you just the way you are. When they're not writing, you can find them making handmade jewelry, caring too much about video games, or freaking out about their favorite books or TV shows, all of which are chronicled on their various social media accounts. For more information, visit www.kitrocha.com.